Girl On a Train

a Novel

by

A J WAINES

ISBN-13: 978-1490320045

For my Mum
Mary Waines (1926-2012)
who always had a mystery whodunit on her lap

Part One

Anna

chapter one

Sunday Afternoon, September 19th

It was supposed to be a mindless train journey home. Peaceful. Sleepy. Uneventful.

I deliberately chose the quiet coach when I boarded at Portsmouth and Southsea. True to form, most people were chatting inanely on their mobile phones or leaking hissing drumbeats from their headphones, so I kept going, looking for an area without cackling post-hen-parties, toddlers or badly tuned radios. There is nothing worse than being forced to listen to other people's choice of music, except perhaps other people's *children's* choice of music.

As I entered the next carriage, my foot caught in a loose strap and I found myself spread-eagled over a table occupied by four men in rugby shirts, building a tower of lager cans. I managed to extricate myself from a chorus of *Swing low, sweet chariot* without too many innuendos and strode on, leaving whoops and cheers in my wake.

My simple quest for a quiet spot was proving an impossible task. There was far too much exuberance for a Sunday afternoon. I'd anticipated the entire train subdued with a post-Saturday-night slump, not feverish with squeals and giggling. Most people I passed were under twenty, wearing Wellington boots. Then it clicked. Probably returning in droves from late summer festivals on the Isle of Wight. It was the mud caking everything below the knee that gave them away. I was glad my music festival days were over - well, camping out at them at least. Memories of waking up with a soggy backside had put me off sleeping under the stars for life (having pitched the tent after dark and failed to notice the *terra* wasn't *firma*).

Was it too much to ask for a seat that wasn't surrounded by dangling wet socks, Indie band posters or discarded soya-milk cartons? I clambered over several three-storey rucksacks, complete with sleeping-bags and rolled up foam mats piled high in the gangway, and settled for an empty airline seat next to a woman looking out of the window. I slung my overnight bag on the rack, dropped my handbag between my feet and sat back with a not unjustified sense of achievement.

I gave a cordial glance to the woman beside me and felt an immediate kinship with her. She didn't seem to be part of the raucous melee and looked to be in her late twenties, like me. My smile, however, was wasted as she failed to register my presence. She wore the kind of fixed stare that made me want to flap my hand up and down in front of her face and ask *Is anyone there?*

Her straggly hair had a stiff fringe like a yard broom that looked like it would move all at once if touched. Someone should have told her that the specs were all wrong; they were chunky like the ones you get in joke shops that have a plastic nose and moustache attached. The right style might have lifted her appearance out of the plain zone into one bordering on pretty.

There was something else, however, that struck me as soon as the train left the station. She was edgy, agitated, checking her watch every few moments. I heard her sigh several times and her neck craned back and forth as she looked up and down the aisle. As I tried to settle into my novel, it started to become distracting and after about five minutes, annoying. I turned Michael Bublé up high on my iPod in a bid to block her out.

Before long, the guard appeared. 'Waterloo… Waterloo…' he hummed, like the Abba song, as he clipped tiny boxes into the corner of our tickets. My shoulders dropped. Little Ms Fidget was going to be beside me all the way to the end of the line. As if to confirm my fears, she wriggled in her seat, drummed her fingers on the edge of her bag, sniffed, pushed up her glasses and then started the cycle over again.

I remembered I'd bought a Sunday paper at the station, so I pulled down the supplement from the rack and offered it to her. Her hands were shaking as she took it and she made an attempt at smiling, but I noticed the magazine stayed rolled up beside her seat. I saw, too, that she hadn't removed her anorak even though the heating was set for arctic conditions. Was she ill? Mentally unstable? She clung to the overnight bag on her lap as if it contained the crown jewels, although the bag itself looked shabby, made of worn green fabric with a chipped ceramic key fob dangling on the end. The initials read E.S. I tried to entertain myself by imagining what name they stood for, but couldn't get beyond Ena Sharples.

I took a deep breath and tried looking out of the window, but it was difficult to focus without seeing *E.S.* at the edge of my vision, jiggling about. Her left knee was bouncing up and down and she had started clearing her throat in a nervous tic.

I was beyond the stage of staring at her and tutting loudly. By now, I was on the verge

of suggesting, none too politely, that she needed to get a grip and SIT STILL, but without warning, she turned and lifted her hand. I took it to mean she wanted to leave her seat and it crossed my mind that she might not speak English. She gave me a tentative, but swiftly retracted smile as I stood to back up and I watched her hurry away clutching her bag.

The train shot into a tunnel and when we came out the other side, it was as though someone had lain a grey cloth over the windows: the carriage sank into a dusky gloom. Grey slashes of rain were ravaging the window panes like the slits of a knife.

The change in the weather took me straight back to the day Jeff and I got married. It was a freak June day of downpours and we'd spent most it trying to avoid trailing my dress through brown puddles. My hair was ruined, the flowers drenched. In the end we surrendered to the rain and embraced the way fate had decided to grace our day with its own brand of crystal confetti. I remember holding Jeff's hand as we emerged from the church; how we both tipped our heads back in unison, letting the warm spray refresh our skin, like a special blessing.

That was four years ago. Two of them spent without him.

In the haven of blissful stillness the woman left behind, I turned to get my first view out of the window, but by now the scene was blurred; reduced to green, brown and grey blobs masquerading as countryside. As it turned out, it didn't seem to matter anymore - without the irritating side-show, I found myself able to concentrate on my novel at last.

After a while, I even began to think that the woman had moved carriages and wasn't coming back, but as soon as the idea entered my head I caught a glimpse of her earnest figure, easing its way back against the tide of people.

I stood for her again and a waft of heavy perfume drove me back into my seat. It was so strong I had to smother a cough. It didn't take her long to start up the jittering again. By now, it had mutated into a form of Chinese torture; the anticipation of her next wriggle being just as bad as the event itself. In the end I couldn't stop myself from saying something.

'Sorry, I can't help noticing you seem a bit... unsettled...are you okay?'

The woman looked startled. 'Me? Oh...no. I'm fine,' she said. Her voice was wispy and fragile, with the slight lift in intonation I always associate with south London. She didn't make eye contact, instead her eyes were wide and busy, flitting from place to place as if she was following the path of a hyperactive insect.

I was about to respond with something more cutting when my phone beeped:

Apols for texting on day off - bla, bla - need you to step in with feature asap. Call me. Joan. URGENT.

Needless to say, I was glad of the distraction.

'Work,' I said, sending my eyes up to the ceiling - although to be honest, I was playacting in a bid to try to engage with the woman and get her to stop fiddling.

Her smile conveyed a vacant empathy; the kind of smile someone gives you when they aren't listening to a word you're saying. I muttered something about needing to return the call, but she was already staring out of the window again. I punched in Joan's number.

'Got a pen?' said Joan. No introductions; never one for idle chit-chat. Before I answered, she was speaking again, 'I need two thousand words on bullying in the workplace, by first thing Wednesday. You up for it?' She spoke with the speed of a voiceover rattling through the small-print on a commercial. 'The original writer's gone off the rails with it,' she said. I could hear her tapping her pen against the phone, eager for my response. 'Needs a complete rewrite...'

I became a journalist because I like tracking down the truth - the raw nuggets of reality that lie under the sham and bluster with which we smother our lives. Writing felt safer than being a detective or a private investigator - no weapons, no scaling high walls or wasting hours lurking in shop doorways - besides, it meant I could make my own coffee. Most of all, though, I liked playing with words. They are alive and magnetic; I liked shifting them around from one spot to another, like a kid transfixed with Lego.

'Anna, are you there?' Tap, tap, tap.

The thought of writing a feature on bullying brought on about as much enthusiasm as a desire to yawn, but I had to take it. Work was thin on the ground these days. As a freelance, I couldn't afford to turn anything down.

'No problem.' I said, trying to adopt a sparky tone. 'You want a particular angle? Same-sex bullying? Homophobia? A racial slant?'

'Find some recent trends and stats. Nothing wish-washy - get some decent quotes from experts - an educational psychologist, occupational therapist and psychiatrist, if you can.'

I was in the middle of saying, 'I'll see what I can do,' when I realised she'd already rung off. Editors seemed to live at a different pace to everyone else. Just talking to her left me exhausted.

I pulled out a spiral notebook and wrote *Bullying in the Workplace* at the top and underlined it twice. My mind went blank. I stared at the title and underlined it again. Out of the corner of my eye, I saw the woman next to me glance down at what I'd written.

'Are you an investigator?' she said, out of the blue.

I blinked rapidly, startled by her unexpected interest. 'Journalist,' I said. 'Lifestyle pieces mostly, with a psychology angle if I can manage it.'

She looked intense. 'You investigate crimes?'

'Er, not really. Not now. I started out as an investigative journalist, but the work's been drying up lately. It's terribly competitive.' Her face came to life, her eyes alert and focused. We must have hit on a subject she was interested in, so I carried on. I was prepared to give her a blow by blow account of my entire life-story if it stopped her fidgeting.

'What kind of crimes?' Her voice was brittle, as though she couldn't get enough air into her lungs.

'A broad range...let me think...stalking, phone-hacking, doping in sport...' Her gaze was still fixed on me. 'But, in the last year, I've been making the most of my degree and focusing on popular psychology.'

'Would you follow up cold police cases..?'

I pointed to my notebook. 'Well – not now...like I said, I'm—'

She sat forward. 'Have you ever done that?' The words came out like sniper fire. She had started tightening her fists, as if she was squeezing a small rubber ball. 'Looked into an unsolved crime? Brought someone to justice?'

'I helped the police track down a ring of joy-riders, once - and a gang of youths who vandalised a high-rise block in Balham. Digging around beneath the surface - that's what I like best. The adrenalin of the chase. The features I write now are less exciting, but the money is more consistent. I seem to spend most of my time talking to answer-phones, trying to get quotes.' I ran my pen along the wire coil of the notebook. 'That bit's a drag. Experts never say what you want them to say.'

'Digging around beneath the surface…' she muttered, echoing my words. I thought she was going to say more, but her attention palpably wandered off again, so I returned to my notes.

Next thing, she'd dropped something on the floor and was scrabbling around trying to find it. She came up with a small bottle of perfume, the source of the pungent smell that was still coating the back of my throat like a layer of creosote. She looked embarrassed; for the first time possibly aware of the irritation she'd been causing me and slipped it into her bag.

A background headache that had been brewing ever since I took my seat decided to settle in for the day. I tried to ignore that too. Back to bullying. An hour passed and we pulled into Winchester. More people bundled on to the train and looked in vain for empty seats. I barely registered when the woman bent down to retrieve the Sunday supplement that had made its way to the floor. I nodded absently as she handed it back to me.

I wasn't expecting what happened after that. We were pulling into the next station, when the woman suddenly got to her feet and made a move to squeeze past me. As her knees made contact with mine, she turned towards me. Her eyes locked straight onto mine, her eyelids pinned back, with a look I could only describe as sheer dread. In the next second, deep tram-lines formed between her eyebrows and her expression shifted. It was as if she was silently imploring me, entreating me. To do what? I had no idea. I was immobile, her gaze pressing me into my seat by some centrifugal force and I held her stare, unsure of how to react. Just as swiftly, she dropped her eyes and the moment passed. With one final glance behind her, she was swallowed up in the bodies at the door.

She was getting off. Something wasn't right.

The train came to a stop. I craned my neck to see if I could see her on the platform. Hardly anyone had left the train and I spotted her, head down, running on her tiptoes towards the stairs, then I lost sight of her.

I shuddered. The woman with a ticket to London Waterloo had just got off at an out of the way place, called Micheldever. The wrong stop. Furthermore, right at the last moment, her face had been charged with terror.

Several minutes passed; the draggy ponderous ones that Sunday delays are made of. A dreary ten minutes later and the train started pulling out. I shifted to the window seat and scribbled a few more notes as a car-park, warehouse and the outskirts of Micheldever slid by in a washed-out blur. I didn't mind in the least about the view; I was revelling in my newfound peace and quiet.

It was short-lived.

Seconds later, there was a massive jolt and the train lurched forward. I watched my pen do a summersault in the air in slow-motion, before hitting the pull-down tray and bouncing into the aisle. Then time switched into double speed and the momentum threw me forward forcing the tray into my ribs, where it tried to take a slice out of my chest. My forehead smacked into the back of the chair in front, before I lost touch with my seat altogether and tumbled to the floor.

The carriage screeched and careered from side to side, then came to an abrupt halt with a loud thud. There was a horrible grating sound. I heard startled cries around me and bodies were scattered into the aisles, legs and arms scrabbling for support. Someone muttered something incoherent behind me and I realised he was praying.

I could hear my own frantic voice filling up my head.

Oh my God, is this it? I'm not ready. Please. Not yet.

There were a few moments of silence in the carriage as everyone seemed to hold their breath. We were still rocking ominously like the ground was slowly sinking under the rails. The lights flickered and I heard a distant straining sound as though something was buckling. I half expected the train to tip over on to its side and I scrambled back onto my seat, taking hold of the arms, gripping hard.

Don't let me die. Please…

Silence. Nothing happened.

The rocking gradually steadied into a sinister creaking lullaby and finally stopped. Then the lights went out altogether. An 'ooh' billowed through the carriage, like we were all watching a gruesome horror movie. The power seemed to disconnect and we were completely still. It was as if the train had died and we were left sitting inside an inert shell.

I tentatively ran my hands across my side. My ribs burned, but I didn't think any were broken. A bump was rapidly swelling above my eye, but when I took my hand away there was no blood. I could hear people moaning, asking each other if they were all right. A man holding a handkerchief over his nose was trying to lift a young woman off the floor. As the red stain rapidly inked its way across the white cotton, I handed him a wad of tissues from my bag.

'What happened?' I heard a young woman shout.

'I think it might be a derailment,' came a man's voice.

'Did we hit something?'

A small girl was howling, having cracked her forehead on the corner of a table. An adult was soothing her, blowing cool air on the bump. Thankfully, the jumble of overstuffed rucksacks had cushioned the blow for many people. I stood up to see if anyone else needed help, but most people seemed to be either on their feet by now, or had returned to their seats.

A deadpan voice over the PA system broke through the mounting hum of speculations.

'This is your driver speaking. There's been an incident on the track, but I can assure all passengers that there is no danger. Please stay calm and in your seats. Do not attempt to alight from the train. I'll bring you further announcements as soon as the situation becomes clearer. My colleague will be walking through the train if anyone requires assistance or first aid. Thank you.'

A buzz of conversation followed like a swarm of bees breaking into the carriage. I looked out of the window. I was in the fifth of eight coaches and as we were on a stretch of track that was straight, I couldn't see the front of the train. We were not far from Micheldever, with fields either side. The most obvious explanation occurred to me and my stomach flipped. Someone must have jumped in front of the train.

A fragile calm hovered over the carriage as people realised they weren't going anywhere for some time. I reached down and picked up my pen from the floor. I stared at it barely aware of what it was for. My phone had picked up Joan's brief by now, so I had everything I needed to make a proper start on the feature, but I couldn't seem to get my brain to engage with the pen, the pen to engage with the paper. I was having trouble controlling the fluttering panic under the surface of my breathing, like moths trapped inside my chest.

For some obscure reason, I found myself returning to the fidgeting woman with the initials E.S. attached to her bag. At first, it seemed that by getting off early, she'd made a lucky escape, then I remembered her face.

Images of her tormented frown wouldn't leave me alone.

chapter two

Everything was at a standstill. No lights, no heating. Barely any sound. No one in my carriage appeared to have any serious injuries and a blanket of resignation settled over us. Those who had been standing were now sitting on the floor leaning against their rucksacks. A girl of about seventeen eventually took the free seat beside me and fell asleep, with her feet, clad in muddy yellow socks, tucked beneath her.

At 16.45 there was a crackle and a voice over the PA system told us that we were going back to the previous station. A loud moan rose up in chorus as the train began to back up slowly, grinding to a halt at Micheldever again. The guard then asked us all to take our belongings and leave the train, but to remain on the platform.

I bundled my notes into my handbag, took my holdall from the rack and followed everyone out into the open. A few passengers were still receiving first aid for nose-bleeds, minor cuts and bruises. Three police officers appeared and started talking gravely to train staff. A sick shiver shook my stomach. It didn't look good. Someone was either dead or seriously injured.

The rain continued to batter down on the roof of the station and I started to feel a chill seeping through my bones, so I went inside the waiting room. It was the size of a bunker and there were no seats left, but at least it was warm. As I stood by the door, I realised I was directly alongside the coach in which I'd been travelling. I remembered the white sticker with 'Coach E' printed on it, hanging off the window near my seat. I was idly observing people coming and going, when I noticed a man looking furtively up and down the platform before jumping back on the train. He seemed to go unnoticed by the officials who had left the doors open, but made it clear the train should remain empty. He appeared to be around thirty-five; agile and just under six-foot, carrying a rucksack and wearing a beanie hat so I couldn't see his hair. The belt of his long beige raincoat swung behind him.

He pulled up his collar and I watched him walk along inside, looking like he was counting the seats. He then stopped right at the spot where I'd been sitting and dodged down looking for something. I didn't recognise him from my carriage. He disappeared altogether for a while and then came out of the next door along. I could see there was nothing in his hands, although he might have had time to transfer something into his rucksack. I went out on to the platform, cupped my hands around my eyes and peered in at the point where I'd been sitting, trying to work out what he might have been looking for. Perhaps someone had asked him to find something they'd dropped or he was simply looking for an abandoned newspaper to read, while we waited for the next train. As I turned, someone bumped into me heavily from the side. I was expecting an apology, but instead I felt a burning pain in my arm and an elbow shoved me into the side of the train.

Losing my balance momentarily, it took me a second to register what had happened. Then I blinked and came to my senses. My handbag had gone.

'Oi!' I cried. 'Stop! That's mine!'

I spun one way, then the other, but the man had been swallowed up into the tornado of people on the platform. There was so much disarray as hoards of passengers flapped about not knowing when they would be on the move that his actions had gone unnoticed.

Clutching my forehead in panic, I scanned the whole length of the platform, checking the stairs and the barriers. Nothing - except people milling around. I was sure of one thing: it was the same man, wearing the tight-fitting hat and raincoat. I was convinced of it. The same man I'd just seen on the train searching for something near my seat.

I suddenly grasped the enormity of the incident: my purse, tickets, phone, iPod, my house keys, my notes for the feature. They had all gone. Hampered by my holdall, I hurried along the platform in the vain hope that I'd spot someone making a dash for it. But he could have run for the lift, headed over the bridge, gone through either exit - I didn't know where to start. I remembered the cluster of transport police at the front of the train and rushed in their direction.

A broad officer, closest to me, darted round reaching for his truncheon in an instinctive gesture. He relaxed as I started my bullet-point explanation of what had happened, transferring his weight to one hip and folding his arms.

'Your handbag?' he said, bending down to my level like one would with a child. 'What's happened, exactly?' His eyes were hooded with too much loose skin, like marbles pressed into dried figs. His gaze drifted off into the distance as I spoke, as though I wasn't worth the trouble it would take to focus close at hand.

'He went that way,' I said, pointlessly. The officer turned in the direction of my finger, but didn't take a step. 'Can't you try and find him?' I said, desperation rising in my voice.

He sent a tiresome glance over to his colleagues that suggested he'd had something far more important to deal with.

'Stolen, you say? Okay, let's take a little look around first.'

About time.

He slipped a radio from his top pocket, said a few words into it, then looked towards the exit.

'Can you describe this man?' he said, turning back to me.

'Around six-feet tall, a black woollen hat, beige coat, like a rain mac with a belt - I'd say he was thirty, thirty-five, maybe.' I hadn't seen the colour of his hair - brown, grey? - I wasn't sure.

The officer looked bemused. 'You seem to remember a lot about someone you only caught a glimpse of...'

'Well...I'd noticed the man earlier; he'd got back on the empty train and was poking about near where I was sitting.'

'Poking about?'

He turned to his colleagues and fluttered his eyebrows, then muttered again into the radio. I heard a high-pitched whistle in response. He then drifted away from me, asking people to move out of the way. It felt like it was a charade put on for my benefit, but I followed him.

The officer's radio crackled and he slapped it against his cheek.

'Gent's toilet, you say?'

He beckoned me to follow him and we carved a narrow path between passengers towards a blue door. A station cleaner was standing outside the men's loo holding a mop, propping the door open with his foot. He pointed inside. Moments later the officer emerged holding a black leather bag with silver buckles at arms' length.

My handbag.

The officer took a look at it, unzipped it, checked inside and handed it to me, suggesting I inspect the contents. I took it gingerly. A simmering anger bubbled into an eager rush as I knew instantly that the bag didn't feel any lighter. The first item I came across was my purse. I expected it to feel flaccid indicating that all the contents had been removed, but it was still plump. I opened it; notes and cash still neatly tucked away. I checked the side; cards and tickets still in place. I pulled out my iPod, phone, house keys, notebook - everything was still there. I couldn't understand it.

'Nothing's missing,' I said, biting my lip.

'You sure?'

I checked again. 'Yes.' I was dismayed. 'It's all here.'

'Are you still wanting to file a report?'

'Well…I suppose there's no point now, is there?'

'Okay, madam. That's fine.' He slid his pencil into a well-worn groove behind his ear. 'I wish all my crimes were this easy to solve…' He hitched up his trousers and strode back to his colleagues.

I held the bag in my arms as if it was a beloved cat, picked up my holdall and headed towards the snack stall for a latte. I felt exhausted. I wanted to get home. I'd had enough upheaval for one day.

A further forty tedious minutes passed before I got on a train to London. I could see as soon as I got through the door that I'd have to stand, but I was glad simply to be moving again. I was next to a door, so I was vigilant for the first few minutes, looking out for signs of the earlier incident. We passed a car-park and a narrow path that ran alongside the track - hardly any distance at all, before the train started to slow down.

A voice on the PA broke through the quiet.

'We would ask that you ensure any children are facing away from the left-hand side of the train,' announced the guard, 'that's *away* from the left-hand side of the train until we pick up speed again. Thank you for your understanding.'

There was a ripple of hushed exclamations and I could hear my pulse throbbing in my ears. So, someone *had* been killed.

I recognised a broken farm gate and a pair of chestnut horses from the spot where earlier, we'd been thrown to a violent halt. I then heard the jangle of electronic bells and realised we were approaching a level-crossing. Others were craning their necks as I saw the lights flash and a red and white horizontal barrier hold back a short row of cars. There were police officers and figures dressed in orange crouching beside the track. I caught sight of what looked like a red blanket beside the rail, before we began to pick up speed.

Without thinking, I took my phone out of my bag and rang Caroline. Poor Caroline. It wasn't her fault, but she was the reason I'd ended up in the wrong place at the wrong time.

'Are you all right?' she said, after I'd given her a heavily edited version of what had happened.

'Yeah – just worn out. Apart from the nasty scare when we all thought we were going to die and the interminable hold-ups, I had a horrendous journey sitting next to this really annoying woman.'

'Annoying, how?'

'She wouldn't keep still – faffing about, jiggling around - drove me nuts.'

'Well – you're safe and sound now, that's the main thing.'

I reflected a moment. 'I wondered if you could look out for any mention of it on the local news this evening? The London news won't cover a small story like this in Hampshire.'

'A suicide…' she said, tentatively.

'Don't know yet.'

'Are you sure you're okay?' she said. I knew she meant emotionally, not physically. The mention of a fatality couldn't fail to throw her back to the same place it did me, but now wasn't the time to dredge up my feelings about it.

'How about you?' I said. 'You managed to get dressed, yet?'

'Oh, sure. Finishing that last bottle of Merlot helped.'

I could picture Caroline standing with one foot resting on the other wearing rolled-down pink socks and a chiffon ditsy dress, her slender arms scooping up her wavy hair. Even at her worst, she managed to retain that most elusive of qualities: uncontrived elegance. I wished I looked that stunning on a *good* day, never mind when my heart was breaking.

It was a rerun of the same old story. The previous week, Caroline had moved out of the Brighton flat she'd started sharing with Martin - an episode that lasted exactly two weeks - to stay in the holiday flat her mother owned, in Southsea. Luckily for her, the demand for seafront accommodation had been patchy that summer. Martin had a lot going for him; a thriving vintage wedding-car business for one, but he had a habit of blowing hot and cold when it came to his commitment to Caroline.

Matters were further complicated by Martin's more than healthy relationship with Pam, his ex-wife. Four children under ten didn't help. It kept Pam and Martin inexorably enmeshed and Caroline forever trying to make her mark, like trying to hammer a foothold into an icy slope with a slipper.

During the course of the weekend, she had wept, shrieked, stomped around, broken a photo-frame, a mirror and a pot plant. She had come up for air and wept again. She was going to finish it. She was going to tell Martin where to put his engagement ring. She was going to be rid of him for good - this time.

Anger made her blonde hair flash from side to side, like a blazing flare on a boat in distress. I was easy to see why she was an actress, although in the last few years, most of her work had been in advertising.

'Martin says I'm self-centred and I should understand that sometimes his boys come first,' she continued. 'I've tried - I really have - but Martin says…'

I wanted to remark that Martin said a lot of things that weren't worth the auditory effort required to take them in, but I didn't. *Don't stir* is my motto, especially when it's someone else's favourite custard.

The train blared its horn as we hurtled through a tunnel and shook me back to the present.

'You still there?' said Caroline. 'I'll phone shall I? If there's anything about the train incident on the news?'

I thanked her and rang off. The rest of the journey was uneventful, which was just as well as I barely had enough energy to drag myself home to Richmond.

If you could ever describe any part of Richmond-on-Thames as being run down, I'd just moved there. In the early stages of Caroline's turbulent relationship with Martin, she and I shared a flat together in Brighton. But she'd hardly spent any time there - except to mope when Martin failed to come up to scratch - and I'd decided it was time to move on. Besides, I'd always wanted to be back in London.

The old Victorian house on Finlay Road had been up for sale for years, but had so much wrong with it that no one would touch it as a property purchase. The owner had decided to split it into three flats for renting and it was snapped up straight away.

I lived at the top in a converted attic. There was a small sitting room, kitchen, bathroom the size of a wardrobe and an unusually large bedroom with awkward sloping corners at every turn. Apart from the damp patches (and mould inside the linen cupboard), the turbo-charged orange-swirl carpets and the constant round of things that didn't work (like the cold-running shower and the dodgy spin on the washing machine) - it was perfect.

There hadn't been a drop of rain in Richmond. It made what happened earlier feel like it took place on a different day altogether. Once I'd made a cup of tea, I was tempted to call Caroline again to explain more about my troubled journey home. I picked up the phone and dropped it down again. I wasn't sure I could cope with another round of vitriol about Martin. In any case, I was supposed to be learning how to be on my own.

The doorbell rang; shrill and intrusive. I was tempted not to answer it; I was too depleted to play at being a welcoming host. On second thoughts, however, it might be the landlord about to barge in regardless.

'Greetings,' said a short bald chap standing on the step. He was wearing a suspicious amount of unmatching tartan - a waistcoat, tie and cummerbund - but he didn't sound the slightest bit Scottish. 'I live downstairs - at your service.' He gave a little bow. 'My real name is Terry, but everyone calls me Squid.' He sounded more like he was from Essex.

I wondered who 'everyone' was. And why he was bothering me.

'Landlord said you needed the toilet seat fixing - and I'm your man.' I could see him looking past me, keen to get on with it.

'Right. Yes. I'm Anna Rothman. Just moved in.'

He picked up his toolbox and came inside, assiduously wiping his feet on the mat even though it was perfectly dry outside.

'Don't like to see a young lady struggling by on her own,' he said.

'I'm not struggling,' I said, more sharply than I meant to.

'You independent women, these days - you don't need us men anymore. It's all about getting on in your careers, am I right?'

I wanted to put him straight and tell him that I'd been happily married until disaster struck two years ago. I made him a cup of tea instead.

He'd finished the job and was on his way down the stairs, when he turned to make what I thought would be one more sexist comment.

'My wife died last year,' he said. 'So I'm a lonely, grumpy old bugger, but I won't bother you unless you need help.' A lump caught in my throat and I was almost apologising for words I hadn't actually uttered, when my mobile rang. He gave me another bow and left.

'How's it going?' I said, tentatively. It was Caroline. I sat on the edge of the bed, then moved into the sitting room. It was strange with all this space to myself. I wasn't quite sure how to make use of it all.

'Martin rang full of remorse and promises, but I'm staying in Southsea for the time being to see how things go. I'm not going to relax until he's delivered some long term follow-through.'

She sounded serious. Maybe this time she was putting her foot down over Martin's propensity to drift back to his ex-wife like a homing pigeon. I hoped she'd stand her ground. Caroline had given him too many second chances already. 'Anyway, you were right, there was an item on the news,' she said.

'Go on...'

'A death on the line at a level-crossing just outside Micheldever.' She said it like she was reading a line from a recipe.

'No more detail than that?'

'Wait a minute…I wrote it down…here we go. Exact words…the reporter said, "A young woman was struck and killed by a train at a level-crossing just outside Micheldever, this afternoon. The woman, who has yet to be identified, was pronounced dead at the scene. British Transport Police are liaising with local police to investigate the incident." That's it.'

'The woman wasn't named?' The mysterious disappearance of the restless E.S. was still playing on my mind, although I didn't like the way my brain was putting her in the same frame as the fatal incident.

'No. Look, I'll record the local news for the rest of the week, if you like - it's really easy with Mum's new machine.' She stalled. 'You okay? You sound a bit low. Has it knocked you for six?'

'Just tired. I had such a weird afternoon. First there was this odd woman on train…then there was the awful panic with the emergency stop. Then I had my bag stolen—'

'Your *bag* stolen! You didn't mention that.'

'But it was weird, because we found it again - a policeman helped…and there was nothing missing.'

'What? Did you see who it was?'

'Vaguely. A guy in a raincoat. I don't think the police caught up with him…in any case, he abandoned the bag without taking anything, not even the money.'

'How very weird...'

'The same guy had slipped back on the train after we'd stopped and was snooping around near where I was sitting.'

'Anna, it sounds spooky. Perhaps you should tell the police.'

'I sort of did, really - when it happened, but nothing's missing. There's nothing to go on, is there?'

'I should turn your bag upside down and check for sure, if I were you.'

'Yeah…perhaps you're right,' I said, looking over at it sitting innocently on a chair by the door.

As soon as I closed the phone, I tipped the contents of my bag out onto the sofa. Everything I expected to see was there, plus a few old sweet wrappers, a loose two-pence coin, a handful of my business cards, a foil strip of painkillers and a few balls of fluff. Overdue for a proper clear-out, but no, nothing missing.

Then I noticed something I'd never seen before. It was a gold locket. I poked at it with the end of my pen, as if it was a large insect. There was no chain, just the heart-shaped locket itself, about an inch wide. I picked it up and rested it in my palm. *Where had this come from?* It was tarnished, but looked and felt like solid gold. I tried to open the catch, but it wouldn't shift. I tried to prise my nail between the edges and after several attempts managed to snap off my nail. I winced, holding the item in my closed hand. I could feel it getting warm.

I thought back over the weekend and wondered if perhaps it belonged to Caroline or her mother and had found its way into my bag by accident. I pictured Caroline; tried to imagine it hanging around her neck, but she wasn't a locket sort of girl - more into modern bling - diamante rings and chunky necklaces. Come to think of it, that was all I'd ever seen her mother wearing too.

I lifted it up and examined it. It looked old, possibly antique with a delicate line of dots running around the edge. I wouldn't rest until I'd got it open, just in case there was something inside, but I needed something thin to force it. I glanced around the room, but there was nothing I could use that wouldn't damage it.

A thought suddenly struck me. I dropped the locket on to a cushion, as though it had given me an electric shock. *What if the guy in the raincoat had left it there? Maybe he'd stolen it and needed to hide it somewhere?*

But it didn't add up. Why abandon the bag when I'd got nowhere near him? Why not put the locket in his own pocket or rucksack? The unexpected discovery made me sift through every other item, but there was nothing else.

I recalled the key fob on the agitated woman's bag. The initials E.S. Did this belong to her? I checked the locket again, but there was no engraving on it. I sat back, bunching up the cushion on my lap, mystified.

I ran through what I could remember of the hour or so we'd been sitting together. At the time, I'd done my utmost to block everything out; now I wanted to retrieve as much as possible. I remembered that I'd given her my magazine, that it had dropped to the floor. I remembered how she'd left her seat, clutching her bag, to go to the toilet. What had happened then? She'd come back to her seat. I'd had the text from Joan and had called her back. We'd talked a bit about my work.

What then?

I'd been writing down ideas. I'd got to the point of ignoring her. Then she'd got up suddenly as we pulled into Micheldever and she'd left the train. No, she'd dropped the bottle of perfume and bent down, first. Plenty of opportunity to slip the locket into my handbag.

I sat upright, feeling light-headed. I could see again the beseeching stare she'd given me as she left the train. Now, like then, it made my heart sink.

All of a sudden, I wished I wasn't alone. I needed to sound this out with friends, work out what I should do. I was tempted to reach for the phone, but I stayed still. No. I couldn't defer to other people all the time. I'd done enough of that in the last two years. It was time to learn to stand on my own two feet. I'd lost all faith in my own judgement, my own intuition. I'd gone from being headstrong and sure of myself, to tentative and meek. A flat-packed version of myself. I wanted the old Anna back. She'd been out to lunch long enough. No, I was going to cope with this on my own.

I went to the kitchen and began boiling a kettle for some pasta. There were still piles of boxes around the place, but gradually the place was looking less like a warehouse and more like a home.

As the penne danced around in the pan, my earlier suspicion was starting to solidify. The one that said E.S. was the same woman who'd been killed under the train. I didn't want to go down that path. There had to be a different explanation.

A wave of dizziness caught me by surprise and I grabbed the worktop. This was the point where Caroline would have rushed to get a bucket and offered me something inappropriate, like a large brandy. I sat down and dropped my head between my knees. False alarm. I was just fine.

That night, I laid the locket on my bedside cabinet. It made it look like it belonged to me. As I tried to sleep, all I could hear was my brain clattering away like the inside of a noisy factory. Eventually, I got up and wandered on to the landing in my nightdress. There was a full moon. I hadn't yet bought a blind for the skylight and the blue-grey glow was making the globe appear as though it was generating its own mysterious aura from within. It was trying to turn everything in its path to silver. I stood in the light, wondering for an eerie moment if this was how it would feel to exist on a different planet. Or how it might feel the moment you die and don't belong to the earth anymore.

I wondered if that was how it had felt for Jeff.

The moment when his spirit took off in another trajectory and spun away from our planet into a parallel place somewhere, on the other side of space, where the air is like mercury and colours are always shadows, like this.

I breathed in the shafts of light, trying to reach him across the ether. Unbeknown to Caroline, the weekend I'd just spent with her had been a bittersweet milestone: exactly ten years from the time Jeff and I met. Ten years since he walked into my life and almost literally bowled me over.

He was working in a bakers in Covent Garden at the time and ran a trolley stacked with bakewell tarts over my toes. I felt like I'd had an electric shock, but it was nothing to do with the pain in my foot. It was one of those weird moments when you want the world to freeze-frame so you can savour it; knowing with certainty that something special, significant, sensational is taking place. It was something to do with the way he swung round and his thick rose-gold hair settled in slow-motion on his shoulders. The way he covered his mouth when he realised what he'd done. It was our beginning.

I shivered. A shadow in my peripheral vision shifted and made me jump. A figure was standing in the shrouded doorway of the sitting room. It suddenly crouched down. I sucked in a sharp breath and brought my hand to my chest.

I was stunned into paralysis, waiting for something to happen. Nothing moved. *Should I make a run for the front door? Where were my keys?* There was no sound. No one else breathing. The figure stayed crouching on the floor. A small figure. Very small indeed, I realised, as my eyes grew accustomed to the low light. And totally immobile.

I cursed myself. *What an idiot.* A gust of wind had blown my silk dressing-gown, hooked in the middle of the doorway, off its hanger. I put on the light to be certain, dropped the dressing gown in a heap on the sofa and shut the sitting room window.

My lungs were still powering like a steam train when I got back into bed.

Welcome back to being young, free and single. Caroline wasn't in the next room anymore. I was going to have to get used to moments like this.

chapter three

I was folding clothes in my bedroom on Tuesday morning, when my mobile rang.

'I'm back in Brighton,' said Caroline, triumphantly. 'Martin's turned over a new leaf. His ex is off-limits. It's going to be much better.'

That was quick. 'Good,' I said, pulling a face. I was glad she couldn't see me. I'd witnessed Caroline's U-turns before.

'There was more on the news about that train you were on,' she said. 'That's why I'm phoning. I wrote down the name of the woman, who... you know, was killed. Hold on...'

There was a rustle of papers.

'Here it is. Elly Swift.' I couldn't help but gulp a loud gasp of air. 'You okay, Anna?'

Elly Swift...*E.S.* - the frightened woman who had dashed off the train several stops too early. It must have been the same one. 'Said she went... um...under the train. They're still investigating...but they're implying,' she took a long breath, 'that...it was...suicide.' I couldn't speak for a second. 'Anna, you still there?'

'Yes, sorry. I think it was the woman I was sitting next to.' My throat was suddenly parched; the words splintering as I spoke. 'The one I was so mean about...'

It was Caroline's turn to sound shocked. There was a faint, 'Oh.'

'Was there anything else?' I said.

'There was an appeal for information from anyone who was with her that day...from one o'clock onwards, they said, in the final hours leading to her death.'

'Right. I'd better see the police, then.'

'Anna, it's awful. Especially after—'

I knew she meant Jeff, but that she wouldn't actually say his name. Caroline, like everyone else I was close to, knew that something like this would press some tender buttons for me. None of them knew what it was that drove Jeff to suicide; luckily the word itself appears to be constructed entirely of barbed wire, so that when people hear it they tend to keep their distance. For those who pry further, pulling the word 'depression' out of the bag comes in handy. It is sweeping and cavernous enough for people to nod sympathetically and get the picture. The wrong picture, as it happens, but it was Jeff's secret and I felt I had no right to drag it into the open.

'I'm okay. Listen, you're not missing a gold heart-shaped locket, by any chance?'

'A what?'

I explained what I'd discovered in my bag. 'Maybe yours or your Mum's?'

'Not mine, definitely. Pretty sure it's not Mum's, but I'll call her and check. You found it in the bottom of your bag?'

'I think she might have left it for me,' I said.

'How extraordinary,' she said, with animation. 'It's starting to sound like a mystery drama.'

'Except, from where I'm standing, it's a bit too real.'

'Yeah. Sorry.' She cleared her throat. 'Are you sure she left it there? I mean - it could belong to anybody. The chain could have snapped in a crowd and it could have fallen from someone's neck into your bag.' It sounded pretty unlikely. 'In any case, when you see the police, hand it over, Anna. It's too creepy.'

'We'll see,' I said.

'Don't go doing anything stupid,' she said.

'Like what?' My voice was heavy with indignation.

'I *know* you, Anna, you're like a dog who gets the scent of something and you won't let it be.'

I didn't like to admit that she was right. In terms of my job, it was a valuable trait to have. Plus, I always seemed to be on the lookout for distractions these days. After I put down the phone, I picked up the photograph of Jeff and I in the rain at our wedding; the one I kept on my bedside cabinet. I stroked the glass. I always thought Jeff would die a tragic death on his beloved motorbike. I never ever imagined it would end as it did. If only I'd done more to comfort him, reassure him that I loved him, to show him that we would have got through his despair, together.

When I think back over our two years of marriage, I see only magical days brimming with companionship and humour. We were like grown-up kids drawn together by our skewed brand of humour. It was a perfect match; the way a plug fits snugly into a socket. I'd never had that kind of connection with anyone before, or since; it was as though the two of us had discovered an exclusive language that no one else could get the hang of. Jeff could have me doubled over in the aisles of a supermarket, a library or at the bus-stop with one single throwaway comment - usually an irreverent stage-whisper involving a garment someone was wearing or an acute observation of human nature. Jeff noticed things in a way I never did. His mind turned to quicksilver when it came to wit; he managed to deliver hilarious quips with the velocity of a thunderbolt.

In spite of this, I'd always known that our relationship was different from that of other couples. If I'm honest, there was an abundance of tenderness and fun, but little in the way of romance or physical intimacy. Sex was always an afterthought, initiated by me, which Jeff turned into a giggling match or game of some sort. In its place, there was a togetherness about everything we did; a delight in each other's company. We wore each other like a pair of treasured comfy slippers.

If only Jeff had hung on. If only he'd let me work through it all with him. Let me in. I missed him. Every day. I felt like my heart would forever be frayed around the edges.

I thought about Elly Swift and wondered what kind of desperation she must have been going through in order to take her own life. I'd tormented myself over Jeff, of course, anguishing over the exact moment when he knew he was going to end it all; when he must have started putting together his lethal plan, deciding how he'd do it, finding a bridge...

The worst thing about the way Jeff's life ended was that when he hit the water, he would have spent his last moments bitterly cold and alone - and the death of someone you love should never be like that. I closed my eyes and saw images of his body floating, face down in the midnight water. Then I pictured Elly. A soggy, broken bundle lying across the railway tracks. Left out in the rain like forgotten laundry. For some reason, it seemed far worse than dying when the sun was shining.

Had Elly made up her mind to kill herself before she gave me that haunting stare as she left the train? Had she known that she was going to head straight to the level-crossing and jump in front of the first train that came along?

I kissed Jeff's picture and lovingly replaced it.

Like a dutiful citizen, I rang the police. Because the incident had taken place in Hampshire and was being handled partly by the Transport Police, the desk sergeant asked me to turn up in person at the police station near Waterloo.

Before I left, I picked up the locket from my bedside. I had to get it open. Why else would the woman on the train have left it for me? I'd relived our encounter many times by now and I was sure it came from her. There were at least two times when I remembered her scrabbling around on the floor between our seats and my bag was open near my feet the whole time. And it put her final pleading stare into context. She was asking me for help.

Getting into it turned into a major operation. It was like trying to prise open a stubborn oyster. So far I'd succeeding in buckling a pair of tweezers and bending the blade of a paring knife. I found a thin screwdriver and tried to jam it between the sides of the locket, but it slipped and the tip gouged a thin line in the gold on the back. *Damn.* I didn't want to spoil it, although I had to remind myself that its owner wouldn't be seeing it again.

I tried a different screwdriver, but it was still too thick to get a proper purchase in the groove. I had a go with pliers and a Stanley knife, but only succeeded in making two gashes in my thumb. I resorted to wearing gloves, but couldn't get a proper grip anymore. It wasn't budging.

There was no way around it: I wasn't getting into it. I'd never know what was inside. I'd simply have to hand it over and let the police take it from there. I grabbed my jacket and left the flat for the next fast train to the city, my mind fizzing with questions I'd probably never know the answers to.

It was raining when I got outside Waterloo station; a relentless, heavy rain that creeps inside your cuffs and collar even when you have an umbrella. I'd forgotten that my boots had a tiny slit in the sole. I tried to avoid the puddles, weaving my way along the pavement like a battery-operated toy, but my left foot was wet even before I'd reached the first junction. A bus pulled into the kerb and sent a bucket full of water over my feet for good measure. I swore under my breath at the driver, turned the corner and gave up avoiding the puddles after that.

I reached into my bag and rubbed the locket gently with my fingers. Why had Elly left it with me? Why not go to the police, if she was frightened about something?

There was a police van parked outside and a chunky white motorbike with battenburg markings behind it indicating I'd got the right place. As I climbed the white tiled steps that led to a modern looking building, an officer came out of the glass doors and passed me on the top step. He looked like he had bad news to deliver; too preoccupied to hold the door open for me.

My stomach turned into a hollow pit as I caught the grave look on his face. I'd got used to my personal tragedy, gradually over time. I'd worn it like an ill-fitting waistcoat that becomes familiar in its discomfort over the years. But I still had days when a song or a scene from a film, or a moment like this would jolt me straight back to that time. The morning when I opened the front door and found a policeman standing on my doorstep, looking at his shoes, with his hands clasped in front of him. When I knew before he even drew breath. Knew my world was about to explode in my face when he opened his mouth to utter those savage words: *We've found your husband - I'm afraid he's dead.*

The door swung back and forth a few times before I reached it. I held the cold handle and closed my eyes tight, willing the distressing memory to go back where it came from.

Once inside, I was greeted with the oily smell of new carpets. I dutifully wiped my feet on the rubber mat and approached the desk. Two male officers wearing high-visibility waistcoats were talking to each other. Idly chatting, I should say. One leaned forward and nudged the other as if he was telling a dirty joke. They both chuckled, seemingly oblivious to my presence.

I turned around to look at the interior. Alongside the 'Have you see this man?' posters were stylish king-sized photographs of operations involving helicopters, car chases and criminals being handcuffed beside a train. It was a pity that the *We-are-true-professionals* image didn't extend to the reception desk.

I cleared my throat and put my hand on the wooden top. The chit-chat dried up and the officers turned to me in one synchronised movement.

'And what can we do for you, madam?' said the one on the right. He leant across the desk like he was picking me up in a bar. He had cropped blonde hair and a spoon-shaped bruise under one eye, and bore an uncanny resemblance to the e-fit I'd just scanned on the wall a moment ago. I pulled back an inch or two.

'It's about a death at a level-crossing in Micheldever. Last Sunday. A TV report said you were looking for witnesses.'

'You witnessed it?'

'Well, no, but I was with the woman who died, just before she…'

'You'd better come through, then.' He said it in a lacklustre, tiresome tone that suggested he was hoping I had something more catastrophic to report. It must have been a slow crime day.

I was taken through to a corridor and then into a small bare room.

'Someone will be with you in a minute,' he said, without offering me a seat. I leant against the table, which smelt of freshly sawn wood and heard the clock crisply spit out each second.

A young woman breezed in. 'Sorry to keep you.'

She wore a black skirt and white short-sleeved blouse with one of those chequered cravats that reminded me of the Formula One flag. She introduced herself as WPC Cilla Lane and invited me to take a seat. 'I'll take a statement here and make sure it gets sent through to the officers dealing with the incident at Micheldever,' she said. 'Let's start with your name…'

I explained who I was and how I'd met Elly; how she'd seemed nervous and fretful as I sat next to her on the train. How I'd seen she had a ticket to Waterloo.

'You're sure about that?' she said.

'Yes. I remember the ticket collector humming the destination of each passenger. Elly's was the same as mine. She was already on the train, so she must have got on at Portsmouth Harbour.'

She scribbled on a clipboard in front of her.

'What else can you tell us?'

I took her through the order of events in as much detail as I could remember.

'And you talked to her?'

'A little. She wasn't very forthcoming.'

'How did she seem?'

'Like I said, anxious, frightened, even.'

'But she didn't say why?'

'No. It was right before she left that she looked most afraid – then she was gone.'

'Did she tell you anything about what she was going to do next...after she left the train?'

'No.'

'Right. Is there anything else?'

A sliver of a gap. *Yes.* 'No, that's about it.'

Yes - she gave me this. That's what I should have said, followed by the surrender of the locket that was lying at the bottom of my handbag. Only, something held me back. A fierce inner voice insisting that I mustn't relinquish it. Instinctively, I folded by hands over my bag to reinforce the fact that there was nothing inside that could possibly be of any interest to WPC Lane.

She ended a sentence on her report with a flourishing full-stop. I took my time and didn't get up.

'We talked briefly about journalism,' I said. 'She wanted to know if I ever got involved in unsolved cases or miscarriages of justice. There was definitely something bothering her, but I didn't ask outright what it was…'

She made a brief note. 'Anything else?'

I let out a long breath. 'There was one odd thing,' I said. I hadn't thought of it until a few moments earlier. Not until I was going back through the story out loud, step by step. 'When Elly got up - presumably to go to the toilet - she came back wearing perfume.'

The officer stared at me, her pen frozen in the air, waiting for me to explain.

'Well, if I was going to take my own life,' I continued, 'I wouldn't bother with perfume. I mean, if you're in the depths of misery, you're not going to spritz on the Estee Lauder to make sure you smell nice, are you..?

'I'm not sure people always behave rationally when they're about to commit suicide.'

She gave me a superior look that suggested I knew nothing about such matters and shouldn't make sweeping statements. She pulled out a form from the back of her clipboard and started ticking boxes. 'We're nearly done,' she said, without looking up.

Something about the tone of her voice jolted me into a harrowing flashback. Not to the incident on the train, but to the enquiry after Jeff's death, two years ago. The thought of it sent a steel clamp around my throat. I'd felt pummelled by the police questioning at the time; enduring rounds of interviews, endless probings into Jeff's movements the night he died, his state of mind, his possible motives for wanting to kill himself.

I remembered the relentless aching in my face from crying; my puffy eyelids, bloodshot, scratchy eyes and pounding headache. I hadn't thought anyone was capable of discharging so many tears over such a prolonged period of time. I remembered the nights I'd half woken up thinking I'd imagined his final departure, reaching out for the warm hollow of his back. I recalled the robotic way I'd tried to carry on with normal life and how challenging even the simplest acts had become - like cleaning my teeth and finding his toothbrush still leaning against mine or hearing his voice cheerily saying we weren't at home when I played back the answer-phone.

I didn't know he'd taken a train. I thought he must have gone off on his motorbike somewhere. I hadn't realised he'd gone as far as Bristol. Why Bristol, for goodness sake? Who or what was *there* for him that he would gravitate in that direction to end his life? They were the questions that still haunted me.

But the rest, I *did* know. It was no mystery. There was no question that Jeff's death was suicide. An open and shut case. His parents blamed me of course; I never told them the truth. I was prepared to take the brunt of their wrath, fending off accusations of being a *bad wife, not making him happy, dragging him down* - to protect his privacy. It was one small precious thing that still held us together - our last secret.

WPC Lane shrugged as she shuffled her papers together. 'You just don't know,' she said, mostly to herself.

She was right about one thing: there is no way anyone can say for certain what's 'typical' behaviour before a person commits suicide. But, still, there was something about putting on perfume before you know you're going to die that didn't sit properly for me.

'She was certainly distressed,' I said, 'but it seemed more than that. Like she was more *frightened*, than in despair. She kept looking into the corridor like she was expecting to see someone. Someone she was afraid of. She rushed off the train, as if she thought someone might be following her…'

I was leaning towards her over the table, adamant, realising my voice was too loud. She gave me a disapproving look and put up her hand, ready to fend me off. It was only when I sat back that I realised something. Until a few minutes ago, I'd assumed Elly had committed suicide. But, the more I thought it through, the more doubts started to stack up. In that instant, I knew Elly hadn't done it. She hadn't killed herself. I knew it with every bone in my body.

The officer ticked a few more boxes on the statement and my mind took off on its own as I waited. What if when I got the locket open, there was something inside that was really important? I'd have to come back here and admit I lied. Or I'd have to act on what I found myself. What if the locket was empty? Then what?

WPC Lane slid the statement towards me, asked me to check it was accurate and sign it. I noticed that my opinions about Elly's state of mind had been omitted. Like every good police officer, WPC Lane had stuck to the facts. She stood and thanked me for coming.

'If anyone needs to follow this up, an officer will call you,' she said.

'If?'

'Obviously - I'll make sure your statement is added to the file, but there is already substantial evidence to suggest it was suicide.'

'Substantial evidence?'

She rested her hands on the table and gave a shifty look behind her, aware she shouldn't be saying what she was about to tell me.

'It will all come out at the inquest - I've seen the report. Apparently, Ms Swift had left a note - a suicide note - on her computer. She was on anti-depressants. Her parents weren't surprised.' She lowered her voice. 'There were…family issues. I can tell you this, because it was all over the news earlier this year. You might remember it? A young boy in the family went missing in March.'

Tiny filaments in the far reaches of my mind were lighting up.

Almost as an afterthought, she added, 'and she'd attempted it before. Twice...'

I caught myself staring into space. A family tragedy, a suicide note *and* two previous attempts. WPC Lane had enough evidence backing up her suicide theory to make it sound more than plausible. Perhaps I wasn't seeing the wood for the trees. Perhaps, I didn't *want* Elly to have taken her own life.

WPC Lane cleared her throat, but I stayed seated, aware I was keeping her waiting. Might Elly have been so distraught about the boy's disappearance that she was unable to carry on? Whose child was it? Was it Elly's son? Wouldn't WPC Lane have said so, if it was? If Elly wasn't his mother, why multiply your family's trauma by killing yourself? There had to be something else. But, there again, WPC Lane had just told me the police had found a suicide note. My head started spinning off in all directions at once and I faltered as I stood and had to grip the table.

'You okay?' said Cilla Lane, her papers pressed against her chest.

'Sorry. Yes.' I stopped on the threshold. 'She was scared,' I said, 'for her safety.'

'Did she actually say anything about anyone following her or being in danger?'

'No...' I conceded.

'And didn't you say yourself, that she was behaving oddly, irrationally?'

I knew for a fact that I hadn't used those words.

'She seemed frightened, not irrational. With the benefit of hindsight, everything she did spelt out the actions of someone who was fearful, afraid...'

'Of course she'd seem like that if she was planning to end her own life...Ms...er... Rothman.' I'd seen her eyes dodge down to her papers before she said my name. 'I've worked with suicides. I've helped talk people down from bridges before. Ms Swift sounded in exactly the same state of mind as I've seen in those cases. Petrified they might not do it properly and end up in unbearable pain. Terrified that there seems to be no other way out. Frightened about what dying will actually feel like...'

She took hold of the door handle, waiting for me to leave and spoke into her radio, effectively ending our encounter. There was an awkward moment. I wanted to ask more. I wanted to ask about the suicide note Elly had written. About what the police knew about her previous attempts, but WPC Lane took off down the corridor, before I had chance to draw breath. I was back outside in the rain before I knew it.

As I headed back to Waterloo, it was hard to say why I felt compelled to get involved. Elly was a stranger to me, I had no obligation towards her. She hadn't actually *asked* me for help. Nevertheless, her situation stirred something in me, not only my innate curiosity and hunger for the truth, but a desire to do my best for her. Elly knew I was a journalist, interested in scratching below the surface. She was trying to tell me something.

In addition, there were too many loose ends as far as I could see - too many to let this be swept under the carpet so soon as suicide. Why spray on perfume? Why leave a locket in my bag? Simply too many unanswered questions for me to be satisfied Elly had taken her own life.

As I splashed headlong through the puddles, I considered what, if anything, the police would do as a result of my statement. It sounded like they had already concluded it was suicide. The case was effectively closed. If so, my version of events would count for nothing and would sit neglected in some box-room somewhere gathering dust.

As I rounded the corner and blended into the hubbub of activity at the station, I thought about how safe and uneventful my life had been lately. Work wasn't fulfilling enough to hold my interest these days and I had time on my hands. Besides, I was overdue for a taste of what I did best. I hadn't known until that moment that this was what I'd been looking for. A crusade I could launch myself into. A worthy investigation. Then Elly had come along; unappealing to start with, but now full of intrigue. It was time to get the bit between my teeth and upset a few apple-carts for a change. I'd been hiding under my comfort blanket for too long. In truth, ever since Jeff died.

In the end, however, there was one thing that swung it for me, utterly and completely. The haunting imploring look Elly had given me when she left the train. I couldn't shake it out of my head. It was an emotional tug I couldn't ignore. In spite of Caroline's warnings, I couldn't let this rest.

As I stepped on the train at platform sixteen, I knew there was one thing I could do. The first port of call was my laptop. I could track down details of the missing boy in the press.

That would set the ball rolling.

chapter four

I spent the next couple of days dividing my time between the feature for Joan and reports about the missing boy. His name was Toby Delaney. There were several accounts and I read them all. From subsequent reports it appeared that the four-year-old boy was Elly's nephew, abducted at the end of March. A desperate picture started to emerge as Elly was interviewed, describing the way her family struggled with the torment of his disappearance.

I skimmed through the remaining news items stopping each time Toby's name appeared again, hoping for an update that said they'd found him safe and sound. The last one was just two lines, dated ten days ago, and said he was still missing. I tried to imagine Elly's sister, her parents - and a heavy wash of tragedy slid over me. That poor family - so much loss to cope with.

I made a note of one detail in particular. It was the name of the church from which Toby had been taken. St Stephen's catholic church in Stockwell. The boy had been snatched from the Children's Liturgy group, the catholic version of Sunday School, on March 21st.

I scrolled back up to the name of the paper. There was a journalist I knew who wrote regularly for the Lambeth Gazette. I'd come across Denise Lunn at a conference last year, giving a talk on freedom of information at the BBC and we'd subsequently exchanged a few emails. I sent her a quick message, giving sketchy reasons for showing an interest in the abduction case, hoping she was the one who'd written the article.

The phone rang.

'Mum says it isn't hers.'

'Sorry?'

'The locket.' Caroline was crunching her way through an apple by the sound of it. 'She's never had one.'

I think I already knew that would be the case. 'And there was an update on the train thingy…I went back to Southsea to collect the rest of my stuff and made a note of it…definitely suicide, apparently. They took a while to identify her, because she had no ID, no bag…'

'No bag…mmm - that's interesting.' I pictured the tatty green holdall glued to Elly's chest.

'There's no CCTV at that level-crossing, it's due to be installed next month - so there was no footage the police could look at. It was raining and there weren't many people about, but apparently witnesses said a woman just rushed on to the track without warning at about five to four. It was one of those half-barrier crossings. No one said she'd been pushed.'

'Did it mention how many people were near her? Who actually saw her?'

'No…that's all they said. Except the funeral's on Monday.'

She said she would listen out for any further reports, but I had a feeling there would be no more media coverage. Case closed.

'The police think it's suicide, but it isn't,' I said.

'Anna - you're not going to do anything stupid, are you?'

'Of course not.'

I knew she had my best interests at heart. *Avoid anything that's going to dig up old wounds* was one of her mottos, although she wasn't that good at following her own advice.

'Just leave it to the police, Anna, I mean it. The woman's dead. It all sounds very dodgy to me.'

I said something noncommittal and ended the call.

I sat immobile after I'd put down the phone, thinking about Elly's bag. Caroline had said it wasn't there when she was found. I had a clear vision in my mind of Elly scuttling towards the stairs in the station, cradling it like a baby. At what point did she become separated from it? Did she simply drop it? Or was someone else involved?

I needed to get that locket open.

It wasn't the quickest route to where I was going, but I wanted to take advantage of the unexpected heat-wave.

It was one of those late summer days trying its best to convince everyone that winter would never seep through and ravage the earth. Except, as I cut across Richmond Green, I could see that the change of season had already started. Bundles of leaves were congregating under benches and beside an ice-cream van, swirling occasionally in the light breeze, protesting that they still had life left in them.

The jewellers was straight out of Dickens' London. The first thing I noticed was the pristine brass letter-box sitting low in the brown door to the right of a rounded bay window. There was a matching brass pull-grip handle; the sort that makes a definitive clunk when the door is opened. Dark varnished wooden panels ran under the window and multiple shelves inside displayed everything from wedding rings to silver hip flasks. There was even a gold chess set. It wasn't a shop I'd ever spent any money in, but I'd spent time outside daydreaming.

When I entered I expected to see an elderly man with wild white hair and a stoop, dressed in a striped waistcoat, but instead, a young man with tousled gelled hair looked up as the bell tinkled. His shirt collar was rolling under at the edges, making it look like it was poorly ironed and the knot of his pink tie was hanging too low, revealing his top button. Instead of the smell of silver polish, an aroma of cheap after-shave hung in the air.

He stared at me sharply; the look of someone caught doing something he shouldn't.

'I'm sorry, I'm not here to buy anything,' I said. 'Just hoping you might be able to open this…'

I unfolded the crackling tissue paper and laid Elly's gold locket on a leather pad on the glass counter.

The man peered at it, then picked it up to get a closer look.

'It's not worth much,' he said.

'I'm not bothered about that, I just want to get it open.'

'What's inside?'

His voice had a nasty disparaging edge to it and as he lifted his lip into a sneer, I noticed one of his front teeth was gold. It should have befitted a person working in a jewellers, but for some reason it exuded a lack of trustworthiness.

I hesitated. 'I don't know.' He raised his eyebrows. 'That's why I'm here.'

I was half expecting him to ask if I'd stolen it.. He spread his hands on the counter. They were calloused and thick around the joints. I noticed tattoos of seagulls on his thumbs. He looked like he was in entirely the wrong profession; as if by accident he'd turned up here for work today, instead of the local used-car showroom down the road. He stared at the locket and sighed, making it clear that it was going to cause him a considerable amount of unnecessary bother. I waited.

'Can you do it?' I said, poised to retrieve it.

He bent down behind the counter and slid open a drawer, pulling out an implement that looked like something a dentist would use.

'I'll have a go.' He didn't sound encouraging.

He disappeared through to the back of the shop. I moved two or three steps closer to his point of exit, hoping to be able to watch his every move, but a heavy curtain flapped shut behind him as though he was part of a conjuror's show. I was annoyed by his vanishing act. I'd hoped he would have performed the operation on the locket in front of me so I could be sure he didn't damage it. Besides, I wanted to be the first to see exactly what was tucked inside.

I suddenly had a vision of something untoward falling out or something so small it would get brushed to the floor and lost forever. My mind ran through a list of likely objects hidden inside: a lover's photograph or lock of hair being the most obvious. What else might one keep inside a locket? A tiny love-note? A gemstone? A cash-point pin-number?

Now the locket was out of my sight, I realised how protective I'd become of it. It was like handing over an injured bird to someone clumsy and insensitive. I didn't like the idea of it being prey to this man's seemingly heavy-handed approach, but I didn't have any choice. I couldn't shift the conviction from my mind that he didn't want me to see the botch job he was going to make of it.

I braced myself for the man's return, expecting to hear the locket was empty or impossible to open. Moments later, the curtain swished. The jeweller was looking pleased with himself. He placed the locket on the leather mat and beside it, he laid something else. I leaned closer.

'I think you might need a magnifying glass,' he said, holding his own tantalisingly out of reach, like a dummy above a small child. 'Have you got one?'

'I do…at home…as it happens.'

He looked disappointed, as though he'd been on the verge of making an unexpected sale. 'Thank you…for your time,' I said.

'Right,' he said, rubbing his hands together. He moved towards the till and for one horrible moment, I thought he was going to charge me. 'Maybe see you again, then.' I gave him a brisk stick-on smile and muttered *not if I can help it* under my breath as I made for the door. 'Have a nice day,' he crooned, in a corny American accent.

As soon as I got outside, I took a quick look at the item he'd found. It was neither a photograph, nor a lock of hair, and as far as I was concerned, it didn't shed any light whatsoever on my quest to discover more about what happened to Elly.

I went straight home. I put the locket on my dressing table and pulled out my great aunt's old sewing box. Before I could put my hands on what I was looking for my phone rang.

It was Denise Lunn, the journalist who worked for the Lambeth Gazette. She hadn't covered the story about Toby's abduction herself, but she knew who had. She gave me the number of a reporter called Stefan Kendrick, saying he was a 'decent guy' and wouldn't mind me contacting him.

I decided to make the call first, before devoting whatever time I needed to the contents of the locket.

Stefan Kendrick answered on the second ring in a hushed voice. I explained who I was.

'Is this about the Stockwell abduction story?'

'Denise Lunn said you'd covered that story. I hope it's okay to—'

'Yeah, yeah. No problem. But the story has gone cold lately.' I could hear a lot of background noise and footsteps echoing down a corridor. It sounded like he was inside a hospital. 'Listen, I'm tied up for most of the week. Are you free on Sunday at all?' I told him I didn't have any plans. 'Can you get to Streatham Vale cemetery around nine in the morning?'

It struck me as a strange time and place. 'Sorry about the unsociable hours. I'm covering an exhumation - it should be done and dusted by nine. I'm going straight from there to catch a plane to Frankfurt, and I won't be back until Thursday. We can liaise then, if that's better.'

'No. Sunday morning will be fine.'

I didn't mind an early start. I didn't want to wait any longer than was necessary.

'Foley Road, near Streatham Common station. See you at the main gate. If I'm not there, send me a text on this number. Come earlier if you want to see some action. I'll need to get you in, as they tend to bring the coffins up before the cemetery is open.'

What a way to spend your Sunday morning, I thought, digging up a dead body. Not often you get an offer like that.

'I might take you up on it. When will it start?'

'At sunrise. About seven.'

Even for something as fascinating as an exhumation, that was too early for me.

'I might make it for eight,' I said, my heart already fluttering at the prospect.

'You'll need a strong stomach - sometimes the lids are broken.'

'I think I can handle it.'

I was intrigued and not a little enthralled by the prospect. I was a tough cookie. I'd seen dead bodies before and although I'd had a more than passing acquaintance with death through Jeff than I would ever have wanted, it had toughened me up. Would Stefan be having his breakfast before or after the raising of the coffin? I knew which my preferred option was going to be. Better to be on the safe side.

I returned to the item that was inside the locket and took it, together with the magnifying glass into the kitchen, the room with the best natural light.

It was a neatly folded scrap of the thinnest tissue paper, with a design on it drawn in pencil, like a floor design of a house. I screwed up my eyes.

There were six rooms and in the smallest one there was a tiny cross. X marks the spot? At the top, in small handwriting were the words, *The Flower Girl's House.* There was nothing else on the sheet. No address. No clue as to the location.

I sat back, my lips twisting into perplexed frustration.

Where was I supposed to look? And what was I looking for?

I thought there'd be more than this. I wanted to help Elly. Under the disappointment, another feeling was coiling around my throat. It took me a moment to identify it. Then it broke through, like a cobra arching its flat head above the undergrowth. Guilt.

Even though we had only exchanged a few words, I felt like I was letting Elly down. She'd talked to me about whether I investigated crimes - she'd obviously been sounding me out to see whether I'd help her. Instead, I'd got nowhere at all.

But, by now I was hooked.

I stamped my feet as I stood outside the imposing black gates. It was cold and windy. I should have brought my gloves. Clumps of leaves tried to wrap themselves around my feet as if seeking their own place of warmth and I could see trees inside the cemetery straining against the wind, flutters of foliage falling with every gust.

Two police officers stood inside with their backs to me. One held a paper coffee cup, the steam coiling into the air. I could have done with one of those, too - not to drink - just to warm my hands. I couldn't risk consuming anything. I didn't know what was going to happen this morning; how close we'd get to the coffin, what state it would be in - but making a fool of myself by throwing up wasn't going to be part of it. I'd always had a particularly sensitive sense of smell. It was great in bakeries and coffee shops, but sometimes it didn't work in my favour.

A man came striding towards the gate. He had a quick word with one of the officers and pointed my way. A grin dominated his round boyish face and he had dark choppy hair that looked like it had been hacked at with kitchen scissors and then backcombed. Somehow, it seemed to suit him; made him appear laidback, happy-go-lucky, a little cheeky.

He ambled towards me wearing blue drainpipe jeans, a black shirt and brown jacket; an odd colour combination I mused, but I liked the look of him even before he'd opened his mouth.

'Anna?'

His hand caught mine in a sideways squeeze rather than a formal handshake and he pulled me down the path. 'You haven't missed much,' he said, 'the coffin is still below ground. I'm Stefan, by the way.'

'You make me sound like a necrophiliac - I'm only mildly interested,' I said, trying to keep up with him.

'Ooo - it always starts that way,' he said, sucking in his cheeks. 'We can talk quietly as long as we stay over here.' He stopped at a spot beside a tree that looked down over the site.

Beyond rows of gravestones, I could see a white tent. It looked like it was struggling to hold its own against the gale and I was half expecting it to take off any moment, revealing its grisly secrets inside. A figure dressed top to bottom in a white suit, emerged through the flap, pulled down her mask and spoke to someone the other side of the *Police - do not enter* tape.

'That's the environmental health officer,' said Stefan, pointing in their direction. 'Next to her is the funeral director and there are a couple of bereavement services staff from the council here. It all has to be done following a tight procedure.'

'Why are they taking up the body?'

'The police have ordered it. It's an eighteen-year-old guy they thought had died by accident during a training exercise. Gunshot wound to the head - but the investigation has been reopened. Fresh evidence.'

A death that wasn't what it seemed...it looked like Elly wasn't the only one.

I pulled my coat around me. I felt like I was at least two layers of clothing short. Stefan must have seen me shiver and looped his scarf around my neck in such an easy manner that anyone watching would have assumed we were firm friends.

'Thanks,' I said. 'I haven't seen this time of day for a while.'

Dawn had fully swept through the morning, bleaching away the night-time, leaving a few pockets of mist clinging to the far corners of the cemetery. Outside the tent a light generator was rattling like a tractor. Aside from the swish of leaves, it was the only sound I could hear.

'There's no JCB digger?'

'The bodies are buried too close together for that. They're having to use spades.'

I took a few steps down the bank hoping to catch a glimpse inside the tent but only succeeded in attracting the attention of a police officer, who turned and stood with his hands on his hips.

'We're not allowed any nearer until they've given the all clear,' said Stefan, catching my arm. 'Health and safety.'

Distorted grey shapes inside the tent bent and crossed over each other. It was like watching a surreal shadow-puppet show. A low sun pierced the trees, gradually asserting itself.

'So why the Stockwell story?' he said, shifting his weight to one foot, his head on one side.

I decided to come clean right from the start, about Elly sitting beside me on the train, about the locket I thought she'd left in my bag. As soon as I'd started to explain, I could see why he made a good reporter. He had a soft encouraging voice, warm eyes and relaxed body-language that made me want to tell him everything. He listened without interrupting, standing still, never taking his eyes from me in spite of the activity below us. I could see that, with Stefan, it would be easy to tell the whole truth and nothing but the truth, when in fact, you'd only meant to spill half of it.

As I brought him up to date with the design I'd found inside the locket, the coffin poked out from the flap of the tent.

'Sorry, I'll have to leave you here. Don't go away.'

He took a signal from someone below and scampered down the bank to get as close as he could to the coffin. A couple of officers lifted their arms to indicate he should go no further. He joined them and patted one of them on the back. The coffin had lost its polish and was encrusted with soil, but otherwise looked intact. Four men lifted it onto a trolley and guided it towards the path. I watched Stefan speak to one of the men walking alongside it, making notes on a pad he'd pulled from his pocket. I took a discrete step or two closer, before I noticed a new group of people running down a path from the other side.

Suddenly a row of policemen came from nowhere and formed a barricade to stop the group from entering the exhumation site. They must have climbed over the locked fence at the far side; eight grey faces. I assumed they were family members. Angry shouts carried across the undisturbed graves and a distraught woman launched herself at the police officer nearest the coffin, beating his shoulders with her fists.

'Let him rest!' she shrieked. She howled and railed against the officer's containing grip before a WPC came running onto the scene and put her arms around her. The woman dissolved into weeping. Distressed shouts came from others in the group as the coffin was wheeled past them. A middle-aged woman doubled over and was supported by a heavy-set man.

I could see how upsetting it must be to have their son torn out of his resting place, but didn't his family need to know whether it had been an accident or whether someone needed to be brought to trial?

A figure in a white suit was using a spray gun to disinfect the area around the tent. I could see Stefan holding a small black tube, speaking to members of the group who were leaning against each other, propping each other up, trying to keep in step with the coffin. I wondered how long it had been since they had all been here, watching the coffin descend into the earth. Now they had the trauma of seeing it come back out again.

The coffin made it as far as the side gate without further interference and disappeared into an unmarked white van.

Stefan managed to speak with all eight members of the protesting group without causing further upset or being ushered away. He'd coaxed them into having their voices heard, their objections noted. I watched him bow slightly, with grace and courtesy, as he thanked them before he turned and walked back to join me.

He grimaced. 'Very mixed views about removing the body - his mother especially. She wanted him to stay where he was.'

'What will happen now?'

'There'll be another post-mortem at Tooting Infirmary. They will be looking again at ballistic evidence, bullet fragments, residue, angle of the shot - that sort of thing. Originally, the police thought the gun had gone off in the victim's own hand by accident, now they think the bullet may not have come from his own pistol.'

'I know it must be really disturbing for them, but don't the family want to know what really happened?'

'The problem is - lots of reinvestigations of this kind turn out to be inconclusive. There's no guarantee of a fresh result.' We turned to watch the family walk back in the direction from which they'd come; slow and measured this time, weighed down by renewed grief and anger. 'Sometimes the families end up with an open verdict. No one ever wants that.'

I stared at the broken soil under my feet and took myself back to Jeff's memorial service. It was a simple and graceful affair at a chapel near where he was born. Everyone left wearing a white rubber wristband with the words *In our Hearts* written on it. They also walked away with unanswered questions and confused frowns. I was the only one who knew the truth.

After we were married, everything went swimmingly until Jeff realised there was one fundamental problem in our relationship. I was a woman and he wanted to be with a man. There had been no showdown, no histrionics, no shock discoveries of male porn or finding him shagging another man behind the garden shed. He'd come home from work one night, asked me to sit down and he'd told me.

'There's something you need to know,' he said, like he was about to tell me he'd forgotten to pay the gas bill. 'I'm gay.'

That was it. After two years of marriage, part of me was shocked, appalled, devastated. The other part, tucked away behind a frosted partition, half-knew the truth already, but hoped Jeff would somehow never realise it for himself. Or that he'd get over it. Stupid, really. We'd both been dancing with denial.

Jeff said he'd *known* from the age of fifteen, but he kept thinking it was a phase he'd grow out of, like preferring granary bread to white or having a penchant for salted cashews. There was no question that we loved each other; love comes in many forms - it just wasn't the kind of love marriages are made of.

I accepted the truth, keeping it to myself, assuming we'd work our way through it once the dust had settled. For sure, there would have been a muddy period when we redefined our marital status, but we could have salvaged most of our relationship. Jeff, however, couldn't live any longer with the lie nor could he allow himself to come out of the proverbial closet. Within two weeks of telling me, he was dead. The truth was like a wall of fire to him that he couldn't bring himself to walk into. To Jeff, his little secret represented unforgivable betrayal and deception involving not just me, but his parents, his broader family - and himself. He couldn't bear the shame for having lived the lie for eight years. He couldn't face the forced bravado on his mother's face or the crest-fallen look on his father's, so he'd taken a train to Bristol one Friday night and jumped off the Clifton Bridge.

A sharp gust of wind snatched Stefan's scarf from my neck and brought me back to the here and now. I had to run two steps to catch it. Stefan smiled, but he didn't say anything. He seemed to know my mind was somewhere else. I thought about the locket and strange little map sitting on my dressing table. Caroline had said Elly's funeral was tomorrow and Stefan had told me there'd been an announcement in the local paper to say it would be a cremation.

The family of the dead teenage boy glided away into the distance. I reflected on how awful it would have been for me if there had been mystery and controversy surrounding Jeff's death. Knowing it was suicide was bad enough, but it made sense – to me, at least. Not knowing why or how he died would have been intolerable.

Maybe I was wrong to interfere in Elly's life. Once she was cremated there would be no second post-mortem, no second chance to reinvestigate. No going back. Maybe, if I kept on digging I'd simply come across layer upon layer of unanswered questions and confusion. Or worse, I'd come across information that no one wanted to hear.

The truth wasn't always a blessing.

'You okay?' said Stefan, as we made our way back to the gate.

'Yeah…' I said, in a way that sounded more like *not really*.

Why was I doing this? Why was I here following the trail of a woman I'd spoken to for about five minutes who'd irritated the hell out of me? I shrugged to myself. Because something in me wanted to fight her corner, perhaps because I saw something of myself in her; uncertainty, vulnerability, isolation.

'Let's grab a quick coffee,' he said. 'I passed a place round the corner.'

'Don't you have a plane to catch?'

'It'll wait,' he said, smiling.

chapter five

As we left the cemetery and headed for the café, I noticed Stefan's hair hadn't shifted an inch in the buffeting wind, whereas mine had turned into a blackout curtain obliterating my face. I clamped my hands down on it and pulled it apart so I could see to cross the road.

I was grateful for the warmth inside the café, but it didn't have much else going for it. The staff were monosyllabic, the tables were scattered with grains of yesterday's sugar and bread crumbs, and my wooden chair seemed deliberately shaped to cause discomfort to my rear end. I felt like I was sitting on a camel. It screeched like fingernails on a blackboard, when I hitched it closer to the table. To round things off, the coffee was weak and reminded me of stale cigarette butts. Stefan didn't seem to mind. Or perhaps, slightly more worryingly, he didn't notice. His quick cup of coffee became the full works: bacon, sausages, beans, fried eggs, toast and waffles. He offered me a taster and tucked in after I shook my head.

'Tell me what you want to know about the abduction?' he said, working his knife and fork like he hadn't had a decent meal in weeks.

'Can we backtrack a bit first. Have you got time?'

'My plane is in a couple of hours - I'm used to cutting it fine.'

'What do you make of this?'

I flattened the map out on top of a clean napkin.

'Where's it from?'

'Elly left it in a locket, when we were on the train.'

'No note with it?'

I shook my head.

'You sure it came from her?'

'It's the only thing that makes sense.'

'So - what do you think she wanted you to do?'

I squinted, thinking about it. 'Look after the locket - or look after whatever is marked with an X...I don't know to be honest.'

'And you think this is the connection with the boy, Toby? Elly Swift was his aunt?' He was buttering his toast. I nodded. 'Not a lot to go on,' he said. He shook the pepper pot, but nothing came out. He leant across to the next table and swapped containers. Stefan stood his knife and fork on end, like a small child. 'I know Elly Swift lived in Brixton, so why had she been on a train coming back from Portsmouth?'

'And what made her rush off at an earlier stop and dive under a train?' I said, running my nail around one of the red checks on the table cloth.

He shook a dollop of tomato sauce over his sausages. It came out like red cement.

'Was it the despair of someone who was suicidal - or someone who was scared stiff?'

'You see - that's what bothers me. The police have only talked about suicide. It doesn't add up to me.'

He tucked into the second egg. It burst and the yolk trailed into the bean juice, like lava sliding into a river.

'Let's come back to this,' he said. 'What about the abduction?'

'It's Elly's parents I want to talk to, really. Did you meet them?'

'Yes. Meg and Dennis Swift. He's an odd character. Seemed like he was miles away. She was distant as well, in a different way. Detached and doll-like. Funny pair. Of course, it was Irene, the boy's mother, I was most keen to talk to.'

'The boy, Toby, he was taken from the Sunday School at the church, right?'

'Yeah. St Stephen's catholic church in Stockwell. Irene and Elly went there. The parents aren't religious. I interviewed Elly - she seemed a bit fanatical about the church-going. It appeared she didn't have many friends and saw the church as a kind of second home.'

'That's useful. I could speak to people there. Find out more about who Elly was. I want to know what the map refers to.' I pinched a slice of his sausage. 'What happened to Toby?'

'St Stephen's has a class called Children's Liturgy - what is effectively a Sunday School for younger children. It runs alongside the ten o'clock mass in the church hall.' He stopped for a moment to deal with a particularly chewy piece of bacon. 'The kids do some colouring and then go back into the church, later on, as part of a procession.'

Stefan rested his knife and fork on the side of the plate, although he hadn't finished.

'Toby didn't come back in after the sermon. He went missing somewhere between the hall and the main church.'

I sucked in a long breath. 'How far apart are they?'

'There's a corridor that connects the two, but also an outside door, so people can get straight into the hall without having to go through the church itself.'

He stirred his coffee as if hoping it might improve the colour. It looked cold by now. He picked up his knife and fork again instead. 'Others remember him sitting at a table drawing a picture of an egg - they were making Easter cards - at about ten twenty, then their recollections of him start to go sketchy.'

'And that was in March?'

He nodded, wiping his mouth with his napkin. 'Six months ago…'

'Nothing since?'

'Not a dicky-bird. The police have interviewed about two thousand people, searched local premises, warehouses, basements, scrap-yards. I've got a mate in the Met who does a bit of inside checking for me and there's nothing. Everything has drawn a blank.'

'What do *you* think?' I said.

Stefan tugged a white chunk of bacon from his mouth and left it on the edge of his plate. It split into two, looking exactly like pulled teeth.

'I don't think they'll find him alive. Not now. It's been too long. I don't think the family is involved. Irene and Frank seem a stable couple, they've got two older boys and there have never been any problems. Nothing involving social services or the police. No problems at school. We raked it all over, but the family are clean as a whistle.'

I drifted back to the anguish and distress I'd witnessed in the cemetery that morning.

'I don't want to stir up anything without due cause, but I do want to speak to Elly's parents - find out more about her. It's the only way I can think of to get any answers.'

He shrugged. 'You don't think Elly killed herself?'

'No - I don't.'

'Why are you so interested?'

'I used to do investigative work - been out of the loop for a while and I've missed it. You know, grappling with pieces of a jigsaw that don't fit together, apparent facts that don't add up.' I rubbed my chin. 'There was a sequence of odd events that day and I can't let it rest.'

'What do you think happened?'

'I think the man in the raincoat was looking for something Elly had with her. I think he followed her off the train and took Elly's bag - it wasn't found at the scene according to the police - and I know for certain she was desperate not to be parted from it.'

'Okay, then what?'

'When our train was sent back to Micheldever, stationary and empty on the platform, he got back on, to look for something there. He can't have found it.'

'You think Elly and this guy are linked?'

I thought about it. 'He was searching where she was sitting…'

'And then he tried *your* bag?' He'd remembered my sketchy outline from earlier.

I nodded. 'Presumably it wasn't the locket he was after, or he'd have taken it.'

He wiped his last triangle of white toast through the remaining red juice on his plate and held it, dripping. I glanced at the plastic clock on the wall and wondered why he was taking the risk of missing his plane.

'Do you think he killed Elly?'

Suddenly, there was a loud pop from the table next to us. I jumped and brought my hand to my chest. A child's balloon had burst. The little girl started to wail and a woman pulled her onto her knee.

'I hadn't really got that far, but it's a good question, although I can't see yet how he could have got to the level-crossing and back in such a short space of time.'

'What do you think you'll get from speaking to her parents?'

'The police said Elly had written a suicide note. I'd like to know what it said. I'd like to know their view about Elly's death.'

'Okay.' He screwed up his napkin and tossed it on the plate. 'I'll give you their contact details, but I'd suggest you wait until after the funeral tomorrow.' He leant forward. 'And you mustn't say you got this from me.'

'Of course. Thank you. They'll probably refuse to speak to me, anyway - yet another prying journalist - but it's worth a try.' I took the scrap of paper he handed me. 'I'll ring first.'

He checked his watch and went for his wallet.

'I've got to dash. Let me know how you get on. Ring me if you think I can help. It's no problem.'

He was already paying for the bill, before I had chance to manoeuvre my scraping chair out of the way. I held out the money for the coffee as we left the café, but he refused to accept it.

'You can buy the drinks when we've got to the bottom of all this,' he said, zipping up his jacket. He waved as we went our separate ways. 'And mine's a champagne,' he shouted over his shoulder.

I headed for the train station glad of his interest in Elly's story. He must be a diligent journalist who hated having loose ends. In any case, he sounded like a sensible and experienced guy to have on-board.

When I got home, I unfolded the details Stefan had given me and placed it next to the other items that belonged to Elly. Another scrap of paper. Another piece of the puzzle.

I had to force myself to wait before ringing the Swifts. By the end of Tuesday, I was pacing up and down, chewing my nails, unable to decide whether it was unreasonable to phone them only one day after the funeral. It's hard to know when a *good time* presents itself after something like this. For me, everything around the time of Jeff's death, funeral and inquest melted into a blur of indistinguishable days and nights. I'm not sure I would have even noticed if the phone had rung at four in the morning. But people were different. I needed a favourable response, so finding a good time to ring was key.

In the end I tossed a coin. Two minutes later, a croaky woman's voice answered the phone - tentative, barely audible.

'Who's calling?' Cautious, suspicious. Understandably.

'I'm very sorry to disturb you, Mrs Swift. My name is Anna Rothman. I knew Elly…'

'You knew her?' The voice was distant and broken as though I was phoning Abu Dhabi and the connection was about to give out.

'Yes. I'm so terribly sorry about your loss. She was a…sweet girl.'

'You knew her?'

'Not terribly well, but yes…' I didn't want to lie, but I was in fear of losing her at any moment. I took a risk. 'She gave me a locket - a gold, heart-shaped locket with dots around the edges…'

Her voice changed. It became fuller and clearer. 'Her locket? She wore it all the time.'

I clenched my fist. I knew it.

'I was hoping it might be possible…to come and see you…if we could talk…'

I could hear a different voice in the background, harsh and grumbling, asking who was on the line. There was a muffled noise and hollow rattle, as if the receiver was being dragged over buttons on a cardigan. It sounded like two people were fighting over it.

'It's okay, Dennis, she was Elly's friend,' said the original voice, some distance from the phone. There was a grunt and Mrs Swift came back.

'I think that would be okay. When were you thinking of coming?'

'Are you in London?' I asked, staring at the address in my hand.

'Colliers Wood, near Tooting.'

'Oh, that's not far. I'm in Richmond. Anytime is fine for me.'

'It can't be for long. Dennis and I are very tired and we've had to talk to so many people lately…about Elly…and about the…other terrible business…'

'Things must have been so tough for you…what with Toby going missing, as well…'

I wanted to sound empathic, sensitive, as unlike their other probing intruders as possible.

'She told you all about that, then?'

'I know how upset Elly was about it all.'

I heard a drawn out sigh.

'You can come on Thursday if you like. Around four o'clock. We'll both be here. Dennis is signed off work at the moment. I'll give you the address.'

I thanked her and put down the phone, my heart racing.

• • •

In spite of living in London most of my life, I'd never been to Colliers Wood. It shared a postcode with Wimbledon, but didn't appear to share anything else: no tennis racquet or strawberries in sight, no central chic village or excuse for a Womble song.

Mr and Mrs Swift lived in a small terraced house near the Tube. Campion Street was lined with cars parked bumper to bumper. It looked like either everyone who lived here took the underground to work or they were all unemployed. The more crumbling walls and boarded windows I came across, the more likely it was to be the latter.

I passed an alleyway where a soggy mattress lay squashed behind an old aluminium dust bin and a pile of crushed soup tins, all chicken and leek, were scattered beside it. Someone had written: *Tanya is a fat slag* on the wall above them. A bicycle missing both its wheels, saddle and handlebars was lying buckled on the pavement, like a giant crushed stick-insect. I pulled my coat close, trying to remember whether I had much cash in my purse.

The curtains to number seventeen were closed, upstairs and down. I pushed open the feeble gate and walked along the path, trying not to look too closely at the broken hanging baskets, smashed toilet bowl and bucket of tar left in the front yard. No one in this household, it seemed, had the inclination for making things look pretty out there. I knew that feeling. After Jeff died, I couldn't bring myself to do anything but the absolute basics for months.

I pressed the doorbell and heard nothing. I could see grey shapes through the two panels in the door, but nothing moved. The obscure glass was heavily patterned with swirls, like the doodling of a child. I tapped gently. A black figure came towards me and the door opened a fraction, jolted to a halt by the gold chain.

'Who is it?' A woman's voice. The voice I recognised from the phone.

'It's Anna Rothman, Mrs Swift, we spoke on Tuesday about Elly.'

She pushed the door closed to release the chain and backed up, without making eye contact. She stooped carrying the burden of grief that had become too heavy for her some time ago.

The first thing that hit me was the smell. A blend of rotten fish and oily animal fur. Close on its heels was the chill. It was freezing and dark. As I walked into the living room my feet felt no give from the threadbare carpet that provided the barest of covering for the floorboards. There was a sheepskin rug in front of the fireplace, the only concession to comfort in the room I could see, but it was more grey than white, the fleece clogged into clumps from years of accumulated dust and grime.

The gas fire wasn't on. Mrs Swift pointed to an armchair covered in flowery cotton, profusely decorated with patches of black animal hair. I perched on the edge, keeping my coat on.

'I'm so sorry to intrude on your grief,' I said, not sure what to do with my hands, but wary of resting them on the chair arms.

'It's not just Elly,' said Mr Swift, standing near the fire. He had perpetual gobstopper eyes as though too much electrical energy was running through his veins and he didn't know how to contain it.

I dropped my head. 'I know about Toby - I'm so sorry...'

'Someone knows where he is,' said Mr Swift, accusingly.

'All the waiting - not knowing - that's the worst thing,' said Mrs Swift. 'At least with Elly...we know.'

A shaggy dog trotted into the room and stretched on the sheepskin rug. It looked a cross between a border terrier and a long-haired goat. It batted its tail at Mr Swift, expectant yelps escaping from its mouth as it dribbled saliva on to his slippers. Mr Swift scooped the dog out of his path with his foot and rolled himself into the armchair opposite mine. The dog whined and curled into a croissant at his feet, his eyes never leaving the man's face. I wondered how long it had been since the poor dog had been taken for a decent jaunt across the park.

Mrs Swift offered me tea and I was left with Mr Swift.

'Someone knows where he is,' he said again, as if by saying it out loud often enough, the words would force the perpetrator into revealing the whereabouts of his grandson.

Mrs Swift came back pushing an old-fashioned wooden tea-trolley with three cups and saucers, rattling like the onset of an earthquake. Aside from the teapot, the pink crocheted tea-cosy must have been the only item in the room that was warm.

'Elly made this,' she said, tweaking the pom-pom on the cosy. 'How did you two meet?' She looked me up and down as she placed a cup beside me. 'If you don't mind me saying, you seem quite…posh for Elly.'

'On a train…' I said. 'We got talking.'

Her mouth formed a circle, but no sound came out.

As Mrs Swift poured her husband's tea, I noticed everything they wore was one shade removed from black. Dennis Swift, wearing charcoal grey tracksuit bottoms with a dark brown jumper, had matching skin that said early fifties, but his body looked like it had lived for longer. He looked like a man who trudged, instead of walked, who dragged his tired limbs through arduous days, hour after hour.

'What do you do, dear?' continued Mrs Swift.

As she leant over, I saw a handkerchief pressed inside her hand. It looked like a long-term fixture, a sort of comforter that was probably clasped in her palm every day.

'I write for magazines - lifestyle pieces, health, psychology - that kind of thing.' I wanted to avoid the word *journalist.* Mr Swift's teacup made a loud crash as he dropped the cup back into the saucer. His eyebrows went up a notch.

'Nothing to write about here,' he said. It came out more like an instruction than an observation.

'Elly was a bookish type,' she said, ignoring him. 'But then you'd know all about that. Part of her problem, I think. Thought she was too good for us. Spent too much time with her nose inside the pages of some old-fashioned drivel, instead of getting on with her life, meeting people.'

I didn't like Mrs Swift's derogatory tone, but I was warming to Elly with every new piece of information I learnt about her.

'She was into those silly puzzles with numbers…' she continued.

'Sudoku?' I said.

'That's them. She was always making up silly codes and cryptic clues, for goodness sake. Like she was talking another language half the time. Thought she was Sherlock Holmes. She'd talked about going to university when she finished school. I mean, honestly, a girl like her! Pah! She had her head in the clouds that one, no common sense, faffing about instead of earning a decent living.'

I wasn't sure what had sparked this tirade about Elly's eccentricities, but I was finding it decidedly inappropriate.

A tiny bell chimed. I looked up to find the source of it: a tambour clock stood on the mantelpiece, telling us it was quarter past the hour. I couldn't imagine how the Swifts tolerated a bell tolling every fifteen minutes. It felt like a cruel reminder that another quarter-of-an-hour had gone by without their grandson being found. Another fifteen minutes their daughter would never see.

Mrs Swift set her empty cup on the coffee table. 'Can you tell us anything more about this awful business?' Her tone had softened. Perhaps she'd seen the look of disapproval on my face. 'Did Elly talk to you? Confide in you?'

I gave them selected highlights from the newspaper interviews Elly had given, about how upset Elly had been after Toby's abduction, how worried she'd been, knowing all the while that it was wrong to let them think I'd learnt it from Elly in person.

As I spoke, they both remained impassive, strangely distanced, like Stefan had warned me, as though all their feelings had been wrung out and used up by now.

'She used to go to St Stephen's church, didn't she?' I said.

'Yes.' It was Meg Swift who did most of the talking. Dennis stared around the room, his eyes settling on various objects for periods of time, his eyes narrowing, as though trying to recall where they'd come from. 'She became Catholic properly about six years ago. Got herself confirmed or whatever they call it. I think she saw it as a way of making friends.'

'I thought it was...don't Catholics have strong views about suicide?'

'Like I say, I think she joined in order to belong somewhere. Like a club. I don't think she was a true believer.' She sighed. 'She gave you her locket?'

I handed it to her.

'She must have thought very highly of you to have given you this,' said Mrs Swift, stroking the gold heart briefly, before handing it back.

It confirmed an important point. It definitely belonged to Elly. There was no doubt about that.

'There was a little drawing inside - like a map - you don't know what it is, do you?' I unfolded a copy I'd made. It was an exact replica, except I'd omitted the cross. There might well have been a good reason why Elly gave it to me and no one else. I didn't want to reveal too much. Mrs Swift took a cursory glance at it. Mr Swift had disengaged himself from the conversation completely and was now staring blankly ahead of him.

'I've no idea. She didn't tell you, dear?'

I smiled. 'We didn't get as far as that.'

She sat still for a moment as if trying to decide whether something was a good idea or not. 'I've got something to show you,' she said. She got up and dragged her slippers across the carpet. She too, could have only been in her early fifties, but she looked twenty years older. I took a quick glance at Dennis, but he seemed oblivious to us. The dog started to snore at his feet making a shuddering, sighing sound that could have been coming from Mr Swift himself.

Mrs Swift returned as my eyes were fixed on a large photograph, standing on the salmon-pink mantelpiece, of a grinning boy wearing school uniform.

'That's Toby. That's our boy,' she said, wistfully. I noticed an inordinate number of framed pictures of Toby vying for attention around the room. The Swifts must have raided their photo album in order to put them on display, as though the more pictures they had of him the sooner he would appear in person. Or perhaps it was a desperate bid to hold on to the past, representing as they did a time when despair hadn't yet blighted their family.

I craned my neck and saw that there was only one of Elly - a family picture with another girl, presumably Irene, Elly's sister, at the centre. The frame sat on the edge of a low chest, hidden from most standpoints in the room by the back of a chair.

Mrs Swift leant towards me.

'She might have liked you to have this.' She held out a book like it was something paltry she'd picked up in error at a jumble sale. It had the words *Holy Bible* printed in gold lettering on the front. 'You can keep it,' she said. 'You were her friend.'

'Well, I wasn't exactly—'

'Elly didn't have many friends.'

She patted my arm. I didn't want to spoil the illusion, so I took it.

'I'm sure you knew that she had a history of depression. Attempted suicide twice before. The police said she'd been seen down by the railway line near her home in Brixton…'

'Really?' I was almost on my feet.

'Witnesses saw her sitting by the line once and another time she climbed over the fence and stood right by the tracks, so it wasn't a spur of the moment thing…'

'I see…'

'Did you know about the note she wrote?'

'No, I…'

Suddenly, it seemed like Mrs Swift had become overly keen to reveal as many personal and private details about Elly as she could think of. Perhaps it was a distraction from dwelling on Toby's disappearance - albeit one that was hardly more pleasant.

'We don't mind you seeing it, do we Dennis?' She glanced across at her silent husband and must have taken his lack of response as consent. 'As you were her friend.'

She disappeared again. Her pace quicker, this time.

'This is what the police printed from her computer…'

She unfolded the sheet of A4 paper on the coffee table. I touched it carefully, lifting it closer to read the words.

I'm sorry, I've had enough. I've tried - I really have, but I can't do it anymore. I don't suppose you'll understand. I can't carry on.

There was no signature and it wasn't addressed to anyone in particular. I sat back, my mind leaping about like a game of hop-scotch. It wasn't what I'd been expecting.

'And this was on her computer?' I asked.

'Written a few days before she died. The police found it. It was the last thing she wrote.'

I read the note again and sat back. She stared at her slippers.

I felt I'd outstayed my welcome and thanked them. Mr Swift didn't rally as I left, so Mrs Swift had to manage all the farewell courtesies on her own. Despite her obvious misgivings about her daughter, I felt a tremendous compassion for Elly's mother, left to cope with the aftermath of two tragic situations single-handedly, by the look of it. I took both her hands in mine as I left. Hers felt cold and fragile - brittle, like I could break them without even trying. I thought I saw the bud of a tear form in the corner of her eye as she smiled.

'I'm glad she had you,' she said. 'I'm so glad you came.'

I felt like I was wading through wet concrete as I made my way back to the Tube. I put it down to a combination of shame on my part for blatantly twisting the truth and an overwhelmingly bleak feeling. As the escalator pulled me down into the earth, there was something fluttering in the corner of my mind, like a daddylonglegs trapped inside a lampshade. Something trying to get through to my consciousness.

What was it? Something about the map? Something about Elly being seen casing her local area, down at the railway line?

Then two filaments joined up inside my brain.

That was it.

There was something seriously wrong with the suicide note.

chapter six

It was late and I didn't know why I was going back there. I came out of Colliers Wood Tube station and started walking towards Campion Street. The vandalised bicycle was still there, the soggy mattress behind the dust bin, Tanya was still *a slag*. It was dark and I didn't feel safe. I kept my head down.

Mrs Swift was smiling when she opened the door. They both were. Perhaps they'd had good news about Toby. She guided me into the sitting room like I was a long-lost relative. The fire was lit and candlesticks and cut-glass vases sparkled in the glow. Mrs Swift directed me to the same chair I'd used before and Mr Swift sat opposite again, smoking a cigar this time. Smiling. He looked over into the corner of the room and nodded his head. I turned and saw a small coffin, standing on the tea-trolley. There was a candle on the top dripping wax. I wanted to tell them not to let the wax spoil the coffin, but nothing came out.

Mrs Swift started bringing in items of Elly's wardrobe for me.

'She wore this dress for her sister's wedding. I'm sure she'd like you to have it,' she said. She started making a pile of folded clothes on the carpet beside me. 'You'll like this - she wore it the day she died.'

Something caught my eye near my left shoulder and I turned.

Elly was sitting on a stool in the corner behind the door.

'She's here…' I said, standing up.

'Who's here, dear?' said Mrs Swift.

'It's Elly, look, she's come back.'

Elly sat quietly on the stool. Her knees were pressed together, her hands on her lap. She wasn't looking at us. She looked sad, staring at her fingers, creases making train tracks on her forehead. Her skin was a strange colour as if a blue light was shining inside her head.

I moved towards her. I wanted to touch her. Stroke her hair. Comfort her.

Once I made the first step, I could see piles of books were standing in the way. I craned my head to see past them, but there were piles more. It was as though an entire library had been emptied out into the room. They were all the same size. Novels by Author Conan Doyle with curious diagrams and mazes on the front.

I tried to push them aside to get to Elly, but each time I managed to tip a pile over another stack appeared. Towering over me now, surrounding me. They started rocking, swaying, toppling towards me.

I fell to my knees. The books continued to tumble, hitting my head with heavy whacks, the spines stabbing my back. I was down on the floor now, huddled in a ball, trying to protect my head as the books came like giant hailstones. Battering me, burying me. I couldn't see. I couldn't breathe. *Help me. Elly, help me.*

I shot up in bed, my breathing loud and laboured, like a cornered animal. I wrapped my arms around my knees and rocked back and forwards, bringing myself back to the here and now. It was 2.15am.

I ran my hand up to my hairline and felt a band of cold sweat. The back of my pyjama jacket was sticking to me. The hard-backed book I'd been reading before I'd fallen asleep had slipped down the pillow. It was digging into my shoulder and I understood why my dream had taken the turn it did. I laughed at myself, but it was short lived as the image of Elly sitting on the stool, dejected and alone, her face glowing blue-grey, stayed in my mind.

I swung my legs out of bed, took a sip of water and went into the hallway. I didn't want to switch on any lights. I didn't want to wake myself up. Through the blind over the skylight, slivers of moonlight were being thrown in a pattern of silvery wands on to the carpet. Everything else was black on black. Silent.

Suddenly, I heard a muffled sound, like an animal scuttling through undergrowth and I reached out behind me to grab the doorframe to my room.

'What the hell?' I hissed.

I felt compelled by now to put on the light, but by then everything was quiet. I checked every room, but there was nothing. My imagination? Home-alone jitters?

I switched off the lights and watched the thin hook of the moon hanging still in the flat black sky beyond the kitchen window. It looked delicate, almost translucent, like a mobile just beyond the pane of glass that I'd be able to touch if I reached far enough. I could see no stars, no other lights up there, no variation in the degree of blackness.

I stood still. All I could hear was the fridge humming. Nothing else. I went to the window and stared at the moon again, transfixed by its solitary shape, isolated and persistent. It made me think of Elly. Made me feel like I was the only person in the world who would help her.

I recalled the look on her mother's face around ten hours ago when I'd said goodbye. Grateful, with an undertone of pleading, not unlike the desperate look Elly herself had given me when she left the train.

I gave the moon one final look and whispered a promise.

I won't walk away. I won't abandon you.

As I went back to my bedroom I felt a wave of peace wash over me.

'Haven't you got better things to do?' said Caroline. She was tetchy. I'd rung too early the following morning. 'It was pure coincidence that this woman was sitting next to you on the train - you were a random passenger she said a few words to. That's all.'

'I can't walk away, Carrie. It doesn't feel right.'

'You should be spending your time socialising, getting to the theatre, exhibitions, dating a nice bloke – not trailing around after dead people.'

'I'm not ready for all that - not yet. You know that.'

'It's been two years, Anna...when are you going to start living a real life again.'

'When I'm ready,' I insisted. 'Besides, this woman was so vulnerable, helpless, alone. You didn't *see* her.'

'What about her friends, her family - why didn't she call on them instead of a stranger?'

'Maybe she didn't trust anyone. Maybe there *wasn't* anyone else.'

She sucked in a breath. 'Is this about Jeff?'

'Jeff? No. Of course not.'

'You sure this isn't some vicarious way of trying to understand why he...'

I tried to explain. 'Listen. I lived through his suicide,' I said. 'I don't think this is the same.'

'People act for different reasons, Anna.' Caroline's voice had mellowed a fraction. 'They have different backgrounds, circumstances - of course it won't feel the same.'

'I know it's too late for Elly, but something about her story is still very much alive. The whole set up doesn't add up and she deserves the truth. Her family, too. They think she killed herself. I know what that does to parents…' I was angry now. I rapped my fingers on the edge of the table. 'No one else is going to help her.'

Neither of us spoke for a few moments.

'Why didn't she just *tell* you what the problem was? Why didn't she just ask you for help, there and then on the train instead of all this secretive stuff?'

'I think perhaps she was going to; she was sounding me out, but she ran out of time. I think she suddenly knew she had to leave the train and it was too late.'

'Supposing she didn't intend to kill herself,' reflected Caroline. 'How would she have known how to get in touch with you? Surely she'd want her locket back, wouldn't she?'

'I hadn't thought of that,' I heard myself whisper.

'Either that, or she really did intend to end it all.'

She had a point. If my instincts were right and Elly *hadn't* intended to die, how would she have known how to track me down? On the other hand, if she was intending to kill herself, she wouldn't have needed to know.

A thought occurred to me and I took the phone into my bedroom.

'I always have business cards lying around at the bottom of my bag,' I said, feeling my way around. 'When she dropped the locket in there, perhaps she took one of them…' I pulled out a small handful. They showed my phone details, email and home address.

'A bit farfetched, isn't it?'

I mulled it over. 'Okay – but she could easily have found out another way – asked which magazines I wrote for and whether she should have heard of me. But she didn't need to, because it was right there on my card.'

'I suppose it's possible…' Caroline didn't sound convinced. I could hear a kettle boiling in the background.

There was an awkward silence. 'I've just thought of something,' I said. She waited.

'You said there was no bag when Elly was found. I reckon the man who was snooping around got hold of it.' I tried to keep my voice steady. 'If Elly had taken one of my business cards and dropped it into her bag, then 'raincoat man' could be holding on to my name and address by now. I could be in danger.'

Caroline laughed. 'Bloody hell, Anna. You're sounding like me! I'm the drama queen around here

- you're the sensible one. It's a lot of *ifs* and *buts* - there's nothing concrete,' she assured me. 'Perhaps, like the police said, she was disturbed and instable and she...took her own life. If it's bothering you - why don't you just drop it?'

'I think it might be too late for that.' I muttered something about needing to get to the post-office and ended the call.

• • •

I didn't have much time to dwell on what we'd said, because by lunchtime I'd been offered a commission for another feature. Shortly after I'd got stuck into it, Squid came to the door.

'I got your message,' he said. 'Things that go bump in the night?'

'Thanks for coming. I'm hoping it's nothing.'

'Let's have a proper check, shall we.'

He put his toolbox on the kitchen table and I made him tea. He checked the pipes and the radiators, the shower, the washing machine. He even reached out of the windows and checked the guttering. Then he asked for newspaper and a dustpan and brush, and forty minutes later, he called me back into the kitchen.

'It's mice,' he said, gravely.

I followed him towards the cupboard under the sink. 'How have they got all the way up here?' I said.

'They climb up into the wall cavity and squeeze through the tiniest gaps where the pipes come inside.'

'I'm not going to kill them,' I said, hastily.

He looked guilty. 'To be honest, I've had them downstairs. I can't kill them either. My wife couldn't bear it.' He scratched his head. 'I can lend you a humane trap,' he said. 'I'll seal all the gaps I can find and I've got some repellent left, as well - you can have the rest of the can.'

I thanked him. 'What was her name - your wife?' I said.

'Nancy.' He scooped back his non-existent hair and I noticed his eyes had gone gluey.

'I'm sorry,' I said.

He smiled and brushed away a tear with the seat of his grubby hand.

'Don't apologise. At least you've taken the trouble to mention her. Most people, when they know I've lost my wife, avoid talking about her altogether, like she never existed. It hurts all the more.'

'Yes,' I said, dropping my eyes. 'I lost my husband two years ago.'

'Ah,' he said, 'Then you'll know. When you love someone you want to talk about them - wherever they are, don't you think?'

I was touched by his sensitivity. His words made me realise that although I thought about Jeff every single day, I hardly ever talked about him anymore.

I thanked him again. When he'd gone I realised he'd cleared away all the droppings and even put disinfectant down for me.

After that, I found myself listening all the time and making impromptu trips into the kitchen to check under the sink, so I decided on a change of scene and took my laptop over to a local café. On the way, I thought about the suicide note Meg Swift had shown me. I'd written it down word for word.

I'm sorry, I've had enough. I've tried - I really have, but I can't do it anymore. I don't suppose you'll understand. I can't carry on.

A creeping suspicion skimmed over me like a chilly shadow. It might have been the last thing she wrote, but I wasn't convinced.

When Jeff left the house that Friday night to catch a train to Bristol, he'd propped a note against my alarm clock. I still kept it folded at the back of my jewellery case. I knew it off my heart:

My darling Anna

I need to let you move on. I don't know how to live like this anymore. Please forgive me. I'll always love you. Jeff XXXX

For a start, Elly hadn't addressed her note to anyone. I found that odd. Impersonal. It was on her computer, instead of being handwritten. She hadn't even put her name at the bottom. Anyone could have got access to her computer and written it.

It wasn't a heartfelt goodbye.

It wasn't a goodbye at all.

By 3.45pm, I was buzzing with caffeine and the feature was more or less finished, but more importantly, I had made two decisions. I would get back in touch with the bereavement therapist who had helped me through Jeff's suicide and on Sunday, I would attend mass at St Stephen's Catholic Church in Stockwell and meet the people who *really* knew Elly. I had a feeling that a lot of answers were lurking inside that church.

What I most wanted to learn was going to be the hardest to find. *Had Elly left suicide notes before? And if so, what did they look like? Were they also impersonal and typed on a computer?* I could hardly storm up to the Swifts' house with questions like those.

As I walked back home, even more were bubbling beneath the surface. Elly had already been on the train when I got on at Portsmouth and Southsea. The train had come from Portsmouth Harbour. *Why write a suicide note and then go off to the south coast for the weekend?*

When I got back, there was a message waiting on my answer-phone. It was from Dr Katya Petrova, the bereavement therapist I'd seen after Jeff died. At last, I might be able to make some progress with Elly's suicide note. She was an expert on suicide and as I heard her richly accented voice saying she'd be pleased to meet for lunch, a ripple of anticipation brushed the hairs on the back of my neck.

Things were moving.

chapter seven

St Stephen's in Stockwell was a Gothic revival church, built in the mid nineteenth century. It stood tall and proud amidst tower blocks and neglected council housing, like a spaceship that had landed on the wrong planet. As I got close to the main entrance, it was as if a wedding was about to take place; a number of women had turned out wearing all the colours of confetti.

The grey stonework on the exterior of the church was stippled with black and pockmarked as though riddled with some kind of virulent disease, but the overall design was impressive; the entrance archway built into a broad bell-tower with four corner spires at the top. The bell was ringing, a lopsided chime on a single tone, like an irregular heartbeat.

Beside it, I could see children fighting in a concrete playground, with stolen traffic cones stuffed into the wheel hub of a van on one corner and a boarded-up shop front with posters slapped over it, on the other. Stockwell wasn't the obvious choice for a Sunday morning in London. This was no tourist trap. I'd be reluctant to wander around here alone even in broad daylight.

As I waited for the congregation to move inside, something about the area was tugging at my sleeve. I reached back in time and retrieved a vague memory of Jeff, leaning against his shiny *Triumph Scrambler*. He used to attend a biker's club somewhere around here. *The Brixton Bones*, they called themselves. It sounded too much like *broken bones* for my liking, but they turned out to be a fairly sedate bunch. They organised rallies, camping breaks, went on ride-outs, to all-night concerts. I'd only met a handful of the guys Jeff mixed with and although a few were verging on the rough side for me (too many tattoos and not enough personal hygiene), the club had a benevolent streak, organising raffles for children's charities and running 'speed aware' campaigns. Jeff used say he was a fund-raiser not a hell-raiser.

I reached the door and stepped inside. I was expecting a figure in black robes to greet me, but instead I was handed a hymn book and order of service by a man wearing an ordinary brown suit. I had Elly's bible in my bag. I wasn't sure why. I'd had a quick look at it on the Tube, but had found nothing unusual. At some point, however, it deserved closer scrutiny.

I steered past a little stone basin built into the wall, watching others dip in their fingers to make the sign of the cross and followed a family of three into a pew near the back. I took the space closest to the aisle. I wanted to get a good view of everyone in front of me.

I'd never been to a Catholic mass before. Neither of my parents were religious, although for some reason my mother always kept a rosary she'd picked up from a market stall outside the Vatican, in her jewel case.

The only time I'd visited churches was as a tourist, in Venice, Rome, Paris. For an inner-city church, the interior was impressive. I wanted to wander around the aisles, stroke the hefty columns, allow my shoes to clack on the sunken flagstones, but for the next fifty minutes or so, I'd be hemmed in following the service.

Behind me, the sunlight was splashing the colours of stained glass onto the white walls and more people were making their way inside. I was ready to get on with it. The bell in the tower stopped and after a short silence a small chime rang out inside the church itself. After a breath, the organ struck up. Everyone stood and the first hymn was underway before I'd found the right book, never mind the right page. The priest passed by in his procession towards the altar and the service began. I scanned the backs of heads in front of me, but the chances of picking out Elly's sister, Irene, were slim, given I had never met her. I'd seen one photograph of her at her parents, taken several years ago. It wasn't going to be a lot of help. Besides, she might not even be there.

By the time I joined in the singing, my lungs were having trouble negotiating an acrid aroma of incense. It was struggling not to splutter. I looked around to try to locate it, believing it to be at close-quarters, but spotted it right at the front, swinging in puffs of smoke from a gold censer in the hand of an altar server.

I pulled out a handkerchief and was forced to breathe into it to stop myself from heaving. One of the drawbacks of having an oversensitive sense of smell.

We moved from prayers, readings, hymns, sections with congregational responses and back to prayers again and I was struggling to keep up. At least it meant it wasn't boring. I watched as others went to the front to take communion; each of them accepting the wafers and wine. I wondered which of them knew Elly. Most people had sombre bowed heads, so it was hard to isolate anyone who looked as though they may have recently lost a good friend.

My chance came at the end when I joined the ribbon of people moving through the back of the church to the hall, for coffee. It wasn't unlike my old school assembly hall, with a stage one end and kitchen hatch at the other. There were flowers at both sides of the stage - and display boards around the room showing photographs of the Pope, missionary visits and a world map with ribbons pinpointing the recipients of overseas aid.

I plucked a cup and saucer from the hatch and stood awkwardly as people formed familiar groups and the chat levels escalated. At the first opportunity, I wanted it to be known that I was a friend of Elly's. I wanted to find out who was in Elly's circle of friends, who would know about her history - anyone who could fill in crucial details.

Someone to my left jogged my arm and my cup hiccupped a splash of coffee onto the floor.

'Sorry, honey,' said a jovial black woman, clutching my shoulder. She was wearing a strong floral perfume. 'Me too big for me body!'

I laughed, brushing down my skirt. 'It missed me. No worries.'

'You're new here, aren't you?' she said, taking in my face. Hers was soft, full, with plump lips painted fuchsia pink.

'Yes. First time.'

'Well!' she said. 'We'll have to do somet'ing about dat.' She let out a loud laugh that came from her belly. 'Me Flora and dis here is Jamilla.' She pulled at the arm of a woman behind us and forced her to spin round, before extending me a gloved hand as if I was someone important. Jamilla followed suit. She looked unperturbed, as though she was used to being manhandled by Flora. They looked like sisters; both in their early thirties, I surmised, wearing bright clashing colours, eager smiles and an early middle-aged spread. Flora kept hold of my hand as I gave my name, placing her other hand on top in a warm gesture. She looked like the sort of person you could run to in your hour of need.

'I was a friend of Elly Swift,' I said, carefully.

I waited for a response, half expecting a blank *Who?* Instead, their smiles shrank, their shoulders dropped.

'Dat poor Elly - weren't it such a shock,' said Flora, making the sign of the cross. 'It terrible - lovely girl - t'ank da Lord.'

'We were painful sorry,' said Jamilla. A large silk carnation was pinned to her purple lapel and I noticed she was carrying a small gold bag, which together with the white gloves and the veil netting crisscrossing her eyes, made her look like she was on her way to a royal garden party.

'I understand she was a regular here.' I was making the place sound like a pub.

'She joined us 'bout six year ago and came every week...right up until...' Jamilla's eyes had a glazed faraway look as if she was trying to find Elly in the distance. 'She was in da choir too...couldn't sing a note, but she always turned up.'

'It was a nasty shock to all of us,' said Flora. 'She'd been uptight lately, clearly worried 'bout somet'ing… but we never found out why.'

'We never would a t'ought she …you know…it… she…' stammered Jamilla.

'Maybe it all got too much for her…dat trouble wid her nephew…' said her sister. 'You know, dat poor bwoy what went missing..?' Their statements passed seamlessly from one to the other, as if they were well-practised at sharing sentences. I got the impression too, that they were relishing their Caribbean accents, which sounded delightfully overplayed for my benefit.

'I know she was distressed about Toby,' I said.

I wanted to drop in a few names. Show them that I was for real. 'Did you see Elly outside of the church at all?'

Flora answered for both of them. 'Yes…she come round for dinner…we took her under our wing…we tried…quiet girl…never seemed to tell us much…' She took a breath as though she was going to say more, but she left the sentence in the air. She paused. 'Ya good friends?'

It was a tricky question to answer. 'We got on fairly well,' I said. I wanted them to trust me, to assume I knew a lot about Elly already. It was going to be a tricky bluff to pull off. 'Is Irene here?'

Flora shot round, scanning the faces. 'Deh she is…' I made a step to move. 'I'll pop back in a minute,' I said. 'Really good to meet you both.'

'Come to choir on Wednesday, if ya fancy,' said Jamilla. 'We're a middle voice short now. Seven on da clock - dis place right 'ere. Sweet singin' music.'

'She means alto,' said Flora. 'Mozart's Requiem.' In the context of Flora's shiny purple skirt, chubby bare legs and glossy heels, her familiarity with the classical composer sounded entirely incongruous. I had the feeling that Flora was a sharper pin than she was making out. I gave a non-committal smile and turned away.

Irene's hair was lighter than Elly's, but I could see as soon as I got closer that judging by her dark eyebrows, straw blonde wasn't her natural shade. She was prettier, too, striking blue eyes and well-defined cheeks. Grief and loss had, however, taken their toll on her body; her wrists were bony, her trousers hung low around her waist and there were purple hammocks under her eyes. There was a general air of neglect about her - unwashed hair, no trace of make-up, crescents of black under her nails. She was leaning against the wall as if she hadn't enough energy to stand unsupported, sipping coffee, surrounded by a group she appeared not to be engaged with. I realised why. She was watching. Watching all the time. The doors. Looking for someone. Looking for her son.

I stopped about two feet away from her.

'Yeah?' she said, as though I'd interrupted something.

'I understand you're Irene. I'm... I was a friend of Elly...'

'Oh.' She sounded disappointed. Her eyes didn't seem to have blinked once since I'd noticed her. It made her appear unreal, like a mannequin.

'I'm so terribly sorry...'

'Frank's not here,' she said, a propos of nothing. 'He doesn't come to church.'

'My name's Anna Rothman.' I held out my hand, but she only looked at it. 'I went to see your parents last week.'

'Did you now.'

'This must be so hard for all of you...I wanted to offer any help...'

'What did you say your name was again?'

'Anna - Anna Rothman.'

'She never mentioned you.' She played with a toggle on her hood and I could tell from the agitated flicks that she was a smoker.

'I hadn't known her long...'

Her eyes narrowed. 'You just turned up today?'

'It's my first time at the church. Elly mentioned she came here. I wanted to see what it was like. Meet people who knew her. She was lovely, but she didn't say much about herself.'

'Why are you so interested?' There was a hostile, frozen chill in her voice. Like Meg and Dennis Swift, she must have had her fair share of hounding from the press since Toby went missing in March.

'I suppose I'm finding it hard to believe that she… ended her life in that way…especially as a Catholic.'

She started chewing the toggle. 'She wasn't a proper one. She was only here because she was lonely.' I nodded. 'And it's Toby, my son, we all need to be focusing on,' she snapped, 'not Elly. She's had her time.'

Her fierce words were so shocking that I took a step back.

'I'm so sorry,' I said, not wanting to show my disapproval. 'I know Elly was terribly concerned about your son.'

'Elly was terribly concerned about Planet Elly,' she said, flicking the toggle away and almost dropping her cup and saucer onto a nearby table. 'She found a way out, but we can't all do that, can we? Some of us have got responsibilities…'

She sounded envious of Elly, as though her sister was in a better place, a place she could never gain access to.

'Your other children…'

Stefan had said she had two older boys. I hoped talking about her family might hold her attention a little longer.

'Frank's got them. Toby was in *this* room.' She stared about her, vigilant, still not blinking. 'And then, suddenly, he'd gone and no one saw a bloody thing - excuse my French.'

She picked up her bag and was on the verge of departing.

'Good to meet you,' I said, but she pushed past me without saying goodbye. I watched her go.

This was going to be harder than I thought. I'd found the right people, but Irene, for one, sounded not only disinterested in Elly's situation, but positively hostile about her. Perhaps her heart was so weighed down with dread about her son that there was no space left for any sympathy for her sister. I needed to find someone who really cared, someone who Elly might have confided in. I picked up my jacket. Maybe, I was expecting too much too soon.

'So - we'll see you Wednesday,' said Flora, giving a little wave as I found myself heading for the exit.

'Yes,' I said, without fully considering what it would involve.

I hadn't sung in a group since I'd ruined a school production of *King Arthur* when I was ten, although I'd never regarded the spectacular demolition of the set on the first night as entirely my fault. The gown foisted on me was too long and the visor on the helmet kept sliding shut. Plus, I'd always seen it as tempting fate to have live chickens on stage. The school couldn't afford to put on a production for at least another two years after that, but thankfully for all of us, I was long gone by then.

Unsurprising, therefore, that the idea of being part of any performance brought a frisson of foreboding with it. As I left the church, however, I could see that getting involved was going to be the only way to make any progress. I had to get to know these people. Far better to mix with them, join them, stand amongst them, than hope for some off-the-cuff revelations from the side-lines. Besides, I'd always wanted to sing in a choir. Caroline would be proud of me. She was always complaining that I didn't have a life, although perhaps turning up as an impostor, as both Elly's friend and as a practising Catholic was taking things a bit far.

• • •

Dr Katya Petrova worked from an office on Harley Street. I'd told her over the phone that I wanted to ask her professional opinion about a suicide note and that it had nothing to do with Jeff. She was kind enough to offer me some time during her lunch break. We met at the reception and walked in the direction of Regent's Park. I assumed we'd find a café, but she surprised me by taking a sharp right turn up marble steps leading to a hotel.

'They do terrific salads,' she said.

The moment I stepped onto the spongy red carpet under one of several glistening chandeliers,

I felt considerably underdressed. Katya raised her hand to someone who recognised her and they waved us through. I trailed behind her, trying to take in the magnificent staircase sweeping in front of me, with its broad steps, gold embellished handrail and vast mural of a woman in a red gown towering above it.

As she strode ahead of me, Katya seemed to be missing the point. Saying they did terrific salads in a place like this was a bit like describing the highlight of Buckingham Palace as the smart forecourt.

We passed a bar and entered a room dotted with palm trees beside tables under crisp white table cloths. A young man was playing a glossy grand piano in the corner. The sunlight gushed through the large windows setting the silverware alight and I lifted my hand to my eyes, temporarily blinded. A waiter showed us to a table with a view across a private square and put leather-bound menus in our hands.

'This is amazing…Dr Petrova, this isn't quite what…'

She cupped her hand over mine.

'Special occasion,' she said. 'It happens to be my birthday, so I'm pleased to spend it with an old friend.'

I was touched and somewhat taken aback that she referred to me in that way. I was also acutely aware that with the absence of any prices on the menu, the next forty-five minutes were going to be ludicrously expensive.

I offered my congratulations and she handed me a basket containing chunks of warm rustic bread.

'I wasn't sure if you'd be able to see me like this... given that I was your client...'

'Oh, it was a long time ago,' she said, waving her hand in a regal fashion. 'Besides, I knew you didn't have any serious psychological problems. You were just a normal person, going through a bad time - that's all.'

She'd always got straight to the point. I liked her for that. In our psychotherapy sessions there'd been no room for long 'therapeutic' silences, no squirming in my seat as I tried to avoid eye contact wondering what psychiatric category she was filing me under.

She poured some water into my glass and a gold charm bracelet jangled around her wrist. She'd told me once that before she trained as a psychotherapist, she'd been a professional ballet dancer and I remember watching her hands after that. She carved elegant shapes in the air that other people's hands weren't capable of and her neck was long, giving her poise and sophistication even before she moved. But most of all, I loved her syrupy Russian accent.

'You wanted to ask me about a suicide?'

I hesitated. 'I'm not sure it feels appropriate - given it's your birthday.'

Dr Petrova wasn't a person to be argued with. 'Nonsense!' It came out elongated: *non-a-sen-a-sa.* Deep, like pure dark chocolate with a shot of rum. It occurred to me that during our sessions together, I'd been as soothed by that tone as I had been by the meaning of her words. 'As long as it isn't too emotional for you.'

'No, it's fine. I hadn't known the victim long. For an hour and a quarter, to be precise.'

Katya looked intrigued. She folded her hands under her chin and rested her gaze on me through her rimless gold spectacles.

'Tell me more.' With her accent, it sounded like a line from a Bond film.

Our salads arrived; mine prawn, hers chicken. They both looked so exquisite, if miniscule, it seemed a shame to disturb the intricate design on the plate. I took a small forkful from the edge and gave her as edited a version of the story as I could. Then I handed over the printout I'd made earlier of Elly's suicide note.

'It was done on her computer and she didn't print it out. What do you think?'

'It is not addressed to anyone. It does not have her name.' She handed it back to me.

'That's what I thought.'

She sliced an egg in two and dipped one half in mayonnaise. She managed to make this small action look delicate and composed.

'It's difficult to say when I've never met the person, but I agree that it's odd to leave a note like this and then go away for the weekend. Most victims are so caught up in the practicalities of what they are about to do that the idea of writing a note doesn't even occur to them, never mind planning a weekend away.' She pointed to the note. 'This seems a little too calculating.'

I told her about the locket Elly had left in my bag and what we'd talked about; how Elly wanted to know if I investigated crimes, followed up miscarriages of justice.

She looked sceptical, her jaw retreating.

'These do not sound like the words of someone about to commit suicide.' She placed her hands either side, stroking the linen with her fingertips. 'This is someone trying to hold on to life, not let go of it.'

I sat back. My lungs were bursting with air as if I'd suddenly been released from a tightly packed lift. 'Really? That's what I thought.'

'Of course, I can't say for definite. But what I would say is…' She tapped her nail against the side of her glass. 'There is a way to be sure, one way or the other.'

I leant towards her, still chewing a sprig of watercress. 'How?'

'You'd need her doctor's notes or hospital records. You'll need to find out when she made the previous attempts you mentioned. How she went about it. What methods, circumstances and so on. In my experience, repeaters usually try the same method again. They rarely swap, say, from cutting their wrists to jumping under a train. They are more likely to try a different knife, cut a few inches either side. The method is important to them. They decide on it and plan it and stick to it. Do you see what I mean?'

I did. It made sense. Perfect sense. The only problem was, I didn't know how I could possibly get hold of Elly's confidential medical records.

She folded her napkin. 'Why aren't the police investigating this?'

'They think it was suicide. It sounds like they've more or less closed the case.' I stared at the strip of orange peel curled at the edge of my plate; the only remains of my tasty, but meagre meal. 'All I've got is speculation - nothing definitive. Not yet, anyway.'

'I wish I could help you more. It's a difficult situation.' She took off her specs and rubbed the flesh at the top of her nose. 'You do know that if she didn't kill herself, it was either an accident or someone helped her along...'

'I know. I'm being careful. And as soon as I get anything concrete...anything at all...I'll go to the police.'

'I'm glad to hear that,' she said. 'Now, let me get the bill.'

I went home feeling at a loss. My encounter with Katya had been helpful and fiendishly overpriced (for her, thankfully), but I'd been left with another seemingly impossible hurdle: Elly's medical records. I couldn't think of any legitimate way I, nor anyone else I knew, would be able to access them.

Back at the flat, there was a strong smell of silicone. Squid had let himself in with the spare key I'd given him and sealed the gaps around the pipes. He'd set a trap under the sink and left a note and a bunch of flowers on the kitchen table.

I made a promise to myself to pop down later and thank him.

Right now, however, I was in need of time on my own.

I went to my bedroom and sat on the bed. Elly's locket, floor plan and bible were sitting on my dressing table, waiting for me. Silent sentinels anticipating my next move. I'd scoured the bible by now. After Mrs Swift had explained Elly's love of codes and clues, I wondered if there might have been something there. I'd looked for underlined words, any page corners turned over, any anomalies. I'd checked the binding, along the spine, even prized away the inside cover. I'd found nothing.

I was becoming obsessed. *Why was I doing this? Barging into the life of a stranger I'd barely spoken to, pretending to be her friend? Had my life shrunk so small that I needed this to fill it? To give it some meaning?* I closed my eyes to try to block it all out.

I started to consider whether there was any going back. I could put Elly's belongings in a drawer somewhere and forget about them. I had not made anyone any promises. There was no one waiting for me to call them, or follow anything up. I could leave everything alone.

But even as those thoughts tried to drag a portcullis down at the front of my mind, something was creeping underneath it, like an invisible gas, persistent, unstoppable.

And wrapped inside the gas were the parting words from Elly's mother.

I'm glad she had you.

As soon as those words reached me, I knew there was no turning back. Something deep within me had made a commitment and I knew I had to follow this through. Find out for certain if Elly had slipped under the train of her own accord or was pushed. That's all I needed to know and once I'd discovered the truth, I'd let it go.

A beeping sound was coming from my phone. I opened my eyes and found a message from Stefan.

Back from Frankfurt. Any joy your end?

I was surprised he'd got back to me so soon, but then like me, he seemed naturally inquisitive. Especially if there could be a story in it. I rang him back and we chatted for a while.

I told him I'd been to Elly's church. He gave me names of people to look out for; Flora and Jamilla I'd already met, but he also mentioned Charlie, Sam and Gillian, Elly's best friend. I explained I'd seen her parents, how they'd given me the bible and about my lunch with Katya.

'You don't need medical records,' he said. 'Just talk to people who knew her. *Really* knew her. They'll be able to tell you about her previous suicide attempts, I'll bet. It's the kind of thing people don't forget.'

chapter eight

I woke up in the middle of the night, but it wasn't the mice who'd broken my sleep. Before I'd gone to bed, I'd been gazing at the little map from the locket. I'd been trying to work out whose house it referred to. Where was *The Flower Girl's House?*

During the night, random images flickered through my brain. I flashed back to the Swifts' home - not a plant in sight. Did Elly have flowers in her flat? I saw a glimpse of the fake carnation on Jamilla's jacket, the flower arrangements by the altar in the church, more on the stage in the church hall. Nothing fell into place. I kept half-waking up, trying to force some connection in my mind. But it was like trying to light a gas-ring without a spark. Nothing came. A total blank.

At three in the morning, I had an idea. What if the flower girl was Flora? In Roman mythology, Flora was the goddess of flowers. The word itself was the generic name for plants. It was a bit obscure and cryptic, but isn't that exactly what her mother had said Elly was fascinated by? Flora had said Elly used to go round to see them. Maybe she'd left something there for safe-keeping?

What I needed was an excuse to go to Flora's house. Get inside and have a snoop around; see if the layout on Elly's map was a match. I didn't have much else to go on, right now - and it would give me another chance to ask about Elly's previous suicide attempts. Problem was – how to get an invitation?

It was a few minutes after 7pm when I got to the church on Wednesday. The side door was open, but as soon as I stepped inside, I could see through the glass panels that the hall was dark. My heart sank. Had the choir rehearsal been cancelled? I was about to leave when I heard distant sounds coming from inside. I gently pushed on the door and stalled a moment while my eyes adjusted to the darkness. Everyone was sitting quietly in the flickering shadows; about thirty-five people engrossed in footage on a projector screen on the stage. I slipped into a spare seat at the back.

Flora had heard the door squeak open and beckoned me towards her on the second row.

'We're getting' in da mood,' she whispered. 'This is from Rupert's camcorder. His wife took a video of our last concert in Bromley.' I was looking around trying to work out who Rupert was. 'Rupert's our choral master,' she said, as if reading my mind, pointing to the short guy with ginger hair who was operating the projector.

The camera panned across the expansive choir and I spotted Flora, then Jamilla, both standing tall, their chests bursting with song.

'Was this taken before or after Toby went missing?' I said, keeping my voice lowered.

Flora thought for a moment. 'February - so, before,' she said, offering me a mint.

I picked out Irene, barely opening her mouth, looking bored. I wondered if being sullen was her natural attitude and not simply a reaction brought on by Toby's disappearance.

The camera found Elly in the altos and I felt a flush of heat burn my lungs. She looked exactly as I remembered her, but was smiling, holding her music high, looking transported and joyful. The camera swept passed her and she was gone.

'You know who's who?' said Flora in a hushed voice.

'Er…no. Not really,' I said, gripping the edge of the chair. 'Elly didn't say much about her life here… to be honest.'

'She was like that,' she said, sadly. 'Used to keep everyt'ing separate – in compartments. Like she never mentioned you, for example.'

'Right…'

'But you seem a nice gal – so I don't mind tellin' you who her friends were.' She sniffed. 'Well - that's Charlie.' She pointed to the left of the screen. 'Poor love is going blind, but no one is supposed to know. He and Elly saw each other now and again, outside church.' I was yearning for the notebook that was buried inside my bag, but knew as soon as I laid it on my lap, it would look all wrong.

As the camera lingered on him, I could see that although Charlie was holding the score open in front of him, he hadn't glanced down at it once.

A dour man, looking shifty, came into the shot. 'And that's Father Brian. You'll remember him from Sunday. He's very…aloof - not well pop'lar, you might say.' The picture wobbled and pulled out again. 'And, that's Sam Braithwaite on da end,' said Flora, 'Did ya know him?'

I felt myself cringe. 'No…another omission.'

'He was Elly's ex-boyfriend. He's supposed to be comin' over to fix our oven door, but he keeps puttin' it off.'

'Right…' I said.

'They spilt up a while ago. How long would it be? July, maybe. When did you first meet Elly?'

'After that,' I said, vaguely. 'Perhaps that's why she didn't mention him.'

The camera pulled back and I found myself searching for Elly again, but I didn't have time to pick her out before the picture swept back to Charlie, the guy hiding his secret. In spite of the thick lenses in his spectacles, he was extremely good-looking. He was wearing a loose white shirt and blue tight-fitting chinos. His soft blonde hair was swept into a wrapa-round fringe that I knew I'd be constantly pushing out of my eyes if it belonged to me. He had what I would describe as classic public schoolboy looks; high cheekbones, blue eyes, pointed nose. I'd bet fending off advances from fawning women was one of his main pastimes. It seemed, however, that he and Elly had only ever been friends.

Flora was nudging me.

'That's Gillian Falkney,' she said, as the camcorder panned in again. 'She was likely Elly's best friend - at deh church, dat is.' She emphasised the final words, not being sure of my personal standing with regard to Elly.

Gillian was plump, wearing an all-encompassing dark smock and flat lace-up shoes. I noticed she was singing with the tenors, her diminutive shape overshadowed by lofty male figures on both sides. She looked lost and out of place. Her face had a pained expression, like the whole performance was too much for her and she was waiting for it to finish. I couldn't help think that she was someone who would always find it hard to fit in, whatever she was involved with.

The picture stuttered, then the film abruptly finished and the screen went white. There was a ripple of applause.

'Five minute break, everyone,' called out Rupert, in a strong Scottish accent. 'And then straight in with the *Agnus Dei.*'

a J Waines

There was a loud scraping of chairs as people started clearing a space in the centre. Flora handed me a plastic cup of orange juice.

'You sung Mozart's Requiem before?' she said, flicking the pages of her score and sending a welcome waft of cool air towards me.

'No. Never. I'm not really—'

A woman walked towards us holding a pile of music. 'Soprano? Alto?' she said.

'Er…I'm not—'

Flora leant across me and pulled one out. 'I reckon you're an alto,' she said. 'You'll be fine. Jamilla will stand next to you. Just follow her.'

I was too preoccupied looking around the room at this stage to worry about singing. If the worst came to the worst, I could mime. I needed to focus on the real reason I was here. Seeing Elly on the screen, so fresh and full of life had spurred me on. I turned full circle, sipping my juice, and spotted Charlie and Gillian, but couldn't find Irene or Sam.

'Who's that?' I said, nodding towards a young girl who was the centre of attention in a small group by the serving hatch.

'That's Linda. She's about nine, me t'ink.'

I watched the girl try to do the splits. Her circle gave her a polite round of applause for her efforts. 'She's in the sopranos, but to be honest, she's not good enough. We've brought her into da fold.

Parents have whole heap o' problems. It's her uncle who picks her up at the end of choir practice. He seems the only one to take interest in her. Terrible sad, but they're well fond o' each other.'

The girl looked older than nine to me. She was chunky in a strong, rather than chubby way, with short pixie hair and a small ring in her nose. I watched her desperately trying to keep her audience by attempting a cartwheel, but she lost her balance and crashed into the table holding soft drinks. She was obviously hurt. I could see her bottom lip tremble and her chin start to quiver, but she tried to laugh as others helped her to her feet. She limped to the hatch for a mop and cleared the spilt drinks without being asked. Tough cookie, I thought.

I excused myself to go to the toilet. The loos were just alongside the entrance and as I stepped alone into the foyer, I remembered what Stefan had said about the boy going missing. He'd explained how the hall led to the main church via a corridor, but also had its own exit. Standing in the foyer, I could see how easy it would be for a young boy to be taken to the toilet and then swiftly bundled outside. I checked left and right. From where I was standing just by the outside door, I was out of everyone's line of sight from both the hall and the church itself. It was the perfect spot for an undetectable abduction.

As I stared at the exit, a thought shot into my mind making me swallow hard.

Whoever took Toby *knew* the layout of the church, knew the timing of the Children's Liturgy, knew when the youngsters would be traipsing back through the corridor to join the main service after ten o'clock. That person knew there was an unlocked outside door, leading to a small courtyard and straight on to the main road.

Wondering if I'd hit on something, I delved into my bag and pulled out the copy of the tiny map I'd found in Elly's locket. Did X mark the spot where the killer took Toby? Was it a clue to his abduction? I studied the map and walked along the corridor. I backtracked into the empty church, but nothing about the map and the layout matched up. False alarm.

I walked back and looked out onto the grey courtyard, judging the distance to the road. It would take thirty seconds to pick up a boy of four, get him out of the door, through the gate and into a parked car waiting by the pavement. *Thirty seconds.* No wonder no one had seen anything. It was too easy. I went back to the hall.

By the end of the rehearsal, I felt pleasantly exhilarated. Standing beside Jamilla had been my saving grace. There were four in the altos, but she had enough voice for all of us. She made sure she sang loudly in my direction to keep me in tune, pointing to where we were in the music.

'When we get closer to da performance,' Jamilla whispered to me, 'other choirs in da area join forces with us, bumpin' up da numbers.'

It made me feel better knowing I'd have more voices to hide behind. By the time we'd run through the *Agnus Dei* six times, I was actually starting to get the hang of it.

'You're a bahn natural,' she said, squeezing my arm.

'I think that's an overstatement,' I said, just as Flora approached me, wearing a hopeful expression. I knew before she opened her mouth, what my answer would be. 'Good gal!' she said, slapping me on the back so hard I started to cough. 'We have ourselves a new alto,' she announced to the group and I earned myself a cheer.

New people entered the hall; family members coming to take the singers home.

'That's Lewis Jackson,' said Flora, 'Linda's uncle.' I turned, but saw only the back of a figure wearing a bomber jacket, carrying a motorcycle helmet. 'He doesn't do mass. Or choir. He used to come now and again with his sister six or seven years ago, but when she went off the rails and her husband ended up in jail - he stopped turnin' up. Now, he's only here because he's Linda's taxi service. He's mates with Sam, Elly's ex. They're both policemen. Always handy, me t'ink.'

I made another mental note. It would be good to get some background from them at some point. If they lived locally, they may even have been involved with the abduction case.

I looked at Linda again, her face tough-set as though preparing herself for the harsh realities of the outside world. She was linking arms with her uncle, pointing down to her bloodied knee. She reached up to kiss her uncle who leaned his head towards hers.

'Linda's bin comin' since the start of the year. Maggie - that's Lewis's sister, was pushing for it. "So that at least one member of the family has a chance of turning out decent", she said.' Flora frowned. 'Not sure it's helped all dat much wid Linda's behaviour. She's a wild one.' She leant towards me, conspiratorially. 'Fact is, Linda is a bright kid with an overactive imagination. Too much time bullying da girls, teasing da boys and annoyin' dem teachers.' She sighed. 'I caught her readin' one o' dem graphic comics in church the other day - ya know - pictures, instead o' words.'

I was in the kitchen the following day, about to kick the washing machine - the only way to jog it into the spin cycle - when my mobile rang. It was Stefan.

'You free this afternoon? I'm in Putney covering last night's robbery on the high street. Isn't that your neck of the woods?'

I scratched my head. 'Putney…Richmond…kind of…' I wasn't sure if this was some kind of date or whether he had information about Elly's case to give me. I didn't know how to play it. 'I'm just finishing off a rewrite for *Yoga and Health* magazine—'

'I've got something for you…on those queries you asked me about. My mate in the Met got back to me…'

That swung it for me. 'Brilliant.' I took a look at my watch. 'Half-past four outside Putney railway station?'

Fine rain had been spitting on and off since morning, but as soon as I left the house a pelting downpour broke through, battering my umbrella as I bolted for the station. Stefan was waiting by the flower stall when I got to Putney, under an awning that was periodically tipping panfuls of water over innocent bystanders. I dragged him under my brolly just before the next burst of water erupted from the canvas.

I couldn't help wondering why he was sticking his neck out for me in this way. Was it purely because he thought there was a story in it or was there something else?

We dodged from doorway to doorway, until he pulled me inside a small steamed-up café on the Upper Richmond Road.

'This do?' he said, without waiting for an answer.

He ordered drinks and we settled by the window, smug now that we were dry. I wiped the inside of the windowpane with a napkin so we could watch people leap out of taxis and scatter down the street, pulling up their collars and holding newspapers over their heads.

I'd thought about Stefan on and off since we'd first met at the cemetery and by now I knew something for sure. I really liked him. I thought he was smart, attractive and relaxing to be with. He had lots to talk about and had no trace of arrogance or showmanship about his success as a journalist.

But I also knew something else - there was no spark. Not for me, at least. It was a tricky situation to manage. Did he fancy *me*? Was that an ulterior motive for getting involved? From a selfish point of view, Stefan was proving to be a valuable asset and I didn't want to blow him out and miss further information about Elly's case. On the other hand, I didn't want him to think I was interested in him, then complain I'd been stringing him along.

It felt too early to broach any of this. It seemed too personal and potentially embarrassing for both of us. I wasn't ready to lay my cards on the table just yet.

'I managed to speak to my mate in the Met,' he said, squeezing water out of the cuffs of his jumper into his saucer. He looked pleased with himself.

'Thank you. That's amazing. I really do appreciate it.'

I'd sent Stefan an email earlier in the week with three questions I'd been battling with that I had no hope of answering on my own.

'Apparently Elly Swift's prints are the only ones on her computer. And it was password protected.'

I was dismayed.

I leant on the shelf that served as a table running the length of the window and turned up my nose. 'So they are still sticking to the suicide theory? It's all wrong somehow.'

He shrugged. 'The police - the Hampshire Constabulary and British Transport Police - they're both dealing with the case - they're definitely running with that theory.' He flipped open his notepad. 'Your next query...' he said. 'I managed to speak to the reporter in Micheldever who interviewed the witnesses at the level-crossing. She said their statements were sketchy, but apparently there was a tractor in the queue. There were three or four cars behind that and six or so pedestrians right at the front, waiting to cross.' He glanced down at his notes. 'One witness said there was one man beside him with a noisy dog, Elly, another woman, a boy and a young girl with a bike. Another witness said she thought there was another woman.'

'I remember it was raining heavily - like this,' I said, waving my hand at the window. 'You can see why the witness reports were sketchy.'

'And my contact said most of the pedestrians had umbrellas...' Several figures scurried past us holding their umbrellas low. It was hard even at this close range to make out whether they were men or women.

'It would have been noisy, too, wouldn't it?' I said. 'A tractor, the alarm sirens at the crossing, the dog barking...'

'She said the witnesses saw the train approaching and that Elly staggered on to the track right in front of it. She was bent double - someone used the word "disoriented". Consensus was that she looked in distress, her face appeared distorted. But no one heard anything or saw anyone behind her. No one saw anyone drag or push her...'

'But, they weren't in the best position to say for sure, were they? I mean, look at these people out here.' I gestured towards the figures bumping into one another on the pavement. 'How much would they know about an incident taking place literally three feet away from them? They've all got their heads down and their umbrellas are severely restricting their views.'

'But, at the level-crossing they were standing still, waiting, watching...'

'There was no reason for them to be watching *each other.* They'd be watching the train, the barriers. I still think something must have happened. Right before their eyes.' We were silent for a moment. I tried to picture the scene. A huddle of jostling people getting wet, eager for the train to pass. I tried to imagine what might have happened. *Did Elly trip? Over the dog? A pedal of the bicycle? Did someone say something to her?* 'What do you make of the way they described her?' I said.

He shrugged. '"Bent double," he read. "Disoriented." "Her face distorted." If you were going to commit suicide, that's how you might appear to other people, don't you think?'

I thought for a moment, one knee jiggling up and down on the high stool.

'No - it doesn't quite fit. This was a woman in fear for her life, not intending to end it.'

I told him how I'd discussed Elly's suicide note with Dr Petrova. As I spoke, Stefan opened a sachet of sugar and started sprinkling it into a doodle on the window shelf. 'I think the police are taking Elly's depressed background too readily into account and jumping to conclusions.'

'You know what the police are like - they won't react unless there's new evidence. There's nothing new.' He tapped the sachet of sugar. It was empty. I balled my fist and banged it on the window ledge. Stefan's sugar doodle leapt into the air.

'I can't bear it!' I said, struggling to keep my voice down. 'Flora, one of Elly's church friends, said the inquest will take place soon. It's all being hurried along. We've got to *find* something.' I tossed the hair out of my eyes. 'I was at choir practice, but I couldn't find the right moment to bring up Elly's previous attempts.'

'It's not easy.'

'I'm running out of time.'

He gave me a sympathetic look.

'Your final query was about the other witnesses. The ones who saw Elly casing the railway line near her home in Brixton?'

'And?' I sat upright. I'd forgotten I'd asked him about that. 'What did you find?'

'There were three separate sightings.' He sounded definitive, as if this was more than sufficient to give weight to Elly's suicide theory.

'Who saw her? Who are these witnesses?'

'Er...they were all under thirteen.'

'Kids? I don't believe it.' I slammed my palm into my forehead. 'What kind of testimony does that add up to?'

Stefan shrugged. He looked like he'd given up. I couldn't understand why he didn't have the same reservations I did. I thought he'd be more sceptical about her suicide than this.

It seemed to me that the so-called evidence was falling to pieces, but the problem was there was nothing sufficiently conclusive to shake up the police. 'It's so bloody frustrating,' I said. 'So much that's hard to prove. So many loose ends that don't quite fit together. Don't you think so?'

'Maybe you should stick to being a journalist,' he said.

I rounded on him.

'No way!' I hissed. 'I'm in this for the long haul, whatever it takes.' I rubbed my eyes. I was tired. I hadn't been sleeping well. Every time I shut my eyes, I saw images of Elly or her mother - their looks always imploring, beseeching, grateful. 'I saw her - she was frightened. It wasn't simply anxiety about what she was about to do - she kept looking behind her on the train. She was expecting someone. The guy in the raincoat.'

I was shouting now. I looked behind me, aware that a hush had stifled the chatter in the café and people were watching us.

'Okay!' he said, raising his hands as though I was holding a revolver. 'But there's no concrete link between the guy who pinched your bag and Elly,' he said, calmly. 'I know you saw him looking suspicious, searching for something on the train, but he could have dropped his lunchbox. You didn't see him anywhere near Elly. And your bag was returned - there was no crime.'

I pressed my hands over my ears. I didn't want to hear anymore.

'Not helping,' I said.

'I know, but it *is* what you're up against.'

Was Stefan trying to block me? Discourage me?

'I thought you wanted the truth,' I said, despondently.

'I do. I'm just being realistic. I know what the police will and won't respond to. There's nothing new you can use.'

I knew he was right. I also knew I wouldn't get anywhere by snapping at him and forcing him away. 'Why don't you come over for an early supper,' I said. 'It won't actually be edible, but you can wash it down with a glass or two of Merlot.'

He stretched and hesitated a moment, his hands on his knees. 'Thanks. That would be great.'

The rain had eased into a drizzle, so we managed to get back to the station and over to Richmond without getting soaked.

There was a note through my door when I got back. It was from Squid. It said I had a visitor waiting in his flat for me. A visitor? Who on earth would this be? I left Stefan with a glass of wine and went downstairs.

'We've been getting on like a house on fire,' he said, as Caroline slid into sight behind Squid with a wave. I asked him to join us, but he said he had a food mixer to fix.

'I was in London for an audition,' said Caroline, as we climbed the stairs. 'I wanted to see your new place.' She stood on the landing. 'Bit small isn't it?'

'It's perfect for me,' I said. 'This is Stefan.' I didn't quite know how to introduce him. 'He's helping me with some investigations,' I said, cautiously. She sent me a withering look.

I sorted out the meal and filled glasses. Caroline started by asking Stefan a few questions about his work and before long they were engaged in animated discussions about the theatre. I turned into a waitress merely presenting the food. In the silences, I caught them exchanging cautious glances. Like prowling animals, they were checking each other out.

By the time Stefan left, we'd all had a lot of wine and were slapping each other on the back like old pals. He took a taxi all the way back to Camden. He was obviously getting a better freelance income than I was.

'He's sweet,' said Caroline, as I started the dishes. She had her face hidden by an open cupboard door, but I caught her look as she went to find her coat. It was a smile I hadn't seen before. Her lips barely moved, but they conveyed something furtive, private, unspoken. I realised after she'd gone exactly what it was. It was a secret knowing.

I felt like I'd mixed two lethal substances together and I had no idea how to cope with the aftermath.

chapter nine

I was surprised to get a call the next day from the Swifts, telling me the date of Elly's inquest. I'd left them my card but never thought for one minute they would use it. The inquest was going to be Monday week, October 18th, and I knew straightaway that it clashed with an interview I'd been planning for months, with Helen Mirren. She was only going to be in London a few days before heading back to L.A. If I cancelled it, I'd have to pay my own way over to Hollywood, which would more than wipe out my commission fee.

I had to admit that things had slowed down recently on the writing front. Not just because fewer of my pitches were being taken on board by magazine editors, but because I'd been distracted of late and hadn't produced enough feature ideas in the first place.

I couldn't afford to lose the interview with Ms Mirren; it represented a potential hike in prestige as well as a healthy fee. I knew the way the inquest was going to go, unless before then, I could come up with some compelling new evidence.

I told Mrs Swift I wouldn't be able to come to the inquest and she didn't seem surprised; she had heard of Helen Mirren and seemed to understand my dilemma. She asked me to visit them instead. She said she had *a few things I might find interesting*. It sounded ominous, and I had mini flashbacks to my weird dream where Mrs Swift had started handing over Elly's clothes. I couldn't imagine what Mrs Swift had up her sleeve, but I couldn't turn down the possibility of new revelations. Plus, if I felt bold enough, I might be able to broach the subject of Elly's previous suicide attempts. I could end up receiving short shrift, but her medical history was one of the hazy areas that needed some light thrown on it. Although, as I'm sure Stefan would hastily point out, it still wouldn't count as evidence as such.

They were happy for me to come over the same day, so I forced myself to sit down and write one new pitch for a potential feature, sent it off to *House and Garden* magazine and left the flat.

Nothing had changed since my last visit; the curtains throughout the house were still drawn, the Swifts were still wearing the same shade-away-from-black clothes and the tea was just as insipid. The poor black and white mongrel looked as forlorn as before.

After the tea (and scones heavily enriched with baking-soda), Mrs Swift looked like she was about to get to the point, but before she'd finished clearing our cups, there was a sharp rap on the front door.

'Are we expecting anyone?' she said to her husband. Mr Swift's eyes didn't flicker. They stayed firmly fixed on the silver bars of the unlit gas fire.

She left the room and I heard the voice of a man in the hall.

'Didn't realise you had company,' said the man, having stepped past her into the sitting room. 'It's freezing in here. Why don't you put the fire on?'

His eyes brushed over me, ignoring me, as though I didn't exist until I'd been introduced.

'This is a friend of Elly's,' said Mrs Swift. She didn't give my name, perhaps she couldn't remember it. 'Frank's come to collect some of Elly's things.'

He jerked his chin in my direction by way of a greeting. He was wearing blue decorators' dungarees and muddy builders' boots he hadn't seen fit to remove at the front door. He was broad with wide shoulders; a chubby shiny face and wisps of thin blonde hair made him look like an overgrown toddler. He didn't hold out his hand to me and I wasn't disappointed; his fingers were covered in dried plaster.

'Stuff for Irene,' said Frank to no one in particular. 'I mentioned it to Dennis last week.'

'Mentioning things to Dennis doesn't always get through,' said Mrs Swift. 'Dennis's smoke signals are a little vague these days.'

We all turned towards Mr Swift, propped up awkwardly in his armchair like a dummy waiting to go in a shop window.

'Which things did you want?' asked Mrs Swift, poised to accompany Frank upstairs.

'Don't trouble yourself - I can go through it myself.' He turned to leave the room.

'We brought a load of stuff over to you last weekend,' said Mrs Swift, blocking his path. 'Irene didn't say she wanted anything else.'

'Must have changed her mind.' He put his hands on his hips. It made him look aggressive, although he was trying to hold a smile on his lips.

She folded her arms, unwilling to back down just yet. 'Why didn't Irene come? Then she could pick out what she wanted.'

'She's busy with the laundry.'

He clapped his hands together sending a puff of dust into the air. 'I haven't got long.' As far as he was concerned, the matter was settled. Reluctantly, Mrs Swift moved aside.

'What's left is in the back bedroom,' she said. He went straight upstairs. I noticed he hadn't brought any bags with him.

Mrs Swift made another pot of tea and took a cup up to Frank, perhaps to check on what he was doing. She wasn't the only one who felt uneasy about Frank's visit. Something about it didn't ring true for me, either. We sat sipping the bland tea in silence and it occurred to me that Mrs Swift was waiting for him to leave before she addressed the real reason for inviting me over.

Footsteps eventually came down the stairs. Frank was carrying a large cardboard box. Two sleeves of a cardigan hung over the edge, limp, lifeless. Like Elly.

'Was that the lot from her flat?' he said, looking innocently back up the stairs.

'Not everything. Paul's transit wasn't big enough. There are still a pile of books and stuff.'

'You should have asked *me*.'

'We didn't like to trouble you…what with…'

That faltering sentence was the closest either of them got to mentioning Toby.

'Let me know when you want to get the rest. I'll see if I can get the van for half a day.'

Without waiting for a reply, he was gone.

We both sat staring at the carpet for a few seconds, as if making sure Frank had really left. I heard an engine fire up outside the window. Meg Swift offered me a ginger biscuit.

Mrs Swift was quiet for a moment and I had a feeling she might have forgotten why she'd invited me. Then she looked up, and said 'Right,' decisively, like she was about to tell me a story, her arms wrapped around her knees, poised on the edge of the chair. 'Elly probably didn't tell you this, but if you can't be at the inquest…' She tailed off like she'd got lost. She cleared her throat. 'Like I said, she didn't have many friends – and if she gave you that locket…well, she must have thought very highly of you. We thought you should know.'

Although she used the term *we*, there were no signs of collaboration from her husband. Mr Swift had been present the whole time just like my last visit, but he hadn't actually been *with* us. He stared at the dog, then at the carpet, travelling around his own private world inside his head. It was as though his life had turned into one extended sleepwalk. I remember after Jeff's death, waiting for the day when I woke up to find that the upheaval had died down and life had gone back to normal. Except, the harsh reality hit me after several weeks that there was never going to be a normality to go back to.

'Elly's previous attempts at suicide will probably come out. It won't be very pleasant.'

I couldn't imagine any inquest that would be.

'I don't remember seeing you there,' she said, absently. 'At the funeral.'

I said the first thing I could think of. 'I was out of the country - sadly.' It was plausible, given my job. The real reason, of course, was that it took place before I'd inveigled my way into Elly's life.

Mrs Swift's voice drifted in again. 'It helps to put everything into context. Makes what she did less of a shock, I think.'

'Okay...'I said, nodding, waiting.

'Elly was always a difficult child,' she said. 'Ungainly, withdrawn, quiet - and she didn't make much of herself. She wasn't a credit to us, like Irene.' She sniffed. 'She was miserable the whole time, claimed she had some sort of...depression...since she was about eighteen.'

She spat out the word *depression* as though it was a crime, a particularly corrupt one. 'Elly took her first overdose at nineteen.' She turned up her nose. 'She was in her flat and took painkillers with lots of alcohol, silly girl.' I bit my lip, finding Mrs Swift's flippant tone hard to tolerate. 'She passed out and woke up two and a half days later.' She let out a hollow laugh. 'No one knew a thing about it.'

I rubbed my forehead trying to hide my rising anger. I was silently horrified. That poor girl, regarded in the family as nothing short of a disappointment, was being insulted for managing to fail even at suicide. Her own mother seemed to find something ironic and amusing about it.

'The psychiatrist said it was because she had low self-esteem, was lonely - that sort of thing, but Elly didn't make the effort to pull herself together. She didn't *try* to make friends. Always in a world of her own, painting these little figurines - make believe.' She pointed to a shelf displaying several vases. I got up to take a closer look. Tucked away at the back were four dusty plastic models. 'From *Lord of the Rings* or *Star Wars*, or what have you.' I lifted one up. They were exquisitely detailed. I couldn't help but feel sad. No wonder Elly had spent her days engrossed in fairytale worlds; real life wasn't very kind to her and that included her mother and her sister, from what I'd heard so far.

'There are boxes of them still at her flat.' She brightened. 'You can have them if you like.'

I politely declined her offer. I wasn't sure what hundreds of fantasy figures, such as Bilbo Baggins and Luke Skywalker were going to tell me.

'She finally got involved with the church,' continued Mrs Swift. 'We were all telling her what she should do, but she went and had another go shortly after her twenty-first birthday.'

She made it sound like Elly had been making attempts at bungie-jumping. 'God knows how she got hold of it, but she used a drug called oxy-something-or-other. It's for ongoing pain and normally only given to people who are on their death beds. She took that with valium and some other drug, washed down with vodka. Stupid numskull.' She scratched her knee. 'Her boyfriend had just finished with her. I told her there were plenty of other fish in the sea.'

And I bet that helped, I thought, so thunderously inside my head that I wasn't sure for a second if my words had actually slipped out of my mouth.

'Elly was just negative about herself, a misery-guts for no real reason.'

She sounded just like Irene. I made a noise that was meant to sound like I was weighing up what she'd said, but it came out more like a protest.

'What did the doctors say - her GP?'

'They agreed that she wasn't psychotic and it wasn't even proper depression. She was a bit of a recluse, different from the rest of us. Saw herself as badly done to.'

Another sharp stab of fury took my breath away. Mrs Swift should have been standing by Elly, not denigrating her, criticising her. I forced myself to look at Mr Swift to distract me from the storm brewing inside my lungs. His face was grey, as impassive as ever. His thumb twitched.

'And what happened after her second attempt, when she was twenty-one? That must have been a while ago,' I said, wanting to get this over with.

'Well. We thought she'd finally seen sense and got herself together. She got a decent job at that wholefood shop in Brixton, she got herself a cat. She joined that church. She'd been a lot better, until recently. Obviously, there was Toby. That shook everyone up dreadfully. Then there was a break up with Sam, another boyfriend.' She tutted and sent her eyes skywards. 'The blues must have started up again…and this is where it ended…'

I could see how anyone hearing this version of events would take no time in deciding that Elly's final appointment with death had been deliberate. That's what her parents had decided. That's what the police had decided. It was a neatly packaged explanation that made complete sense. But it only made sense, if you excluded all the pieces of the picture that didn't fit. I checked on one of those pieces, right there and then.

'This may seem an odd question to ask, Mrs Swift, but did Elly leave suicide notes…you know…before?'

'Yes.'

'The same sort of thing? Typed on a computer?'

'I'm not sure she had a computer then. No. I think she wrote them out herself. I might even still have them…' She got up and went to a bureau in the corner of the room. There was a rustle of papers and she came back with two folded sheets.

'Not sure why we've kept these. I suppose there's not much else.'

She handed me both notes. I recognised Elly's neat script. The first read:

Dearest Mummy and Daddy

I know you don't understand what I'm going through. I'm so unhappy, I can't carry on anymore. I need to be at peace. I'm sorry to let you down. Yours Elly X

The second read:

Dear Mummy and Daddy

I can't find any reason to keep going. I feel so alone. There's no point. It doesn't mean anything. I don't expect you to understand. Please don't be sad. I'm sorry I have to go. Yours Elly X

By the time I'd finished reading, my throat had swelled into a fat ball of flesh and I couldn't speak. A drip fell on to the page and I realised it was a tear.

'I'm sorry,' I whispered, fearing that I'd spoilt the note. Mrs Swift was stroking the dog and looked like she hadn't noticed.

I handed them both back and went to my bag for a handkerchief. I blew my nose loudly, unashamed of my emotional outburst. In fact, making a point of it. It was a well-deserved expression of grief for a girl whose loneliness and misery had never been fully acknowledged. Only judged.

Mrs Swift waited patiently for me to clean myself up. Mr Swift was still fixed on some random object in the room, unavailable. They were both residing in their own individual plains of denial, I concluded. In their eyes, Elly's demise had nothing whatsoever to do with them.

It was time to go. I thanked Meg Swift, but didn't linger at the door this time. My view of her had completely shifted. The sadness I'd seen during my last visit, I realised, had been for herself, not for Elly. My crusade was going to be for Elly alone, from now on.

I found myself wanting to run as I got through the gate, to escape the poison that was distorting the person Elly was. She'd been shy and reserved, brought up in a family that didn't appreciate her gifts and looked down on her, regarding her as a second-rate daughter. No wonder her self-esteem had been rock bottom.

I called Stefan. I didn't want to be alone after what I'd just been through. He answered straight away. Relief made me gabble my words.

'She definitely didn't write the suicide note,' I said, before introducing myself.

'Okay, Anna. Slow down.'

I explained about my visit, about Elly's previous attempts and the notes. I described how she'd addressed both notes personally to her parents, signed them with a kiss, had expressed her sorrow and reasons for doing what she did.

'Plus, Dr Petrova, my old psychotherapist, said that it's very rare for people repeating suicide attempts to change their methods,' I said. 'Elly took overdoses, she didn't throw herself into the path of trains…'

'What are you going to do?'

'Get in touch with the police again. Tell them everything I know. See if they will see sense.'

'Good luck.' He sounded like I needed it. 'Tell me how it goes.'

• • •

As the Tube trundled its way north, for some reason Frank came into my mind. I could see him standing at the bottom of the stairs holding the box of Elly's things and questions drifted into my head, like wasps through an open window. *What was the real reason for his visit? What was he looking for? Was he the man in the raincoat?*

chapter ten

I held the line for ages before finally reaching Cilla Lane, the officer who had taken my statement at Waterloo station. It took her a few moments to work out who I was and which case I was referring to. Once we were finally on the same page, I told her I had further information.

I told her everything I had discovered since looking into Elly's death, still omitting to mention the locket, but including the fact that I'd discovered that witness statements at the scene didn't match; that they couldn't even all agree on how many people were waiting at the level crossing.

'And the witnesses who said they saw Ms Swift loitering around a railway line,' I said. 'They were *children* - they're not reliable.'

I could hear the dismissive overtones in her voice as she soon as she responded.

'I don't know how you got hold of this information, Ms Rothman, but it hasn't been released to the public. And, I'm afraid, I don't see how it changes anything.'

'But the suicide note bore no resemblance to the other notes she left.'

I heard no reply, just breathing - breathing that sounded riddled with desire to go and do something more important. Then, it was as though she made a decision.

'I shouldn't really be telling you this, but the suicide notes *were* similar - the wording was very similar. She used exact phrases she'd used before. We had a forensic linguist check this one against the others. She confirmed it was written by the same person.' I knew she was telling me this in order to score points rather than to be helpful.

'I've spoken to a suicide expert and…the methods…the…' I was running out of impetus, out of hope.

'Ms Rothman, I'm not quite sure what your concern is in all this, but perhaps you should attend the inquest on October 18th. I can give you the details. All the reports suggest that Ms Swift died as a result of suicide. The case will be closed unless there's new evidence to suggest otherwise.'

That word *evidence* again.

As far as I was concerned Elly's chequered psychiatric history made no difference to my belief that she didn't kill herself. Elly hadn't been deluded. The fear I saw ravaging her face didn't only exist inside her head. No. Elly's fear was real. The menace was standing beside her, outside, in the world, as clear as the man who stole my bag. It was all connected. I just didn't know how yet. Having seen her original suicide notes, I *knew*, not just believed, that Elly did not commit suicide.

I'm not sure whether either of us said goodbye, but the next moment the phone was purring in my hand. I snapped it shut and flung it into my bag. *Bloody nerve of the woman!* I considered ringing back and asking to speak to a more senior officer, but that word *evidence* was like a massive tomb of concrete blocking my way. There was no way around it. I was stuck.

I sat in the kitchen, staring at the tiny map where X marked the spot. I had to find an excuse to get inside Flora's house. It was the only clue I had.

In the end, all it took was a phone-call.

Flora and Jamilla lived in a one-bedroom flat in a concrete high-rise in Stockwell. It was barely big enough for one, let alone two of them and neither could be described as petite. They even shared a bed. Outside, the rough, stippled walls were daubed with red and black slogans in Arabic and drips from the gutters, year in and year out, had formed solid lime scale trails, like stalactites, above their front window.

Inside, however, it was like stepping through the back of C.S. Lewis's wardrobe; everything opened up. There was no resemblance to the poverty-debased landscape Squid and I had just walked through.

To say Flora and Jamilla were house-proud was like saying bees like honey. The fairy-lights and rows of porcelain mermaids, dolphins and hanging seagulls weren't exactly tasteful, but they certainly made an impact. Like Alice in Wonderland, I felt huge and was terrified that with the swish of my coat or whoosh of my sleeve, some precious object would fall to its grave.

Before Squid and I had taken off our coats, they were plying us with Jamaican ginger cake and iced coconut drops on a tray so close to the gas fire, it looked like the pink icing was melting. I had a surreal moment of concern when I feared being fed so much that I wouldn't be able to squeeze back through the doorway into the outside world. Squid was in his element; two gracious women pandering to him. He looked like he was settled in for the whole day.

So far, my plan had gone without a hitch. I'd remembered Flora saying she'd been

waiting for someone at the church to fix her oven door. I happened to know a keen handyman and that was my passport to getting inside the place.

My first concern, however, was that it wasn't a 'house' at all, but a tiny flat. I made an excuse to use the toilet and took the miniature map from my pocket. Emerging with it from the bathroom, I surveyed the space. It was all wrong. Nothing like the map. I couldn't believe that after all my efforts, I'd taken off on a wild goose chase.

As Squid fiddled with the oven door, chatting to Flora, Jamilla showed me some of the trinkets.

'These are from Spain,' she said, holding up two donkeys made of raffia. 'And this was Elly's favourite…' She put a tiny pixie sitting on a box in my hand. The wings were as fine as a butterfly's.

We turned to another shelf and I spotted a collection of painted figures.

'Did Elly paint these?' I asked.

'Yes. They're from *Star Trek* and these,' she bent down to another cabinet, 'are from *Batman.*'

She invited me into the compact bedroom where fantasy creatures were collected into scenes on the tops of cupboards and shelves. On top of a dolls' house were jigsaw puzzles and games. The sisters were certainly big kids at heart. A trait they must have welcomed in Elly.

Squid called out to say the job was done and we got ready to leave. The encounter ended with everyone happy - except me.

When I got back to my flat, there was an odd smell.

It was my heightened sensitivity. I was picking up something oily in the air. I couldn't place it at first, then it made me think of Jeff. Engine oil. Motorbikes. Someone had been in.

Holding my phone in case I had to make an emergency call, I checked every room, but they were all empty. I went into my bedroom, cautiously, not sure what I was going to find. My eyes went straight to the dressing table, but the locket was still there. So too, was Elly's bible.

I searched around, my senses on alert for anything unusual, untoward. My slippers neatly aligned beside the bed, my pyjamas folded on top of the pillow. My library book on the bedside cabinet, the glass of water from last night on top of it. Nothing out of place. The flowers in a vase on the edge of the dressing table, the talc and perfume beside them. The talc I hadn't used for a while.

I moved over to the dressing table, staring down at the objects that were lined up. Hairspray, deodorant I'd used that morning, hand-cream. Nothing different. I came back to the talc and looked at it carefully. There was a crescent shape of shiny wood at the base of the cardboard container. I hadn't dusted in a while and ran my index finger over the edge of the table top. It drew a line - a shiny wood line where the dust had cleared.

I knew then that the objects on my dressing table had been moved.

I pulled the first drawer open. It was stiff and as I pulled, the jars and bottles on the top wobbled. The deodorant and the perfume toppled over. I could see now why there was a crescent of dust-free wood by the talc. Someone had been through my drawers and had displaced the containers that had fallen over as a result. Only very slightly.

I stopped where I was, thinking about fingerprints and pulled out a tissue in order to avoid gripping the other handles with my bare hands. I had nothing of value in those drawers, but I checked anyway. Nothing seemed to have gone or been disturbed.

I looked round for my laptop. It was where I had left it, by the window. The rest of the room seemed the way I remembered it.

'Are you absolutely sure someone's been in?' said Caroline. She sounded impatient. Like she had somewhere else she wanted to be.

'I know for certain things have been moved,' I said. 'Someone's been opening my drawers.'

'*Moved.* So nothing's actually missing or damaged?'

'It's very discreet. You wouldn't know unless you were looking closely.'

I took the phone with me down the stairs to the front door and looked closely at the lock. It wasn't sophisticated, only a basic Yale, but I could find no scratches or marks to suggest anyone had forced it. I remembered I'd given Squid a key, but he'd been with me all afternoon.

'You're really convinced about this, aren't you?' said Caroline. She made it sound like I was seeing devils and ghosts where there were none. 'You're sure you're not getting swept up in the drama of this weird riddle you're involved in?'

'Overreacting, you mean?' I stared hard at the carpet. 'You don't think I should I call the police?'

'Nothing's missing, Anna! There are no sign of a break-in - nothing's been disturbed - except perhaps a couple of jars fell over. It's hardly going to get the blue lights flashing, is it?'

She had a point, but I knew I was right. I went down to Squid and he produced the spare key which he said had 'never left his pocket'. He asked if I wanted company, but I didn't feel like being sociable.

I spent the night on my own hugging a cushion with the latch pressed down on the front door so that even with a key, no one would be able to get in. I kept the TV on low, listening to the creaks and groans of the flat, drinking Chablis in small quiet sips.

I didn't sleep well that night. Every time I shut my eyes I saw images of the man at Micheldever station, imagined him creeping up the stairs, poking around in my room. *Looking for something.* It had to be him. He must have found my business card, the one Elly must have pinched from my bag on the train, just as I'd thought. He knew where I lived.

I pulled up the duvet but it felt like a thin veil, giving me neither comfort nor warmth. I tried to stop listening, but it was like telling myself not to think of a blue elephant. I heard the leaves hissing in the breeze outside, the branches scraping the windows of the flat below, cars passing, the intermittent rattling of the pipes, gurgles from the radiators. I thought I heard the patter of mice, but I didn't mind. It was far better than the constant thud, thud, thud of my quivering heartbeat.

• • •

After mass on Sunday, Jamilla wrapped her arms around me in an impromptu greeting. In a single breath, I felt like I'd consumed a bottleful of lily of the valley. 'You gonna be a proper reg'lar?' she asked.

'I hope so,' I said, feeling mean. I had one reason for being there, albeit it a good one, but it had nothing to do with Catholicism.

'Flora's around here somewhere,' she said, lifting her head. I broke away to rinse my hands in the Ladies' and I could hear a soft whimpering, like an injured dog, coming from one of the cubicles.

'Hello?' I said. 'Is someone there?' I tapped on the door of the cubicle and waited. 'Are you okay in there?'

Nothing happened and I was about to leave, when Flora stumbled out. Her hat was at a precarious angle and her face was glossy with tears.

'Flora! What's happened?'

She looked on the verge of collapsing. I grabbed her waist, certain that if she keeled over she would take me with her. She slumped into me, squashing the fake flower pinned to her lapel. I dragged her out of the cubicle and tried to shuffle her towards the wall.

'What's happened?' I said, again. 'Are you ill?'

'No darlin',' she said. 'I don't want her to see me like dis.'

I reached behind her and pulled a paper towel from the dispenser. She took it greedily and began mopping her face. I waited for her to explain. 'Jamilla…' she said, trying to breathe between rasping sobs.

'Jamilla?'

'Jamilla, she—'

She broke off, unable to hold up her head. She was having difficulty getting oxygen into her lungs. I was in two minds about rushing for help, but couldn't rely on Flora remaining upright. Flora wheezed another breath trying to get the words out.

'Jamilla, she got…she got cancer.' As she said the last word her foot buckled underneath her and she slipped further down in my feeble grasp. I flashed back to only moments earlier, when her sister had welcomed me with a generous hug like she hadn't a care in the world.

'Flora. I'm so sorry.' I was half hugging her, half holding her up.

'I don't want her to see me upset. She's got enough to deal with.'

'When did you find out?'

'Last Wednesday, before choir practice. I don't know how she was able to turn up and sing like not'ing had happened. Praise da Lord.' She sniffed. 'I had to keep a brave face on…couldn't say anyt'ing. But I can't do it no more.'

'Okay…okay.' My arms couldn't support her weight anymore. 'You lean against the sink and I'll go and get a chair,' I said.

She didn't object. I found an abandoned seat in the foyer and dragged it into the confined space.

'Shall I get you a glass of water?'

'I'm all right. I'll be all right in a minute,' she said, contradicting herself. 'The hospital says it's bad. She only got 'bout six months…to live…'

Her face fell in, like a crumpled airbag and she tried to smother her howls with her scarf. I held her, half rocking her, my backside crushed against the sink.

She went on to tell me about the tests Jamilla had undergone, the ordeal they'd both gone through not knowing for sure during the last five weeks. She recounted the exact words the specialist had said to them, the brutal prognosis and the futile treatment that she would be offered anyway. The words poured out. Anxiety did that sometimes. You can keep the cork stuffed into the bottle for a while, believing that you're coping, and then suddenly when you least expect it, the pressure erupts and you blurt it all out to a virtual stranger.

I rubbed her back, squeezed her arm. Her body was both firm and jelly-like at the same time.

'She's so brave,' I said. 'You both are.'

'She's a fighter - that one.'

'That's good. She'll make the very best of this, won't she?'

She looked up, her eyes a little brighter. 'You're a kind girl,' she said. 'I'm glad Elly had you as her friend. Poor t'ing.'

She straightened her hat in the mirror then turned to me and held me briefly at arms' length. 'I'd better go back in. She'll be wond'ring what's happened to me.'

I felt Flora's firm, but gentle hands gripping my arms and it felt in that instant that she was the one holding me up, supporting me, instead of the other way round. I swallowed hard and felt the shame pass down my throat, like sour medicine. Flora had confided in me and I was still harbouring the lie about my true motives for being there. I'd broken into their little pious community like a conniving thief.

'I've got a confession,' I said. I heard my own words and was taken aback, as though they'd come from someone standing behind me. Suddenly the space felt claustrophobic, airless, the combination of air-freshener and Domestos making me feel giddy.

'A confession?' She laughed. 'Me t'ink you in the wrong part of the church for dat!' She was almost fully recovered from her weeping by now.

I looked down, considering whether to back-track. I hadn't planned this declaration, but now I'd started it was going to be difficult to bluff my way out of it.

'I *did* know Elly,' I said. 'but not that well. I was with her on the train just before she died. In a round-about way, she asked me for help. To cut a long story short, I don't think she killed herself. Well, I *know* she didn't and I'm here to get to the truth.'

'Oh, my…' she said.

As soon as she responded, I began to see how unfair it was to be burdening Flora with Elly's tangled web - my tangled web - at a time like this. I felt I was stealing Flora's attention when Jamilla was head of the queue. But Flora was made of sterner stuff.

'Tell me 'bout it,' she said, leaning forward on the chair. Her eyes were bright and sharp, like a cat that has spotted movement in the undergrowth.

'I don't think she went under the train of her own accord, Flora, I think she was pushed.'

Her jaw dropped. I told her everything. It all came tumbling out, first Flora and now me, spilling our secrets, like coins cascading into the tray after a big win on a one-armed bandit. About the locket, the little map, the way my bag was snatched, the so-called suicide note, how I was certain I'd been broken into. Everything. I let down my guard and gave away my secret.

'My word…' she said. 'There seems to be a lot more to this than meets da eye.' Rather than having added to her troubles, Flora's eager expression suggested I'd given her a special gift.

'I'm sorry I didn't come clean right from the start. It's been difficult to know who to trust.'

'No. You were being careful. There's noth'ng wrong with that. Me and Jamilla will help you all we can,' she said. 'Clear dat poor girl's name, if you're right. Jamilla will like dat.'

'You will keep it quiet though, won't you? If someone at the church knows more about this than they should, I don't want them alerted.'

'You t'ink someone here killed Elly?'

I reached out to turn off the tap that had been dripping ever since I walked in, but it wouldn't tighten any further. It occurred to me in that instant, that Flora might pounce on this opportunity to involve herself with my 'investigation' as a means of escaping Jamilla's terminal illness. I didn't know her well enough to know whether that would work to my advantage or turn out to be one hell of a terrible mistake.

'I don't know,' I replied. 'But St Stephen's seems to be at the centre of it. For now, anyway - until something else comes to light.' She crossed herself. I lightly touched her arm. 'You didn't hear Elly mention something called *The Flower Girl's House,* did you? It was on the little map in her locket.'

Flora tipped her head to one side.

'I can't say I did,' she said. She took my hand by way of thanks and led me back to the main hall.

'And if there's anything I can do…for you or Jamilla,' I said, 'let me know. I'm often free during the day, I can come with you to hospital appointments, get shopping for you, that sort of thing.'

Before I could say more, there was a crash from the back of the hall.

'It's Linda,' said Flora, throwing her eyes heavenwards.

I craned my neck to look behind her and saw Linda lying flat with a tablecloth over her legs sprinkled with cups and saucers - most of them in small crooked fragments.

'Linda, you silly girl!'

'You hurt yourself, Linda?'

'Linda - just calm down!'

'You all right, darlin'?'

A circle formed around her as people began picking up pieces of broken crockery. Linda had achieved today's moment of fame, for sure. She slid out from under the table cloth into a sitting position, looking like she had no idea where she was. Flora went to get a cloth.

'Her grandfather's in hospital,' said an onlooker, as if this explained Linda's failed attempt at a backflip. 'Someone needs to keep a better eye on her.'

Flora had pointed Mrs Weedon out to me before. She was holding an old fashioned handbag in front of her knees with both hands and wearing a felt brown hat with a small feather clipped at the back. With her round glasses, pleated tweed skirt, olive green cardigan and 'sensible' lace-up shoes, she looked like she was playing the part of someone's aunt in a play by Agatha Christie.

'Isn't her uncle here?' I said.

'He doesn't stay for the services. He's the taxi service. She's probably practising some new Kung-Fu trick to try to impress him,' said Mrs Weedon. 'She adores him, you know. She's always trying to win him over as neither of her parents have time for her, but she doesn't need to bother. Her uncle doesn't have kids of his own and he's made it perfectly clear he'd jump at the chance to take over as a father to her.'

'She looks boisterous,' I said.

'She's been excluded from school,' she said, folding her arms, looking smug to be the bearer of gossip.

'What did she do?'

'Stole the deputy head's watch. She's pinched things before. I think it's attention seeking. Mother is an alcoholic, father's in prison…you know the story.'

'Downward spiral, I imagine.'

'When they found the stolen watch, they found a pile of nasty graphic comics in her locker.' Mrs Weedon raised an eyebrow. 'Violent, brutal, adult stuff. I don't know where she's getting it from. Someone needs to tell her mother.' She flared her nostrils 'Her uncle is the saviour in that family,' she said. 'He's helping out now that her father's gone back to jail for stealing antique lanterns, a coal scuttle and two benches from a pub in Esher. Oh - and clobbering the landlord half to death while he was at it.'

'Oh dear.'

She shrugged. 'I know. What hope does she have? She's a feisty one all right. Always in trouble. Lewis has got his hands full. She's a right old nosy parker for a girl of her age, I can tell you. I often find her poking about in places she shouldn't be. Little busy-body.'

I made a mental note of that last piece of information.

As we spoke, I was aware that a shape had appeared at my shoulder. I turned to find Father Brian standing a little too close than socially appropriate, holding a small square of cloth.

'Sorry - didn't mean to interrupt.' He glanced over to Mrs Weedon with an apologetic smile. 'You were a friend of Elly's, I believe?'

I hesitated, not sure what was coming next. 'That's right…'

'This is hers.' He held out the cloth, which I could now see was an embroidered sampler showing a nativity scene. It was crudely, but lovingly worked with several lumpy knots on the surface and missing stitches. 'I wondered if you might pass it on to her parents. They don't come to the church. Irene didn't want it.'

He laid it over my hands in an odd sort of quasi-religious gesture and glanced again at Mrs Weedon before walking away. I folded the square carefully and put it in my bag.

'I didn't know you knew Elly Swift…' she said, stiffly, as she made a move towards the door.

'Yes. Did you?'

Her eyes didn't light up. 'I don't like to speak ill of the dead and all that, but she made mistakes that girl.'

'Mistakes? How do you mean?'

'Well, when the father of a missing boy needs… consoling, you don't…take advantage.' She stretched her eyes wide open in a knowing look.

'Frank? Irene's husband?' I said, confused by what she was getting at.

Mrs Weedon looked about her, making sure we were out of earshot of anyone else.

'Yes. Frank all right. Only a month or so after Toby was snatched, Ms Swift muscled in and had an affair with him.'

She said it as though Frank had been carried off into the night against his will. 'He wasn't in a position to know what he was doing, at the time,' she continued. 'As soon as he came to his senses, he did the right thing.'

It took a moment for what she'd said to sink in. She was telling me Elly had had an affair with her brother-in-law, right under her sister's nose.

'Did Irene know?'

She rubbed her chin. 'No one said a thing about it, including Irene.'

I wondered how it was that Mrs Weedon knew all about the affair, but I didn't want to delve further into her seedy scandalmongering. She was relishing being the source of sordid gossip too much.

I feigned the urge for a hot drink and moved away. At the hatch, I spotted Flora chatting with a group of people. She looked happier now. Laughing again, her arm hooked around someone. It looked as though finally telling someone about her sister's fatal condition had allowed her shoulders to drop back into place again, her whole body to sink down and let go.

I noticed Linda's uncle talking to a man with a walking stick and I stood beside Linda, hoping to engage her in a little chat-chat to see if she could fill in any pieces of the puzzle. According to Mrs Weedon, she was the eyes and ears of the place.

'You like coming here?' I said, by way of introduction.

'It's alright. Nice biscuits.'

'Do you know everybody?'

'Mostly.' She was swinging her arms around like she was doing backstroke. 'The best bit is the drawing. We do that when the grown-ups are in church.'

'Do you remember the little boy who went missing?'

'That was ages ago.'

'March. Were you here then?'

'Yep. I remember seeing him. We were all drawing Easter eggs. He did a pretty one. He got a toffee for it, I think.'

'Did anything seem strange that morning? Any people around you didn't know?'

'They asked me this before. I don't think so.' She squeezed her eyes shut as if she was listening to her favourite tune. 'All I remember was Mrs Weedon - she's the one over there that looks ancient - and Father Brian, whispering by the font.'

'Did you hear what they were saying?'

'Uncle Lewie says it's rude to listen, but they were saying something about...buying old ropes. I don't know what it meant, really.' Her thumb slipped into her mouth and she looked woefully at the floor. 'I wish he was my Daddy,' she said, out of the blue. 'I don't have a proper Daddy.'

'Someone said he wasn't around much,' I said, carefully.

'He's locked up for doing bad things.' She pulled a face. 'Mum says I mustn't steal stuff at school anymore.'

'I don't suppose you'd like it if someone stole something you felt was precious.'

'That's what Mr Jenkins, the headmaster, said.' Her eyes narrowed. 'I don't have nuffink, really. Except Uncle Lewie. He's the best thing ever.' She clapped her hands together like she'd won a prize.

She ran over to him, all smiles. Our private chat was over.

On the way home I pondered over Linda's words. *Buying old ropes,* she'd said she'd overheard. Then the penny dropped: *money for old rope.*

Could it be that Father Brian and Mrs Weedon were in cahoots over something?

chapter eleven

It was around a ten minute walk from the church to Stockwell underground. I'd only got round the first corner when I had the feeling I was being followed. I couldn't put my finger on what it was that gave me that impression; it came from nowhere with a prickle on my scalp. I heard no footsteps and when I took a quick look round there was no one behind me, but there was a chilling feeling, the sense of a figure lurking on my heels, casting no shadow, making no sound. It sent a shiver of foreboding down my neck that made me edgy, made me hasten my step.

I pulled my bag to my chest and folded my arms over it, picking up my pace into a jog. I ran on to a road lined with shops, several of which were open; a delicatessen, launderette, newsagent. I kept close to the shop-fronts, keeping my eyes forward, not daring to check the reflections in the glass.

I got to the Tube out of breath and leapt on the escalator. Heavy footsteps hurtled behind me and I screwed up my fists, ready for a tousle, but they charged straight past. Once I got down, the spaces filled up. There hadn't been a train in a while, so people were backing up on the platform. I mingled with the crowd, able to get my breath back and calm down.

I'd arranged to meet Stefan for an update, so I took the first train north to Camden Town. Despite questioning his reasons for helping me, I was still keeping him in the loop. After all, he was all I'd got.

He was holding a pink ice-cream as I went over to greet him.

'Is that for me?' I said.

'Sorry, no - but I can get you one.'

'I'm only teasing.' I glanced up at the moody grey sky as a gust of wind whittled down the front of my coat. I shivered. 'It's not really ice-cream weather. Where's the nearest café?'

We started walking towards a neon sign, but had to loiter outside until he'd finished his cone.

'Strawberry?' I said.

'Sour cherry,' he said. 'Actually, it's a bit weird.' He dropped the rest of it into a bin

and we went inside. It was lunchtime, but people were still tucking into late breakfasts: bacon and eggs, omelettes and beans. I ordered two hot chocolates and we took seats at a small table at the back. I took a shifty look around, scanning faces, judging whether it was safe to talk in there.

'You look antsy,' he said.

'I'm sure someone was following me when I left the church.'

I also told him I thought someone had been in my flat.

'Are you certain?'

I screwed up my nose. 'I was at first. Now, I'm not so sure. Might be my overactive imagination.'

I rested my forehead on my folded arms, feeling sullen and fraught. And tired, desperately tired. I'd had fractured sleep last night following the undetectable break-in and before that, I'd been on edge ever since I'd come back from Portsmouth. In fact, ever since I'd come across Elly. That was exactly three weeks ago now. It felt far longer than that.

'Keep a lookout,' he said. 'You never know.' His forehead collapsed into a frown. Like he was gearing himself up to say something awkward. 'How's Caroline?' he said. He'd tried to make it sound offhand, but it had come too early in our conversation.

'She's fine. Why?'

'No reason, just…'

The skin in his left eyelid flickered and began a dance of its own accord. 'Do you think she might be interested in…going to a film or something?' He held his mouth open, waiting for me. 'Do you think?' he said, again.

'I'm afraid she's seeing someone in Brighton. But things have been…how can I put it…up and down between them,' I said. 'It might be worth a try, but don't tell her I said that. You'll need to tread carefully.'

He cupped his chin, looking pensive. At least I didn't need to worry anymore about him having any romantic intentions towards me, although I still wasn't sure why he was going out of his way to 'help' and whether I could trust him. I supped the hot chocolate, waiting.

'I spoke to Harry, my mate in the force, about which officers were working on the Toby abduction case.' I sat up straight. I'd asked Stefan if he could check whether either Sam or Lewis had been assigned to that operation. 'Neither of them were involved. Sam is in traffic division and Lewis was working on a drugs' bust at the time. Neither of their names come up on any of the reports, except as witnesses.'

'That's useful. Thank you.' I wiped the corner of my mouth with a napkin. 'I've just heard from a young girl at the church that the priest could be involved in some dodgy money-making. Either that, or she's been watching too much TV crime.' Stefan laughed. In spite of vague misgivings, I couldn't help liking him. 'I know. What have I got myself into?'

I leant into him, exhausted and resigned, and he squeezed my shoulder.

At times, without my permission, recollections of Jeff swam up to the surface. Almost anything could trigger them. This time, it was the way Stefan pulled me towards him. For some reason it made me think of Jeff's tendency to talk in his sleep, his refusal to eat fish, the way he had of calling my name.

I tore myself away and rested my head on my folded arms, drifting into thoughts of our life together. Underneath all my memories of Jeff's mannerisms; his quirks, the moments we shared together, I hadn't really known Jeff at all - not properly. Not enough to realise our relationship would never make him happy, not enough to see how much pain he was in, or to be able to predict he would take such a radical and definitive step to end his life. But Jeff was one of those people who once he made up his mind about something, he followed through - even when he had doubts and lacked courage. He wasn't a man of half measures.

Something stirred in me as I thought of him, like molten lead trickling down my back-bone, thickening my resolve. I was going to follow through for Elly, whatever it took. I wasn't going to give up.

Stefan was staring at the dregs of his hot chocolate. I could tell from his earnest expression that he was seeing something else.

'Why are you so involved in this?' I said, daring at last to ask him directly. 'We barely know each other and you've already gone out of your way for me several times.'

He pressed his fingertip into a small pile of spilt sugar, lifting a clump of crystals.

'It's the reason I got into investigative journalism in the first place.'

I waited.

'My mum was killed in a car crash in Greece when I was eleven. The investigation was a shambles. First, they said it was an accident, then it was caused by a truck driver, then it was high levels of alcohol in her blood. The police were useless. We were put through the most hellish situation - not knowing the truth, not being allowed access to the reports. It matters *how* someone dies, doesn't it?'

'Absolutely.'

'It makes a difference to the brand of grief you feel, the people you can blame, the way you sort it all out inside your head.'

'I know.' I put my hand over his.

'That's why I get a bit obsessed when a crime crops up with loopholes. I want to find out more, dig and dig - even if it has nothing to do with me. It's a latent energy, borne of anger and confusion. I was too young to do anything for Mum. By the time I was old enough, there was nowhere to go to find out the truth.'

His fist clenched under mine. I realised how lucky I was - if death can ever involve good luck - that Jeff's death had been so straightforward. Others may have been confused, but for me there had been no lingering questions, no hovering doubts.

I felt a pendulum swing inside me from guilt to relief. Stefan did have his reasons for getting involved in the case, but they were entirely above board. I'd done him a grave disservice. I told him about my beloved husband, in as much detail as I could without revealing the reason he took his life. I still felt that was Jeff's secret, not mine. I told him about how it linked me to Elly's situation. By the time we were ready to leave, I felt that no matter what, we were going to be firm friends.

'I need to go,' he said. 'I've got some work to do and then I'm supposed to be reviewing a play in the West End.'

'What's on?'

'Ibsen. Not my cup of tea, to be honest.'

I grabbed his sleeve. 'Oh my God, that's it.'

'What?'

'I might be wrong. I'll tell you when I've checked.'

• • •

It only took a few words to Jamilla on the phone and then I went straight over to Stockwell, to be greeted by another round of pastries and cakes. I took a chocolate brownie to be polite, but slipped it straight into my bag. I couldn't eat a thing. Not until I'd found what I was looking for.

Jamilla took me into the bedroom and moved aside two jigsaws and a game of Scrabble.

'If you'd asked me in da first place, not Flora, I'd have told you straight away. She doesn't know Elly gave it a special name.'

'So, this is *The Flower Girl's House*?' I said.

Jamilla carefully removed the lid. Inside there were six rooms laid out exactly like the plan in Elly's locket. In each room there was miniature furniture, in Victorian style, and tiny dressed and painted figures. There was a grand piano in the parlour, a dog by the hearth, even a chain hanging from the cistern in the bathroom. The detail was remarkable. *The Flower Girl's House* had been Flora's all right, but it was her *dolls'* house. It was only when Stefan mentioned Ibsen, and I thought of his plays, that I made the obscure mental leap. The kind of leap Elly might make.

'You t'ink der's something here that Elly left, on purpose?'

I nodded, scrutinising the contents.

Flora joined us. 'Elly did all the work,' she said. 'Ain't it beautiful?'

I knelt down and peered into the different rooms. There were detachable rugs, cushions and tiny lamp stands. I was so taken by the intricacy of it, that I almost forgot I was looking for one room in particular.

I held up the map. 'According to this, there's something in the nursery.'

It was a small room, with a cradle the size of a thimble, a rocking horse and a single picture hanging on thread on a pin in the wall. I carefully lifted everything out and stared at the little fantasy objects.

I turned each one over in my hand. The more I tried to see something emerge the more I started to feel the crackling energy drain away from me, like a bath with the plug snagged from the hole. It didn't mean anything. Everyone had been right. Elly's world was whimsical, unreal. It was make-believe, like her mother had said. Elly hadn't left me any clues to anything. There was nothing to find.

And yet, some niggling residual impulse in my brain was still thrashing about - a fish on dry land refusing to die.

Then I saw something. The picture was disproportionately large in comparison to the other items.

'Did Elly paint this?'

'Yes - she did all da miniature portraits,' said Flora.

I'd brought my magnifying glass with me, just in case, and held it over the back of the picture. A scrap of paper was loose on the back and I gently tugged it. Flora took a sharp intake of breath and I nearly ripped it. Gradually a thin sheet of tissue paper was peeling away. As I teased it out, it opened up like a concertina, forming a square sheet.

'Praise da Lord,' said Flora. 'Elly did leave somet'ing, after all.'

I took the flimsy paper to a table and flattened it out. It had a grey design on it, about the size of a plastic CD cover. I held the glass over it to try to make out the detail.

'It looks like some kind of brass-rubbing…like an insignia or emblem.' I squinted, trying to get a better view. 'Here…'

I handed Flora the magnifying glass.

'You're right, it's a pencil rubbin' - a pattern of some kind. What's it for?'

She handed the glass to Jamilla. It was the kind of design you might find on any number of things: a jewellery box, large cigarette case perhaps, or a tankard. I turned the sheet over, but there was nothing on the back. We looked at it again, trying to identify the separate components, all wearing the same mystified expression.

'There are swirls and coils and a kind of heart shape here…and here,' said Jamilla, 'with four petals crossin' in the centre.'

I strained to see.

'And a bird shape at the bottom,' I said. 'It doesn't look like there are any initials or dates.' It had been painstakingly done, but it meant absolutely nothing to me.

I straightened up.

'Except this,' said Jamilla. She was pointing to the top of the square. 'Run ya finger over dis.'

I stroked the space and sure enough there was a clear indentation where someone had pressed hard with a pen on a page above it.

'It's a cross,' I said.

Flora touched the sheet. 'Not just a cross - a crucifix,' she said.

'You're right.' I stroked the other sides of the page and found another symbol at the bottom.

'What d'you think this is?' I said, handing it to Jamilla.

'It's…like a little flower…'

She passed it to her sister. 'Yes - a daisy.'

'What are you going to do now?' said Jamilla.

'I don't know.' I puffed out my cheeks. 'Do you know anyone who might know what it is?'

She looked blank and shook her head. Then her face brightened. 'Dolores might. She lives downstairs. Doesn't she know someone who works at the British Museum?'

Flora agreed.

When I left, I had the pencil rubbing and a new telephone number in my bag. The chocolate brownie, however, didn't make it as far as the Tube. I'd got my appetite back. It had gone in three mouthfuls, before I'd even left the estate.

As soon as I got home, I dialled the number, but got through to a voicemail. It wasn't good news.

I rang Flora.

'The name you got from Dolores, Tessa Bennet, isn't available for another three weeks,' I said, disappointed.

'Yeah - after you left, Dolores said she forgot Tessa was on a dig in Monte Pallano. East coast o' Italy. She's sorry 'bout dat.'

'Would Dolores know of anyone else who could help?'

Flora said she'd check and phone me back, but the news didn't get any better.

'No. Just Tessa,' she said, out of breath, a few moments later.

'No worries,' I said, thanking her.

I couldn't believe after all this, that everything had ground to a halt. There was no way I could put this on hold for another three weeks. An energy had been sizzling through my body ever since I'd found the pencil rubbing. I couldn't seem to switch it off.

I stared out of the kitchen window at the maze of overlapping roofs and back-alleys wondering what it all meant. Elly had left behind a trail of obscure clues – to what? Why did it have to be so convoluted? Was this going to help explain her death or was it just a silly game Elly had invented to pass the time?

I wouldn't know the answer unless I found out what the pencil rubbing was all about. Perhaps then it would become clear.

Maybe I didn't need Tessa Bennet, I decided. Maybe I just needed her name.

• • •

There were coach loads of people queuing up outside the British Museum the following morning, but it didn't detract from the awe I felt stepping into the place. Under the huge glass canopy, the light spilt through like a sky heavy with snow, giving the space an eerie glow. It sent geometric patterns across the walls like a spider's web. There were broad Roman arches left and right with Ionic columns reaching the roof. Even the floor was white marble, sending the light back up from its shiny surface. I inhaled the impressiveness of the place and went to the information desk on the right - and came out with my blatant lie.

'Hi. I'm a friend of Tessa Bennet - Roman artefacts - I know she's away on a dig in Italy right now, but she said someone else might be able to help me.'

The woman I spoke to looked barely sixteen, with a dithering air of ineptitude, making me think she was on her first day of work experience. 'I'll just... see if...'

She stood, twisting to and fro with her weight on one leg, her finger pulling at her lip, waiting for a colleague to finish showing a man directions on a map. After hushed words together, the older woman came my way.

'Roman artefacts?' she said.

'I know Tessa Bennet is away,' I said, 'but she said I should come down anyway and see someone else.'

'About what?'

Her tone was officious, bordering on downright unfriendly. Her glasses hung around her neck on a chain, nestling into her ample bosom. I was glad I wasn't in the girl's shoes, having to kowtow to this woman's no doubt unreasonable demands all day.

'I have a pencil rubbing that I'd like identified.'

'Have you contacted us about this already?'

'Sorry?'

'You need to check with us first and send us an image - you can't just show up -

we don't have the resources.' She gave a small nod, snapping the heels of her shoes together, as if to indicate that our encounter was over.

I leant over the counter. 'It's really important. It's part of a police investigation.'

She hesitated. 'Is it now? And who, exactly, are you?'

'I'm a journalist - here's my pass.' I handed her a laminated card with my photo and details. 'Tessa said you were all really helpful here and it would be fine.'

'What era are we looking at?' she said. 'Roman, is it?'

'I'm not sure. I think I'd need an expert to take a look at it, first.'

She turned up her nose as if she'd suddenly found herself transported to a farmyard.

'I'll see if anyone's free.' She picked up the telephone, running her finger down a list of names. 'We're all very busy, you know,' she sneered, over the rim of her spectacles.

I forced an apologetic smile, but it didn't linger.

She turned her back to me as she spoke into the mouthpiece. Then I saw her nodding reluctantly. She turned round and gave me the sort of look reserved for someone scruffy and unkempt who has, against all odds, been admitted to the private party after all. She led me across the courtyard into one of the galleries and told me to turn right, go down two flights of stairs, turn left, turn right and then find a door marked D17. I was sure she was giving me the most roundabout directions, but set off, pleased to see the last of her.

I'd walked only a few steps when someone joined me at my elbow, carrying a box-file.

'Heading for D17?' he said.

'Yes - I've been sent this way.' I pointed into the distance.

'It's quicker down here,' he said, pushing a door to our left marked *Private.* 'I saw you with Mrs Nettle - she's a bit of a battle-axe.'

'Dark Age or Neolithic?' I said.

He laughed. 'I'm Morris Whitlock.' He held out his hand. 'Finds Adviser for Iron Age and Roman artefacts.'

He took me down some steps and into a warren of warm white corridors, normally out of bounds to members of the public. 'D17 is part of the Centre for Anthropology,' he said. 'We've got specialist curators there who provide opinions on individual pieces or small collections.' He pushed through a set of double doors. 'We don't do valuations, though.'

He slid a small ID card into a slot outside another door and it buzzed, letting us through. 'Every year thousands of objects are discovered by people with metal-detectors - or just out walking. You must have found something important if Mrs Nettle - she of the stinging variety - has sent you down herself. A find is it?'

'Sort of.' I didn't want to go into detail if I was going to have to repeat it all to someone else.

A phone in his belt chimed and he answered it.

'That's right, she's with me now,' he said. 'No problem. I can deal with it.'

He turned to me. 'That's my supervisor. Apparently, this is police business. I can take a look at it, if you like. A weapon is it?'

'No - it's a pencil rubbing from something. It's very vague, but it's part of an ongoing investigation, so it's very important.' It seemed that the word *police* had been passed on in some form of Chinese whispers, lending me an authority I didn't deserve, but wasn't about to dispute.

We entered a room that resembled my old chemistry lab at school, except the bunsen burners had been replaced by computers and sophisticated microscopes. We walked past people in white coats, poring over trays containing fine soil or sand, holding jugs and vases under special blue lights. There were tripods leaning against the wall and several hi-tech cameras nestling on the filing cabinets.

'We've got various computer packages for our work,' said Morris, making a full sweep with his arm. 'Statistical packages, the SPSS programme, Anthropac and Autocad mapping tools.'

He seemed oblivious to the fact that he was talking to someone who didn't have a clue what he was talking about.

'Right - this is my work-station.' He put down the box-file and perched his backside against the desk. 'What have you got for us?'

I pulled out the folded pencil rubbing and flattened it down on the table.

Morris looked at it first without any form of magnification.

'It's certainly not Roman.'

He called over a colleague and they discussed it as if I wasn't there - pointing to it, rubbing their chins. They might have been talking gobbledygook for all I knew. Morris clicked the mouse on his computer, opened various files and scrolled down. They both nodded and he turned back to me.

'It's probably Victorian.' He slipped the sheet under a microscope and invited me to look. With a small implement like a metal toothpick, he pointed to the individual shapes. What Jamilla originally thought were heart shapes were in fact leaves and the bird at the bottom was clearly a peacock.

'It's from a piece of decorative cast iron,' he said. He showed me a photograph on his computer screen of an iron staircase inside a stately home. 'You could find this kind of ornamental ironwork almost anywhere: railings, gates, manhole covers, mirrors, garden furniture - and very common in churches.'

'In churches?' I said, with interest. I pointed out the indentation of a crucifix at the top. 'There's another mark at the bottom.'

Mr Whitlock turned up his nose. He was more interested in the rubbing itself.

'Lots of ecclesiastical possibilities,' he said, hitching up his trousers. 'Railings around a tomb, iron screens between sections of the church, gates to a crypt - as well as outside, of course, around tombstones, covering a well…' He turned to his colleague who looked noncommittal. 'We'd need an encyclopaedia of decorative ironwork - they do exist - it would pin down the exact design, possibly the maker. Tell us what it might have been used for. It looks Italian, but I'd have to check. It would take a lot longer to date, I'm afraid.'

'That's okay. I…we…don't need that,' I said, sliding the sheet out from under the lens.

'You'll be requesting an official written report?' he said.

'Er…no, not at this stage.' I collected my bag from the desk. 'Thank you so much. You've been brilliant.'

'But, you *are* from the police?'

'Me…no, not exactly. Thank you so much.' I turned to go, hoping my profuse gratitude would make up for the fact that somewhere along the line they'd mistaken my identity.

'But, Mrs Nettle said…'

I was out of the door before I could hear the end of his sentence.

I hurried along the corridor, trying to retrace my steps from earlier. I went wrong a couple of times, but eventually emerged near the main concourse, where

Morris had first caught up with me. Then I bolted for the main exit.

• • •

I was too fired up to go straight home, so instead of getting the train back to Richmond, I took a detour and caught one to Kew bridge. A brisk walk might help me to assimilate what I'd learnt from Morris Whitlock. It might also help me get a decent night's sleep.

On the way, my phone rang. I had already told Stefan about the dolls' house, the pencil rubbing and my proposed trip to the British Museum.

'They said it's a design from a piece of ironwork.' I said, sparkily. As soon as I said it, I realised how vague it sounded.

'Connected to what?' he said. His tone was flat and unconvinced.

I tried to sound positive. 'Well…there was another reference to a flower, at the bottom…and a cross at the top…it could be from a church…St Stephens…' I knew I was making unfounded leaps, but I couldn't afford to lose Stefan. 'Toby was taken from there… and St Stephens was Elly's second home…it would make sense for Elly to refer to it.'

'For what reason?'

'Maybe there is incriminating evidence...left somewhere...about Toby's abduction - after all it does look like someone has been trying to find something - on the train, in my bag, in my flat...'

'Then why didn't Elly just go to the police? All you've had so far is a series of nonsensical clues. The locket with a map to the dolls' house. Then another piece of paper with a design on it - nothing concrete. It's starting to look like the deluded product of a mind that was in a world of its own.' Stefan was starting to sound like Elly's mother.

'But, this was how Elly's brain worked. You can't deny that she was leaving a trail of clues...'

'Yeah...but to what? And for whom? They weren't originally meant for you.'

'Like I said... the clues might be connected to Toby's abduction.' No reply. Nothing but a crackle. I ploughed on regardless. 'I thought you'd be interested. It was your story.'

The phone hissed and popped and I thought he'd gone.

'Of course I am...but...'

His voice was coming and going. 'I can't hear you, Stefan? Can you say—' I realised I was speaking to thin air.

I was about to press *last-call-return*, but I didn't get that far.

chapter twelve

It happened so quickly. There were no warning sounds, no ominous shadows. One minute I was alone, passing the opening to a small park, the next, someone was yanking back my hair. My phone was still in my hand, but I felt it fall the same moment as a sharp scorching jab shot through my arm. For a second I thought I'd been stabbed, but the searing pain was the intense jolt of my bag being snapped from my arm, the friction burning my skin. Just like last time.

Within seconds I was surrounded by figures dressed in grey and black hoods. Young figures. I could see pairs of eyes dodging, lowering as I turned, but nothing else. No detail, nothing distinctive or memorable - except that they were kids. Six of them - the seventh one with my bag under his arm, was already making a run for it. No one said anything. All I could hear was my breathing, rough and amplified with fear.

The others hovered around me in a ritual circle, standing too close, making sure I didn't follow the bag. One of them pocketed the phone. As soon as the figure with my bag reached the corner, they broke apart and ran too, scattering in different directions.

It happened so fast that I didn't know what to do. My brain was having trouble keeping up; it was busy dithering around trying to process what had taken place. I'd been accosted and my bag had been taken. *I'd been mugged.* My purse. My phone. My memory stick. My house keys. The drawing of the iron design. I couldn't see myself getting the bag back intact this time.

Like the theft at Micheldever station only three weeks ago, I felt plunged into a shivering state of shock, into utter loss, like suddenly finding myself in the middle of the ocean in a rowing boat without oars.

I needed to phone the police. I didn't have a phone. I needed to catch a train. I didn't have any money or travel card. I needed to get home. I didn't have a key to get in. The steps I needed to take were thwarted at every turn by the fact that my bag had gone. It suddenly seemed like my bag had everything inside it for my entire survival. Without it, nothing in my life could possibly function.

I felt like dropping to the pavement and curling into a ball.

Before I sank any further into the ravages of self-pity, I came to my senses. A flash of urgency, like a fire alarm going off inside my brain, jarred me into action. If the kids had my purse, they also had my address - and my keys to the flat. They could walk right in and help themselves.

I bolted to the junction and spotted a phone box. *Please God, let it be working.*

It stank and the mouth piece was scorched, but it purred when I lifted it. I dialled 999 and reported the incident. A police officer asked if I lived alone. She suggested I contact the landlord and when I said I didn't have his number, she looked it up for me. I rang him straight away reversing the charges. He said he'd wait for me at my flat. Thankfully, I wasn't far from home, so I half ran, half speed-walked in record time.

The Landlord was waiting outside in his van when I got back. He came in with me to check I was safe. Nothing seemed disturbed. Before long, I was crouched over a cup of tea, smudging the name of a local locksmith with my sweaty finger, in the yellow pages.

As soon as I'd put the phone down after arranging the new lock, I rang Stefan.

'That's two muggings and a break-in,' I said. 'It's getting beyond bad luck, don't you

think?'

'Except....they were a bunch of kids...it could have been a random mugging. They

might not have been after anything specific.'

'You don't believe me...' I squeezed the phone like it was a life-line.

What was it going to take for him to realise this wasn't all inside my head?

When I put down the phone, I felt lonelier than I'd ever felt. More lonely, even, than during the days following Jeff's death. At least then, people understood and sympathised with what I was going through. Now, the police, Caroline and Stefan, all looked at me as if I was nothing but a scaremongerer.

Jeff would have seen what was going on. Jeff would have known that Elly's clues were worth pursuing.

I felt like I was carrying lead in my boots, but I dragged myself to the police station to fill out the forms following the mugging. I didn't hold out much hope of ever seeing my bag or the contents again, but it meant I wouldn't be charged if someone used my credit cards and I could make an insurance claim. There was only one plus point in the nasty business; at least I'd taken the insignia to the museum earlier that day. It had gone now, but I'd learnt what I needed to know from it and I'd looked at it so many times, I was able to sketch a pretty good copy.

I was exhausted when I went to bed, hopeful that my weary body might help my mind to wander off, taking me towards a horizon of blissful, blank whiteness. But, when I closed my eyes I knew it wasn't going to be that easy. Sure enough, I lay there listening for sounds, my ears twitching at the slightest noise. The radiator, the water heater, the guttering, the mice? I kept sitting up, thinking there were noises at the front door. I was counting down the minutes, the hours, until I'd have a new lock. I cursed myself for being such a child. The snick was down on the inside of the front door, so no one could get in, even if they had a key.

I slipped in and out of light dreams, unable at times to work out if I was awake or sleeping. Elly's enigmatic clues came towards me, like signs above a motorway. The locket, the map, the dolls' house and the ironwork rubbing flashed in red neon lights in the darkness under my eyes, over and over again.

I still had no idea what it was about, but I knew I was in the middle of a complex and dangerous situation. I had the feeling I was up against someone with cunning and persistence. I couldn't believe by simply changing the locks my troubles were going to be over.

I don't know when it was I finally got to sleep, but daylight was already sneaking through the gaps in my curtains.

Choir practice was called off on Wednesday. I'd been out to buy a new mobile phone and found the message from Flora on my landline, asking me to call her back.

'The hall is being painted and there are ladders and dust sheets everywhere,' she said. 'Father Brian says it a health and safety t'ing, so we can't go in.'

Damn. It meant I'd miss the chance to talk to people and ask more questions. Flora must have wondered why I sounded so upset.

The upside was that the choir were meeting at a pub, instead, and I was invited. I thanked her, taking down the location of the King Alfred. Stockwell was hardly my ideal setting for a quiet drink, but at least it would give me the opportunity to speak to people in Elly's life, fill in some of the background.

The King Alfred in Stockwell lived up to, or rather matched, my expectations. It was a neglected Victorian building with tiles the colour of bile peeling off the outside, under the graffiti. The inside wasn't much better; the overall impression was dark, cramped and predominantly brown, including the nicotine-stained net curtains and bar stools strapped together with parcel tape.

There was a threadbare trail across the carpet, like a narrow brook, leading fittingly to a bucket under a drip in the once-white ceiling, where a patch had turned beige and was dangerously close to collapsing altogether. The jukebox was right under the dart board and I didn't fancy anyone's chances of selecting a single without getting spiked in the backside. Needless to say, there was no music playing. To say the place was 'run down' was like saying 'the M25 gets quite busy'.

I brightened a little when I saw familiar faces sitting around tables opposite the bar. This, together with the fact that nobody in the place was, as yet, threatening a punch-up was probably about as good as it was going to get. I found a space between Flora and Jamilla and discovered as I sat down that the banquette had broken springs between the cigarette burns. I didn't want to touch anything and found myself checking how clean the glass was, when Flora handed me a rum and Coke.

'We don't often come here,' said Flora, 'but it's local for most people. The young ones like the idea of being able to meet somewhere they can let their hair down for a change.'

I glanced across at Jamilla, who looked tired today, but was trying her best to be jolly. I lowered my voice. 'How are you bearing up?' I said to Flora.

She held her hand up and rocked it from side to side.

'Oh, you know - good days, bad days, darlin'.'

'There are some new faces tonight,' I said, hoping to put some names and background information to them.

Flora indicated a young man sitting next to Sam Braithwaite, the policeman.

'That's Steven Hawes. He's got one o' dem chequered pasts. Been inside for fraud recently.'

I watched the man sip his beer. I hadn't heard his name mentioned by anyone so far. His eyes, like dark beads, moved too quickly, shifting over the top of his glass in all directions, as though he was expecting something unpleasant to happen. He was picking persistently at a small wart under his chin, as if hoping it might peel off.

'How come he's part of the fold?' I said. There are some people who seem to have the innate look of a criminal; a mean furtiveness about the eyes, loose haggard skin and a tightness in the jaw. Steven Hawes was one of them. Instead of bringing myself to strike up a conversation with him, I decided to see if Stefan could run his name past his mate at the Met, for more information.

'He knows Gillian. She used to visit him in prison. It must make t'ings a little awkward now Gillian and Sam are an item – him bein' a policeman.'

I turned to Flora, scanning her face. She discretely nodded her head towards the woman sitting on Sam's knee.

'That's Gillian?' I said, keeping my voice low. Gillian was known to be Elly's best friend; the one I hadn't spoken to yet and Sam was Elly's ex-boyfriend. It seemed rather soon, slightly indecent I felt, for two of the closest people in Elly's life to have moved on without her so quickly. It made me feel like they had squashed Elly out. 'Sam and Elly split up in July, is that right?'

'About then. Bad business though. She dropped him, but he kept making out it was the other way round. I think it got to his macho pride, if you know what I mean.'

'How long have he and Gillian been together?'

'Not sure. A few weeks?'

Gillian barely looked the same person as the one I'd seen recently on film. She'd lost a couple of stone for a start, her thick mousy hair had been lifted into blonde and she was wearing a short denim skirt in place of the frumpy smock. The new romance had certainly done wonders for her self-image.

'Had Elly and Sam been serious, do you think?'

'Doubt it. They'd only been going together a few months. I'm not sure it was the romance of the year.'

I watched Sam stroking Gillian's hair. They looked playful and giggly together, but Sam looked like he was in charge. He had a thick neck, like a racing driver, and his biceps, visible under the short sleeves of his t-shirt, were solid and well-developed.

'You don't like him?' I whispered.

Flora had to consider the question, which effectively answered it.

'He doesn't give much away 'bout himself. Seems to have some kinda sense o' humour...' I watched

Flora struggle to find anything more positive to say about him. Sam pretended to let Gillian fall backwards, before catching her at the last minute. 'I don't t'ink he treated Elly well.' She sniffed. 'He's married.'

'Is he now?' That put a slightly different complexion on the situation. I looked at Sam's left hand and saw no ring. 'Did Elly know?'

'She must have found out somehow. She said it was the reason she split up wid 'im.'

'So, presumably, Gillian knows as well.'

'Dats for certain. Elly was made o'different moral fibre, though. She knew right from wrong.'

Presumably, Flora hadn't heard about Elly's fling with Frank.

Out of the corner of my eye, I saw Gillian slide off Sam's knee. I guessed she was going to the Ladies, so I gave Flora a quick sign with my thumb and followed her.

There was only one cubicle, so I waited in the corridor a few moments before going in. It smelt so damp that I could almost feel the spores landing on my skin. She flushed and the cubicle door opened. I stood back and cleared my throat.

'Are you Gillian Falkney?' I said.

'Yeah.' She pushed down on the soap dispenser, but nothing was coming out.

'I'm Anna. I was a friend of Elly's.'

'I know. Sam pointed you out to me.' She didn't seem ashamed to mention his name. 'I was her best friend.' She said it as though she expected me to challenge her.

'You must miss her terribly.'

'Yeah, well. Life has to go on, doesn't it?' She threw the paper towel in the bin. Her accent was northern; I put her somewhere in the Newcastle area.

'This might sound like a really odd question, but before she died, did Elly talk about being frightened of anyone?'

She turned to the mirror, tweaked her hair. 'Elly was always a bit paranoid. It's just how she was. Jumpy, always thinking people had something against her. She was convinced someone was following her. She was doing an evening class at Lambeth College and she said the tutor was stalking her.' She reached behind her and adjusted her knickers. 'She was *your* friend. Didn't she tell you any of this?'

'I didn't know her that well. We only met recently.' She scrunched up her nose. 'When did she start being jumpy?'

'She started the course in April, but she only mentioned it a couple of weeks before she died.'

'Lambeth College?'

'Yeah - near Clapham Common. She started doing some sort of business course. She thought it might help with job prospects.' She turned her back to the basin and leant against it. Given the state of the surrounding tiling, I wasn't sure that was such a good idea.

'Do you know the name of the tutor?'

She folded her arms. 'What is this? You sound like a bloody reporter.'

'Sorry. There's a lot I don't know about. I was shocked when she died.' I hesitated. 'Were you?'

'I knew she'd tried to top herself before, but I thought that was all in the past. She seemed to have got herself together, although obviously things didn't work out too well…with…Sam.'

She straightened up, looking like she'd had enough, keen to get back to her boyfriend.

'Do you know anything about the shop where she worked? Anyone she mentioned?'

'Only that they're a weird bunch of vegetarians. It's on Electric Avenue. You didn't know about *that* either? What kind of friend were *you*?'

I could have asked her the same question. She yanked open the door and left.

When I rejoined Flora, the pub had filled up with youths who looked like they'd already had several pints too many. They shouted and elbowed each other and the landlord started playing loud rock music as if to drown them out - only it made them shout even louder. Flora said a band was playing in the area that night. I scanned the walls and spotted a torn poster and went over to take a look. It was advertising a band called *The Flying Undercrackers,* playing at the O2 Academy in Brixton. I'd never heard of them. A man wearing a tired suit and tie passed me as I returned to my seat and told me they were renowned for their offensive lyrics and harrowing stage show - only he used more graphic language.

'Sounds entirely miss-able,' I said.

'Load a shite,' he said, careful not to raise his voice.

When I got back to the group, I couldn't hear what anyone was saying anymore. There was no point in trying to speak to Sam, even if I was able to pry Gillian away from him. When he stood up to get drinks, I tried to think back to the man wearing the raincoat who had stolen my bag at Micheldever station. *Had it been Sam?* I watched him lope towards the bar. The man I remembered was a tad under six foot, I was sure of it. Sam looked about the right height. Perhaps Elly and her lover had exchanged letters? Or maybe Elly had kept a diary he wanted to get his hands on? Sam was married and perhaps he wanted to stay that way. I thought too about Frank, Toby's father, the guy who had turned up at the Swifts' to collect Elly's belongings. He and Elly had had a brief fling shortly after Toby went missing. If that had been committed to writing in the form of a love-note, letters or a diary, Frank wouldn't have wanted Irene getting her hands on it - but was he the guy in the raincoat? I tried to think back to the figure in blue dungarees, standing at the bottom of the stairs. Hard to say.

I glanced over at Steven Hawes. I'd seen him stand to talk to someone he knew. Being an ex-convict, he was an obvious choice as suspect. I tried to compare him to the man I remembered at Micheldever. He, too, looked about the right height and build, but he didn't look the sort to own a raincoat. Nevertheless, I couldn't dismiss him on that basis. Everyone seemed to fit. It was hopeless.

Shortly afterwards, I made my excuses and headed home.

That evening I came down with a nasty bout of flu - I blamed it on hygiene standards at the King Alfred.

I didn't resurface until the weekend. In the meantime, the only call I had was from Caroline. She brushed over my illness in order to tell me her news.

'This is absolutely it, this time,' she said. 'He has well and truly blown it.'

She didn't need any encouragement to fill me in with the details. It boiled down to what it always boiled down to. Martin hadn't paid Caroline enough attention, hadn't been as available as he should have been and - always the death-knell - had been spending too much time with his ex-wife.

'It's definitely over,' she said. 'And before you ask, things got better for about twenty minutes,' she said, never one to underplay a situation.

Many people questioned my friendship with Caroline; she was ruthlessly self-obsessed, high-maintenance and verging on neurotic. But she'd been the glue that held me together after Jeff died, with her no-nonsense approach to (other people's) problems. Surprising, she also showed me a depth of compassion I never knew she was capable of; holding me, spending time with me, never expecting anything back. It was worth putting up with her grating complaints and capricious changes of heart, for that alone.

Through the gummy fog of death-bed flu, I grasped that her plans were to move to London and she'd already been looking at flats in Clapham. I knew one person who would be pleased to see more of her.

On Saturday morning, once the locksmith had been, I went to Brixton to visit the shop where Elly used to work. Her colleagues told me Elly was kind. Shy. Considerate. They knew of no skeletons in her closet, knew no one with whom she'd fallen out. I came away with nothing I didn't already know.

I needed to get back home. I hadn't had any feature commissions for a week and hadn't done anything about procuring any new ones. It was a slippery slope. In my business, you had to keep a high profile with editors or they forgot who you were and moved on to some new highflier eager to get a foot in the door. I needed to be careful. Elly was taking over my life. I was literally walking in her footsteps now, everything I did was for her, or more exactly for some elusive truth that lay just to one side and slightly behind her. Out of reach, like a relative in an old photograph no one recognises.

On the way through Brixton market I had a call from Stefan. He had already managed to work his magic. As a result, he had tracked down the enrolment details for Elly's course and could even give me the name of Elly's tutor. I didn't ask how he'd done it. Aside from his contact at the Met, he had a unique trick of being able to delve into the sorts of private places to which most people had no legitimate access. I was just glad, now I trusted him, to have met him at a time like this.

I had a gift for him, in return. I told him that Caroline was now single and moving to London. I could hear the broad smile in his voice when he said goodbye.

The college was only ten minutes' walk away, so I thought I would see if by any chance Dr Trevor Bell was teaching that afternoon.

• • •

I used my pass again to get through reception, saying I was doing an interview for *Time Out* magazine. Fortunately, he was giving a lecture on marketing on the first floor. I waited outside until it was over, then going against the tide of students, went inside to find him. He was clearing away marker pens from an overhead projector.

'If you leave them lying around, they'll be gone in five minutes,' he said. He seemed to think I was the lecturer for the next group. I introduced myself and explained that I knew Elly.

'I understand she was a student of yours,' I said.

He didn't meet my eye. Instead, he busied himself with papers on the table. I noticed his tie was riding at half-mast.

'The name doesn't ring a bell, I'm afraid. Hundreds of students pass through these doors every year.'

'I understand she was in your tutor group - that would consist of only twelve students, I believe.'

'You *have* done your homework,' he said. 'I wish my students were more like you.'

We were walking down a corridor. He stopped at an office with his name and two others on it. 'Who did you say you were, again?'

I held out my pass, changed tack and explained I was doing a piece on suicide for The Samaritans. 'Cheerful subject,' he said, dumping his briefcase on a desk. The room was empty. He offered me a seat by the window.

'I can't offer you coffee, I'm afraid,' he said. 'Unless you want it powdered from a machine.'

He looked the sort to keep a flask of brandy hidden in his inside pocket. The sort who would never share it. 'How do you think I can possibly help?' I noticed that an elbow patch on his tweed jacket was peeling away and when he ran his hand through his greasy hair, I saw no wedding band. He wore crumpled corduroy trousers, the colour of mulled wine, that were dusted on the knees with white animal fur. I put him at about fifty. A confirmed bachelor with a longhaired cat, from first appearances. I was turning into Miss Marple.

'I'm looking into a number of suicide victims, talking to their family and friends, to see how evident it was that they were about to take their own lives.' He nodded, vaguely. 'Elly Swift was one of your students. She enrolled in April this year. She committed suicide on September 19th.'

'I think I do remember, now. Plain girl, easy to overlook.'

'I wondered if you might have any records about her - how often she attended, how well she was doing on the course, how she fitted in - that kind of thing?'

'I probably do have, somewhere.' He glanced behind him at a row of filing cabinets, but he didn't make a move towards them. 'Perhaps I could fax something to you,' he said.

'I'm afraid I'm on a very tight deadline, Dr Bell. I'd be very grateful if you could get any details for me while I'm here.'

He reluctantly got to his feet and pulled out one drawer, then another. He drew out a manila folder and turned the first sheet on its side to look at it.

'She didn't miss a class...until...obviously...'

He pulled out another sheet. 'Coursework reasonable, nothing exceptional. She didn't really stand out.'

'What were your personal impressions of her - from what you can remember?'

'Like I said, she was an easy person to overlook. Quiet. Didn't say a great deal. Problems at home, I understand. Something about a young boy going missing earlier in the year.' He prodded the page. 'I've got a note of it here.'

'Anything else?'

'No - I don't think so.'

'Did she seem different in her last class - that would have been mid-September, just a few days before she died?'

He shook his head. His memory seemed fully restored now. 'No. Nothing different.'

I asked for the names of people Elly used to mix with in the group. He referred to his sheets but said he couldn't remember. I thanked him for his time.

I left feeling distinctly ill at ease. It couldn't have been more obvious. Dr Bell was definitely hiding something.

chapter thirteen

I drifted in and out of bizarre dreams that night; half planning what I was going to do at the church the next day, half finding myself in strange rooms, caves and tunnels, that didn't belong to St Stephen's. At one stage I was wandering around a crypt, which opened out into a massive cemetery, like the one I'd visited with Stefan in Streatham.

I kept running through ideas in my mind about what the pencil rubbing referred to - where I was going to find it. And what it would lead to.

Morris Whitlock at the British Museum had said the ironwork *could* be found inside a church, but could equally be located in any number of other places. It could be that Elly had hidden incriminating letters from a lover, or a diary, but even *I* had to admit that whilst either Sam or Frank might be keen to get their hands on some such item, it was decidedly extreme to follow Elly all the way to Portsmouth, or indeed to kill her for it. Surely, it had to be more than that.

Was this treasure trail all about Toby going missing? Would there be evidence of some kind that wasn't sufficiently conclusive to take to the police? I'd pinned my hopes on finding something at the church, but maybe it had nothing to do with that. Maybe what I was looking for was at the wholefood shop, in Elly's or Flora and Jamilla's flat like before, or somewhere else entirely.

Another thought occurred to me. What if Stefan was right and there was nothing to find. That would be worst of all.

I fretted, sticky with sweat and threw off the duvet. Then shivering, reclaimed it again. I tried a foetal position, but wasn't comfortable, flopped over on to my front, but couldn't breathe. Finally, I tossed myself on to my back and stared at the ceiling, watching the headlights of passing cars flash across it, like search lights.

Tomorrow was the last day before Elly's inquest. I needed to find something concrete *now* to show the police before her demise was recorded in stone as suicide.

I arrived early at the church and had to walk twice around the block before I saw Father Brian unlock the main door. I began my search straight away. Trying to look like a curious tourist, I started at the back on the right and worked my way up to the altar, looking for anything that could be a match for the ironwork rubbing. I stopped at metal plaques, chests to scrutinise the metal locks and the collection boxes embedded in the wall.

I looked up at the organ and examined every partition - the font, the pulpit - although much of the detail was carved in wooden panels. I got as close as I could to the altar - and the chalices and cups - the heavily worked front of the bible. I went into the individual chapels along the side of the church, checking the iron railings, any detail on boxes, cupboards, doors, light fittings.

As I approached the steps to the crypt, a strong smell of emulsion paint caught the back of my throat. I could see pots of paint and rags stored down there. I climbed down the stone steps leading to a gate. It was locked, but the key was in the hole. I pressed my face against the railings, cupping my hands around my eyes, but it was too dark to see anything except shadows and recesses. A musty smell rose up and I turned away. A tour down there was definitely on my itinerary once the service was over.

At the back of the church on the left, I noticed a door that wasn't quite closed. I'd spotted it before and wondered where it led. People were filing in now, but most were preoccupied with their families or kneeling in private prayer. When I was sure no one was watching, I slid inside.

It was a windowless room, with jumbles of items at every turn: baskets, vases, dusters, forgotten umbrellas, stacks of chairs, tubs of cleaning fluid, a mop and bucket. Several jackets clung to a lopsided coat-stand in one corner, which also held an anorak and pair of overalls. A rubber glove was lying beside the sink on the draining board, alongside a shovel and an electric toothbrush. I detected the gritty, old-fashioned smell of Vim.

I couldn't see anything bearing the ironwork design, but I would need more time to check all the shelves and cupboards.

I heard the organ strike up. Time for one more task before mass.

I found Flora in the ladies toilet this time, trying to hold her skirt in place with a safety-pin.

'Blinkin' zip gone and broke on me,' she said, attempting the almost impossible task of pressing the pin through the thick tweed while breathing in sufficiently so that the two sides met. I offered to help, but didn't hold out much hope.

'You remember the pencil rubbing we found in the doll's house?' I said, as I grappled with the waistband. I felt like a sheep-shearer trying to pacify an unwieldy ewe. She nodded, trying not to let the air out of her lungs. 'Do you think something in the crypt could be a match? What's down there?'

'There might be a chest down there, for one o' dem reliq'ries perhaps. I'm not sure. It's usually locked, but the decorators are keeping their gear down der for the time bein' - and Father Brian is leavin' it open for dem.' I nudged her to take in another breath. 'You won't catch me settin' one foot down in dat place.'

'Ghosts?' I said, playfully.

'Oh, my word, no. Me no worried 'bout a few old souls joinin' me for comp'ny. It's dem creepy crawlies I'm talkin' about. Why da Lord had to go and make so many of dem, I'll never know.'

I loved the way, when Flora got the least bit emotional, it enriched her dialect. With one final stab I managed to get the pin in place.

'Is the church open all the time?' I asked.

'No way. Not 'round 'ere! Only ha'f an hour before mass - and for confession and evenin' vigil on Saturdays. The rest of the time it's locked, apart from de holy days of obligation, but der are only a handful of dem each year. After the services - sometimes there's a cleaner and Father Brian does paperwork an' stuff.'

As we went into the main church, I asked about the other rooms leading from the church. Flora pointed out the different doors; the Sacristy, the music room, meeting room and the one I'd entered earlier, the flower room - none of which were labelled.

'The only one that isn't locked is the flower room,' she said. 'It's just a broom cupboard. Not'ing of value in it.'

'Yes - I noticed.'

By then, people were filling up the pews. I had to put my mission on hold.

Flora edged me to one side as we were drinking coffee, after mass.

'I heard somet'ing interesting the other day. I forgot to say,' she said. 'Millie, one of my friends, over there - she said she knew somet'ing 'bout Elly.'

'Go on.'

'She said she saw Elly and Father Brian having… bitter words a few weeks before she died.'

'What about?'

'Elly told her she'd seen Father Brian takin' money and that Father Brian had got all hot under da collar about it.'

She stood back and sucked in her cheeks as if to say: *Who would have believed it?*

'Father Brian taking money? That sounds awkward.'

'Millie said Elly had been asked to return a robe she'd mended to the Sacristy and she saw Father Brian taking ten pound notes from the safe and putting them straight into his own pocket. Elly said he made up some story about not having any paying-in pouches and going straight to the bank, but it was a Sunday. Besides, the money always gets counted in the presbyt'ry first.'

'Mmm.'

'It was before your time, dear, but we had a few cases of bits and pieces goin' missin' in da church for a while.'

'And you think Father Brian might have been the culprit?'

'It's possible, don't you t'ink. I've never liked him,' she said, as if that sealed the matter.

Did Elly perhaps have proof of a case of serious embezzlement? Documents? Photographs? I scoured the hall and spotted Father Brian talking solemnly to a couple I hadn't seen before. I tried to picture him as the bag-snatcher at Micheldever station. It was hard to be certain, but he didn't look tall enough. His movements were slow and ponderous. To my mind, he didn't quite fit.

In conspiratorial tones, Flora said, 'Do you think he killed her? Should we call the police?'

I shook my head vigorously. 'No - no. Leave it with me. You've done really well.' I patted her arm and she straightened up with pride. I was going to have to keep Flora on a tight rein or she could turn out to be a liability.

'Here's trouble,' she said, tipping her head towards a couple behind us. It was Linda and Lewis, her uncle. She was carrying his helmet like it was a trophy.

As I took a sip of coffee, Linda backed into me with considerable force and sent the cup and saucer on an abrupt journey towards the ceiling. Gravity took charge and they crashed to the floor, sending boiling liquid and shards of crockery skating across the floor.

'For God's sake, Linda,' said Lewis, instantly squatting down beside me. 'I'm really sorry. She's a firecracker. I can't leave her for one minute before something gets broken. Are you hurt? Did you get scalded?'

'No, I'm fine.'

His voice was soft and lilting. I wouldn't have known he was a policeman; his body was less broad and bulky than Sam Braithwaite's. He certainly moved with agility, however. He'd been at my side in an instant after the mishap and his tight trousers revealed pronounced thigh muscles like those of a dancer.

'Get a mop and a bucket, Linda - don't just stand there.'

She flounced off and a few others joined in the now weekly ritual of clearing up after her.

'I'm really sorry, everyone. I'll pay for replacements. I know it's not the first time.' Lewis pulled a face at me and there was something both charming and cheeky about it. 'She's been reading too many of those fantasy comic books. Thinks she's Wonder Woman or something… '

She came back with a cloth and he grabbed her round the waist and lifted her up, then started tickling her. Their mutual affection was palpable; a tight, binding energy I'd never known with anyone in my own family. In a thunderbolt moment, it reminded me of Jeff; we'd gone to the Turkish baths in Paddington one summer and our session in the Russian steam room had dissolved into a tickling match. I lost - and ended up in the ice-cold plunge pool. Jeff had to endure twenty minutes of a hefty masseur walking on his back, to make up for it. Despite her obvious problems, in that moment I envied Linda. She had someone devoted to her, fighting her corner.

I was about to walk away, when Lewis turned to me. 'I've not seen you before. You new here?'

'Started coming a few weeks ago,' I said, finding myself fiddling with my hair. 'I'm in the choir, too.' I was sounding like a self-conscious teenager.

'That's quick work. I don't attend myself, just come to ferry this bundle of tricks. I'm her uncle, Lewis Jackson.'

We stood and made small talk for a while. His dark hair was short but thick and he still bore the leftovers of a summer tan. He looked like an outdoors man; the skin on his hands and face was coarse and rugged, like it had battled the elements. In that way, he reminded me of Jeff. Perhaps it was the telltale sign of a genuine biker.

'Come and say hello to Anna,' he said, dragging Linda away from an attempt to do a handstand.

'Hi. We met before. Can you do Robatics?' said Linda.

'It's *acrobatics*, Linda,' said Lewis.

'I used to love the vault at school,' I said, 'but that's all, I'm afraid.'

'Cool. I don't do school at the moment.'

'Right,' I said. Linda had told me about the stealing, but I didn't know if I should refer to it.

'Still get effin' homework,' she said, in a mock grumpy voice.

'Linda! None of that - I've told you.' He glared at her and she shrank back, a hurt frown crossing her face.

'How long have you been...dropping Linda off here?'

'I used to come now and again with my sister about six or seven years ago. This one was too young then, of course.' Linda had slipped her arms around his waist and was nestling her face into his armpit. Lewis tidied her hair. 'Then Maggie got into problems with...stuff...and Stan got put away...and it fizzled out. Maggie wanted Linda to get involved, keep her on the straight and narrow. So I started bringing her at the beginning of the year.'

'Uncle Lewie's a policeman,' said Linda, looking up at him.

'Is he now? That's comforting.' I kept my eyes on Lewis and pointed to the helmet in front of him on the floor. 'Is the bike part of your job?'

'Yes. I'm lucky. I get to do what I love at work.' He tapped it with his foot. 'There's still plenty of boring work behind a desk, mind you.'

'Are you and Sam in the same department?' I said.

'No. He's Stockwell, I'm Brixton. I see him around. You know him?'

'Oh, no,' I said. 'Someone said he was also a policeman…I just…'

'He's on a course today,' he said.

'On a Sunday?'

'Advanced motorcycle training. The Met don't have traditional days off like the rest of civilisation. Thankfully, I got mine out of the way last week.'

'I was married to a motorbike enthusiast,' I said.

He laughed. 'You'll know your crank shaft from your brake shoes, then - and the feel of WD40 in your hair?' He looked like he was about to reach over and touch a few strands of mine to check. 'Perhaps I can take you for a spin sometime.'

'I don't think—'

'Go on.' He curled his lip.

'It's been a long time…'

'You look like a girl who needs a bit of adventure.'

'Is that so?'

I turned away feeling my cheeks prickling and my heart fluttering against my rib-cage. It was a sensation I hadn't experienced in a long time. A very long time.

I was one of the last to leave, but I didn't go home. I wandered over to the local playground and sat on a swing, killing time. Some kids were firing an air rifle at cans on a wall. I waited for twenty shots to hit their target and then retraced my steps.

The place appeared to be empty, with only four isolated candle flames beside the altar piercing the still air. They looked both vulnerable and triumphant struggling to hold their own in such a vast space.

I crept along the side of the church, checking to see if I was alone. As I passed the Sacristy, raised voices came from inside. I stopped to listen, aware that I'd have to instantly duck behind a pillar if the door opened. The male voice was that of Father Brian. The other took me a few moments, but I recognised the whine as Mrs Weedon's. It was like listening to a tennis match; words were being flung back and forth between them - short and hard - but I couldn't make any sense out of them.

It was too risky to loiter in that spot and, in any case, I couldn't hear well enough, so I moved on towards the crypt. When I got there, I realised my mistake. I didn't have a torch. I looked around. I could hardly pinch one of the sacred candles from the altar. Another idea occurred to me. I went into one of the smaller chapels and found the tiers of votive candles. I took one, lit it from a candle that was already alight, and carefully shielded it with my hand as I crept back towards the crypt. It took an age to get there without blowing out the flame.

I descended the steps, unlocked the gate and climbed down to the mossy stone floor. The air was thick with woody, dank smells. A haven for mould and damp. I rubbed my sleeve. It was like walking into a freezer.

The tiny flame was barely better than nothing. It cast light for about three inches, so I had to be on top of objects before I could make out what they were. I crouched down to piles of rubble and broken stones. Tins, ladders and dust sheets belonging to the decorators were stacked on one side.

Squinting into the darkness, I managed to make out two waist-high stone vaults. I knelt down to read the inscriptions and to look around for anything resembling the design on the ironwork rubbing. Two stone figures loomed beside me, one missing an arm, the other with a broken shield. Another was covered with a long cloth. I bumped into what I thought was a cupboard, but it turned out to be a battered old upright piano.

It was hard to get a sense of the full extent of the space, let alone check for any chests, fancy ironwork or hidden hidey holes. The candle seemed to be struggling to stay alight. I tipped a few drops of wax onto the floor to stop the wick from drowning. I didn't know how long I'd have before Father Brian decided he'd had enough for the morning and locked up. It was unlikely to be long.

I hurried as far forward as I could, scouring the nooks and recesses, as I went. Peering through the shadows, I saw shelves and alcoves, but under closer inspection, most held only matted cobwebs. To the far right at the back, an area was sectioned off with scaffolding, where the floor above appeared to be collapsing. I found nothing there but broken stones and a pair of wooden ladders. There was a faint hum in the distance, perhaps it was traffic.

I was about to turn back when, with the dying rays of my flame, I came across a recess and made out a large wooden casket. *Could this be it?* I ran my fingers over the top. It was indeed engraved. I was just about able to pick out the design carved into the wooden lid, but it bore no resemblance to the one on the rubbing. I ran my fingers over the clasp at the front, feeling now, more than seeing, and then suddenly the weak flame went out and I was surrounded by thick curtains of nothing but black.

I froze to the spot, my ears automatically becoming my main source of orientation. Then I heard it. A distinct shuffle behind me. I felt the saliva in my mouth shrivel up. Having got used to the sound of mice in my flat, I knew it wasn't rodents. It was distinct and crisp. Like a footstep. My breath seemed to jam in my throat. Another footstep, then a beam of light criss-crossed at the foot of the steps.

I had to think fast and I couldn't see a thing.

From my cursory survey, the crypt appeared to consist of only one room; I had found no annexes or passages leading from it. No doors, no low windows, or grilles to let in the fresh air. It was several meters underground. There was no other way out.

I took tiny blind shuffles forward as quiet as I could, my arms wavering out in front of me, like a zombie from a horror movie. It gave me an idea. It was the only place I could think of to hide.

A flagstone sloped a little and I stumbled, hoping I hadn't made a noise. I touched the edge of a shelf and held on to it getting my bearings. I felt an insect scurry over my wrist and wanted to snap my hand back, but forced myself not to react.

The torch light gradually got closer, and whoever was holding it was searching every nook and cranny just as I had been doing. Could this be the same person who had grabbed my bag at the station? Who had pushed Elly under the train? I didn't rate my chances, if he found me. A cobweb stuck to my lips and I tried not to cry out. I compelled myself to move in slow motion and finally, my foot reached something soft and I picked it up. It smelt of emulsion. I only hoped it would work. He was checking everything, but surely he wouldn't check here.

I knew it was possible. I'd seen street performers doing it, day in day out.

The footsteps came closer. I heard the man's breathing, slow and deliberate and could almost feel his body heat. The beam flashed up as high as my eyes. Surely he'd realise? S*tay perfectly still. That's all I had to do.* Then he was almost touching me. He brushed his sleeve past my arm and I squeezed my eyes shut, trying to keep my body as straight as possible. I couldn't hold my breath any longer and let out a slow jerky exhalation, but he was past me by now, moving towards the back of the crypt.

I was tempted to make a run for it, but I couldn't rely on my legs to hold me up. He'd catch me and drag me to the floor before I'd made it to the steps. I had to wait. Stand still and wait. He shuffled around behind me, lifting, moving, opening things. I heard him swear and walk briskly past me. Then I heard him run up the steps. The light disappeared and all was quiet.

I heard footsteps cross the floor above and then disappear altogether. Still, I waited. I didn't dare move, just in case. Then I let my arms drop and pulled off the sheet that had been draped over me. I threw it over the adjacent statue and patted it on the head. Thank goodness they were life-size.

As I made my way in the dark towards the steps, I noticed the humming sound again. Then it stopped altogether. Tiny creaks and grating noises took its place. They reminded me of the radiators Caroline and I used to complain about in our old flat. Central heating. The pipes contracting. I'd noticed pipes under the floor in the church - the heating must have switched itself off.

With a sudden flash, I knew what Elly's ironwork rubbing pointed to. *What an idiot!* I'd been so close. All I wanted to do was rush headlong around the church, but I had to check that the man with the torch had gone and Father Brian wasn't skulking around, poised to order me out.

I slowly emerged from the crypt, scanning full circle. Once I was confident I hadn't been seen, I started at the altar and followed the line of the ironwork air vents. My epiphany in the crypt boiled down to the central heating. Everywhere in the church, there were pipes running under the floor with ironwork grilles inlaid over them. Designs with leaves and swirls, around six inches wide. I'd walked over them every time I'd been here. The patterns varied in different parts of the church, I just had to find the right section.

I followed the iron border down the side of the church, through the chapels and right round the other side. The patterns were similar, but nothing quite matched the one in my mind with peacocks at the bottom. I had to blink as my eyes began to roll the black designs into one long fuzzy blob. Then I was back at my starting point. I'd been around the whole church. There was no match.

Lurking in my subconscious was the little indentation on the bottom of the Elly's pencil rubbing – a flower - and I smiled to myself. There was one other place. Every little sign Elly left meant something.

I slipped inside the unlocked flower room, following the iron pattern around the edge of the floor. The design in here was based on the same pattern as the pencil rubbing, but seemed elongated. From the hazy sketch in my memory, this wasn't an exact match either, but close. I followed the air vent round, tracing the pattern as it repeated itself. I shifted boxes and chairs out of the way to see if the design altered. The vent then disappeared under the cupboard in the corner. I shoved against it, but it was too heavy to shift. I was exhausted, hungry and emotionally wrung out, but I wasn't about to give up. It had to be around here somewhere. It was definitely the right sort of design.

I heaved against the cupboard. It was built of heavy oak. I hesitated. I couldn't guarantee I had time to empty the whole thing out. I tried to rock it slightly and as I did so the bottom drawer shifted an inch or two towards me. I pulled the drawer out completely. Underneath there was no solid base, only slats to hold the bottom drawer in place. The vent continued underneath it into the corner.

A wave of euphoria swept over me, like a child spotting a pile of gifts Santa has left under the tree for Christmas. I held my chest; I was breathing so fast, I was almost hyperventilating. A section of the iron grille, right in the corner, looked different. It was around six inches square; a separate tile-shaped piece. I ran my fingers over it and felt myself chewing on my own heartbeat.

It was loose.

I lifted it out and saw a small space underneath. I put my hand in, felt around.

Then I found it. A hidden box. Wide-eyed, I slid it out. I clutched it to my chest and without warning, burst into tears. The relief and sense of triumph felt unreal, as if I still couldn't quite believe it.

I shook myself. *Just hold it all together until you're out of here.* I set the box down on the draining board. It wasn't heavy, about the size of a large brick. Pretty, inlaid with mother-of-pearl. I lifted open the lid and stared inside.

It wasn't what I'd been expecting. On the top were two spongy colourful items inside see-through plastic bags. But, underneath I saw something else. I didn't dare linger, but I swiftly flicked through it. It was all here. Elly's story - her diary. *I'd found what I'd been looking for at last.*

chapter fourteen

Elation, like fireworks, detonated inside my lungs as I clutched the book that held Elly's missing secrets. Everything she didn't want getting into the wrong hands. The answers to the mystery of Elly's life - and hopefully her death - that had kept me obsessed for weeks.

I heard a sound in the church and hastily replaced everything and closed the lid. I slid the box into my bag. It sounded like someone was sweeping outside the door, then I heard a low cough. I opened the door, trying to look nonchalant.

'Just needed to wash my hands,' I said, rubbing them as though they were still damp.

Father Brain looked incredulous, but carried on sweeping. I said a cheery goodbye and left.

Ten minutes later, I was on the Tube to Camden.

'I ran you a bath like you asked,' he said, as I breezed past him at the door. I clambered past a bike in Stefan's dingy hallway and headed up to the first floor. 'You've found it?'

All I could think of on the way over was lying back in bucketfuls of steaming hot water. The mouldy stench of the crypt had permeated every layer of my clothing and then seeped into my skin. I asked Stefan for frothy bubbles and a stiff brush to cleanse it away. His Radox, followed by coal tar soap was perfect.

Once I had polished off my second bacon sandwich, I put Elly's box on the kitchen table as though it was a precious archaeological find. 'Take a look at this,' I said, presenting my treasures.

'You said there were some weird things inside,' said Stefan. 'Where did you find it in the end?'

I explained as I pulled out the two plastic bags and put them on the table.

'What the—?' he said, holding up the first bag. His eyebrows slid together forming two deep grooves.

'It looks like a child's toy,' I said. 'A penguin.'

'And these?' He grimaced, holding the other bag at arms' length.

I shrugged. It appeared to contain a crumpled pair of ladies' panties.

'Nice,' he said, pulling his mouth down at the edges. He dropped them on a chair.

'Why are they in bags?'

'Look - I don't know.' He was winding me up with all his questions. 'Here's the pièce de résistance,' I said. I laid the diary on the table - my winning hand.

'So this is it,' he said, with deference.

'Definitely the same writing that was on the map in the locket. And there are also these…' I handed him two envelopes with torn flaps that had been squashed right at the bottom of the box. 'See what you make of these - I've not looked at anything yet.'

'Okay,' he said. 'You get reading her diary and I'll look at these letters.' He turned to a coffee pot gurgling on a hot-plate. 'Strong black?'

We each took a sip and got to work, poring over the pages on the kitchen table like teenagers sitting an exam.

After a few minutes, Stefan broke the silence.

'I don't know how on earth these are connected to anything,' he said, 'Just soppy love letters that get a bit explicit in parts. Looks like one is a reply to the other. Neither of them are signed.'

'Sentimental value?' I said.

He peered over my shoulder. 'Doesn't look like her writing,' he said.

'Maybe Elly was looking after them for someone.'

'Or maybe,' he tapped the side of his nose, 'she was blackmailing someone.'

I snorted. 'Doesn't sound like her style. I don't think Elly was that kind of person.'

'And you met her for exactly how long? An hour and a half?'

I dropped my eyes. 'Something like that. But I've spoken to people she knew.' He sniggered at me for trying to stand up for Elly's character. 'The diary starts in January this year and I've got to the part where Toby went missing, but it doesn't tell us anything new.'

'Can I have a flick through?'

I handed it to him reluctantly. He glanced at a few pages, thumbed further into the book.

'What are these dates?' he said, laying the book down flat.

I tossed my hair back. 'Looks like Elly was doing a bit of snooping of her own.' I stabbed my finger on the top of the list of dates and times; mostly Sundays, some Saturdays.

'"Sunday, June 27th, 11.15am", "Saturday, 3rd July, 7.45pm", he said. 'What do they refer to?'

'It says here these are the times when Elly saw Father Brian or Mrs Weedon handling cash.' I sat back. 'She was keeping tabs on them.'

Stefan starting reading; he was as curious as I was. '"*I'm certain they're working together. Strange, because they always ignore each other, perhaps it's a purely business arrangement. I've seen Mrs Weedon taking money 'for church expenses' a couple of times and Father Brian's definitely taken wads of notes from the safe, again. I nearly got caught, staring through the keyhole. I think Mrs W might have seen me coming out of the flower room, too. Bet she doesn't know about my little hidey hole, but I'll have to be careful. I'm thinking of telling Sam. He'll know what to do.*"' He straightened up. 'How about that?'

'This links in with what Linda said.' I ran the end of the pen over my lips. 'Looks like Mrs Double-U and Father Brian were skimming money from the church funds and Elly found out about it.'

Stefan turned away, thoughtful. 'It sounds like a paltry operation, but if either of them knew the details were recorded in Elly's diary, they'd be pretty keen to get hold of it, wouldn't you say?'

'Together with Frank - you remember I told you he had a fling with Elly? - it gives them all a motive to get their hands on it. I can't rule either of them out as the guy who grabbed my bag at Miceheldever - although I think Father Brian is too short.'

'Those letters,' he said. 'Definitely not Elly's writing. One is addressed to someone called "Fed" and the other is to "Gladiator".'

'Yeah - she mentions those names in here. I'll look at them later,' I said, slapping my hands over my ears. 'Let me get on.' I wanted to get through the rest of Elly's diary, grasp the whole picture. I could hear Stefan twitching in the background. 'Make yourself useful,' I said, pointing to my empty mug and he sprang into action.

As he put the refilled mug in front of me, I put my hand firmly on his arm.

My words felt icy cold on my lips. 'Elly was raped.' Stefan narrowed his eyes and sunk heavily into his chair. A bubble of bile rose in my throat. 'That's why the knickers are here - there's...sperm on them,' I said. 'She never went to the police. She never reported it. She was ashamed.'

Stefan lifted the plastic bag and laid it reverently on the table.

'We mustn't open it. DNA. Did she say who did it?'

'Not yet. She keeps just saying "he".' I quickly scanned the next page. Apart from finding a name, I didn't want to focus too much on the details; it felt too intimate, too intrusive.

I needed a bathroom break and when I came me back, Stefan's head was buried in the diary.

'Oh, boy,' he said. 'I've got the rapist. It's not a name. It's in code. LB92.'

'LB92, who on earth is that?' I sat back, tired by now of Elly's little puzzles.

'I don't know. She says here that he is the one who raped her two years ago.'

I flipped the book round to face me. 'This is important, especially if that's all she's used to identify him.'

'Maybe it's his initials and a house number.'

'Or part of a vehicle number plate?' My brain was turning to papier-mâché.

'Elly and her bloody codes,' huffed Stefan.

He dragged his laptop in front of us and punched LB92 into his search engine, but neither of us were hopeful. 'Nearly quarter of a million hits,' he said, his enthusiasm flagging. 'From pet safety vests to photocopying paper. It's too vague. I'm not sure how to narrow it down.'

'I'll have a look,' I said. 'You carry on reading.'

I tapped London into the computer and played around with car registration numbers, but got nowhere.

Stefan made a croaking noise. 'It goes peculiar from here onwards,' he said.

'What do you mean?'

He laughed. 'Well - it stops making any sense. There are long gaps between the words - it seems to disintegrate into gobbledegook.'

'Where?' I peered over his shoulder. He pointed to a page about a third of the way through the book. From then on there were only two or three words on a line. The rest was blank.

'I don't believe it!' I exclaimed.

'It's not in invisible ink, is it?'

'Hold on,' I said, lifting the book close to my face. I touched the page. 'These aren't gaps,' I said. 'It's partly written in Braille.'

'You're joking?'

'I think so.' I ran my fingertip along the lines. 'Feel it - there are little bumps on the paper.'

He did the same. 'It's half handwritten - half in Braille,' he said, throwing his hands in the air. He got to his feet. 'How incredible. This woman was completely crazy.'

'No, she wasn't,' I said. 'She was very clever and careful. What better way to keep it secret?'

He shrugged. 'You need two people to read it - a blind person and a sighted one. Know any blind people?'

'As a matter of fact, I do. Elly's friend at the church. Charlie.'

Stefan stretched. 'Looks like he's our next step.'

I slumped forward on to the table, knocking over a bottle of tomato sauce. I couldn't believe that I'd been asking questions, searching, delving, snooping, putting myself in danger, racking my brains for weeks - and after all that effort we'd ground to a halt.

'Look, before I go completely doolally,' I said. 'What have we learnt here?'

'Okay,' he said. 'There are three separate issues. There's someone desperate to get hold of all this,' He held out his arms to encompass Elly's diary, the toy, the knickers and the letters - and we know that Frank, Father Brian, Mrs Weedon, Dr Bell and Sam - all had motives for at least one item here.'

I tapped my pen against my notepad. 'Then there's Elly's death. Was it an accident? I certainly don't think it was suicide.'

'Or was it the man in the raincoat? He could be one of the diary-chasers.'

'And finally, there's Toby's abduction - an entirely different event that just *happens* to involve the same family.' I took a deep breath. 'In theory - we could be looking for three separate perpetrators: a thief, an abductor and a murderer.'

'Or we could be looking for one,' he said, massaging the bridge of his nose. 'The abductor - who was after Elly's diary, or these letters, and ended up killing her.'

'My head hurts,' I said. 'Let's get out of here. Take a break. Maybe some fresh air will help us think more clearly.' I stood up, weary and defeated. 'I'll take a look at those letters when we get back, see if I can see where they might fit in.'

'I was wondering if…' He faltered.

'What?'

'Shall we take the stuff with us and head over to south London?'

'I was thinking of visiting Elly's grave later.'

'Okay. Why don't we do that on the way.'

'Any particular reason why you want to come over to Richmond?' I said.

'It's Clapham, actually,' he said, rubbing his eyebrow and hiding his face.

'Nice one,' I said, slapping his backside. I was glad that at least one good thing might come out of all of this. 'In case you didn't know already, I should warn you that Caroline is a bit of a handful.'

Stefan drove us to Norbury. I rang Flora and asked for Charlie's number, but he wasn't answering. I left a message asking him to call me back, saying it was about Elly.

I wanted to see where Elly's ashes had been scattered, wanted to visit her final resting place. Flora had told me that a stone plaque had been placed where she had been cremated. It was beside a specially chosen rose bush in a Garden of Remembrance. The family hadn't wanted any memorial, so the members of St Stephen's had clubbed together and paid for the rose to be planted and the plaque to be engraved. It was four weeks since Elly had died. I was still no closer to proving it was anything but suicide and the inquest was tomorrow.

The garden was situated behind a small chapel, which had a traditional graveyard on three sides and a grassy slope on the other. We walked through a stone archway, past an obelisk and sunken tombstones leaning over like old men's teeth.

Stefan left me alone for a moment, walking the other way to smell the few stray roses that remained at this time of year. I found the right spot. There was a cigarette butt beside her stone. I flicked it into the bushes. The plaque simply read: *In loving Memory*, with Elly's name and the date she died. I crouched down and ran my fingers over the letters of her name.

'We're getting there, Elly.' I whispered. 'You haven't made it easy, girl.'

The rose bush beside her plaque was heavily pruned, but one single late apricot-coloured bud remained, trying to unfurl. It made my heart ache. This small innocent bud was striving to be seen, desperate to have a place in the world. The analogy with Elly did not pass me by.

I leant over and breathed in the faintest waft of honey. It reminded me of the strong perfume Elly had worn on the train. Either someone had been very thoughtful or it had been a coincidence. I stood up.

'I'm sorry it's taking so long,' I whispered, as I walked away.

I couldn't believe that after so much effort, Stefan and I were barely any closer to finding out how Elly had died. That, after all, had been the real reason for our investigation. Along the way, we'd picked up queries over Toby's disappearance and the knowledge today, that Elly had been raped. I wondered what else awaited us in the, as yet, unread pages of her diary.

• • •

Stefan dropped me off at home before driving to Clapham. I hadn't seen it yet, but Caroline had found a flat near the mainline station and had started moving in her belongings. Stefan was 'invited' to help.

My flat felt lifeless and cold. It was too quiet. Like how it had felt once when I threw a birthday party in my teens and no one showed up. I missed Caroline's overblown brand of melodrama. Missed Jeff's affectionate banter even more.

Having waited for this moment, I was stuck without Charlie's help. What if he didn't read Braille? What if the rest of Elly's diary still didn't make any sense? My initial euphoria at finding Elly's box had given way to trepidation. I wasn't sure if I wanted to unwrap the secrets it held anymore. Wasn't sure what I was going to find.

I switched on the television and pretended to watch rugby. I hated rugby. I flicked over to a black and white film; something to do with ships and submarines, but I couldn't tell what was going on. I couldn't settle. The stillness around me felt too thick. False. I kept feeling that someone was about to jump out from behind a door or leap out of a cupboard. I checked the mousetrap under the sink, but it was still empty. There'd been no sign of my little intruders for several days.

There wasn't anything further I could take to the police. What we'd read in the diary so far was all hearsay and speculation. Perhaps simply the dizzy way Elly's mind worked. I looked at the clock. Nineteen hours before the inquest.

I had failed her.

The following day, I was supposed to have an interview with Helen Mirren at 11am. Her manager rang at 9am to change it to 2pm - then her agent called at 12 to cancel it altogether. She was indisposed. I rang Southwark coroners court straight away, only to find that Elly's inquest had already taken place. I couldn't help wondering if anything new had emerged, anything I should know about. I spent the rest of the day chewing on stale crisps, half-heartedly watching television, waiting for Charlie to call. The phone never rang.

I spent all Tuesday morning working mindlessly on features, before I left the flat to find a local newsagent.

I flicked through the paper and found the right page:

> *An inquest held yesterday at Southwark Coroners Court, SE1, heard how on September 19th this year, Ms Elly Swift, 27, of Brixton, fell under an oncoming train outside Micheldever at 15.53, taking her own life. The coroner, Mr Charles Ripley, said "I consider that the balance of her mind was disturbed by reason of depression and anxiety." Her parents, who were at the inquest said: "Elly brought joy to her family and friends in her short life and will be sorely missed by us all."'*

I slapped the paper down and left the shop, a headache drilling fiercely into my forehead. It had started to rain and everything felt like a mess. I wondered who it was who had written the Swifts' statement at the end, because I knew for certain that it hadn't come from them.

When I got home I ran to my bedroom and threw myself onto the unmade bed. I was glad I was on my own. I couldn't hold it in any longer. I cried and cried, my head hurting so much, I felt like the sinews inside must be snapping. The tears soaked my pillow, my hair, my sleeve and still there were more.

I cried about Elly, about Jeff, about my inability to have made any difference for either of them. I'd let Elly down just like I'd let Jeff down.

I opened my jewellery case; the place where I kept Jeff's suicide note. I unfolded it, kissed it and laid it on my damp pillow. Then I leant under the bed and pulled out my box of photographs. I tipped them onto the duvet and flicked through them trying to feel close to Jeff, trying to taste the happiness we once shared, allowing the love I still felt for him to fill up the holes I could feel gaping inside my head, my heart, my soul.

There was one I loved of him as a teenager, long before we'd met. He was astride his first motorbike in front of Ayers Rock in Australia. The expansive shot looked like an advertising poster; the sun made the bike sparkle and he looked at once shy and bewitching in his tight white t-shirt.

There was a more recent one of him on a bike trip, sitting cross-legged in front of a tent, squinting into the camera, holding a tin kettle. It must have been just before we got married. He looked earnest, like he missed me.

After two years, he was slipping away from me; his clothes, his voice, the smell of him - long since swept away. Even with pictures like these I was finding it difficult to reach him. *You are getting harder and harder to find. You are stepping further and further away from me. You're shrinking into a past that I don't recognise anymore. Come back...*

Another snap, not long before he died.

I had to look twice at the last picture, not believing what I was seeing. As the truth sunk in, I could barely breathe.

The impact was so great, I felt like I'd been flung against a wall.

This isn't right. This can't be true. I must be mistaken.

The muscles in my neck, arms and legs were taut, crackling.

I was staring at a photograph of someone standing beside Jeff who I now recognised. Someone who belonged to my current life, since I'd met Elly, not to my life then, with Jeff.

It put a whole new spin on everything.

This involves me, now, not just Elly.

I'm no longer on the sidelines in this terrible mystery - I'm right at the centre of it.

Part Two

Elly

chapter fifteen

The stalls were in place by nine forty-five. Fifteen minutes to go.

Elly filled two plastic cups with orange squash and carried them over to the tombola stall. Flora and Jamilla were running it, which probably meant that everyone would walk away with a prize. From the first day Elly stepped into the church, they had taken up joint responsibility for the position of her Fairy Godmother - they even remembered her birthday. Flora had once told her that 'Friendship is God's way of apologising for our families'. Elly wasn't sure if she should feel blessed or heartbroken.

Today, Flora was dressed in Pink with a capital P. Every part of her outfit was the same baby-girl shade, apart from her tights which were white, but took on a pinky-brown hue due to the tube-map of varicose veins decorating her legs. Elly was concerned that Flora hadn't yet tried to sit down in the pencil skirt. Flora's hips weren't pencil thin and she wasn't sure if the silk's tensile properties would pass the test. The box-jacket topped off with a fascinator under bee-keepers' netting, conspired to make her look like an overweight doll.

There was no malice in Elly's observations, she just liked to see things as they were. Saying it out loud was another matter altogether. Elly was careful to make sure her words didn't always match her thoughts.

Flora gave the tombola box a practice twirl and straightened the cashbox for the tenth time. She was unable to keep still, as if attending her very first party. She reminded Elly of a girl at infant school who ate too many cupcakes at an Easter Parade and threw up over the teacher's new handbag.

The church hall was set out for the usual fund-raising affair; a raffle, bric-a-brac, toys, books, drinks, cakes and games, involving miniature netball hoops, quoits and skittles. Father Brian was standing in front of the 'recreation' area, pacing up and down, straightening the side-netting. He looked about as comfortable as an undertaker at the dodgems. He hated this kind of thing. Elly had once overheard him telling a nun that having to lower himself to church fetes brought on severe migraines. But the money for fixing up the church had to come from somewhere. God didn't have much spare change - although Elly couldn't help thinking, having caught him at it before, that a small cut might well end up lining Father Brian's own pockets for his trouble.

Elly, on the other hand, had been looking forward to spending her day off among friends. The church was her new home - poles apart from the one she grew up in, where she'd felt neither accepted nor embraced. She knew Irene wouldn't be there. Far too busy at the weekend looking after the boys, cleaning, cooking, being a good wife. She caught herself sliding into a mean silent tirade about her sister and dragged herself back. Irene would be plagued every day with dread and terror about her lost little boy. She'd been through hell with Toby. It wasn't fair to have a go at her.

Elly found herself at Terry's book stall. There was a hardback she had her eye on: *Secret Writing* - all about designing and cracking codes. She was spellbound just flicking through it. If she'd sold enough raffle tickets by the end of the day, she'd treat herself to it. When Terry's back was turned she tucked it under an old encyclopaedia and hoped no one else got there first.

Her parents had never understood her relationship with books - or with puzzles, games, fairy tales or imaginary worlds, for that matter. Come to think of it, she'd never seen Irene read anything other than celebrity gossip in cheap weekly magazines. Sadly, it meant Irene's children weren't being introduced to the enchantment of literature, folklore and legends either.

It would be Max's birthday soon, Irene's eldest. Elly gravitated towards the toy stall, hopeful there might be a jigsaw or game suitable for a present. Money had been tight lately, now that the landlord had put the rent up. It would have to look new, though. She didn't want Irene thinking she was scrimping; couldn't bear the backlash of snide remarks that would follow if the gift was noticeably second-hand.

Gillian was behind the stall, together with Charlie. Elly pulled her to one side as Charlie was busy fiddling with a box on the floor.

'Be gentle with Charlie. He'll have difficulty seeing the prices on things.'

'I know,' she snapped. 'I've put everything that's one pound at his end of the table, so it should be easy.'

Elly nodded and starting browsing the kids' stuff, realising before long that she was picking her way through playthings for a boy half Max's age - a folded paddling pool, a bag of marbles and a wooden Noah's ark with clip-in animals - as if in search of a gift for Toby.

She turned and leant against the table, pressing her fist into her mouth. She hoped Gillian hadn't seen the way her face had changed colour. Toby was always there, in the background, like a little face at a distant window, standing on his tiptoes trying to get noticed.

'You okay?' said Flora suddenly at her side, never one to miss a trick.

'It's Max's birthday soon,' she said, avoiding her eyes. 'What are boys of ten interested in, these days?'

She knew Flora would have about as much clue as she did, but it took the conversation to a safe place.

'All kinds of stuff they shouldn't be,' she said, helpfully. She stared down at the table. 'Table-tennis? Etch-a-sketch?' Flora was even more out of touch than Elly. At least Elly would have suggested a play-station, had her purse stretched that far. Flora gave her a pained smile and shuffled back to the tombola.

Elly lifted up a few items and put them down again. It was difficult to tell with Max and Irene's eight year old, Alex. Since they were born, Elly hadn't had much contact with them. It wasn't for want of trying. She was rarely invited over and her offers to baby-sit were greeted with feeble excuses, such as *the little one's got flu* or *Mum's already offered.* Irene didn't seem to trust her. Didn't want her in the house. She'd once overheard Irene telling Frank that she thought Elly was a liability. *She's got head problems, that girl - I don't want her contaminating our boys.* Contaminating?

Elly had hoped things might have changed when Toby went missing; she was desperate to help, to do something practical, be supportive. Surely, as a family they should be pulling together, but it wasn't only metaphorically that the door had been closed in Elly's face.

'We're too upset for visitors,' said Irene, who answered the doorbell one afternoon, holding a sumptuous chocolate cake.

'But I'm family, you don't need to—'

She was going to say *go to any trouble*, but wasn't given the chance to finish her sentence.

What Elly found strange was that since Toby had disappeared it was as though she'd finally got to know him. She'd spoken to his teachers, parents of his friends, his playmates, kids down at the park, pored over photographs - and she'd discovered an adorable little boy. It was a sad and tragic irony that Elly had found him, now that everyone else had lost him.

Elly pulled a walkie-talkie out of the pile and something fell to the floor. It was soft and didn't make a sound. As she reached down for it, a sharp pain stabbed her chest like she had suddenly inhaled thick acrid smoke.

What was this doing here?

Instinctively, she pressed the penguin to her throat in a protective hug. She smelt it, stroked it. It was the soft toy that used to belong to Toby. He used to call it Pengy. He'd had it with him the day he'd gone missing and no one had seen it, or him, since.

She held it out in front of her. Perhaps it wasn't Toby's after all, perhaps it was a common toy and there were lots of them about. She took a closer look. No - there was no doubt. Elly remembered the detail: the bowtie Irene had added made of blue ribbon, the grey felt wings, the knitted blue hat. Most significantly, Toby had chewed off the top button on the penguin's jacket. She pulled at the tiny thread that remained. It was definitely his.

She looked behind her, unnerved, cautious. *Had someone seen her with it? Was the person who took Toby a regular church-goer?* She felt queasy at the thought. Everyone had always assumed a stranger had come into the hall that Sunday in March and led Toby away.

Holding the toy close and keeping her back to the centre of the hall, she slipped behind the table to join Gillian, who was in the process of counting out change.

'Do you happen to know who brought this?' said Elly, finding her lips tight and her mouth dry.

'Er…' Gillian leant on one foot. She looked down at the tray of coins, losing count. 'What?' She scratched her nose. 'How would I know? Does it matter?' She gave Elly a sharp stare that said she had more important things to do.

Elly was lost in thought. *Why now?*

'Can I buy it?'

Gillian absently took the money, keen to get back to putting the finishing touches to her stall. Elly put Pengy in her bag and made her way back to the serving hatch, nearly bumping into Linda, who was standing on one foot, swinging her other leg out behind her.

'Get ready,' said Elly, 'They're all coming in.'

Before Linda could reply, the doors were opened and the mob descended on them like the first day of a Harrods' sale.

• • •

That evening, Elly opened her business studies' books at the kitchen table and tried to catch up with college work. Juggling full-time work at the whole-food shop, an evening class and commitments at the church wasn't easy, but everyone had told her that keeping busy was good for her mental health. She wasn't so sure anymore. She couldn't help thinking that having more time to reflect and relax might not be better.

Elly's past had become a place she knew she'd travelled through, but could no longer fit in to the topography of her life. It was a surreal and barely understood landscape to her. It was like knowing you'd been to the moon, but having no idea how you'd got there. Or how you'd got back. She was only glad it was all over.

She found it hard to envisage how wretched she must have felt when she was younger. Even with Toby missing and the stupid run-in with Dr Bell, she would never describe herself as depressed these days. The GP still had her down for anti-depressants, but she hadn't taken one in over a year. It was hard for her to remember those two points in her past when she'd attempted to end her own life. Hard to match those up with the person she was now. That former self was someone else: fragile, lost and out on a limb. Someone she'd been glad to leave behind when she joined St Stephen's six years ago and started to turn her life around. She'd been truly saved. Less by God - than by Flora, Jamilla and Gillian. Her personal Angels.

Rereading her notes, she couldn't help but see Trevor Bell in his patched up tweed jacket, as he strutted at the front of the lecture theatre, his shiny face melting under the spotlights. *Creep.* She could imagine the rubbery, rancid smell of him, the way he put his face too close to hers when he spoke.

He'd duped her into thinking he took all his students to the local pub to *see how they were getting on.* It was a con. She'd innocently turned up at The Falcon with her file under her arm and he'd plied her with drinks, rubbed his thigh against hers (pretending there wasn't enough room on the seat) and then taken an excessive interest in the skirt she was wearing. *It suited her. Made her look slim and elegant. It went nicely with the tights she was wearing - or perhaps they were stockings?*

She felt a stale, bitter taste in her mouth as she tried to swat him out of her mind and get back to the text.

He'd insisted on taking her home, insisted on seeing her inside the door. *Did she fancy making coffee? Did she want to get an A+ for her next essay? Did she want to sit beside him on the sofa or was the bedroom more comfortable?*

There she was, twenty-seven years old, reduced to standing shoulders hunched inside the front door, beside a bloke at least twice her age who was after a quick grope. She'd been taken advantage of before - and it wasn't going to happen again. She'd bundled him out of the flat and slammed the door in his face. It wasn't a gainly act. She'd had to grit her teeth and press her hands into his jacket, turn her face away and push. He'd given in like a sack of wet putty and had nearly fallen down the fire-escape. Serve him right if he broke his leg. Or his neck. Let him explain that to his colleagues. Afterwards, she'd felt pleased with herself - liberated and strong. She'd written in her diary that night about it being a turning point. *I'm not going to let anyone walk all over me, ever again.*

Back to the marketing book, the same sentence. She wasn't getting very far. She thought again about leaving the course. Perhaps it was her best option; she didn't feel she had enough reserves to play stupid mind-games with Ding-Dong-Bell for another three terms. In any case, she shouldn't have to. She closed *Principles and Practices of Marketing* and found the college prospectus instead. She'd never really liked the idea of Business Studies anyway; it had been Frank's idea. He'd said it would help her get a better job. Maybe she didn't want Frank's idea of a better job, thank you very much.

French, Italian, English classics, drama. There were plenty to choose from. Perhaps even a course at university. That would knock her mother for six. The idea of learning more about novels or psychology sent a shoal of tiny fish up her spine.

Or maybe something entirely different. She was enjoying learning Braille with Charlie. It was like writing in code and it helped him, too. Gillian was doing a yoga course at Wandsworth college; she should ask her more about it. Gillian had demonstrated one of the positions last weekend and it hadn't seemed too complicated. The Warrior, she thought it was called; a triangle shape pointing sideways. Elly and Mandy had both had a go at it.

'There are no men there, for a start - women only,' Gillian had said, holding up her fist. She knew about Elly's reasons for wanting to quit the business course. 'Dirty old codger,' she'd said.

'Maybe you should learn kick-boxing or a martial art,' Mandy said. 'Then you can give these creepy blokes what's coming to them.'

Elly knew little about Mandy Cunningham other than she liked a strong ale, lived in Portsmouth and spent the weekend with Gillian, now and again.

They'd apparently met at college in Nottingham and from there, Gillian had become a librarian and moved to London and Mandy, a hairdresser in Portsmouth.

Things had taken an interesting turn after that, as they'd sat in a pub a week ago, off Wandsworth High Street. Elly couldn't remember how the conversation had got there, but before long they were talking about Toby's abduction.

Elly hadn't realised that Mandy had been staying with Gillian the weekend in March when Toby had gone missing. In fact, she'd been at St Stephen's church that very morning, although neither she nor Gillian had known about the abduction until later. The police weren't called until around 11am, once it was clear that Toby was nowhere to be found and the congregation had largely dispersed by then. Gillian had subsequently been questioned, but failed to mention that her friend had been with her for mass. Mandy had gone back to Portsmouth a few hours after it happened. It turned out she'd been a key witness, never interviewed by the police.

For a week now, Elly had been replaying their conversation, struggling with what she should do about it.

'You weren't well the weekend Toby disappeared,' Gillian had said, 'do you remember?'

Mandy pulled a face and rubbed her belly. 'We'd had that dodgy Indian takeaway the day before,' she said, 'and I'd had the runs all night - it was awful, but I was determined to get to mass on Sunday.'

'Do you remember anything unusual?' Elly said, 'now you know what happened?'

'The thing was,' said Mandy, 'I had to keep leaving the service to go to the loo. As you know, the Ladies is just by the church hall. I remembered seeing the kids doing their drawings, through the glass in the hall door.'

'The children came back into the main church at about 10.20am,' said Elly. 'That's when people with Toby started to lose track of him.'

Mandy drummed her fingers on her mouth. Her lips were plump, a natural cherry colour. Together with her corn-coloured hair, which was tied away from her face in intricate plaits, she reminded Elly of one of the Von Trapp girls from *The Sound of Music*, although she couldn't have said which one. It gave Mandy an aura of sisterly dependability.

'You know, I *did* see a little boy.... but I'm pretty sure it was *after* 10.20 - more like 10.40. I'd just taken some *Imodium* and wanted to remember the time. He was waiting by the bins at the back. I did think it was a bit odd - him being on his own like that, but I was rather preoccupied getting to the toilet, I'm afraid.

He looked like he was waiting for someone, holding a blue toy.'

Elly held her breath and didn't dare speak. She didn't want to break Mandy's train of thought.

'Yeah,' said Mandy, nodding, the picture in her mind obviously getting sharper. 'It was after all the children had gone back into the church. The hall was empty. I looked again when I came out of the loo, but he'd gone.'

'That could be really important to the police, Mandy. I don't think anyone knew he was out by the bins. You say he looked like he was waiting for someone?'

'I'd say so. Standing about on the spot, looking inside.' She nodded. 'Yeah - waiting for someone.'

Gillian was almost on her feet, ready to leave. Elly reached up and dragged her back down again. 'This is really important,' she said, the words shooting out like greyhounds from a starting gate. 'This means Toby knew who it was. It wasn't someone from outside who took him - it was someone inside - someone he knew, we all knew, from the church.'

Mandy held up her hands. 'I can't be absolutely sure about the time. I was feeling queasy and feverish, remember. I might have got the order of things mixed up.'

'Can you remember anything else?'

Mandy pulled her mouth to one side; a misty, far-away look in her eyes.

'I heard the sound of a motorbike backfiring after I left the boy to go back into the church. It gave me a shock. It was nearby. I thought it was a firework at first.'

Elly stared at the intricate red carpet on the floor of the pub, seeing nothing but a blur.

Lewis Jackson had told everyone that he hadn't been at the church once he'd dropped Linda off at 9.50am. Apparently, he didn't need to come back to collect her, because she was having lunch with a group of girls from the Brownies.

Sam also had a motorbike. *Did any of the other church-goers use a motorbike?*

'And I saw the back of someone…a man…'

'A man?' Elly reached out and grabbed Mandy's wrist. 'Where? When?'

'Look, I'm not sure, okay?' She shook herself free.

'What did he look like?'

'I only saw the back of him…by the church hall… he was looking inside, so I didn't get a good look at him.'

'What colour was his hair? How tall was he?'

She puffed out her cheeks. 'It was a while ago. I didn't take much notice at the time. Brown hair, I think. Around six foot maybe, wearing an anorak, so it was hard to make out his build.'

'Was he with Toby?'

'No. I think it was before I saw the boy near the bins.' Mandy grimaced. 'Must have been an earlier dash to the loo.' She gripped the edge of the table. 'Look, it was ages ago. I can't be sure about the details, the timings, the exact order of things.' She shook her head. 'I didn't know at the time I was supposed to be remembering everything!'

It wasn't until after that conversation last weekend, once Mandy had returned home to Portsmouth, that Elly came to a decision. She'd take a trip over there and show Mandy stacks of photographs of people from St Stephen's. There'd been various outings over the years and there was cardboard box in the flower room with piles of pictures from choir concerts, church plays, Bishops' visits and so on. Everyone involved with the church would be in there, somewhere. One of them had to be the man Mandy had seen by the hall.

She'd do more than that. She'd take her camera when she next went to church and snap some fresh shots of the church hall, the foyer, the corridor outside the toilets, back door, courtyard and the bins. She'd take those along to Mandy too, to see if any of them jogged her memory. Surely, with that barrage of images, a little bell would go off inside her head?

Surely, something there would nudge her in the right direction? Then they'd go to the police.

Elly returned to the college prospectus on the kitchen table, but she couldn't concentrate anymore. Her thoughts kept sneaking back to Portsmouth, Mandy, the man with Toby.

Only a week to go.

Even if it led to nothing, it would be good to have a break, to get out of London for a while. Gillian was coming too. They'd make a girlie weekend of it, just the three of them. Elly hardly knew Mandy, but they were easy in each other's company and Elly didn't feel judged. And Gillian, she was Elly's special friend; she never expected anything of her or tried to coerce her into being different. She accepted her for who she was - a rare quality, Elly had come to realise. Not to mention the fact they all enjoyed a tasty beer and a laugh. Ever since Toby went missing, Elly had felt like she was in quasi-mourning. She was sure God wouldn't mind if she had some fun for a change.

chapter sixteen

'You're both so kind,' said Elly, after mass. 'But, I've got leftovers from yesterday's tea to finish.' She reached out and squeezed Flora's arm. 'Thank you for asking.'

'Are you sure? It's da full works - curried callaloo, boiled yam and Jamilla's multi-storey boiled-wheat dumplings,' she said, licking her lips. 'We can't tempt you?'

Not this time. Elly had to be firm. She intended to finish her post-mass coffee and be on her way. It was the day after the bazaar (which after a polite start had turned into a cross between a jumble-sale and a bun-fight) and she wanted Sunday afternoon to herself for a change; time without jolly chit-chat, customers and business books. Time to enjoy her own company. She could hardly believe she was thinking such a thing, but she wasn't afraid of being alone anymore. Of sitting still inside her own head. This new realisation had only hit home in the last week or so and she wanted to hang on to it. It brought a giddy sense of freedom and possibility, like a fresh breeze taking away a longstanding, rotten smell that had seemed like it would never shift.

For some unknown reason, she'd felt like she was blossoming lately, itching to branch out. She felt physically stronger than she had done in years, as if her legs were more solid, her lungs were more elastic. It was hard to pin down exactly where this surge of rejuvenation was coming from. Was it because she had finally reached a stage where she felt she had a place in the world? Was it because she'd shown Ding-Dong-Bell where he could shove it?

Regardless of the cause, she liked this feeling of demanding more say in her destiny. With the backing of her friends and the support of a patient and forgiving God - say Amen to that - she was ready to forge ahead with plans of her own, instead of spending her life flitting about like a damaged moth, fitting in with everyone else. It was time to stride out in the world. Make a fresh start. *Boldly go where no man has gone before.* Well, maybe not that drastic, but at least find new activities - such as learning to play tennis or taking singing lessons so she could do justice to Mozart's Requiem. Thinking about where she really wanted to live. *Was Brixton the best place?* What she wanted to do. *A different job?*

Ideas that until recently had seemed impossible - *how can you think of yourself when Toby's still missing?* - were now flashing up on her radar.

It was like waking up from a long turbulent sleep, opening your eyes and finding yourself in someone else's skin. There was so much she wanted to do. Change her appearance for a start; the tie-dye hippy look had had its day. She wanted a new hair-cut; something in a sleek bob would be nice - and a more stylish pair of specs. She'd always bought the cheapest for herself - just as her parents had done (strange how she'd never noticed that Irene was always given items in the next-but-one price range), but now it was time to invest in herself. Give herself a chance. As soon as she was back from Portsmouth, she was going to scrimp and save and start booking appointments.

She'd also had enough of the likes of Frank, Sam and Dr Bell. They were life's leeches; draining away her virtue, taking advantage of her goodness. For their own selfish ends. It was time for that chapter to be over.

She finished her coffee and went over to collect her bag. As she reached it, she tipped her head on one side. Curious. Elly was convinced she'd left it zipped up. Surreptitiously, she checked inside, not wanting to look like she mistrusted anyone at the church, but being aware also that with the side door open anyone could stroll in from the street. Her purse was there, her keys, diary, her phone and Pengy; Toby's toy that she'd felt unable to leave at home. All there. False alarm.

She was on her way to the door when Charlie took her to one side.

'I heard something that you might be interested in. Irene isn't here, so I thought I'd tell you.'

'Go on.'

'The Sunday Toby went missing, Sam was away. Apparently, he bragged to Gillian about having the perfect alibi. He was on a police training course all day in St Albans.'

'Thanks, Charlie. That could be helpful.' Unless Mandy told her otherwise, that was one name she could cross off her list of suspects.

Charlie knew she'd lost faith with the police by now and was trying to do her own private sleuthing. Elly hadn't, however, told him yet about Pengy, nor Mandy's recent revelation about seeing Toby waiting by the bins. She wasn't going to tell anyone - except her diary, of course - until she knew more about what it meant.

'Do you happen to know if anyone, apart from Sam and Lewis, uses a motorbike to get to church?' she asked, knowing that with Charlie's gradual loss of sight, hearing was fast becoming his main means of interpreting the world.

'I don't think so - never heard another one. You should check the car-park. I know Sam has a bigger bike than Lewis, it makes a rougher, deeper sound.'

Elly left the church and walked to the underground, through the car-park. There were a handful of cars left and a bicycle chained to a signpost. The push bike had been abandoned for months, gradually losing parts like a carcass being picked off by vultures when everyone's back was turned. If Sam hadn't been in London that Sunday, and if Charlie was right, there was only one other person at the church with a motorbike and that was Lewis. Only he claimed he wasn't there at the time Toby went missing. Surely the police would have followed up everyone's whereabouts that morning? Just because Sam and Lewis were police officers, they weren't above the law.

Elly felt inside her bag as she rode down the escalator and gave Toby's penguin a quick squeeze. She had no idea why it had turned up again or who had brought it to the church. Without knowing that, it wasn't going to be any use to the police.

All the more reason to get to see Mandy next weekend. Elly found herself crossing her fingers as she climbed on the train. At the same time, she sent up a little prayer: *Please God, let Mandy remember something important that leads to Toby being found.*

Hyde Park was dotted with figures coiled on the grass. It was warm enough to sit for a while and not come away with a damp patch on your behind. An Indian summer. Special luxury.

Elly bought an ice-cream from the café beside the Serpentine. She drowned out the inner dissenting voices: *you'll spoil your appetite* (mother), *how can you treat yourself when Toby is still missing?* (Irene) with loud slurps of chocolate and banana. Sitting on a bench by the river, she watched people stepping off the wooden jetty into their boats, wobbling as if on a high-wire as the water rocked them, until they made it to their seats.

The last time she'd been here, Sam had insisted they take a boat themselves. It must

have been the middle of April. After the church trip to Cornwall where they had ended up sitting together on the coach and before she knew it, Sam was calling her his girlfriend. Elly couldn't recall any point when she had agreed to that new arrangement, couldn't remember taking part in that particular decision herself. Like most choices in her life until now, it seemed to have been made when she was out of the room, putting the kettle on.

She couldn't say she fell for Sam. It was more like she'd gone along with it. He'd seemed powerful at the time, a protector. Now his big presence seemed like bulk, lagging, extra weight you added, like a padded jacket, to make you look more substantial. Inside Sam himself, she discovered there wasn't much to hold on to.

He had no sensitivity. Everything about their relationship was on his terms. He led the way, ran the show and she followed. She was so used to other people telling her how things should be done. *Such a nice man. You'll be safe with him, he's a policeman.* Sam was comfortable, familiar, easy. It was safe to trot along behind him like a puppy.

They had split up briefly in early May. Elly felt she was just going through the motions with him, so she called it a day. It was after that when the unfortunate encounter with Frank took place. After Toby went missing, when Elly tried to reach out to her family, the only person who seemed appreciative was Frank. He was frightened. He should have been there for his little boy. Five or six weeks after he'd gone missing, Frank went into meltdown. He was a terrible father and needed comfort, he said. It took ten days for Elly to see it for what it was. It wasn't comfort, it was sex. Cheating. *How could she have been so naïve?*

As she crunched the last of her cornet, she knew she was fed up with all that now. Fed up with having no say in her life. *She* was going to be in charge from now on. Luckily, no one else had been party to their ludicrous fumblings. She'd dusted herself down and ended up back with Sam in June, finishing it in July when she found out he was married. *Married! What a nerve? How could Sam come before God every week and ask for forgiveness when he was 'playing away from home' behind God's back? Didn't he realise God could see everything?*

She pulled her diary out of her bag and flipped back to the end of March, to the entries she'd made around the time Toby went missing. She wanted to make sure that when she went to Portsmouth she had as much detail as possible to jog Mandy's memory.

Toby didn't come into the church at the usual time of 10.20. Irene couldn't see any sign of him at 10.30, but Mandy spotted him near the bins in the courtyard at 10.40. Elly sighed, trying to make sense of the order of events. Where was he during those twenty minutes? Hadn't Irene checked everywhere?

Mandy's memory was vital. Her recollections of that morning could turn everything around, but more than anything, she needed Mandy to make an identification. She needed Mandy to point out a specific face. She was counting down the days until she could get to Portsmouth.

This coming week couldn't go by quickly enough.

Chapter seventeen

Elly didn't notice anything was wrong straight away. She got back from work the following day, just after six o'clock and emptied the washing machine, hanging up the damp clothes on the rack in the sitting room. Only four days to go before she'd be getting off that train in Portsmouth. She was watching the news, when something in the room caught her eye. If she hadn't been so jumpy after finding Pengy, she probably wouldn't have noticed.

She got up and walked towards the bookshelf in the corner. The lamp had been knocked over. She straightened it and stared at the books. Elly had a rule about bookshelves: *never lie books flat across the top - always stand them upright.*

She bent down and noticed a copy of *Bridget Jones's Diary* lying horizontally across a row of other books. Elly knew for a fact that she would never have left it like that.

Someone had been in.

Her pulse thudded inside her head, roared inside her ears.

She stood on the spot, chewing her thumbnail, afraid to move for a moment. Afraid to make a sound, even though she'd already been home for ten minutes, crashing around. She tried to think who else had been at the flat recently. *Who would have taken a look at her books and put one back on its side?* Gillian had popped in on Friday evening, but they'd stayed in the kitchen and hadn't come through into the sitting room. She thought again. Flora had turned up with some cakes the previous week but hadn't even come into the hall.

There had been no one else.

She moved to the front door, shivering, finding herself creeping and listening with every step. She checked the lock. There was no sign of it having been forced.

Shaking now, she went into every room checking each window. There were no broken panes of glass. All the windows were still locked. She scanned every item to see if anything had been moved or was missing.

Nothing seemed to have gone. Her jewellery case was open where she'd left it on the dressing table. Her grandmother's diamond ring was glinting under the angle poise lamp. Her second-hand laptop was sitting beside her bed. The television was still telling her the news in the sitting room, the old stereo system on the shelves beside it.

She dropped to the sofa, pulling her knees into her chest into a tight ball.

Was someone after Pengy? Did someone at the church bazaar see me buy it? Was someone putting two and two together, thinking I knew a lot more than I actually did?

It was a bit of a coincidence, otherwise.

Just as well she'd had the penguin with her all day in her bag, she concluded. She hadn't wanted to be separated from it for the time being. It was all she had of Toby. By having Pengy by her side all day, it was like having him with her - that sweet sunshine boy - holding his hand, not letting him out of her sight. Perhaps Pengy was a good omen, a talisman. Maybe it could act as a homing signal.

She put the toy on the kitchen table and pulled out a roll of unused freezer bags. Sam said the police sometimes used them as evidence bags, if they stumbled on an unexpected crime scene. She put Pengy inside and squeezed her fingertips along the seal. Seeing it inside the bag made her heart swell with grief. It was reduced to a piece of evidence now. A soulless item to be tagged and logged and thrown in a box labelled, 'Abduction: Toby Delaney'.

The truth of the matter was that it might indeed have evidence of some kind on it. She should have thought of that before, but had been too swept up in the emotional attachment of it. After analysis, it might still be able to point to where Toby was being held or to who had taken him. She had to be practical.

She considered whether to call the police, but there was no evidence of a break-in and the soft toy on its own was not enough. Elly thought about Mandy, hoping that by Sunday there'd be a big fat piece of new information to take to the police.

She went back into the sitting room and noticed another book on the shelf under the speakers. *The Horse Whisperer.* It had been pushed back into the row of paperbacks with its hard cover trapping another book. Someone had definitely been in, carefully looking for something. *If they weren't looking for Pengy, then for what? Why pull out the books?*

She sat on the edge of the sofa. *Think about this.* Reaching down, she pulled her diary out of her shoulder bag and rested it on her lap, her hands lying over it, guarding it, shielding it. *Was it this that someone was after?* Her mind snapped back to having coffee after mass, on Sunday. She'd had the distinct feeling someone had been in her bag. Her diary had been in it. *Had someone read it? Found something they didn't like and decided to come back for it?*

It had been with her all day at the shop. Sometimes there were a few moments in her lunch-break to scribble a few lines. Perhaps she should be more careful with it. She certainly wouldn't want it getting into the wrong hands.

Who would have thought her diary would have turned out to be so useful? She'd never thought of it as anything other than a private place to pour out her soul, but now she was seeing it more like a useful document. Everything about Toby's disappearance was recorded. It was so easy to forget things, get dates mixed up, get facts wrong - but with a diary it was all there in black and white. There were records of everything else too. It could prove to be a godsend, especially with part of it in Braille. That had started out as fun, but was an excellent way of hiding incriminating and secretive passages.

Suddenly a thought struck her, making the hairs on her arms prickle.

She rushed to the bathroom to check the laundry basket, reaching under the cloth lining at the bottom. She sank to her knees on the rug. Everything was still there. The two letters and the knickers she'd been wearing that disgusting night, way back. They were still lying inside a freezer bag. Another makeshift evidence bag. She pressed her hand on her breastbone with relief.

She remembered checking on the computer - it was months ago now - how long DNA survived in sperm on items of clothing. She recalled the surge of triumph she'd felt when she'd learned that under normal conditions it remained intact for years. The rapist didn't know she hadn't washed the knickers she was wearing that night and had put them instead, straight into a polythene bag. He didn't know she had two handwritten letters that spelt out his secret - stolen from his hotel room. They weren't worth anything to her, but they meant a lot to him. All of that was recorded in her diary, too. She'd kept everything just in case. A kind of insurance policy in case he ever got nasty again.

No one knew she'd been raped two years ago. She hadn't reported it at the time, not just because of the shame of being a rape victim, but because she was catholic and it was a sin. Because she'd already brought shame on her family with her two…'difficult' episodes…the two not quite successful attempts to finish herself off.

She'd wanted to leave that shame behind, wash herself clean, not pick up more of it. So, she hadn't told the police. Recently, however, she'd had regrets. She found herself still reliving that dreadful incident at regular intervals. Odd moments, such as when she was kneeling in church, peeling carrots or watering her pot plants. She'd see her knickers lying torn around her ankles, feel the dirtiness of him like a bucket of excrement chucked all over her. His silage smell in her hair, pressed into her skin. Her dress ripped. Her eyes swollen with tears. She'd vomited several times afterwards and still couldn't get rid of him, then gently washed and rewashed her throbbing vagina with the hotel's rough budget toilet paper.

She hadn't told a soul. It's probably the only crime where you consider whether to tell anyone or not. She'd decided against it. She'd had no support, no aftercare. She'd gone through her waking nightmare entirely alone that night, and ever since.

The only way she could cope on the odd occasion when she saw him, was to totally cut off from her emotions. She imagined a steel wall around her, keeping her protected in her own safe capsule. Thankfully, he did his best to avoid her, too. He'd never been one for socialising, so no one seemed to question it.

Earlier in the year, she'd pulled out her diary and written it all down, every moment that she could recall, hoping for some kind of exorcism. She'd forced herself to squeeze out every detail like crushing a rotten grapefruit, hoping that by getting it out of her system in words, it might leave her alone.

It hadn't worked, but the way she thought about it had changed.

Now, she no longer felt she was living with the secret shame of it. She knew it wasn't her fault. She was the innocent victim. There was no shame in that. But still she hadn't made the call. Was it too late? Two years. It would hardly stand in her favour. She could end up in court making a complete fool of herself.

There was also something else. Someone would always harbour those cruel words *no smoke without fire.* She could imagine that *someone* being Irene. Or her mother. She knew only too well that something didn't have to be true for it to be believed. Elly didn't want the stain of that in people's minds.

When she went to bed she made the decision to make a call first thing in the morning. Not to the police, but to a locksmith. She was going to get an expensive five-lever deadlock fitted. *I have to feel safe.* Use some of the birthday money Flora and Jamilla had given her last month. She'd have to buy the furry winter boots she'd promised herself, another time.

She went to bed in her jeans and kept the light on all night.

• • •

Elly woke with a jolt on Tuesday morning. Instantly convinced someone was breaking in again, she leapt out of bed and grabbed the nearest weighty object she could find. A shoe.

She hovered behind the bedroom door, realising stupidly that she should have gone straight for the phone. Or something far heavier. What kind of damage was she going to do with a moccasin? She listened, holding her breath, shaking like she'd suddenly been transported outside and was standing knee-deep in thick snow.

Another sound. A scraping sound. She cocked her head. *Was it inside the flat?* There was a shout. *No, it was outside.* She heard the sound of a wheelie bin being shunted down the back alley. *Definitely outside.* Bin Men.

She let out a noisy breath and flopped back on to the bed.

A few minutes later and she was on the phone to her landlord, who agreed to a new lock as long as Elly was the one footing the bill. The locksmith said he'd be there the next morning. That meant one more night, cowering under the duvet.

That evening after work, Elly opened the front door with coiling eels in her belly. *Had someone been back in the flat again?* She'd taken her diary and Pengy in his freezer bag to work that day, hidden them in a broom cupboard at the back of the shop and left them there when she'd come home. She couldn't risk keeping them in the flat - not until she'd had the new locks fitted.

The door opened with its usual stuttering creak, like a football rattle. The flat felt cold and echoey, as if no one had lived there for weeks. It didn't even feel like it belonged to her anymore. She checked every room. Nothing seemed out of place, but the idea of being on her own made her feel edgy and sick. She couldn't stay there. She went straight to the phone and rang Gillian.

'I can't tonight.'

'Oh,' said Elly. It was a tiny sound, plump with surprise.

'It's my Mum. She's not well. I'm going to stay with her.'

'I thought your parents were on holiday in Ipswich.'

There was an odd silence. The kind where, had they been face to face, eyes would have been averted.

'They are…they were…they had to come back.'

'How awful. Is it serious?'

'I don't know. Some kind of kidney thing.'

'Shouldn't she be in hospital?'

Another empty space.

'Yeah…she might have to be. Anyway, I'm seeing her tonight. I'm really sorry. You could always stay with Irene.'

Elly rang Flora.

'Of course you can, darlin' - get yuhself over here.'

A smell of ginger cake greeted her as Flora opened the door. The sisters sat either side of her on the sofa, plying her with a selection of goodies dripping in cream and honey, as she recounted the horrors of the past couple of days.

'And you told da police straight'way?' said Jamilla.

'Well - the break-in was very subtle - I didn't actually—'

'You *must* tell them,' said Jamilla.

Making a formal report felt like a waste of everybody's time. She was saving her big moment at the police station for when she got back from Portsmouth.

'What do you t'ink they were after?' asked Flora, pressing her fingertips into the scattering of crumbs on her plate.

'It's difficult to say,' she said.

It was only difficult to say, because Elly didn't know how much to tell them. Flora and Jamilla were adorable, but when they got hold of people's private details they often passed them around like bread at the Last Supper.

'Nothing of value has gone. The lock wasn't damaged. There was no mess.'

'Dreadful to-do,' said Flora. 'Another piece of cake?'

As the figures in some dance competition floated across the TV screen, Elly drifted in the opposite direction, away from the bright lights and applause into a fearful underworld inside her head. *Was someone after Pengy? Or her diary? The letters? Or something altogether different?* She shook her head in confusion, then quickly looked up to see if Flora or Jamilla had noticed. They were both engrossed in the programme, rooting for a boy who kept doing the splits.

Elly tried to work out who would know she kept a diary.

Gillian, Sam, her colleagues at the shop, Irene, Charlie, Flora and Jamilla.

More to the point, who would have reason to be concerned about what she'd written?

She was surprised to realise there was an accumulating list of people. Firstly, Sam, who had put rumours around that *he* dumped *her*, but more significantly, wouldn't want his wife to know he'd been unfaithful. Having details of the affair, with dates and places in Elly's diary, could be seen by him as a liability. Or by anyone else who wanted to make life unpleasant for him, for that matter.

Then there was Father Brian. He and Mrs Weedon made an unlikely couple, but she was involved too, skimming money from the church funds. Elly'd said that as long as it stopped, she wouldn't say anything. Would he be desperate enough to get his hands on her diary and remove all traces of his ungodly act? Unlikely. How would Father Brian even know she kept a diary?

Dr Bell. He had some unbecoming behaviour to be ashamed of and there was the stupid fling with Frank. He certainly wouldn't want that leaking out to Irene.

She returned to the other awful business from way back. Not only had she never told anyone she'd been raped, she'd never revealed what she'd seen that night. Never told anyone she had taken the letters. Never given away the 'big secret' - the *reason* for the rape, the brutal threat to keep her quiet. But it was all there in the pages of her diary. Did *he* know about it? LB92?

Flora started clapping and Elly realised the programme was over. It was only eight o'clock but she felt exhausted.

'We'll have supper in a jiffy,' said Flora.

'Supper?' *Hadn't they just eaten enough to keep them going for a month?*

'Oxtail stew 'n cabbage wid butter beans,' she said.

Elly managed to ease her lips into a smile and instinctively rubbed her stomach by way of apologising to it in advance.

chapter eighteen

Elly had a good excuse to leave early in the morning. What a shame she had to meet the locksmith, she said, as she zipped up her overnight bag. It meant she had to forgo the fried dumpling with salt fish and plantain fritter on offer for breakfast. Just the smell of it had sent her on her way.

One thing was for sure - Flora and Jamilla ate well. They might live on a run-down estate, but they weren't anywhere near the poverty line. Both of them had managed to work their way up to respectable jobs; Jamilla was a pensions' administrator and Flora was a manager in soft furnishings in a department store. They'd both gone beyond the expectations of their families, but always kept one foot firmly planted in their Jamaican roots, expressed in the food they ate, the clothes they wore, the dialect they used. Elly admired what they had done, how they had made something of themselves from humble beginnings. It was exactly what she intended to do.

By nine-thirty, a shiny new lock had been fitted to her front door, to British Standard 3621:2007, according to Mr Buckfast, who kept repeating it like a mantra, no doubt to justify the seventy-five pounds she'd had to pay for it. It should have put her mind at rest, but she wasn't convinced.

Elly walked to work, not in the usual unseeing blur of commuter sleepwalk, but with her head craning from side to side like a mobile camera, her eyes working fast, taking in all angles, spotting every movement. Her heart was a tight elastic coil, her brain cells on high-alert. When she arrived at the shop she felt like she'd crossed the Alps. Fear did that to you. It made small things seem insurmountable. Insignificant things seem suspicious.

She hid the two letters and DNA evidence she'd brought with her next to Pengy and the diary in the broom cupboard and spent the day looking over her shoulder. By five o'clock, she'd managed to persuade Bernie and Denise to walk her home. She wrapped all the items in a plastic carrier bag and pressed it to her chest under her coat, as her minders flanked her on either side. They stayed for fennel tea and by the time they'd left, Elly had come to a decision.

The four priceless items were going to have to live somewhere else from now on. Keeping them in the flat was too dangerous. Even with a new lock, her flat didn't feel safe anymore. *Would the intruder return to the scene of the crime? Why not? They presumably hadn't got what they wanted.* They could easily smash a window next time - and there were no good hiding places - no loft, no cellar - and she knew that carrying anything in her bag left her vulnerable on the street. Earthfoods itself, had been broken into a few times recently. That didn't feel safe enough, either.

The television was showing a rerun of *Antiques Roadshow* and Elly stopped and watched it for a moment. An expert with a white quiff and spotted dickie-bow was examining a small box with an intricate lid inlaid with pearl. Something about it looked vaguely familiar.

Ah-ha. *That would do nicely.*

From under the bed, Elly slid out a cardboard box; the storage space for items she'd never found proper homes for. At the bottom was a wooden box. Her grandmother had given it to her before she died; a pretty Armenian box with a mother-of-pearl design set into the top. She'd never found a use for it. She knew exactly what she had to do next. She blew off the dust and opened it. Two old three-penny stamps torn from envelopes fell out. Apart from those, it was empty.

She took her diary and held it over the box. Perfect fit. She squashed the letters into the bottom of the box first, tucked the diary on top, then added the bag containing her knickers, followed by the bag holding the penguin. The rosewood lid snapped over them with a satisfying clunk, like a coffin. It was as though that space was made for them. There was no key, but where it was going, no one was going to find it without a little help.

• • •

'What's with all this cloak and dagger stuff?' said Charlie, as he met her at the exit to Stockwell Tube station. Elly had the box in a rucksack strapped on her back, having walked swiftly along the most populated route to Brixton underground and fiercely held the bag close the rest of the way.

'Thanks for agreeing to meet me. It's probably better if I don't tell you,' she said. 'No one's hurt or in trouble - that's all you need to know.'

She'd decided there was no point in revealing her secret plans to Charlie. He wasn't the right person to hold on to the evidence for her; he was going blind, he'd never be able to read anything, apart from parts of disjointed sentences in Braille that wouldn't make sense.

'Fair enough - but you will tell me if you're in any trouble, won't you?'

'Of course. It's about Toby's disappearance… loose ends.'

He slapped his hands over his ears.

'Stop - I'm not supposed to know anything,' he said. 'Hear no evil, see no evil, speak no evil - is that the right order? Anyway, I'm a safe bet on the second one…'

Elly squeezed his hand and they started walking towards the church. 'How have things been going? Did you get to see the specialist?'

'Mr Sharp says I could lose eighty-five percent of my peripheral vision by the end of the year and I'll only be able to make out dim shapes in degrees of grey. I haven't been able to pick out colours for six months now.'

Elly couldn't imagine how terrifying it must be to have your entire world rapidly disintegrate into meaningless shadows. 'Shall I come to read to you again next Tuesday?'

'We could do some more Braille as well, if you like.'

'Grade two is useful,' she said. 'More like shorthand. Yeah - we'll do some of that, I'll read the paper and then we could take Peppy out.'

'He likes you.' He stared ahead of him, holding her arm, like a couple in love. 'I'm starting the training with a white stick next week and Mr Sharp is talking about some new GPS technology.'

Elly found an odd irony in Charlie's situation. There was a strange equation at work which would allow Charlie to see less of the world, but meant the world would see more of his misfortune. 'How do you feel about people knowing? It's always been…an issue for you.'

He clicked his tongue with resignation. 'I've got to face up to it, haven't I? If I keep hiding the fact that I'm nearly blind, I'll end up helpless.'

Elly was blinking back tears by the time the church came into view. Charlie showed a level of courage she knew she'd never find within herself.

'By the way,' she said. 'I won't be at mass on Sunday - I'm going to Portsmouth.'

'Sounds intriguing. Anyone special?'

'No, it's not like that. I'm hoping to come back with some good news about Toby, with any luck.' She grabbed his coat sleeve to prevent him going inside the gate. 'And I've decided to leave college. That business course is doing my head in and the tutor is a creep.' She pictured the draft 'goodbye' note she'd hastily written on her computer before she left. She'd add the finishing touches when she got back from Portsmouth and post it to Dr Bell straight away.

'Good for you. Take charge of your own destiny - that's what I say.'

They walked into the courtyard.

Elly had deliberately timed it to arrive early and only three members of the choir were waiting in the hall. She left Charlie with them and slipped away into the main church. Candles cast small ponds of glowing orange and the central gold candelabra sent out shards of white light, like a sparkler on bonfire night. It looked unreal, unwavering, as if it could never be extinguished, but left the corners gloomy and uninviting.

She needed somewhere safe to hide the Armenian box, somewhere no one knew existed and she'd already found the ideal place. It was ready waiting for her. It had been fun drawing the little map to hide in the locket and sticking the pencil rubbing to the back of the tiny portrait in Flora's dolls' house. It had been a game. She hadn't seriously thought she'd ever need to make use of it.

She'd only need two minutes and then she could turn up to choir practice as usual. Making sure she wasn't seen, Elly turned towards the back of the church and slipped into the flower room.

She followed the iron vent on the floor that ran over the central heating pipes to the point where it disappeared under a hefty cupboard at the far corner of the room. She pulled out the bottom drawer to reveal the continuing pattern of the iron grille underneath, with the replacement piece at the end. Shifting it aside she uncovered the concealed compartment: a tiny hidey-hole built into the floor. She'd discovered it months ago when she'd been helping to tidy the room.

She lowered the box down into the hole and put everything back in place.

That was it. Job done. All those years engrossed in Enid Blyton and Nancy Drew had stood her in good stead. She'd always enjoyed treasure hunts - she just hoped if anyone ever had to follow her clues, they'd be able to unravel them all. She'd have to hope she'd get enough warning to choose the right person, if she *was* indeed in danger. More so, she hoped it would never come to that.

She tucked the locket inside her blouse so it wasn't visible - it wouldn't be leaving her neck until she was back from Portsmouth - and left the flower room. As she crossed through the back of the church, she dragged her feet to muffle the sound of her heels that clopped like horseshoes on the stone floor.

She laughed silently at herself. *I'm going to far too much trouble here. I'll be back for the box myself, just as soon as I have that bit more evidence from Mandy.*

Choir practice dragged that evening. Mozart's Requiem sounded like a tuneless dirge; the notes were reduced to meaningless sticks bobbing up and down on the page like miniature puppets in front of her eyes. Elly found it hard to take her mind away from the box, hoping it was safe. Hoping no one had spotted her.

As they handed in their scores at the end, Gillian seemed in a rush to get away. Elly caught up with her in the corridor.

'How's your Mum?'

'She's…she's okay. Thanks.'

'She still at home?'

Gillian looked distracted, as if she was looking for someone.

'That's right. Yeah.'

Elly lowered her voice and was about to tell her about the box, but as she started to speak, she noticed

Gillian was taking tiny steps backwards, like a child retracting from an incoming tide.

'Sorry?' It appeared that Gillian hadn't been giving Elly her full attention.

'Are you still coming on Saturday? To Portsmouth to see Mandy? I was thinking of catching the ten o'clock train from Waterloo…'

'I forgot to say,' said Gillian. 'I can't after all. It's Mum. I'd better not. Sorry. I'm sure Mandy won't mind.'

Their conversation had brought out tiny salmon patches on Gillian's cheeks.

Elly had one final question. 'I know I asked you before, but can you remember who brought the blue penguin to the bring-and-buy stall.'

'That soft toy you bought?'

'Yes - it could be important.'

She was staring at Elly as if she'd asked whether she'd seen King Kong recently.

'Crikey - I'm not sure. Let me think. It turned up quite late, I remember that.' She shifted her weight to her other leg with a sigh. 'I think it was Steven Hawes…'

'You sure?'

'No - wait - the other one with dark hair. Lewis. Lewis Jackson.'

'Yeah?'

'I can't be certain, Elly,' she snapped. 'I've been worried about my Mum.'

Elly let her walk away. She'd noticed her friend becoming increasingly distant during the past few weeks. Was it simply because her mother was ill? Or had Elly done something to upset her? It felt like a crack in the earth that was growing into a chasm and the separate chunks of turf were sliding away from each other.

As she turned to go, Elly heard a scuffle behind her and spotted a shadow skulking on the outskirts of her vision. She turned her head and it darted out of sight, but not fast enough. Elly recognised the figure. It was Linda. She definitely hadn't been there a moment ago. Elly thought of going after her, but there was no point. What did it matter if Linda had overheard the conversation?

As she strolled out into the cool night air, her rucksack considerably lighter, she felt as if a more substantial weight had been lifted from her shoulders. All being well, she'd be back on Sunday evening to collect everything, ready to go straight to the police. By then, she was hoping Mandy would have identified Toby's abductor, or at least remembered some vital piece of information that they could report. As she passed through the gate, she made the sign of the crucifix with her fingers crossed. A double-whammy of hope.

chapter nineteen

It was blowing a bracing gale when Elly stepped out of the station at Portsmouth. The first thing she noticed was the clatter of ropes, as they batted against the masts in the harbour. The second was the impact of the sweeping expanse of water to her left and the majestic rigging of HMS Warrior, ahead of her. Behind her rose the white Spinnaker Tower; slim and elegant like a rocket about to launch.

The air smelt different; it wasn't just salty with seaweed, but seemed more expansive somehow, as though without London exhaust fumes, the air itself could breathe more fully.

Elly descended the steps, filling her lungs. Being here was already a success. It was a relief to get out of London; to escape the rut of domestic weekends, leave behind the trail of loss and uncertainty about Toby that had plagued her for months. She pulled the single sheet from her pocket and followed the map through the bus terminus around to the right. She crossed through an airy shopping centre and reached the quayside, edged with awnings, chairs, tables and parasols belonging to a row of newly-built restaurants.

It was like the Mediterranean; white powerboats carving feathery grooves into the sea, while people sat with their limbs outstretched, their faces tipped to the sun, sipping cocktails. She followed the line of the quay past more shops and exclusive flats, through the ferry terminal for the Isle of Wight and into the quarter marked Old Portsmouth.

Within meters, the lanes became narrow and cobbled, the flats became cottages leaning into each other, world-weary, holding each other up. Every lane led to the sea front, where Elly could see two pubs facing the harbour in an area signposted evocatively as Spice Island. She'd bring Mandy over later for a drink. It was a shame Gillian wasn't with them, but she was sure Mandy wouldn't take much persuading. If there was one memory that stuck in Elly's mind about Mandy, it was the alacrity with which she knocked back a pint of real ale. It belied the cute, sugar-coated image she associated with the rest of her demeanour.

As she approached the tiny cottage next door to a lone gift shop, she realised how little she knew about Gillian, never mind Mandy. Gillian was Elly's best friend, but she knew nothing of her family, her early life; their tacit agreement not to probe into 'family' territory was part of what had brought them together. They'd met when Elly joined the church and she'd instantly recognised in Gillian another lost lamb trying to fit in, trying to find her place. Gillian was a librarian and loved books, too. She understood Elly when she raved about some obscure literary writer and even passed on books that had been withdrawn from her branch library, when they weren't too battered.

In the early days, they'd both been overweight and frumpy with spots and low self-esteem and Elly felt an immediate kinship with her, more so than she'd ever felt with her own sister. They'd been on diets together, fitness campaigns, shopping sprees, goading each other with glamorous items that were entirely beyond their price range. Elly pictured her friend when they'd last spoken. Gillian had certainly moved on, probably more radically than she had. She'd lost over a stone, wore short skirts now, had a new air of confidence that still eluded Elly. She was chuffed for her, it wasn't a source of envy, although Gillian had certainly been acting strangely recently. Elly made a mental note to ask her about it when she got back.

Elly arrived at Mandy's cottage and rapped on the bronze knocker. Nothing happened. She rapped again and began to wonder if she'd come to the wrong house. There was a muted thud from inside and the door slid open a few inches. Mandy wasn't wearing what Elly had been expecting; instead she saw a dressing-gown wrapped around her shoulders and wrinkled pyjamas. A sheen of sweat on Mandy's skin caught the light and she squinted like she'd been sitting in a cupboard for hours.

'Didn't you get my message?' Mandy said, in a way that conveyed: *You shouldn't BE here.*

Mandy was holding on to the door as if without it, she'd crumple into a heap on the doormat. Elly barely recognised her at first. She could have been Mandy's older sister, or even her mother. Her (usually) perfectly plaited hair was tossed like coarse string over her shoulders.

'I'm so sorry,' said Elly. 'I didn't know. You got flu?'

Mandy stood where she was, lacking it seemed, any energy to take further action. Not even a nod. 'Let me make you a nice hot drink,' said Elly.

Those words were sufficient to swing it in Elly's favour. Mandy backed away and disappeared up the stairs on all fours without another word.

Elly stepped along the hall, which smelt of menthol and was overly warm. She bobbed under a low wooden beam and took a quick look in the two rooms on her right. Everything that involved fabric was decorated in a tiny 1970's Laura Ashley floral print. Elly remembered wearing a blue smock in a similar design when she was at infant school. Mandy must have got a job-lot; the curtains, sofa cover, blinds and cushion covers were all in the same pattern. It made the limited space seem all the more cramped. Even the carpet and wallpaper followed suit in a wash of yellow flowers. Every day, Mandy must feel like she was waking up in a meadow of wild buttercups.

Elly found the kitchen. It was odd poking around in a virtual stranger's home. She swung open cupboard doors and pulled out drawers in order to work her way into Mandy's domestic mindset. Nothing was where she expected it to be: mugs were under the sink, tea bags on the fridge, teaspoons not in a cutlery drawer, but standing on the window ledge in a cup. The sugar, milk and kettle were likewise each housed in the least obvious places.

Elly was considering whether a stranger would find her own kitchen equally maze-like, when she suddenly remembered her recent intruder. It sent a shudder across the back of her neck as if someone had brushed her skin with an ice-cube. The idea of leaving her flat unoccupied for two days suddenly felt irresponsible. She forced herself to whistle passages from Mozart's Requiem to block out menacing thoughts.

She found Mandy propped up against her pillows, gradually sliding down the lumpy slope. Elly plumped them up and offered her the mug.

'I think you've had a wasted journey,' whispered Mandy, as though Elly hadn't already worked that one out. 'I can barely breathe, let alone think.'

'It's okay,' said Elly, the reality of the disappointment settling on her like a heavy downpour.

The busy Laura Ashley pattern was prevalent, but more subdued, in the bedroom - but only because of the poor light.

Elly sat on the edge of the bed. 'How long have you been like this?' she asked, helping guide the tea to Mandy's crusty lips.

'Since yesterday. Ken's had it, but he's back at work today. I *did* phone you and left a message.'

Elly didn't know which number she'd used, but the call hadn't reached her. 'Can I get you anything else? A hot water-bottle? Glass of water?'

Mandy shook her head, then dropped it back on the pillow.

'I just need to sleep.'

'Right,' said Elly. 'That's fine. I'll go.'

'Listen,' Mandy said, her clammy hand grasping at Elly's. 'There's something you should know.'

'What?'

'She didn't want you to know…but I think…' Her voice tailed off and she closed her eyes.

'Who didn't want me to know. What are you talking about?' Elly watched Mandy's fluttering eyelids and wondered if she was being delirious.

'Gillian…she's been seeing Sam…'

'Sam?' Elly stood up straight.

'Braithwaite.'

'Yes - I know who Sam is.'

Elly reflected for a moment. It would explain why Gillian had been distant with her recently. She felt a wave of relief that this was all it was. 'She can have him. He's not my type. He's married, anyway.'

'Perhaps I shouldn't have told you.'

'No, it's fine, honestly. I'm glad you did.' Elly leant closer. 'Can I leave something with you?'

Mandy frowned. 'The pictures,' said Elly. 'I've got photos of all the regulars at the church and snaps of different parts of the church itself. I'm hoping something might jog your memory.' Mandy didn't respond. 'About the guy you saw…the day Toby…'

'The boy…' she said, as though muttering in her sleep.

'Yes, the boy.' Elly felt a band of sweat gather under her fringe and wondered if you could catch flu that quickly. 'You might remember something important. That's what I'm hoping. There's also a list of times and order of events the day Toby went missing - who did what. Please call me as soon as you're well enough to look at them. I'll leave my number again and my email address.' She tapped the carrier bag she'd left on the bedside table. 'It might mean us going to the police.'

Mandy stirred again, but neither opened her eyes nor said anything.

Elly raised her voice a notch.

'You must look at them as soon as you can.'

'Mmm…I know…I will,' she said, turning over. 'But I'm not sure I know anything.'

Elly scribbled a quick note to explain everything and left it on top of the bag. She stroked a strand of Mandy's hair away from her eyes and slipped away.

Elly walked towards the water and entered the pub on the corner, the frustration at her wasted trip oozing into her veins like the sea water-logging a small boat. She'd saved up her hard-earned wages for this and it was turning into a washout. She barely registered the sloping timber floorboards and collection of ship's lanterns brightening up the interior. She ordered a port and slumped by the window on a wooden bench.

It was starting to sink in how much she'd had pinned on this weekend. How she'd hoped Mandy would pore over the photographs and suddenly look up with a flash of recognition. How Mandy would press her finger into a face in one of the pictures and say: *That's him.*

Elly could only hope that once Mandy was less feverish she would take her time to examine the pictures, take it as seriously as Elly. The package she'd left beside Mandy's bed was like a lifeline to finding Toby, a trail of clues which once they had a few more pieces, would lead the police right to him, sitting on the floor in a warm house playing with a toy truck on the carpet.

She remembered the last time she'd seen Toby. They were in the church hall and he was showing her a new colouring book that Frank's mother had given him. It was just before mass that dreadful Sunday. He was wearing denim dungarees with a hammer embroidered on the front and a red anorak that made him look like Bob the Builder's right-hand man. He was sucking a juicy chew bar that disintegrated into long pink uncontrollable strings, creating a sticky mess on everything he touched; his sleeve, his pocket, the floor, his hair. Under his arm was Pengy.

Who were you waiting for by the bins in the courtyard, that day? Whose hand were you holding when you left the church hall?

She finished her drink and left to check into the B&B she'd booked. She'd phone Mandy in the morning to see if she was any better and in the meantime do some sightseeing. She wanted to see the Mary Rose. Hoped it would take her mind off her consuming disappointment.

As she wandered through the quiet back streets, she realised there was one positive side to her trip. She wasn't having to look over her shoulder every few steps. It was the closest she'd felt to freedom for as long as she could remember.

chapter twenty

Ken answered the phone.

'Mandy's not well enough to see anyone,' he said.

'Okay.' That was that. 'Sorry I bothered you.'

Elly closed her phone and finished packing up her overnight bag. She'd decided to catch an earlier train home. There didn't seem any point hanging around any longer and the sights of Portsmouth had lost their lustre under an all pervasive prickly blanket of despondency.

It was cooler and spitting with rain when she left the B&B. She'd managed to find the cheapest on offer and the threadbare carpets and bald candlewick bedspread had done nothing to challenge its one-star rating. Even the mattress felt damp. She was glad to be out of there, even though the weather seemed to have jumped a season overnight.

There were fewer people around the quayside today and those who were, scurried under cover and out of sight. There was no one enjoying a promenade or sipping drinks by the water. The Mediterranean magic had gone. It was like a different place altogether. Portsmouth had returned to being a dull city in a damp English autumn.

Remembering that when she got home a pile of laundry and last week's ironing awaited her, she treated herself to an early lunch. Delay the inevitable for another couple of hours. She found a wine bar on the way to the station and ordered the cheapest pizza, sitting by the window to get her final views of the sea. The water was grey today, like a man who yesterday had hired a smart dinner jacket, but today had reverted to his dirty raincoat.

Portsmouth Harbour station was busy when she arrived. Scrambling past crowds of young people leaving a trail of mud behind them, she managed to find a seat next to a window. As the train pulled out, Elly fumbled for her phone. After her disappointment, she wanted to hear a familiar voice; to tell Charlie or Flora that she was on her way home. She checked her overnight bag and all her pockets. *Damn.* She remembered now. She could see her mobile sitting on the bedside table in the B&B. *What an idiot.* She'd made the call to Ken and gone and left it there, in a daze.

She rolled up her coat and stood to put it on the overhead rack. As she turned, she caught sight of someone. A face that shouldn't have been there. Time got caught in a freeze-frame for a moment, then all the strength drained out of her legs. He was staring at her from the end of the carriage, a few feet away. She flinched as though she'd been slapped in the face. *What was he doing here?*

She dropped down into the seat, her knees giving way. By now her heart was stamping against her ribs, her blood hot inside her ears. *He's on the same train. How did he know I was here? Linda knew, Charlie knew, Gillian knew, Flora knew - if Flora knew, perhaps everyone did.*

She squeezed her knees, trying to work out what to do next, ducking down in the seat even though she knew he'd already spotted her. *What was he going to do?*

She didn't dare look up, didn't dare move. *Was he after the diary? The letters? The evidence? Did he think she'd found out more information from Mandy?*

In an instant she felt boxed in. Trapped. There were people everywhere. She couldn't get out. There was nowhere to run to, nowhere to hide.

All Elly could focus on was getting off the train, but as it pulled into Portsmouth and Southsea station, she didn't move. She clung to the seat as if afraid it might catapult her into the air. Right there by the window with all these people around her, surely she was safe. Hemmed in, but safe. He couldn't harm her if she stayed where she was. There were too many people about.

A woman took the seat next to her and Elly felt more cornered. *Did this woman know him? Had he sent her to grab her bag, hoping she'd have her diary with her?* She was starting to feel dizzy, starting to wonder if she was losing her mind. *Was she overreacting?* She was agitated, unable to sit still, wanting to know where he was and not wanting to know at the same time. She had to think. And she had to think quickly.

What am I going to do? She was picking at her nails, struggling not to burst into tears, struggling to hold herself together. She'd been strong so far. She'd been doing so well. Now this had tipped the balance. It was all starting to feel too much for her. Pengy, the break-in, Mandy letting her down - and now this. That old panicky feeling, the one she thought she'd shaken off for good, was starting to creep back. She had never felt so alone.

She checked her watch. The next stop was Winchester, but that would be ages. The woman beside her took out a book and started to read. Elly envied her. The bliss of being able to switch off and escape into a novel. *If only.*

The world passed by the window; fields, trees, farms, houses. A normal Sunday. Other people's normal Sunday. A life she could never have. Safe, free, ordinary. It wasn't fair. Her life wasn't like that. It was like being on a daredevil ride at the funfair that starts out exhilarating, then begins to churn your insides. Her mind was breaking up, careering off into places it hadn't been before, places it shouldn't go; sick thoughts, evil thoughts, deadly thoughts. She wanted to get off.

Her head was about to explode. She was having a panic attack. She forced herself to breathe deeply, trying to remember the yoga technique Gillian had taught her. *In for four, out for four. In for four, out for four. That's it.* She could feel herself shivering.

Let the bad thoughts go. Let everything slow down.

She could feel the velvety seat beneath her, stroked the glass beside her head. Cold, moist. This was real, not what was inside her head. *It's okay.* She was panting, shaking, but she was coming back. *In for four, out for four.*

You must think this through carefully.

He'd be expecting her to get off the train at Waterloo. He'd be waiting for her. He must think she'd got the diary with her. She'd have to do the unexpected and get off earlier, hide in the station and catch a later train home. In the meantime, just in case her plan went wrong, she'd have to make sure someone retrieved the box. Make sure that someone continued the campaign to find Toby and bring his abductor to justice. *Thank God she'd left all those clues! Perhaps she hadn't been so melodramatic after all.*

In for four, out for four.

She needed to move, stretch out - a boiling cauldron was about to explode in her chest. She left her seat to go to the toilet and calm herself down. She stood staring at her image in the mirror, breathing, grounding herself. The train rattled along at full speed; with it, time rattled along at full speed. They'd soon be at Winchester. By now, she was coated in a sticky layer of perspiration, so she spritzed a few sprays of perfume under her collar to freshen up. Then she took the locket from the chain around her neck and hid it in her hot hand, before returning to her seat.

Elly wasn't sure what to do next. It was only a few minutes until the next station and she wanted to get as far away from *him* as possible, as soon as she could. She was holding the locket so tightly that it was cutting into her skin. *Would the woman sitting next to her help?* She wasn't sure, but realised she didn't have the luxury of many other options. She couldn't even borrow the woman's phone, because she couldn't remember any of her friends' numbers.

Just as the thought entered her head, the woman's phone beeped and Elly overheard snippets of conversation. It sounded like she was a journalist. *A journalist. Had God sent this woman to save her?*

Elly bit the bullet and asked if the woman ever investigated unsolved crimes. She was getting frantic now. This woman *had* to be the one to help her.

The woman seemed pleasant, friendly, interested. She talked about writing for magazines, enjoying research; how she'd helped the police get people arrested. She sounded exactly like the kind of person Elly could trust. She had gentle eyes, the kind of eyes that had known loss. *She was the one. She had to be. There was no one else.*

Problem was she didn't have time to explain it all. The whole story was so complex – Toby, the rape, the letters, Pengy turning up – this woman would think she was off her trolley. Elly felt so distressed, she didn't know where or how to start and more to the point, she didn't have time; the train was beginning to slow down for Winchester.

Elly pretended to drop her bottle of perfume on the floor and as she was down there she quickly dropped the locket into the woman's open bag. Then she waited. Tried not to hold her breath. She was feeling calmer. The world was going back to the right speed again.

The train ground to a halt, but Elly knew it was too soon. She couldn't leave yet. She needed to find out where the journalist lived. She needed to be able to get in touch with her once she was safe. Asking for her address outright wouldn't work, especially when they'd barely spoken; she'd think she was a weirdo. She thought again. The woman was a journalist. Freelance by the sounds of it. Surely she'd have business cards with her, probably in her bag. It was worth a try. The train was on the move again; she had ten minutes before they'd arrive at the next station.

Elly bent down again under the pretext of picking up the magazine that had slid to the floor. As she was pretending to get hold of it, she put her hand inside the handbag again and felt around at the bottom for loose cards. Her fingers touched a sweet wrapper and what felt like a thicker card made of plastic. Then she found a thinner card and a pile underneath it, all the same size. She scooped one into her palm and hid it with the magazine as she straightened up. A furtive glance told her she'd got it right. Anna Rothman lived in Richmond. She had all the details.

As the train slowed down approaching Micheldever, Elly rose to leave.

Perhaps she had been overdramatic. Nothing was going to happen to her. Anna would hang on to her locket until she could claim it back, that's all. Anna wouldn't need to do anything more than that. It was all going to be a false alarm.

Anna backed up to let her out and as she did so, Elly sought out her eyes, taking her time, silently begging her to take care of what she'd left behind. Their eyes locked and the moment lasted an age; Anna holding her gaze with query and concern.

Elly turned away and geared herself up to make a dash for it. She watched the passenger in front of her press the *open* button and the door slid across. She jumped on to the platform and hurried towards the stairs. Rain was battering the roof above her. She kept her head down and didn't dare look round. If she was quick, she could be out of sight before the train left the station, invisible from any windows. *He* wouldn't know she'd gone.

As she reached the footbridge, she wished she'd spoken more directly to the woman on the train. *Why didn't I ask her for help, outright? Why did I leave the tiny locket in her bag that she probably won't find for weeks?* As soon as the questions became concrete in her mind, she knew why. Because it was a long and complicated story, because she was terrified and would have stammered and been incoherent, because then Anna would have thought she was gaga and dismissed her altogether. At least this way, if anything did go wrong, she'd have a chance of someone taking up her cause.

She'd got halfway across the bridge when she heard footsteps behind her. Slow and steady at first, then speeding up. Catching her. She didn't turn - instead, she quickened her steps. For what felt like an age there was no one but the two of them on the bridge. Micheldever was a one-horse town and hardly anyone had got off there. She held her bulky overnight bag tight to her chest and broke into a run, but the cumbersome weight of it held her back.

In a split second, he was beside her, making a grab for the bag. She couldn't look at his face. Couldn't bear to meet his eyes. He didn't say a word. She fought for a moment and then as he sharply wrenched it, she let it go. *Best to get away. As he's searching through it, I'll be long gone. Focus instead on getting back to London in one piece.*

She continued to run and assumed he must have dodged back the way he'd come. *Leave the bag. Let him go.* As she clattered down the wooden stairs, the idea of finding a police officer crossed her mind, but she cast it aside. She didn't want to be standing around, didn't want him to be watching, lying in wait, once she was on her own again. Once he'd discovered the diary wasn't there. It was too much of a risk. *Get out. Get away.*

Foolishly, although she'd taken the precaution of moving her valuables to her pockets, she'd left her return ticket in the bag. She'd have to buy another one when she caught the train back. Right now, her priority was escape. *Run. Hide.* Luckily, being a Sunday, the barriers were open at the exit, so she ran straight through and out into the forecourt. She felt like a terrified rabbit, desperately searching for a deep hole.

Rain was hammering down like tall strips of corrugated iron. Her umbrella had also been in the bag. Somewhere to stow away and stay dry - that's what she needed - before she headed back to the station for another London train. She looked both ways. Instinct took her right, towards the car-park.

There was a footpath at the end of it and she could see a small shopping mall and a pub further down, over the other side of the railway tracks. There must be a bridge or some other way of getting across. Still running, skidding on the slippery paving stones, she came to a gate and a gravel path. At this point she dared to look behind her, but saw only a boy coming towards her on a bicycle and behind him a young girl with her hood up, jogging.

Elly carried on trying not to slow down until she reached signs for a level-crossing. A minor road led off into the distance away from the line. She craned her head in that direction, but saw only hedges and surrounding fields. There wasn't enough cover for her to wait around without getting drenched or being seen, so she decided to cross the railway line - get to the shops on the other side. As she got closer to the crossing, bells began to ring, red lights started to flash and with a judder, the half-barrier slid down. She turned and saw the Waterloo train trundling in her direction through a misty curtain of rain.

For a single instant she considered making a run for it. She counted the rails. If she was fast enough, she could get across to the other side before the train got anywhere near her. But she had always been last off the mark in races at school. Knowing her luck, she'd slip in the rain, trip over the rail, end up…*No - that isn't an option.*

She sighed and stood her ground. A few cars had banked up at the crossing behind a chuntering tractor. It set a dog barking beside her. A few others were now waiting, most with umbrellas. Elly shifted her weight from one foot to the other, grateful for a chance to get her breath back. Rain was dripping down the back of her collar and her spectacles were spattered with drops blurring her vision. She gave them a quick wipe against her coat sleeve and checked the footpath again. He was nowhere in sight.

The train rumbled closer and closer, bearing down on the huddled group by the barriers.

All of a sudden, an excruciating pain shot through her right side. She looked down and saw what looked like a mobile phone pressed into her hip. For an instant, she tried to work out how such a thing could possibly be hurting her, before the extreme pain wiped all means of thinking out of her head.

It was as though a thousand volts were shooting through her body, making her muscles judder uncontrollably, rendering her totally helpless. She couldn't cry out, she couldn't work her limbs anymore. She tried to stagger, her body like a rag-doll, away from the source of the pain, stumbling, buckling over, heading nearer the red and white barrier. *Get away from the pain. Must get away.*

She felt herself reeling, not sure which way she needed to go. She couldn't get her bearings. Everything was going too fast for her. Everything was moving near, then far - up, then down. *Get away.* She managed to topple forward, seeing the red and white barrier in front of her, above her, now behind her, everywhere. And a dreadful noise like thunder swallowing her up.

She saw red flashing lights on black, shooting stars on black and then there was a terrific thud and she felt herself exploding into the air and falling at the same time.

There were orange fireworks on black.

Then there was just black.

Part Three

Anna

chapter twenty-one

Wednesday, October 20th

I went to choir practice that week as usual. Charlie had returned my call and suggested we talk after the rehearsal.

I was waiting for him by the side door, when Lewis entered ready to collect Linda.

'Good practice?' he said, swinging his bike helmet.

'We're getting there,' I said.

'Linda behaving herself?'

'Nothing smashed so far,' I said.

His smile faltered. 'Only a matter of time.'

We both watched as Linda practised a pirouette that keeled precariously to one side. 'Crikey, she'll be down in a minute.' He rushed through into the hall. 'Come on, trouble. Time to go,' he said, before the door swung shut.

Linda squealed, ran to him and jumped up, hooking her legs around his thighs. He swung her round as she leant back, completely trusting of his grip. They came out into the foyer together. 'Get your coat. We're off to McDonalds.'

Linda slid to the floor and leapt up and down, chanting, 'Big Mac, Big Mac...'

'She's got so much energy,' I said. As he moved closer, I could smell a mixture of warm leather, bike oil and shampoo. It was oddly comforting.

'*Too* much energy,' said Lewis. 'She's having some tests for ADHD. It could explain a few things.'

He turned to me as Linda ran to fetch her coat.

'How about that bike ride, then?'

'Oh…' I tried to act like I'd forgotten.

'This Saturday okay?'

'Well…' I pretended to scan through my catalogue of non-existent social engagements.

'Tell me where you live and I'll pick you up at eleven.'

'I don't have a helmet...or the right gear…'

'No problem.'

It was all agreed.

As soon as they left, Charlie emerged.

'I had no idea Elly was using Braille to keep a diary,' he said. His golden hair fishtailed in the breeze from the open door. He was using a white stick and walked tall and boldly with it.

'It's part handwritten, part in Braille - keeping everyone on their toes.'

We found a local wine bar. It wasn't ideal - the music was too loud - but at least we could find a corner and not be disturbed. We quickly got into a rhythm whereby I read out Elly's words and he filled in the sections in Braille. I wrote down Charlie's interpretations trying to keep track of where they fitted into each page. It made for a disjointed read, but it soon became clear why the soft toy had been included in Elly's box.

'Elly kept the toy for any possible DNA,' said Charlie, skimming his fingertips across the page. 'She suspected Lewis Jackson or Steven Hawes of being involved with Toby's abduction, because Gillian thought she saw one of them leave it at the bring-and-buy stall.'

I was startled by the sound of Lewis's name. He hadn't been mentioned in the pages I'd already looked at.

'But, there's no case for testing it,' I said. 'One of them could have picked it up from the pavement. It doesn't mean either of them took the boy.' In spite of my indignation, I was aware my palms were wet. 'What's your opinion of Lewis Jackson?'

'I've not spoken to him much, but everyone seems to like him,' he said. 'Sounds like Elly was just desperate to find the boy.' He took a sip of lemonade. A thought occurred to me.

'Does it say who LB92 is?'

'I came across that a few times, but she doesn't seem to explain who it is.'

'Did Elly ever mention it to you?'

He lowered his head, then shook it. 'Nope. Never heard of it until now.'

I had one final question. 'Did Elly say anything else, the last time you saw her? Did she seem suicidal?'

'Not at all. She was excited about going to Portsmouth. She let slip that she was hoping to find something new about Toby. It says here she was hoping Gillian's friend, Mandy, would remember something or recognise someone,' he said. 'I wonder if she found anything, before…you know…'

I squeezed his arm. We were at the end of the book and I realised there was nothing definitive I could take to the police, nothing anyone could use in court.

'Anything else?'

'I know she was fed up with her tutor at college and she was talking about leaving the course.' He sniffed. 'She was on the verge of making a fresh start.'

We were both still for a while. The world carried on spinning even though, like a child on a roundabout that's revolving too fast, Elly had been thrown off. Just when her life was beginning.

It was late, so I walked Charlie home and made my way back to Richmond.

• • •

Saturday was a dry day with copper-coloured leaves reluctantly drifting towards the ground in the faint breeze. Every so often, the sun slid out from behind a cluster of clouds and kissed the earth, creating shadows and definition, making the world deeper, bountiful, lush.

Lewis held out a pair of leather trousers and a jacket when I opened the front door. They were even my size. I hadn't been on a bike for years and the only person I'd ever ridden pillion with was my husband. It was strange putting my arms around this man I'd only just met. He was firm in everything he did, telling me where to hold around his stomach and giving me plenty of time to feel comfortable before he got the engine started. He had a way of making me feel safe as soon as he kick-started it.

But the photograph I'd found hadn't lied. I knew he had some connection with Jeff.

I'd checked it before Lewis arrived and although his dark hair was much longer, Lewis's features were unmistakable. Jeff was leaning against a tree in the middle of the shot, with a man called Pete Brooke on one side and Lewis on the other. It looked like they were in the middle of a park. Jeff had mentioned Pete and I'd once been introduced to him, but I'd never heard him talk about Lewis. I knew I would have remembered; he was too distinctive, even his name was out of the ordinary. When I'd checked the back of the photo for a date, my heart had tripped over itself. It had been taken only three days before Jeff died.

You don't need to travel far west of Richmond before you find yourself in rich countryside. We rode through Hampton Wick and Walton-on-Thames, then up through Windsor; pretty towns in the rich commuter belt with detached houses, bijou cottages and half-timbered pubs. We didn't stop. We got into the swing of the leans straight away, finding a natural rhythm like dancing our first waltz. Lewis took roads close to the Thames the rest of the way and we passed through Henley before coming to a halt in a pub car-park in a place on the river called Goring.

I pulled off the helmet and tossed out my hair. I was lost for words at first, still tingling with exhilaration from the ride.

'You okay?' he said, pocketing the keys.

I stuck my tongue out like a thirsty dog. 'Just brilliant!'

I followed him through to the back of the pub, which overlooked the water from an expansive veranda. There was a superior-looking blue and white boat moored to the left, with bunting and balloons indicating that a wedding was about to take place. A bridesmaid dressed in navy-blue scurried down the ramp and I noticed that most of the clientele around us wore Flora and Jamilla-style outfits complete with matching bags, hats and high heels.

'Someone's special day,' he said.

'It's been pretty special for me, so far,' I said. I hadn't realised how much I'd missed the intense thrill that riding at speed so close to the elements could give you. I'd also underestimated how breathtaking it would feel being so close to Lewis; smelling the rich body oils around his neck, pressing my chest into his back.

We had a ploughman's lunch and I was pleased to see Lewis drank soda and lime rather than alcohol. I watched the river make its way under the road bridge, mesmerised by the lull of it; steady, relentless. We chatted about the ride, the scenery, the bike. I wanted the day to take forever.

'I had a period in my life when I was terribly lonely,' he said, out of the blue.

I looked at him over my glass, supping juice through a straw.

'You'll probably think I'm impertinent,' he said, shifting in his seat. 'But I think I can see something of that in you.'

I pressed my lips together in a tight smile.

'Sorry,' he said. 'It's none of my business.'

'No - it's fine. You're right. Not many people see it.'

'Yet you're full of spirit and there's a sparkle about you, too.'

I felt my cheeks heat up.

'How did you cope with your loneliness?' I said, keen to shift the spotlight back onto him.

'I starting working with people who were worse off than me. Did some stints for the soup kitchens in Soho. Still do. It's a healthy reality check.'

'Is that why you brought me out?' Disappointment was ready to crush my hopes. 'You felt sorry for me?'

'Nothing so gallant, I'm afraid.' He gave me a broad grin. 'My motives were entirely selfish.'

I looked down and swished my straw around, trying to hide a flush of delight.

We talked more about his love of motorbikes. Like Jeff, he called them silver machines. I'd always loved that description. I looked thoughtfully into the distance as I tried to work out how to phrase my next question.

'Does the name Jeff Knowles ring a bell, by any chance?' I said.

'Jeff who?'

'Knowles.'

I scrutinised his face, waiting for signs of recognition.

He squinted into the sun. 'Don't think so,' he said. I saw his eyes were a deep velvet mahogany, like tunnels stretching into another world. 'Who is he?'

'He lived in Brixton - he used to have a bike, like yours. I thought maybe…'

'I don't know every guy who has a bike in Brixton,' he said, leaning back, giving me a sideways look.

He and Jeff must have only met in passing. After all, it was about two years ago. I thought again about the snap showing Lewis standing alongside Jeff. Just because you're in a picture with someone, it doesn't mean you know them. I could think of countless photographs where I'd featured with people I couldn't name or remember meeting.

'He used to ride in *The Brixton Bones.* It's a bikers' club.'

'Yeah. I've heard of it.' He sniffed. 'Not my scene.'

He got up to get more drinks. When he returned, he discretely changed the subject and he asked what I did for a living. I decided to play down my job.

'I'm a writer. Non-fiction. I've written a few health books.'

'You make a living from a few books?' His voice was gently teasing.

'Well, no, I also write features for women's magazines - dieting, lifestyle, you know the kind of thing.' I tried to keep it as vague as possible.

He nodded, flicking at the ice in his glass with the end of his straw. 'You haven't been on a bike for a while.'

'Not unless you count my pushbike,' I said, 'but I haven't even used that for ages. It needs a bit of an overhaul.'

'What's wrong with it?'

'Needs new brake pads, I think. It's sitting in the shed going rusty.'

'I'll have a look at it for you, if you like. If you want to get it up and running again.'

A bicycle didn't inject quite the same level of excitement as a motorbike, but I had fond memories of getting about on it in Brighton, before I'd moved. 'I keep meaning to get it fixed up, but there's no need for you—'

'I'll pop over with my van sometime. It shouldn't take long.'

We took a walk through the village and talked about his job, Linda, the church. I mentioned in passing that I knew Elly, but he didn't seem interested. He said he'd never met her. In fact, because he was only ever a taxi service for Linda, he said he barely knew anyone from St Stephen's.

It was late afternoon by the time he dropped me back at the flat. I invited him in for a hot drink, but he declined. He said he had to be somewhere. I decided it was gallant, although I couldn't help but feel something precious tear inside my chest at the let-down. I thanked him for the ride and gave him a peck on the cheek. He looked sheepish and waved as he got back on the bike, then rode away. I watched him disappear along the street.

Lewis did not know it, but he'd become a bridge between Jeff and me.

A white van pulled up just after eleven on Wednesday morning.

'I've got a day off,' he said, when he'd rung to arrange it. 'The bike should only take about forty-five minutes to fix up. You might as well come over too. We can go for lunch if you like.'

It was only five days since our bike ride. I'd expected to wait weeks before Lewis offered to look at the pushbike. I was surprised he'd even remembered at all. I accepted the lunch offer, hoping I didn't sound too eager. I hadn't felt giddy and tingly like this in a long while.

He opened the back doors to put the bike inside while I climbed into the front. As I stepped up, the strap of my bag looped around the sleeve of a jacket. It was a high-visibility jacket tucked behind the seat. I half dragged it out in an attempt to free the bag, making out the first two letters of the word *Police* written on the back. I didn't think anything of it and was shoving it back inside, when something sharp gripped my intestines. I could see a number in silver digits on the epaulette.

I pulled the sleeve a further two inches into the light as I heard Lewis slam the back door. *LB92.* It was the number I'd seen in Elly's diary.

Before I had chance to react, Lewis jumped into the front seat. He apologised for the state of his van. The passenger seat had a large rip across it with tufts of yellow horse-hair poking through, but I couldn't shift over to the next seat as that had been removed altogether, exposing the bare molding underneath. I was glad. It meant I could stay right next to the door.

There was a bad smell; a combination of damp, stale cigars and rotten cabbage. I was tempted to crack some quip about the van having being used in a recent bank heist, but I was too shaken.

'Sorry, the window doesn't shut,' he said, as I tried to use the flaccid winder. The draught blasting my face made me feel like I was hanging out of a helicopter. Under the circumstances it wasn't such a bad thing. I was having trouble keeping my breathing steady and the gushing air hid my heavy gasps. It also gave me a reason to be shivering.

My brain was refusing to join the dots, but what I'd seen meant Lewis must be Elly's rapist. *Maybe the jacket wasn't his. Maybe there was some mistake.* I wanted to ask about it, but knew the tremor in my voice would give me away. Besides, I was dreading the answer. If it wasn't what I wanted to hear - *decommissioned police gear they let me have - accidentally left behind by a colleague* – then I had the rest of the journey trapped with him. I found myself checking the road signs. My teeth started chattering. Maybe we weren't heading for the garage in Stockwell after all.

He asked what music I liked and all I could think of was, 'anything popular', so he put the radio on. I tried to fake looking relaxed, but it was coming across as restless. He kept looking across at me with a half-smile on his face like he knew something I didn't.

I'd intended to ask him about Toby, but it felt too dangerous. *Were you at the church that day? Was it you who had Toby's penguin?* Hardly safe ground under the circumstances.

We passed a sign for Stockwell and my heartbeat settled a notch. I didn't want to believe for one minute that Lewis was guilty of anything. Surely, LB92 wasn't him and Elly's furtive imagination had been working overtime when she connected him with Toby's abduction.

We arrived at a housing estate and drove round to a row of six garages at the base of a block of flats. I let out a lungful of air I'd been holding in for the last half-mile and hoped Lewis hadn't heard.

I tried to stop my hands shaking as I grabbed the handle and got out.

'It's my sister's garage,' he said, pointing halfway up the concrete high-rise to our right. 'She lives up there on the fifteenth floor.'

He swung the garage door overarm with a loud clang and wheeled the pushbike inside. The place was unexpectedly tidy with a yellow *Citroen 2CV* on bricks taking centre stage and the motorbike we'd ridden on Saturday near the wall.

Should I make my excuses and get out of there now I was free to make a run for it?

He bent down beside the pushbike and spun the pedals.

'Okay. New brake pads, tyres need pumping up, a good oil and clean up,' he said. 'Shouldn't take me long. Maggie knows you're here, by the way. She said she'd get a cuppa ready.' He straightened up. 'Fancy going up? It's flat number one-one-three in Trevellian Tower.' He pointed to the entrance. 'The lift's working.'

The relief I felt at being able to walk away was immense. On the way, I tried Stefan's number to tell him what I'd discovered, but I couldn't get a signal.

Maggie opened the door as though it was four in the morning. I couldn't see the colour of her eyes, because she didn't open them wide enough and her hair was in a rough ball over her head. She didn't seem capable of putting words together into a sentence, but led me through to the kitchen where she poured water into the kettle.

'Tea?' she mumbled.

'That would be great.'

'Sugar?'

'No, thanks.' I didn't intend to engage her in idle conversation. I was working out what I should do next.

She seemed to be having enough trouble holding herself up and keeping her dressing-gown closed. Under it, I caught glimpses of rolls of flesh in all the wrong places. It was tumbling over a babydoll nightie like sponge-mix oozing over the side of a cake tin. I remembered Mrs Weedon saying Linda's mother was an alcoholic. I hoped she was getting some professional help, for Linda's sake, but from this morning's performance, it didn't look like it.

'Do you have a phone?' I asked. Getting through to Stefan, or anyone in the outside world was starting to feel imperative.

'Only my mobile, but it's out of juice.'

I thought about feigning stomach cramps and asking her to tell Lewis I'd gone home, but I didn't want him racing after me offering to give me a lift. Until I could think of anything better, I was going to have to make the best of it.

I could see the whole tea-making operation was going to take some time.

'Is Linda here?' I asked, aware that she should now be back at school following her exclusion.

'Out,' she said. She pointed vaguely towards the window. 'Bike.'

Not back at school, then.

I took the two mugs from her. As I passed through the narrow hall, I nearly tripped over a pile of comics on the floor. They had dark, grisly covers.

'Linda's,' she said.

I read two of the titles: *Zombie Apocalypse* and *Porn-Powers and the Vampire Dungeon*. Mrs Weedon had been right. This didn't look like the kind of material a young girl should be looking at.

When I got back to the garage, Lewis had the chain off the bike and was fixing new brake pads. Everything appeared entirely above board. I watched him for a moment, his actions forming bundles of bulging muscle under his t-shirt as he worked. His short nearly-black hair was glossy and thick, like the fur of a bear. As he tightened a bolt he grunted and something raw and hungry enveloped my chest. I didn't want it to be him.

I strolled around the three sides of the interior to distract myself and look for anything unusual. Elly had, after all suspected Lewis of Toby's abduction, although obviously she didn't have much to go on. She'd been clutching at straws.

I didn't want or expect to find anything: Toby's glove? His shoe? His anorak? How likely was it that something so obvious would show up after all this time? But I wouldn't forgive myself if I didn't at least check. I wanted the place to be squeaky clean to set my mind at rest.

There was a bench on the right, with a collection of tools hanging above it: a hammer, wrench, spanners, screw-drivers. The usual. There were tins of oil, paint, plant pots and an old sewing machine on the bench itself. In the corner was a well-used wheelbarrow. There was a tall rubber plant beside it.

'What's that doing there?' I said.

'Maggie doesn't want it. She said it's too big for the flat; she keeps thinking someone is coming up behind her.'

'It'll die without light.'

He straightened up.

'You can have it if you like.'

It was an elegant plant and would have looked perfect in the corner of my sitting room.

'I'll think about it,' I said, tempted to smile.

As I pushed past the 2CV, I came across sacks of compost, a roll of carpet and an ancient cylinder mower that looked straight out of the eighteen-nineties.

'Is this yours?' I said.

He looked over and laughed.

'No. It's my Dad's. He wanted me to sharpen it, but he won't be using it again.'

'Oh?'

'He's in a hospice. Just last week. Linda's gutted about it. And Maggie.'

'I'm sorry,' I said.

As I squeezed past the car, I noticed a nail sticking out of the wall, with several keys hanging from it. Each one had a paper tag on a piece of string, like you find on an old suitcase. I leant closer. In faded script, I could make out *allotment shed* on one, *lock-up* on another and the third read *greenhouse.* On impulse I grabbed the first one and slipped it into my pocket. Wouldn't a shed on an allotment make a great place to hide a small child? It was worth a try. After all these months, I wasn't expecting to find him there, but it would have made a good temporary spot to hold him. He might have left something behind. There was nothing else to go on at the garage: no hiding places - no trunks or wardrobes. Nothing untoward.

I took the empty mugs back up to Maggie's flat. In the interim half an hour it looked like all she'd managed to do was smoke a cigarette. I put the mugs on the draining board.

'I'm very sorry to hear about your Dad,' I said.

'Hospice.'

'Yeah.'

'Cancer.'

'I'm sorry', I repeated. 'Did he live near here?'

'Brockwell Road,' she said.

'Lewis said there's an allotment.' I wasn't sure at that stage who it was who owned it, but the writing I'd seen on the tag looked like it was made with a fountain pen, in a fancy cursive script that few people would bother with these days.

'Pat's,' she said.

'Your father's?'

She nodded, examining her nails.

I wiped my hands on the grubby towel. 'Did your father use it much…in the last year or so?'

She didn't query my odd questions. I doubted whether she'd remember them in an hour's time.

'No. Cancer.'

'Do you go there much? Is it far?'

She shook her head with a vehemence that suggested I'd asked if she'd ever been to the opera. 'Brockwell Road.'

'Right.' I turned to go. 'Thanks for the tea.'

She shrugged and left me to see myself out.

'I'm nearly done,' Lewis said, when I got back to the garage. 'Then we can find somewhere for lunch.'

The gravel under my feet blurred for a second as I thought about having to get back into the van with him. I was standing in a trance, trying to figure out how I could get out of there, when my phone rang. I'd finally got a signal. Before I could speak, Caroline burst through.

'Listen…' She was out of breath, walking quickly. I could hear sirens in the background.

'What? What's happened?'

'Stefan's been arrested. He's at the police station on Cornwall Street. In Clapham.'

'Is he okay?'

I saw Lewis glance up in my direction.

'They won't tell me anything. I thought you should know.'

'Of course.' Thankfully, lunch was now out of the question. 'I'll be right there.'

Lewis was standing inside the garage holding my reconditioned bike, ready to present it to me. He saw my disturbed look.

'Trouble?' he said.

'I'm afraid so. I've got to go. A friend's been... taken to a police station.'

He raised an eyebrow. 'Which station?' he said, propping the bike against the wall.

I started to move away. 'I'll get a taxi.'

'Which station?' He was wiping his hands on a rag.

'Cornwall Street.'

'I'll drive you.' He was already locking the garage. 'It's five minutes from here.'

'Right…thanks.' I couldn't look at him. Just wanted it to be over with.

Lewis knew the area well and cut through the back streets. On the way over, I knew I had to steel myself and ask about the jacket. I had to know for sure. As soon as I saw signs for the police station ahead, I decided to risk it.

I pulled out the sleeve casually and waved it. 'Surplus stock?' I said. 'Or does this belong to you?'

'It's mine, alright,' he said. 'I keep meaning to get the zip fixed. They don't hand out replacements unless your original's in shreds.'

In an instant I felt car-sick and gripped the seat, praying we were nearly there.

He pulled up inches from the main entrance, where only official vehicles were allowed to park.

I got out of the van and ran straight into the police station.

chapter twenty-two

I yanked open the door, running blindly to get away from Lewis. I turned warily to see where he was. He'd started talking to a uniformed officer in the car-park and was leaning back, laughing. Caroline grabbed me in the corridor.

'Hey - not so fast,' she said. 'Stefan's been released.'

Caroline took my distress to be concern for Stefan and held my hand. He came out of a side door with a police officer and signed a form before they waved him away.

'Let's just get out of here,' I said, peering out towards the forecourt. The white van had gone.

'You look white as a sheet, Anna - what's going on?' said Stefan.

'I'm not sure,' I said, as we got outside. 'I need to ask you a favour.'

'Sure,' he said.

'Can you call Harry at the Met? I want to know which police officer is registered with the number LB92'

Stefan let out a loud *Oh-h-h.* 'It's a police identification number,' he said, hitting his forehead with the heel of his hand. 'Of course. All officers in uniform are supposed to wear one on their shoulders.'

'Will you do it?' I realised I was squeezing his wrist.

'Yes - what's the rush?'

'Sorry.' I stroked his sleeve. 'Are you okay?' I said, aware that I hadn't shown the least bit of interest in what had happened to him.

'Yeah - total misunderstanding at the Tube.' He flapped his hand about. 'Apparently, I'm the spitting image of a guy who's been regularly stealing mobile phones.'

We got to the main road. 'I'm heading home,' I said. 'Call me as soon as—'

'Sure. By the way, how was your date?'

I rolled my eyes and said I'd explain later. We were about to part when he stopped me. 'I've got those letters from Elly's box,' he said, holding them out. 'Sorry, I ran off with them.'

I put them in my bag. They weren't my top priority right now. In fact, I'd forgotten all about them. I left the two of them walking arm in arm towards a coffee shop.

I'd only just got home when the phone rang. It was Stefan. There was a self-satisfied loftiness in his voice.

'I've spoken to Harry and I've got something you'll be interested to hear.' I waited, my hands cold around the phone. 'LB refers to Brixton West. The two numbers, 92, means the guy is a sergeant. Harry checked the list.' He sounded triumphant. 'I know who LB92 is.'

'Lewis Jackson,' I said.

His voice was audibly deflated. 'You knew?' he said.

'He raped Elly,' I said, faltering.

'Listen - I've got to go,' he said. 'We've got tickets to a play at Leicester Square, but call me any time after that, if you need to.'

I went to the kitchen and wanted to stay there, pretend the box didn't exist. I felt sick. I wanted to rip the pages from the diary and drop them outside an open window. Watch them fall, like the autumn leaves. Watch them scatter and curl and fade away into nothing.

I opened a bottle of wine and poured a large glass.

How could he? How could Lewis do something so brutal, so abominable? We'd spent the day together on his bike. We'd talked. He'd seemed so…honourable. He'd said he'd never met Elly. *He'd lied. He was a monster.*

I shivered. A thought occurred to me. I went to my bedroom and pulled the box of photos out from under the bed and found the one I'd looked at before: with Jeff, Pete and Lewis. I stared at the snap, looking again at Lewis, then Jeff, back and forth between the two, trying to figure out if there was a connection between them, whether they knew each other. He'd lied about knowing Elly. *Had he also lied about knowing Jeff?*

It was only then that I looked closely at what Lewis was wearing. He had on leather biker's trousers and a blue t-shirt with a logo I couldn't read. I went to my sewing case to find my magnifying glass.

When I looked again, it was unmistakeable. *The Brixton Bones.* The name of the bikers' club Jeff belonged to. The one Lewis said he'd never been part of. Clear as day on Lewis's t-shirt.

Alarm bells were ringing furiously now inside my head. *Was there a link to Elly?* From the bottom of my bag, I dragged the two envelopes Stefan had given me that had been hidden inside Elly's secret box. I took out the first letter. It was obvious straightaway from the language that both sender and recipient were men. I read declarations of undying love, plans for erotic sexual encounters, promises of a future together. Then I opened the second one.

Tears flooded on to the page as soon as I looked at it. I didn't need names. I knew in an instant who had written it. I recognised Jeff's handwriting the moment I unfolded it.

I ran to the bathroom and heaved over the toilet, but nothing came up. I sat there on the floor clutching the bowl, my head so heavy I had to rest it on the seat.

Oh, God.

Jeff had a lover - just before he died. He'd never told me.

I tried to stand, but needed several attempts before my legs would hold my weight. I staggered back into the bedroom. I re-read the first letter: To 'Gladiator' from 'Fed'. I noticed at the end that it warned the reader to burn it as soon as it had been read. I couldn't help but smile. The other man didn't know Jeff as well as I did. Jeff would never have burnt something precious like this. He would have kept it, probably hidden it in the inside pocket of his jacket to hold it close to his heart.

What was Elly doing with these two letters?

I returned to the diary. I'd already read every word with Charlie's help, but I'd skimmed over sections to focus on references to Toby, because that's where I thought I'd find the answers. Now I was seeing it with fresh eyes. With an altogether new and horrifying significance. Another Pandora's box had opened up.

I found myself reading with one hand pressed over my mouth, forcing myself to take in every word. It was like being in a dentist's chair undergoing ghastly treatment, but knowing it was too late to make a run for it.

It started with an entry on February 2nd:

I thought I was doing a really good job of avoiding LB92 and then he caught me by the church hall on Sunday and pushed me against the wall. I think he's worried I'm going to say something. He saw me talking to Sam. I told him I'd keep his smutty little secret from two years ago, but I was really shaken. It brought it all back like it was yesterday. But he doesn't know I've still got the knickers with the DNA.

He doesn't know either, that I took those two letters from his hotel room that weekend we went to sing with the choir. Letters between 'Fed' and 'Gladiator' that make his situation clear as day. I've kept them just in case things get nasty again. A sort of insurance policy.

I remember his exact words after I'd seen him kiss the man that first evening near the hotel. It wasn't just a peck on the cheek, either. He confronted me and said, 'You didn't see that, you understand?' He grabbed me. 'I'm into girls, not guys, okay?' He said if word got out, he'd be finished as a copper. 'It happened to a guy I knew. He lost his promotion - ended up directing traffic. That's not going to happen to me, you understand?' Then he did it.

Suddenly it all started to make sense. Lewis was gay. Elly had seen Lewis in an amorous embrace with a man two years ago, when they went on a church trip. Lewis realised he'd been seen and threatened her, then raped her as a further threat to keep her quiet.

Two years ago. Bristol. Jeff.

Suddenly my head was spinning and I could barely see straight anymore.

No!

I checked the date on Jeff's letter to Lewis; it was dated two weeks before he died. Like a maniac, I started flicking through the pages of Elly's diary, not caring if they got ripped. Elly had made several references to 'that Friday in August when I saw him' and 'August 19th, two years ago'. It suddenly clicked. The day Jeff died. The truth slammed me in the face like the door of a vault.

Jeff and Lewis were together the weekend Jeff died.

I rested my head in my hands. *No, it can't be.*

All of a sudden a rush of questions came at me like trucks hurtling out of the fog on a busy motorway. *Was Jeff's death really suicide? Were they together on the bridge that night? Did Lewis play any part in it?*

I was starting to panic. It was all too much at once and my head hurt as I tried to get everything to fall into place. *Stay calm. Don't rush into anything.*

I stood up and paced around. What I'd discovered had thrown up a torrent of new questions, but was there any evidence? There was the DNA in the semen on Elly's knickers which would no doubt match Lewis Jackson's. It could prove that he raped Elly.

But what about Jeff? There was evidence, the letters, to prove that he and Lewis were lovers, but nothing to indicate Jeff's death wasn't suicide.

And Toby? Nothing. There was nothing to add to the accusations Elly already harboured about Lewis.

What do I do now?

I was desperate to speak to Stefan. He'd know what to do. He'd calm me down and be sensible, but he and Caroline were probably still in the second half of the play. Besides, although I was severely shaken up, the truth of the matter was there was no immediate danger, no immediate crisis. Elly was raped two years ago. Jeff had died later the same night. Another few hours wouldn't make any difference.

The pendulum had swung a hundred and eighty degrees since I'd first stepped on that fateful train to Waterloo. It had started with doubts over Elly's so-called suicide, moved on to Toby's disappearance, to Elly's rape and ended up with tormenting questions about Jeff's death. Jeff's life too. In a matter of a moments, I realised I hardly knew him at all.

I hung back from ringing Stefan until nearly 11pm, hoping that by then their evening would have long been past the point of being interrupted.

'You're up late,' he said, as cheery as ever.

'Did you have a good time with Caroline?'

'Absolutely.' There was a short hiatus. 'She's still here actually.'

I hesitated. 'I won't keep you.'

'It's okay - she's in the bathroom,' he said in a way which indicated he knew Caroline would be there for some time.

'I finished the diary and the letters…'

'And?'

I hadn't meant to dissolve into tears, but I felt my chin start to wobble and my voice begin to break. 'Are you okay? What is it, Anna?'

I gripped the phone, a single flimsy rope; all that was keeping me from tumbling into a deep abyss.

'It's opened up a massive can of worms…for me personally…about Jeff…my husband.'

'Jeff? I don't understand.'

I explained what I'd discovered. I was surprised Stefan could make out a word I was saying. My voice was croaking one moment, barely audible the next. In between, there were convulsive sobs.

I cleared my throat. 'It raises ghastly questions about how Jeff died. I was always convinced it was suicide.' I had to stop to blow my nose. 'Now I'm not sure at all. Lewis was with him that weekend.'

'This is incredible…' I heard his breath judder as though he'd sunk into a chair.

I told him how Jeff had told me he was gay two weeks before he went to Bristol. Now that Stefan had seen Jeff's letter, there was no point in trying to curb the truth.

'You think Lewis—'

'He made it clear to Elly he didn't want anyone to know he was gay. He told Jeff to burn their letters. Maybe Jeff was ready to come out and Lewis wasn't?'

'What about the suicide note?' he said. 'The one Jeff left?'

'Good point,' I said. I'd overlooked that. I knew it off by heart, of course, but it could be helpful to take another look at it in the light of what I now knew.

'Anna - you must be in a terrible state.'

His sympathy set me off again. I wept, unable to speak for a while, holding the phone against my chest. He waited. 'I knew you'd be the one person who would know what this felt like,' I mumbled. 'After what happened to your Mum...in Greece... when none of you knew how she'd died...'

'Too right. Accident one minute, suicide the next. I know a bit about how this feels.'

'I need to know the truth,' I said.

'I know you do - but you must be really careful.'

'I have to talk to Lewis.'

I heard his chair scrape as he stood up.

'No, Anna! You mustn't be alone with him. Look what he's done. I'll come with you.'

'Thanks - but I need to do this on my own. He doesn't know I know all this. He doesn't know I've got the letters - or the diary. I need to make the most of it - to get close and find out what I can.'

'I'm not happy about it - especially now we know what this man is capable of.'

'I'll be careful, okay?'

When he rang off, I went to my jewellery case and snatched Jeff's final note from its resting place. It was only a week since I'd last laid it on my pillow, stroked and kissed it.

My darling Anna

I need to let you move on. I don't know how to live like this anymore. Please forgive me. I'll always love you. Jeff. XXXX

Instantly, I knew something about it no longer felt right. It was like reading something translated into English where the true meaning of the original has been entirely lost.

Dr Katya Petrova had been wrong.

Your note wasn't a suicide note at all, was it, Jeff? I said, out loud. *You weren't saying goodbye to LIFE, were you?* I let the note fall to the floor. *You were saying goodbye to ME.* Heaving sobs violently engulfed my body.

It wasn't just me who was supposed to move on - it was YOU, too, wasn't it?

I was tempted to stamp on his words, but held myself back. I knew I'd regret it. I sank to the bed, clutching my chest. *We told each other everything. I was your soul-mate.* I pulled the pillow close and hugged it. *You were scared of telling your parents, ashamed of the half-life you were living. But you had missed out the vital part.* I found myself screaming the final words: *You were in love with LEWIS JACKSON.*

I got up. I sat down again. Flopped on to the pillow and buried my face in it. I went into the sitting room and grabbed the remains of the wine I'd opened. I glugged it down straight from the bottle.

I walked back and forth, going nowhere. I didn't know how to feel. Didn't know how to think anymore. My version of Jeff had been shattered, dropped from a great height. I didn't have a template in my life for how to react. Shock, anger, hurt - they were the same feelings as before, but now in the light of this blinding truth, they played in an altogether different key. They scraped the back of my throat like cuttlebone.

The motorcycle club - it was the one area of Jeff's life that I played no part in; the one loophole left open within which to betray me. And that was how I now felt. Betrayed.

I punched the pillow, howling like a lost dog.

How short-sighted I had been, how naïve. To think that Jeff and I could muddle along without his sexual needs being met. He'd known he was gay since he was fifteen. I should have realised that he would look for romance somewhere else. I'd been so stupid. Finding out he had a lover should *not* have come as a shock to me. But I was reeling with unbearable pain, nevertheless. I was exhausted by the time my tears ran dry.

I took my mind back to my bike ride with Lewis. It seemed a life-time ago. A shiver made my scalp prickle. Lewis Jackson was the person at the centre of everything. He had a lot to answer for.

He was the person I most needed to speak to.

chapter twenty-three

The doorbell woke me at 8.30am. It was the cavalry. Stefan went through to the kitchen and tipped a selection of warm fattening pastries from a paper bag onto a plate. Caroline had brought over a tin of my favourite hot-chocolate and started boiling milk. I was almost moved to tears. 'Thanks guys, I really appreciate this.' We joined together in a prolonged group hug.

'What are you going to do now?' said Stefan.

Before I faced Lewis, I needed breathing space to think carefully about how I was going to approach him. I didn't want to blunder in red-faced, beating my chest. I didn't want to mess it up - not when it meant finding the truth about Jeff.

'There's something I'd like to investigate.' I reached into my pocket. 'I've got this.'

I held it up tentatively, ready to be reprimanded. Instead, Stefan's eyes lit up. I explained that the rusty key dangling on the string belonged to Patrick Jackson, Lewis's father. That he had gone into a hospice and there was an abandoned allotment shed waiting for us to take a look. I even told him where it was.

'Good work, detective,' he said. He checked his watch. 'We could get over there now, if you like.'

After a quick breakfast, we headed over to Stockwell in Stefan's car. Caroline came too, refusing to be left behind.

Brockwell Road consisted of a row of terraced houses with a boarded-up shop on the corner. Few of the houses looked occupied, with large sheets of chipboard replacing most of the windows. I looked at the map and saw that it was about half a mile - only a ten minute walk - from St Stephen's church.

The allotment was at the end of the street, behind black railings and an old gate which leant against, rather than hung from, the gatepost. There was a padlock, but it was gaping open. Several figures were dotted about inside, tipping out mulch, emptying water-butts, cleaning tools, clearing leaves - the boring work as the season came to a close.

'Do we know which one it is?' said Caroline, staring at the selection of sheds dotted like identical beach-huts across the land.

I turned the tag over.

'It says nineteen on the back.'

There were no designated paths, so we followed the border of turf towards the first row of plots. There were two sheds and a plastic greenhouse ahead of us.

Stefan suggested we split up to cover more ground.

I took a right turn and walked past rows of tall canes, raised beds and hooped tunnels covered in white fleece. At the mid-point there were two sheds beside each other, one was unmarked, but once I'd got close enough I could see that the other had a wonky piece of wood nailed to the door that read: *Stanley*. I peered in the windows of both of them, just in case, but there was nothing unusual.

Caroline joined me at the next intersection.

'What exactly are we looking for?'

'The right shed for a start - and then anything to indicate a four-year-old boy might have been there. Maybe a large chest or cupboard where someone could have hidden him, or something he could have dropped, or signs of food...'

'Is it worth talking to the people here?'

'Only if we don't find Patrick's shed. I don't want what we're doing getting back to the wrong person.' I saw movement out of the corner of my eye. Stefan was waving, beckoning us over. 'He must have found it.'

The shed looked just like the others, a simple shack with a door at the front and one window at the side. The number nineteen was painted in green beside the padlock.

'Before we go in,' he said. 'I've just had a call.' He held up his mobile. He was red-faced and out of breath as if he'd been running. 'You're going to want to hear this.'

We stood in a cluster by a water-butt. 'Harry ran some checks on everyone we've come across so far,' he said. 'I owe that guy big time and he knows it.'

'And?' I said. I was ready to shake him if he didn't get on with it.

'And...one name came up with a red light. Falkney.'

I pulled at my lip. 'Falkney? How do I know that name? I know I've heard it.'

'It's Gillian. But it isn't her. It's Eric Falkney, her father.' He kicked at a stem of chickweed twisting up between the cracks of the paving stones. 'He was arrested, but never charged - get this - in relation to a kidnapping of a *five-year-old girl* in 1999. It was in Nottingham. The daughter of a rich banker. There was a ransom demand that time.'

'Bloody Nora,' I said. 'But this Falkney guy was cleared, you say?'

'Yep. But he later served a sentence for money laundering. That's how Gillian knows Steven Hawes – the guy you saw in that grotty pub in Stockwell. She was visiting her dad in prison and started becoming a regular visitor.'

I opened my mouth to say something and then stopped. My brain was running on too many tracks at once. 'So, where was this Eric Falkney guy the day Toby went missing?' I said. I had Stefan practically backed up against the shed by now.

'This is the interesting bit,' he said, enjoying drawing out the tale. 'Gillian's father had an alibi that Sunday morning.' He looked down and studied his nails. I gave his arm a rough shove. 'He said he was with Sam Braithwaite…'

I stared open-mouthed, taking it in. 'Sam! That's nice and cosy, isn't it? Do they know Sam's connection with Gillian?'

'They do now,' he said, tapping the side of his nose. 'It works both ways; sometimes the Met help me, other times I help the Met.'

Caroline let out a pained mewing sound, staring at us as though we'd launched into Japanese.

I stood in a stupor for a second. 'Hang on a minute…wasn't Sam on a police training course in St Albans, that day? Didn't he have an altogether different alibi?'

'He did, but…wait for it… he arrived late. Said his motorbike had broken down. Eric said he was with Sam in Stockwell between 9 and 10.15am, helping him fix the bike. Sam corroborated that story. Sam is a respected police officer. The police had no reason to doubt either of their statements.'

I sank against the water-butt almost knocking it over. 'Bloody hell…'

'The police are re-interviewing both of them, now they know that Sam is involved with Gillian. I think they'll be looking for evidence that Eric really was still with Sam when Toby went missing. If Sam took off for St Alban's around 10.30, or before, that would leave Eric on his tod, in Stockwell - right time, right place...'

'So, the man that Mandy saw *could* have been Eric...or even Sam?'

Stefan looked pleased with himself.

'Is someone going to tell me what this is all about?' Caroline said, helplessly. 'What connection does any of this have to do with that woman on the train?'

'I'm as lost as you are,' I said, struggling to think in a straight line.

'The police will take it from here,' said Stefan, confidently. 'Let's get on with our little job, here - and see if we can help them cut any corners.'

Suddenly, looking for Toby in Lewis Jackson's father's shed felt like we'd gone miles off piste. Surely, we weren't even on the right planet. I told Stefan as much.

'Let's finish the job,' said Stefan. 'We've got nothing to lose. You never know. Sam and Eric might just check out.'

'Yeah - and my great-grandmother was a maid to Queen Victoria,' I said, dangling the key in front of him.

'Was she?' said Caroline. I lifted one eyebrow and she backed up, handing the torch to Stefan.

There was only room for one of us at a time, so Caroline and I stood outside, trying to look like we belonged there, straightening the netting and pulling out a few weeds. Stefan emerged shortly after shaking his head.

'You take a look,' he said, handing over the torch.

It was musty inside and I heard the familiar scurry of mice as I moved some newspaper on the shelf to the left. It was dated October last year, five months before Toby went missing. I checked the floor, all the shelves, the drawers in the old Welsh dresser, but found only what you would expect to find: gardening tools, broken pots, plastic trays for seedlings. There was barely anything that was personal. No mugs, Wellington boots or even a fold-up chair. It didn't look like Patrick, or anyone else, had ever spent much time there.

I clipped the padlock shut and dropped the key inside my coat.

'I'll have to put it back,' I said, patting my pocket, as we made our way over to the car. 'I need a strong coffee.'

I'd almost forgotten it was choir practice on Wednesday. Even though my treasure hunt at the church was over, people there might continue to shed light on Elly and Toby, besides it was my sure-fire means of 'bumping' into Lewis.

I didn't know how I was going to feel seeing him again. I'd been presented with so many different versions of him recently: Lewis the charismatic copper, Lewis the rapist, Lewis the gay lover, Lewis the man who was with Jeff that final weekend. At least, if the new revelation about Eric or Sam followed through, Lewis wasn't an abductor.

The performance of Mozart's Requiem was coming up in two weeks' time and this was to be our last rehearsal at the church before we got together with the orchestra at Brixton Town Hall. In spite of the upheaval of the last few days, I was looking forward to our concert. I'd started to love the piece and was keen to hear how it sounded when we had a full orchestra backing us up. I was also desperate to take my mind off the tangle of *what ifs* snarled up inside my head.

In the break, I couldn't find Flora or Jamilla. Charlie came over to me. He was no longer wearing his bottle-thick glasses, which instantly raised his attractiveness to pin-up level.

'You look lost,' he said. 'I know that's ironic coming from me.' I put my hand on his arm.

'The sisters aren't here tonight,' I said, hoping he could enlighten me.

He screwed his nose up.

'Jamilla's in hospital, I'm afraid,' he said. 'Lewis took her in on Sunday night.'

My high spirits were flattened in an instant.

'Very bad?'

He shrugged. 'Flora thinks it's the beginning of the end,' he said, apologetically.

I had a flashback to Flora's stricken face when she'd broken down in the Ladies'. I pictured Jamilla's proud, defiant expression, her chubby little body, the way she was the quiet sister, but always ready to speak up for others. Charlie's exact words replayed through my mind.

'Lewis took her, you said?'

He nodded. 'The sisters live near Linda.'

I suddenly had visions of the two sisters being bundled into Lewis's insalubrious white van. 'Lewis didn't take them in his clapped out old banger, did he?'

Charlie laughed. 'No. Flora said they'd arrived in style. Lewis had slapped a blue light on the roof of his Ford Sierra apparently, and ripped through the traffic.'

I explained how I'd recently seen a car on bricks at the garage Lewis used, but that it was a 2CV, certainly not a Ford.

'That's his father's car. Lewis is supposed to be fixing it up for him, but I'm not sure Patrick's going to be driving anytime soon.'

'Yeah. I heard he'd gone into a hospice. His house is on Brockwell Road, I understand?'

'Yep. Standing empty now.'

Charlie pulled out a chair for me at a small round table. I watched Linda make a play to entertain a couple of teenage girls with her kung-fu kicks. One of them poked her in the ribs as she turned her back. In a flash, Linda spun round and grabbed the girl's hair. A scrap followed and in spite of their age difference, it was clear who was coming out on top. Linda landed a full-blown punch in the taller girl's face seconds before Rupert, the choral master, stepped between them.

'If you've got so much energy, you can help Mrs Landy with the washing up.'

Linda scowled at him and flounced away, while the other girl held her nose, trying to decide whether to be brave or burst into tears.

'Linda's getting out of hand these days,' I said, not sure how much of the scene Charlie had been able to make out.

'She's shaken up about Patrick,' he said. 'She's always been a bit wayward, though.'

'Has Patrick always kept his car at Maggie's garage?' I said, an idea playing on my mind.

'Don't think so. Pat has his own lock-up near his house. I think Lewis said he'd moved the Sierra over there a few weeks ago.'

'You seem to know the family well,' I said.

'I was giving Linda extra spelling lessons until my eyesight got so bad.'

I watched Linda again, this time trying to lift a girl the same height as her on to her shoulders.

An adult intervened before there were any broken bones. 'You can't remember where Pat's lock-up is, exactly, can you?'

He folded his arms in mock consternation.

'You're very interested in the Jacksons' cars all of a sudden.'

I hesitated. 'Just nosey.'

Even though it now looked like Eric or Sam were prime suspects, without a conclusive announcement from the police to say someone had been charged, it would do no harm to make some final checks of my own.

'I went there once with Linda to pick up some gravel,' he said. 'There's an allotment at the end of Brockwell Road…' I nodded, able to clearly picture the area. 'The lock-up is beyond it, first road on the right. Pat's is the first one under the arch of the railway viaduct.'

Rupert was calling us back to our places for the Agnus Dei.

After the rehearsal, I deliberately took my time, hoping that Lewis would arrive to collect Linda. I wanted to fix a private time when we could talk. I heard his voice as I was folding the last music stand.

'How's your friend?' he said, coming up behind me.

Lewis stood slightly too close, his rich brown eyes friendly and at the same time lacking warmth. Now I knew that Lewis had brutally abused Elly, being close to him had become something of a dilemma. It also made me question why he was bothering to spend time with me. It certainly couldn't be for any romantic interest, unless he was bi-sexual. It was like being forced to stand alongside a poisonous snake that's also beautiful and enchanting. Part of me wanted to back off, but I didn't want him to see me acting differently.

'He's not behind bars.' I forced the words out between gritted teeth. 'Thanks for taking me.'

He nodded. 'I'll bring your bike back on Sunday, if you like.'

I thought for a moment. If he did so, it left me with the problem of returning the key to Pat's shed, and although Eric Falkney, and possibly Sam, were now top of the list as likely suspects in Toby's disappearance, I still wanted to help myself to the key I remembered seeing to Pat's lock-up. It was still worth a check. More to the point, however, my need to find out what Lewis knew about Jeff's last hours was starting to feel like a lead weight inside my chest. I wanted some uninterrupted time alone with him, even though the thought of being around him, since Elly's revelations, made me decidedly queasy.

'No - I'll cycle back. I've got to start somewhere and I can always give up at Clapham Junction and hop on a train if my legs give out on me.'

'Okay.' He shrugged. 'We can go over on Sunday, after mass?'

I squeezed out a weak smile. 'If that's okay.'

• • •

The next few days dragged by. I wanted to press fast-forward and arrive at Sunday, reach that moment when I could finally get the chance to speak privately to Lewis about what happened in Bristol with Jeff. By Saturday evening, I was like a bull straining outside the ring, hoofing the sand, wanting to get it over with. Restless, pacing around the flat, I took off to Isleworth swimming pool to calm myself down or tire myself out, whichever came first.

The pool was quiet and I was able to swim thirty lengths without being impeded by the stray limbs of splashing children or teenagers showing off. I stopped to get my breath and hung on to the side, staring into the swirling blue water. All of a sudden I found myself seeing images of the broken fuzzy shapes of Jeff's stiff body in the pool. I saw his suede jacket and blue jeans refracted into triangles and squares as if I was looking through a kaleidoscope.

His dark blonde hair fanned out like wet silk. I took a deep breath and dunked my head under the surface to try to make the images go away, but when I opened my eyes underwater, I saw him again. I watched his fixed star shape turn with the movement of the ripples. I tried to remember which shirt he'd been wearing and whether I'd bought it for him. I wondered if when he fell from the bridge, his body floated or sank.

I watched bubbles explode in my face and all my movements became slow motion. I watched the colours of my flesh and my swimsuit smudge into indefinable blurs.

Had Lewis pushed him off the bridge? Had there been a waterlogged handprint stamped on the back of Jeff's jacket as Lewis sent him over the edge? Or had Jeff threatened to jump and had Lewis tried to stop him? Had their fingers been interlocked in a tight grip for a moment as Jeff hung precariously over the edge of the bridge, until the moment when his weight had become too much for Lewis - and he'd let go?

Or was Lewis nowhere near when Jeff jumped from the Clifton Bridge?

There were no more bubbles. My chest was tight. My eyes stung. I'd been down there too long and needed to get back up again. I kicked hard with my legs and broke the surface with a loud gasp, sucking in the air, tasting the chlorine, hearing the echoing shouts - back to life again.

It was quiet when we arrived at the garage on Sunday after mass. There were a few kids kicking a ball against a wall where the sign read: *No ball games*, but most people, it seemed, were either having Sunday lunch or hadn't yet got out of bed. I imagined Maggie would fall into the latter category.

Stefan knew where I was. He'd insisted on me texting him every fifteen minutes.

Lewis unlocked the door and heaved it over his head. As he wheeled the bike towards me, I took a few steps inside and feigned interest in the 2CV.

'A friend of mine had one of these,' I said, running my hand over the bonnet. 'It blew over once on the motorway.'

He laughed. 'People call them prams,' he said. 'This is my father's. It's barely road-worthy.'

'Certainly, looking like this,' I said, pointing to the missing wheels. I walked behind the car, pretending to take a good look at it, heading towards the nail in the wall. 'Can I have a look inside?'

'There's nothing in it,' he said, curiously.

I cupped my eyes and leant down beside the back window. As I did so, I contrived to knock a box of screws onto the floor close to the nail holding the keys.

'Damn. Sorry.'

I bent down beside the nail, making a grab for the tag marked *Lock-up* and hurriedly swapping it for the key I had in my pocket. Lewis was already picking up the scattered screws. I wasn't entirely convinced he hadn't seen me touching the keys, but he didn't react. He stayed beside me on the concrete floor until we'd collected them all.

As we straightened up I decided the moment had come.

'There's something I need to ask you about,' I said. I swallowed. My mouth felt like sandpaper.

'Fire away,' he said, squinting into the sun.

'It's…very personal.' I stood with my feet apart, willing myself to stay firm.

He looked down at his feet, then straight back into my eyes.

'Try me.'

'It's about—'

Before I could say more, a distraught figure appeared at the opening of the garage, flapping and shouting. It was Maggie. One slipper had fallen off and she was holding it in her hand like she was about to give it to someone. She didn't acknowledge me.

'Didn't you hear me?' she screamed.

'What's up this time?' said Lewis in a tired tone, his hands on his hips.

'I need an ambulance,' she cried, hitching up her dressing-gown and pointing to a thin trail of blood dribbling down her knee.

'What have you gone and done now?' he said, taking a step towards her.

'I broke a glass…and I knelt in it and…'

Her words were slurred. She was clearly drunk and could barely stand. Lewis knelt down in front of her, as she rested her arm on his back to keep her balance.

'Go back up and run some water on it. It's just a scratch.'

'But - I'm gonna need…'

'You need a plaster, that's all.'

He turned to me and made an embarrassed grunt.

'I'd better go,' I said. It was clear Maggie wasn't going anywhere without Lewis. I wheeled the bike outside and hopped onto the saddle.

'Sorry,' he said. Maggie stood watching me with her mouth open.

'Thanks again for fixing this,' I said.

As I rode away, I could feel my teeth grinding with frustration. I banged my fist down on the handlebar. *Bloody Maggie.* Just when I was about to get to the truth.

There was still one more place to check before I was done with being a detective. I used all my pent up adrenaline to pedal like a demon and within three minutes had passed the Brockwell allotment and reached the viaduct. It sliced the road in half and under the first archway was a lock-up just as Charlie had said. There were other garages beside it and a boarded-up pub on the corner. I could hear the trains thundering overhead; the arches shuddering as they passed over, shaking green-black gunge down the bricks in large drips. There was a burnt-out car tipped on its side in the corner of the cul-de-sac, with every window smashed. Needless to say, it was a badly rundown area. I shivered.

I took a look back the way I'd come. There was no one about. I rested the bike against the wall and pulled out the key. I wanted to get this over with as soon as possible. Take a look around like we did at the shed, looking for any possible signs of Toby and then get straight out of there.

There was a wooden double door with flaking layers of blue paint. The lock was jammed, but eventually the doors buckled in with a jolt. They swung back creaking like a falling tree. I flicked on my torch and slid inside.

It was bigger than the garage Lewis was using - presumably the reason he'd started using it for his Ford Sierra - but felt entirely different inside. The one at Maggie's place was lived-in, with homely touches, such as a radio and recent newspapers on the bench. Pat's lock-up had a stench of neglect about it, with stale air and cobwebs and a sense of desertion. Just like his allotment shed. All the items inside had a layer of dust over them like volcanic ash and none of the tools were without the crusty patina of brown rust.

a J Waines

There were blobs of oil and brick marks where a car had stood in the centre and the walls were littered with accumulated detritus gathered over the years: a bicycle with one wheel, an old washing tub with a wringer, a vacuum cleaner, broken rake, various household tools. The term lock-up brought to mind all manner of macabre images: chains on the walls and implements of torture, but this place was untidy, perhaps creepy, but remarkably ordinary.

I crept to the back, searching for any signs that a small boy had been there, but everything on the bench and on the floor was grey and tired, as though they had been untouched for years. I was only there out of respect for Elly: she was convinced Lewis was involved, but now we knew about Gillian's father, it was looking like Elly had got it entirely wrong and Lewis had nothing to do with Toby going missing. Part of me wanted it to be that way, even though I knew Lewis was guilty of at least one other disgusting crime.

There was a tall thin wardrobe and next to it, a trunk freezer with a padlock. It was the only object that looked like it belonged to the last twenty years, although it wasn't plugged in. I approached the wardrobe first and eased open the door. A musty waft of old clothes hit me, the dust making me cough. I rummaged through overcoats and jackets - men's clothes. There was nothing else. I turned to the freezer, feeling the weight of the heavy lock in my hand, knowing I didn't have the key.

It was then that I heard a shuffle behind me. At first I thought it might be a rat, but it was followed by a crisp footstep.

'Thought it might be you,' said the voice.

chapter twenty-four

I jumped. It was Lewis. He must have seen me take the key from the garage and followed me over here.

I turned, flattening myself against the wardrobe. He came a step closer. 'What's going on?' he said.

I dropped my head, unable to give any plausible answer. I should have planned for this moment; rehearsed an instant retort to account for my actions, but I wasn't sure I would have been able to come up with anything credible no matter how much thought I'd given it. I'd stolen a key and broken in. Simple as that.

He switched on the light. 'I could arrest you for this,' he said. 'It's called breaking and entering…not that there's much here for you to take.' He put his hands on his hips, a smile breaking out on his face. 'What are you doing?'

He looked around the place as though trying to work out what I wanted.

'I'm looking for something.'

'I can see that. What is it you're looking for?'

'I think you might know the answer to that question.'

He laughed. 'Believe me, I haven't a clue what you're after.'

'I think you should be looking closer to home, Lewis, if you want someone to arrest.'

He put his finger on his lip and tapped it. 'What are we talking about, here?'

I couldn't think fast enough. Couldn't concoct anything clever on the spur of the moment, so I resorted to the truth.

'Someone said they heard your motorbike at the church the day Toby Delaney went missing - you said you weren't there. Elly thought you were involved.'

'Elly?'

He stared at me.

'I knew her. Not well, but enough to know she was really scared…about…you.'

He nodded, leaning against the bench, rubbing his chin.

'Were you there?' I said. 'At the church, that morning? Did you come back for Toby?'

'It's none of your business.'

'It's certainly *your* business - if you hope to clear yourself as a suspect in an abduction.'

He shook his head. 'Clear myself? I hadn't realised I was about to be arrested' He still had a smile on his face. It was smug. I didn't like it.

Before I knew it, the words were out of my mouth.

'I know you raped Elly. I know why, Lewis. Or perhaps I should call you Fed.'

The words came tumbling out. I wanted to wipe the smile off his face. In a bid to score a few points, I'd probably put myself in considerable danger. I'd done it now, there was no going back.

He folded his arms fiddling with a wrench. I realised I should be sending a text to Stefan any minute now.

'What exactly is it you think you know?'

That was sufficient for me to pour the whole thing out. I told him that Jeff was my husband and that I knew Lewis had been with him the night he died. I told him about Elly's diary, the letters.

'I've been to a lot of trouble trying to get hold of those bloody letters,' he said, dusting down his sleeves.

'The problem is, Lewis, I always thought Jeff's death was suicide, but now I'm not so certain.' I took a step towards him, wary, my whole body shaking. 'Were you with him on the bridge that night? Did you push him?'

'Before we get into that, let me make one thing clear.' He looked serious for once. 'On Sunday, March 21st - at the time Toby was abducted, I was with someone. In Brighton. I was nowhere near the church.'

'Can you prove it?'

'I'm not sure I need to - certainly not to you.' There was a sharper tone to his voice now. I squeezed my eyes shut for a second willing myself to keep going.

'Did you have Toby's penguin.'

'Penguin?' He was scratching his head.

'Did you take a penguin soft toy to the church bring-and-buy sale?'

He looked genuinely confused. 'There was a blue penguin. It was in a batch of stuff Maggie - my sister - dug out in one of her annual clear-outs.' He bit his lip. 'I didn't know it was Toby's.'

I was thrown by his apparent sincerity, but he could have been well practised at faking it. After all, he'd lied to me before. I couldn't afford to let it distract me. Not now, when the bubble was about to burst.

'Open the freezer,' I said.

'I don't have the key.'

'Force it then. Or I'll call the police, right now.' I held up my phone, purposefully.

'And who are they going to believe? Little Miss Busy-Body or an officer of the law?'

I could see another reason now why Elly hadn't reported the rape. The odds were stacked against her. Just like they were stacked against me, right now.

'People know I'm here.' I looked down at my phone. 'If I don't ring at a certain time - they'll come looking for me.'

It sounded feeble, desperate, even though it was the truth.

'You probably won't get a signal in here,' he said, softly. 'Anyway, I'm not going to hurt you.'

I wondered if he'd said the same to Elly before he'd pushed her into some grubby corner somewhere and forced himself on her.

'Open up the freezer - then I'll leave.'

'Have it your way. It hasn't worked for years. I've got nothing to hide.'

Lewis took a crow bar from the wall and jammed it under the fastening. He gave it a sharp thrust and the padlock fell to the floor with a metallic thud. We both staggered back as if a bomb had gone off inside it.

It was the smell, the same kind of smell I remembered when I'd found a dead rabbit once in the neighbour's compost heap. Only richer, denser and a hundred times more pungent. The smell of rotting flesh. I put my hand over my mouth and stared as Lewis leant over the freezer and began cautiously unwrapping layers of polythene. I crept closer, finding the stench overpowering, but too impatient to see what was inside.

Lewis snapped his face away in disgust. 'What the f—'

He tried to drag me away, but I refused to move. I edged towards the freezer and looked inside. I saw a squashed up shape wrapped in a red jacket. The body of a small boy. His face wrapped in cling-film.

Seven months of decomposition had taken its toll. His skin was black and there were gaping holes where his eyes should have been. I turned around and instantly threw up. Lewis slammed the freezer shut and threw up, too.

In a panic, I turned and tried to run, but as I got to the exit another figure appeared, followed by several more, blocking my way. It was Linda, with a gang of her friends close behind her. They silently gathered inside the garage, eight of them altogether. Linda closed the doors behind them.

'Linda, sweetheart - you shouldn't be here - what's going on?'

She skipped towards us wearing a frilly skirt and jumper. Her knees were grey and her left sock had sunk to her ankles. Sticky pink patches glistened around her mouth and her hands were so grubby, she looked like she'd been cleaning out a hearth with her bare fingers. All the other kids were dressed in black zip-up hoodies. It was like Snow-not-so-White and the seven dwarves.

I had my phone in my hand, but I was too slow. A boy ran towards me and snatched it, completing a little circle back to his place like a trained dog. They all stood like sentries with their hands behind their backs. None of them could have been over the age of ten.

Linda broke the silence. 'You shouldn't have opened it.'

Her voice was petulant. She made it sound as though Lewis had unwrapped his Christmas gift before everyone was ready. Lewis walked towards her. I wasn't sure what he was going to do. Wasn't sure he knew either. Several boys closed in around him and he let his arms fall to the side and ground to a halt.

'What do you know about this, Linda?' He pointed to the freezer. I knew that abhorrent image of Toby would revisit me in my sleep for the rest of my life.

'I didn't mean to. It was for you. It was an accident. He cried too much, I had to make him stop. I came back and he wasn't breathing anymore.'

Lewis looked so stunned, he couldn't react. He staggered back against a stepladder, using it to prop himself up. I felt my jaw drop, trying to work out if I'd just heard what I thought I had.

'Oh, my God,' he said. It was as if the truth was only just sinking in. 'It was *you*!' he said. 'You took Toby from the church?' He rubbed his forehead in startled alarm, desperately trying to make two plus two come to anything but four.

'It was *for you*,' Linda said, again, thrusting her arms down at her sides.

He prodded his chest. 'It was for *me* - how could it possibly have been for *me*?' His voice was raspy as though he'd been lost in the desert for days.

'Because *you* were going to find him. Rescue him. Then you'd get your big promotion at work. You'd be our hero - everyone would love you for finding him. I was going to leave him in the park and you were going to find him. Just like the story in one of my comics.'

'Oh, Linda...' he buried his face in his hands. 'What the hell happened?'

'Just before the end of the kiddies group, I took him out to the toilet and we hid there for a bit. I said it was a game. After everyone had gone into church, I got him to hide behind the bins, make sure nobody saw him and if he did it right - he'd get jelly snakes as a treat.'

She pulled up her left sock, but it quickly slithered back down again.

'When we left the church, we went to get the sweeties, but Toby was whining, saying it was cold and he wanted to go home. So we went to the shopping centre - it was warmer there.'

Her voice had a proud singsong swing to it, like she'd been chosen to appear on Blue Peter. 'But he was still whingy and kept crying for his mummy, so I brought him here. But, he was crying so much - wailing, screaming - I had to make him quiet. I put the cling film around his mouth. It was just to shut him up when I went out to the corner shop on Brockwell Road to get him a chocolate milk.'

She leant on one leg, swinging from side to side. 'I only left him five minutes, but when I got back he wasn't breathing no more. He'd spoilt it. The plan wouldn't work. So I put him in the freezer. I got that bit from one of my comic books too.'

The gang was circling around us now, like some well-rehearsed tribal ritual. I caught the sight of glinting metal and realised some of them held knives. Linda was holding a mobile phone as though it was a weapon. They slowly herded us to the back of the garage like sheep.

'I only did it for YOU, Uncle Lewie - so you'd be happy. You would have saved him and got a medal. My hero.'

'You stupid girl.' We reached the back wall and Lewis sank to the floor in a crouch, emotionally winded, his head in his hands. One of the boys bent beside him and pulled the phone from Lewis's back pocket before he could respond. Lewis straightened up and turned to me, distraught. 'I had no idea - this is total madness.'

I believed him, but I was amazed at Lewis's lack of initiative: we were getting deeper and deeper into a precarious situation as we stood helpless in the shadows. The kids were armed and seemed to be under Linda's spell; they weren't about to offer us tea and biscuits. It must have been the shock. Lewis had just found out his beloved niece was a murderer.

My survival instinct forced me into action and I made a dash for the doors. As I shoved my way past Linda, she grabbed my arm and jabbed her mobile phone into my elbow. Her actions caused the most unexpected results. A scorching pain, like the slash of a blade, ran from my funny-bone to my neck. It was at once scalding hot and stone cold, numbing the muscles right throughout my body. I jack-knifed and unable to hold myself up, tumbled to the floor. Lewis was suddenly shaken out of his stupor and was at my side, pushing Linda away.

I managed to make my mouth form the words, 'The phone...'

'That's a *stun gun*!' he cried, his mouth frozen into a wide dentist's-chair gape.

I was doubled over with pain. I felt like a shark had torn off my arm. The muscles in my legs juddered and I flopped sideways into his grip. He tried to force me to stand, but having hoisted me halfway he could see my legs were like jelly. He let me slide gently to the floor. The place was spinning and for a moment I didn't know where I was. It was like falling out of bed during a dreadful nightmare, only the nightmare wasn't over.

'Where the hell did you get that?' he hissed.

'On the internet - I used Mum's credit card - it was easy,' she sounded pleased with herself. 'She never knows what I'm up to. You're the only one who cares. I got it before we went to Portsmouth.'

'Portsmouth?' I shook my head like a character in a cartoon who isn't sure if they've heard something correctly or not.

'Yes,' she said. 'We went to follow Elly.' She said it like it was part of a huge game.

I was gradually coming back to life. 'Lewis - were you and Linda on the same train as Elly, the day she died?'

'It's true,' he said. 'Linda and I went to Portsmouth. Linda heard Elly say she was going. Linda told me she'd seen a diary and there was a mention of letters. She remembered one of the names…we used - Gladiator. I wanted all record of…what happened two years ago destroyed.'

He looked ashamed, sorry even.

'So, it *was* you on the train. *You* who stole my bag, thinking Elly had passed the diary on to me?'

'I admit it.' He was hanging his head now, defeated. 'When Elly got off the train at Micheldever, I went after her and took her bag, but I didn't find the diary and then Elly slipped…'

'She was pushed!' I said, vehemently.

He tugged at his hair. 'All the evidence pointed to suicide.'

'Where were *you* when she fell under the train?'

He looked down at his shoes and I was convinced he was about to snap at me about it being none of my business again, but he appeared to be thinking.

'At the station looking for Linda,' he said, in a considered tone. 'I'd taken Elly's bag as she ran across the bridge, but by the time I'd checked it, Elly had gone. I went back to the platform and Linda wasn't where I'd left her.'

I took myself back to that Sunday afternoon. I knew the train had arrived at Micheldever at about 3.35pm. It waited in the station for a while and had then moved off, coming to that chilling halt at the level-crossing, putting Elly's time of death at about 3.55pm. 'You're saying you didn't follow Elly to the level-crossing?'

'Level-crossing? No! I was concerned about Linda. You know what she's like. She's curious, hyperactive. I was worried, even though it was only a few minutes. I could just imagine her doing something reckless, like clowning around too close to the track.'

He looked across at Linda who was practising a handstand against the wall. She kept stopping to turn and revel in her uncle's telling of the story, her cheeks enflamed like highly-polished apples. Her seven guards were waiting patiently for further instructions.

Suddenly his eyes lit up. 'I spoke to a station official. I asked him if he'd seen Linda. That would have been just before 4pm. I swear I wasn't anywhere near the level-crossing.'

'Just before 4pm?'

If he was right, he couldn't have got back from the level-crossing in time.

He couldn't have done it.

Linda suddenly spoke.

'You said you'd had enough of her.' She stamped her foot, pouting, sorry for herself. 'You said you wanted rid of her.' There was an ominous silence. The kind of silence where people look at each other with a frozen stare, because they know something terrible is coming next. 'You said, "why can't someone get rid of her?"' That's what you said. I thought I was *helping.*'

My mind took a strange detour at that moment. I went straight back to a high-school history class, where we'd learnt about the murder of Thomas Becket. I'd always remembered that one fateful statement made by Henry II, 'Will no one rid me of this turbulent priest?' - the apparent throwaway line that was taken by the King's knights to be a royal command and led to Becket's untimely death in Canterbury Cathedral. Here it was being replayed centuries later, with Linda.

'No!' Lewis's voice was strangled.

'I didn't push her,' she said, defiantly. 'I just used the stun-gun.' Linda held up the weapon disguised as a mobile phone. 'She did the rest herself.'

'No - you, you *killed* her,' I said. I staggered to my feet, still holding on to Lewis.

My throat was dry, tight, compressed: the words squeezed out like sharp chicken bones. I was trying to take in the fact that a nine-year-old child was responsible for the death of two people: first Toby, then Elly.

'She fell under the train. I didn't push her.'

'You *made* her fall,' I said. I pointed to the fake mobile in her hand. 'She was in pain and didn't know what she was doing. Just like when you used it on me now.'

'It's worse on the hip,' said Linda. 'I gave her about three seconds…I only gave you a little jab.' There was a touch of belligerence now. I felt a chill creep through my body even though I was no longer on the concrete floor.

One of the gang spoke. 'Come on - what's happening? We haven't got all day.' He was obviously keen to get back home to his chicken nuggets and the latest episode of Shaun the Sheep. The situation was ludicrous. I couldn't believe the two of us, both adults, one of us a police officer, were being held hostage by a bunch of kids. I was trying to work out what hold Linda had over them.

Lewis stood up and finally made an effort to take charge.

'Okay, guys. The fun is over. Let's all clear off home.' He moved towards the doors, but Linda nodded and three of the boys closed in on him. 'I don't want to have to hurt you, lads,' he said. 'But this is over, right now.'

Linda shouted something I couldn't make out and there was a noise like a cork-popping, then a hissing sound. A metal container rattled across the floor and then the light went out. The children ran for the doors, opening them a crack and squeezing through. Linda grabbed hold of Lewis.

'Come on, Uncle Lewie - this will get rid of all the en-vidence and everything will be alright.'

chapter twenty-five

There was a weird moment when I wanted the world to stop so I could correct Linda's pronunciation, but a dense fog was already descending on us. Shapes around me were fast disappearing into what felt like a vat of mushroom soup. It caught in my throat and had me struggling to breathe. I ran to where I remembered the doors had been, but they were shut fast.

I heard Lewis and Linda squabble behind me, as I kicked and thumped the wood as hard as I could. There was a scuffle and I was shoved out of the way. The door opened and I felt a brush of legs against me, then a flash of daylight splintered over me like an explosion. Before I could break free, the door slammed in my face and I was left trapped in the smoke. My eyes were burning and I could no longer keep them open. Streams of tears soaked my face and rivulets of mucus started running into my mouth.

I was not expecting what I heard next. It came from beside my left shoulder.

'It's tear gas.' I couldn't believe it. *Lewis was still inside.* He'd had the choice and he hadn't abandoned me. 'Cover your mouth - breathe under your jacket. Don't rub your eyes.'

We were both caught in an uncontrollable coughing fit, my throat and nose stinging savagely. I could barely gasp any air, spluttering like I was drowning. A wash of dizziness took hold of me. As I staggered around helplessly, the floor came to me meet me with a hard smack.

I was stunned for a moment, but then heard something that shook my body into a new level of terror. It was the crackling of flames. I felt a sudden surge of heat beside me. My eyes were locked shut and I couldn't force them open, but nevertheless, I could see flashes of orange dancing under my eyelids. The place was on fire. I couldn't remember having seen a fire extinguisher. I didn't know which way to crawl to get out.

I felt an arm on my shoulder. Lewis was trying to pull me to my feet. We fell into a contorted hug and he dragged me across the floor. Next thing I knew I was leaning against the front doors. They rattled with our weight.

He was pushing my mouth into the crack between the doors, trying to show me how to get breaths of air. I heard him strain against the doors, pushing hard, trying to force a gap. He was trying to say something between rasping coughs, through the thickness of his jacket.

'K-e-y…'

Yes! I still had the key in my pocket. I managed to pull it out and blindly pressed it into his palm. I could feel great billows of heat soaring behind us now, ready to swallow us up. I tried not to think about any stray cans of petrol that could be ignited any second.

Lewis began what felt like a brave but futile attempt to track down the keyhole. I could hear him stabbing at the door, feel the wood shaking. I knew we didn't have time. I held on to his legs, keeping my face pressed against the tiny sliver of daylight between the doors, coughing and spluttering the whole time. I didn't want to let go of him.

The darkness sank to a deeper black and I felt myself drifting, floating now, reality slipping away. I saw the faces of my parents; my impassive Mum I'd not seen in months, having chosen to move to Inverness, an arduous train journey away, with her sisters. Instead of her usual stern look, her face was soft and open, like it had been before the *shameful business*, as she called it, with Jeff.

There was my Dad, who'd passed away when I was twelve. Years ago, I'd lost the ability to see his face in my mind, but he was here now, as clear and three-dimensional as Lewis had been a few moments ago. He chuckled and reached out his hand and I could smell the pipe-smoke from his ready-rubbed tobacco. It occurred to me that I was about to join him.

Time and space became fluid entities that melted into each other. I no longer knew where I was. I no longer seemed to be anywhere. In spite of the searing heat, my entire body felt cold. Too cold. I could no longer feel Lewis's legs. Could no longer feel anything.

I must have crossed over to the other side.

I was calm. Safe. It was all over. I could go to sleep now. I was drifting for what felt like hours; a serene, quiet nothingness. I was letting go, slipping away. Soft voices, close by, then far away. Then no voices at all. Silence. Bliss.

Then unexpectedly, the darkness fell away into light. There was air, like someone had thrown open the windows on a summer's day. Hands under my arms, dragging me across the ground. Leave me be. Let me sleep. Rising up. Floating in the air. Someone flushing water into my eyes. People talking again. A familiar voice. *Is she breathing?* It doesn't matter anymore. Let me sleep.

Someone took hold of my hand. I thought it was my father at first, but the grip was too slight. *Everything's okay.* I know. Just let me sleep. *Keep her conscious.*

I was breathing again. Rasping, hoarse, coughing, choking. Hard to suck in the air, weight on my chest, too difficult. Can't I sleep? *Keep her conscious.*

'Anna? Can you open your eyes?'

I don't know. Too bright. Stinging ripping across my eyeballs, slicing them in half, like a razor blade.

Seen that somewhere, surreal film. I snapped my eyes shut again, still on fire, too loud. *We're losing her.* Very cold now. Too hard to breathe. Can I go home? Please let me sleep. Someone shook me gently, rocked my face from side to side.

I tried breathing again. Swoops of air. Fresh, wholesome. Burning my throat, hacking, spluttering, alive. Don't let go of me. I want to stay. I fluttered my eyes open again briefly and saw a fuzzy shape that looked like Stefan. *She's coming round again.* I tried again and saw him standing in front of the door of an ambulance. Movement, this time, and colours. A body on a stretcher was being lifted inside with a dark blanket over the top.

'Get the mask on - she's going to be okay.'

Not yet. Something important to say. Something to ask. Listen. I tried to dodge away from the plastic mask coming to send me away again. Stefan leant close, squeezing my hand. I opened my mouth.

'Lew-is?' My voice was unintelligible - nothing but a wispy croak. 'Is he..?'

'You're going to be alright,' said Stefan with a smile.

'No…I…' Everything slipped away again.

When I got home from the hospital, Stefan, Caroline and Squid were all waiting to give me a hero's welcome. Celebrating was the last thing on my mind. What I wanted most was to sink down in a darkened room with a vast, uninterrupted silence and sip warm water, but I forced myself to rally to their kindness.

'I've made some of Nancy's favourite fruit scones,' said Squid.

Stefan handed me a bottle of brandy.

'I brought a Lanson champagne,' said Caroline. 'It's better than Bollinger.' Bubbles were Caroline's answer to everything.

I laughed. It hurt. 'You've been brilliant - all of you.' I made them sit down. It crossed my mind, given their attention, that perhaps I'd had a closer brush with death than I realised. 'You might need to fill in some gaps for me. I think I wandered off for a while.'

'I can't believe you solved the case,' said Stefan. '*Both* of them, in fact - Elly and Toby.'

'You were semi-conscious for two days,' said Caroline. 'Your mother was here.'

Things must have been serious for my mother to make the trip down from Inverness on her own. I had patchy memories of her talking to me, leaning over me, her eyes locked in a point-blank stare.

'Is she still around?' I asked, trying to see if there was a small figure lurking behind the others.

'She left on the early train…as soon as she knew you were going to be fine,' said Caroline, without looking me in the eye.

I ran my fingers along the collar of the baggy shirt I'd been dressed in, remembering that I'd woken that morning to find a small gold Cartier brooch in the shape of an angel pinned to my hospital gown. It used to belong to my grandmother and I knew how highly my mother treasured it. I think it was the closest she could get to letting me know how terrified she'd been. My fingers found the little gold lump and I wondered if my mother had pinned it on before she left, or whether it had been someone else.

'Charlie left some flowers,' she said, carrying the vase of pink roses into my line of sight.

'Flora and Jamilla sent chocolates,' said Stefan.

'Look, stop treating me like an invalid.' I tried to sit up, but my arms felt like they were made of paper. I sank down again, pulling the blanket over me, my head spinning.

'The doctor said you'll feel weak for a while,' said Caroline.

'I don't think my voice will last much longer.' I whispered.

Caroline made a light supper of soup and dumplings, followed by chocolate blancmange and coerced me into eating a few spoonfuls. They were careful not to offer me anything with rough edges. It was as though they were exaggerating every ounce of normality and comfort they could muster, in order to smooth away the harsh reality of my ordeal. I loved them for that.

Later, they left me alone with Stefan so he could fill me in with what had happened. He sat in front of me on a little stool, so I didn't have to crane my neck to see him.

'When you didn't send another text and didn't return my calls, I came straight over to the lock-up,' he said. 'I saw the smoke and called 999. I tried to smash the door in, but I couldn't shift it...' He banged his fist on his knee. 'I ran for help, then the fire brigade arrived. They were there within minutes.'

I looked down at my torn nails, shredded and splintered, from fighting to get out of the lock-up. 'Lewis?' I didn't look up. 'Is he..?'

'He made it.'

I squeezed my eyes shut. 'I'm so glad.'

'He's got burns on his arms and hands and some minor complications with smoke inhalation like you, but he seems okay - physically.' He rested his hands on his thighs. 'Mentally, not so good. I went to see him in hospital.'

'He came good in the end. He tried his utmost to keep me alive.' I had to take a fresh breath between nearly every word.

'He told me about Linda, about the…freezer,' he said.

'It must be a huge story by now.' He nodded. I was glad Stefan would be heading up the scoop. He deserved it.

There were a few moments when all I could hear was my raspy breathing. It was like sitting next to someone who was dying.

You did brilliantly, Stefan. If you hadn't—'

'Yeah - well, we had a good contingency plan between us.'

My eyes were still stinging from the tear gas. My lungs felt like they were stuffed with hedgehogs.

'Besides, things took a new turn when you were in the lock-up. I had a message from my mate in the Met about Eric and Sam. Eric *had* been at the church that morning. He'd dropped by to see Gillian on the off-chance, but she was still in mass. It was him wearing the anorak, all right - the guy hanging around - the one Mandy remembered. He was looking in the hall where the kids were doing their drawings, to see if he could see his daughter. It was Sam's bike Mandy heard. He dropped Eric off at the church on his way up to St Albans.'

'Were the police about to arrest Eric, then, before the truth about Linda came out?'

'They went back to the CCTV footage and witness accounts at the time, but the timings were all wrong. Eric had left the church before 10.20. He was caught on a camera on Stockwell High Street. Toby

a J Waines

was still in the Children's Liturgy group at that time. Sam knew Eric was innocent, but given his dodgy past - he'd lied.' His face tightened into a pained expression. 'That's when I started to get worried about you - being with Lewis. You had a lucky escape, you know,' he said, leaning forward, a sudden catch in his throat. 'If there had been cans of petrol lying—'

'Don't.' I said. I hadn't yet been able to bring myself to fully process what I'd been through. To take in how far I'd travelled along the path that would have ultimately led me to a place where everything was finished, over. To a place that held my father. I knew I'd had a choice at some point during the fire; there had been a strange feeling of being carried into a hinterland, a waiting place, that was neither life, nor death. I'd had to decide whether to cross over or to come back, and I'd chosen to come back - to struggle and stay with life, but I didn't yet have the reserves to examine how close I had come to choosing the alternative.

'Lewis's alibi at Micheldever checked out,' he said. 'The station official logged his concern about Linda going missing at 3.55pm, that Sunday - Lewis said he'd told you. He couldn't have been at the level-crossing when Elly went under the train.'

'No. I know.' I thought for a moment. 'How did Linda get all the way along to the level-crossing in such a short space of time? I know it was only just outside the station, but I can't see how she did it?' It was hard to speak, but I wanted to fill in all the gaps.

'Knocked a kid off his bike and took off with it,' he said. 'Elly had run all the way from the station and your train had hung around a while before pulling out again.'

'Yeah, I remember that.' I could see pale images of the guy on the platform swinging his black and white lollipop as we waited at Micheldever station. 'But, Linda couldn't have known that the train would wait ten minutes at the station…' My brain was having trouble getting the pieces to slot together.

'Apparently, she carried the stun-gun with her all the time and was waiting for the right opportunity. It was all about *helping* Lewis. She knew Elly was trouble for him - she didn't quite know why - but she thought she was doing the right thing for him. When she saw Elly take off out of the station, she decided to go after her.'

'She was so young…I can't believe it.'

'Young, but cunning and street-wise.' He sniffed. 'Linda had been totally off the radar as far as the police were concerned.'

I pictured Linda - nine years old - her skirt flopping upside down over her chin as she practised another handstand. A double murderer. It was still too outrageous to take in.

'Did Linda confess everything to the police?' I said. He nodded. I responded with a coughing fit, which seemed to split my head open. He handed me some water, but I pointed instead to the bottle of brandy he'd left on the sideboard.

'The shit hit the fan in early September for Lewis.' Stefan passed me the glass and leant his elbows on his knees. 'Linda told Lewis that she'd seen Elly's diary at church and had read bits of it. She said she'd recognised Lewis's police ID number and read about Elly calling him a "bad man". She told him Elly had written that she'd had evidence, some "DTA", she called it and there was mention of some "secret" letters.' He raised his eyebrows. 'Lewis panicked and began his crusade to get hold of the incriminating material. Using a special police skeleton key, he broke into Elly's flat in Brixton.'

'And presumably it was Lewis who tried to get into my flat and scared me in the crypt…' My head split in two again as I spoke, but I couldn't stay quiet.

'The flat, yes - but it wasn't Lewis in the crypt,' said Stefan. 'We were right about there being various different people after the diary. That was Frank.'

'Frank?' I tried to sit up, but it was beyond me.

'I don't know all the details yet, but Irene mentioned to Frank that Elly kept a diary and he was terrified his wife would get her hands on it and discover their little fling. That's what he was looking for when he showed up at the Swifts' that day when you were there. He started getting desperate when he couldn't find it, but he knew you were involved. He'd seen you searching in the church. He took Irene home that Sunday and came back to take a look around.

'So - it was Frank that scared the life out of me in the crypt.'

In spite of the sedative, my brain was leaping around like a jack-in-the-box.

'We were right, too, about Father Brian being another one in the hunt for the diary,' said Stefan. 'Mrs Weedon overheard Linda saying that Elly kept a diary "with lots of dates about money going missing in the church". Mrs Weedon told Father Brian, so they were both on the lookout for it. Mrs Weedon had her suspicions about the flower room. She'd seen Elly creeping in and out a couple of times, but she hadn't found the little cubby hole under the floor.'

'What will happen to Lewis?'

'He's reconciled to whatever punishment is coming his way,' said Stefan. 'I think, to be honest, after what Linda's done he's pretty much lost the will to live.'

'Lewis may not be responsible for Elly's death, but there's still the fact that he raped her,' I said.

'We only have Elly's description in her diary to go on.'

'We've still got her underwear.'

I wondered if Elly would ever have reported the rape. Whether she'd want me to do so, on her behalf.

I flipped to the other side of the argument. How much punishment should Lewis suffer? How much punishment was justice? There was no doubt Lewis saved my life in the lock-up, but he had also committed a monstrous crime two years ago for which he'd never been punished. It was too much for my woolly head to get to grips with, right then. Besides, there was still one more piece of unfinished business between Lewis and me to be resolved, before I could make any decisions.

I needed to find out the truth about Jeff.

chapter twenty-six

He took a long time to answer the door, but I'd waited this long, another half-minute wasn't going to make any difference. Stefan had offered to come with me, but I wanted to face Lewis on my own.

His flat was in Brixton Water Lane and like mine, at the top of a Victorian house. My fists were clenched when he finally opened the door. On my way over I'd been determined to stick to my resolve, to probe and pry and ask every personal question I needed to without regard for his privacy. To speak my mind, have it out with him, no matter how painful it became.

As soon as I saw him, my hardheartedness melted. I could see the suffering following Linda's arrest getting the better of him. I could see the grief in the rings under his eyes. In the grey recesses of his sunken cheeks. I'd do what I had to do but there was no need to inflict any more wounds than necessary. The truth was all I needed.

Lewis was wearing an exact duplicate of the shirt he'd been wearing the day of the fire. It was disconcerting, as if he was trying to pretend it had never happened. I had thrown away all the clothes I was wearing that day, although everything I'd worn since seemed to carry a scorched smell inside the fibres. It felt like it was embedded into the folds of my skin. No amount of soap or shampoo would shift it. I'd considered getting all my hair cut off, but I knew it still wouldn't take away the charred smell.

Lewis took me through to the sitting room. He didn't offer me coffee. I was glad. I didn't want him trying to turn my visit into a social call. I sat on the sofa with my coat on.

'I went to visit Jeff's grave,' I said.

'How's it looking?'

'Someone had left fresh flowers for him.'

A hint of amusement touched the corners of his mouth, but he didn't meet my eye. It was two weeks after the blaze, but his hands were still bandaged. There was a crusty raw patch on his face, too, just under his left eye and clumps of his hair had gone, leaving grey gaps like irregular crop-circles.

I recognised the tall rubber plant from the garage and pointed to it.

'You rescued it,' I said.

'It needs a better pot.'

I cleared my throat. 'You remember the question I asked you?'

'Refresh my memory.'

I stared at him. 'Did you kill him?'

He lowered his head, shaking it slowly, but didn't say anything at first.

I waited.

'Jeff wanted us both to come out - and I was stalling,' he said. 'The timing wasn't right. I needed to get a promotion at work first.'

'How long had you been...seeing each other?'

'About ten months.'

I felt like someone had trodden on my wind-pipe. I'd known this was going to be painful. I'd braced myself as far as anyone could for hearing all the little stabbing details that I both did - and didn't - want to know. The reality of it still gave me a shock. With each discovery another piece of my marriage was being snapped off, ripping my heart apart, making it bruised and sore. This wasn't some passing whim. *For ten months, Jeff, you were seeing someone else.* The guy from the motorbike club.

'What happened?'

He could see my hands were shaking. I didn't hide them. I wasn't ashamed of my trepidation.

'Maggie, my sister, was a regular at the church back then. She wanted to go on the choir trip to Bristol. Father Brian's brother is the Bishop of Clifton and there was going to be a big performance at Clifton cathedral of some requiem or other. I went along for the ride. Jeff and I arranged to spend the weekend together.'

He blinked rapidly as if he'd got something in his eye. He certainly couldn't use his bandaged fingers to rub it; they were the size of fat cigars and about as flexible.

'Are your burns bad?' I said.

'They're healing.' He glanced down at his hands like they were the least of his worries. 'Elly saw Jeff and I…in a compromising embrace earlier that first evening, the Friday, the night it happened. I followed her and…well, you know what happened. I was terrified she'd say something.' I brushed over the rape. There would be chance to address that at a later stage. 'I don't know how she got hold of the letters - I only found out about those recently.'

I didn't want to get sidetracked. 'What about Jeff?'

'We met again before midnight at the Clifton Bridge for a walk. We argued. There were tears. I pleaded with him not to break our secret until I was ready. It would have ruined my career, I know it would.'

Lewis's knee had been bouncing up and down the whole time. I'd never noticed him do that before. He stumbled through the sequence of events, not sparing me the details, respectful enough to know I wouldn't want to be shielded from the harsh reality. I admired him for that.

'What did Jeff say? Can you remember?'

'Every word. It's bleached into my memory. He said I didn't love him enough, that I'd never be ready.

He thought I was fobbing him off. He also said he loved his wife and that he'd left you a note saying he was letting you get on with your life. He was berating himself, saying leaving the note was cowardly. He didn't want to hurt you, I could see that.'

I looked away, droplets burning the corners of my eyes. The room went blurred, as though I was underwater. Jeff had thought about me. He really had loved me in his own way. I put my hand over my mouth as if to prevent my distress from flooding the room.

Lewis pulled a handkerchief from his pocket and handed it to me.

'It's clean,' he said.

I blew into it noisily and scrunched it into my fist.

'And you were on the bridge at that point?'

'Yeah. Jeff had been drinking - he was upset. He said if we didn't come out after that weekend, then it was all over.' Large tears flopped from Lewis's chin onto his bandages. 'He climbed on the railings. There are reinforced barriers, but he managed to get over them. He was making an idle threat about jumping to show me how much I was hurting him. He stood right on the rail, it was only about three inches wide. There were lights up there, but it was still too dark to see properly. Jeff said he was going to try a back flip - he didn't, of course. I'm not good with heights, but I tried to climb after him.' His voice dropped to a whisper. 'I thought I had everything under control.' He hugged his knees, burying his face. 'I *didn't.*'

I hung onto the edge of the seat, holding my breath.

'Jeff got fed up after a while. Said he was cold and wanted another drink. Said he'd get down on his own.' Lewis stopped and pressed his hand against his chest, as though unsure where his next breath was going to come from. 'He came towards me and that was it. He lost his balance. He stretched out his hand to me and just fell backwards. He didn't even call out. He just looked surprised.'

My mouth was dry and I could feel my heartbeat thundering in my mouth, my head, my chest - everywhere.

'I didn't push him. I can't prove it, but I didn't push him.'

He held his head in his bulky hands.

'Didn't you go down and find him? Didn't you check...'

'I could see...once he'd hit the water...'

'But you said it was dark. You didn't run after him?' My questions came tumbling out one after the other, like a row of toppling dominoes.

'You can't scramble down the bank on foot. It's a sheer drop.'

'He could have been unconscious...'

Lewis shook his head. 'I saw him hit the water...'

'How can you be absolutely sure?'

'Okay.' His jaw jutted forward like he was about to face the enemy. 'When a body falls from that kind of height, it goes from roughly seventy-five miles an hour to nearly zero in a split second. The force of impact causes the internal organs to tear loose. People break their necks, skulls, ribs, their heart gets punctured.'

My eyes were wide in horror.

'The only way he could possibly have survived is if he'd fallen feet first, and believe me - he didn't. If the fall didn't kill him, then he would have drowned straight away. When you hit cold water the instinct is to take a deep breath.' The room went still and silent as though all the air had been sucked out of it. 'He was dead, Anna.'

'Shit…' My head fell into my hands and everything was wet. I sobbed uncontrollably, finding it hard with my lungs still sore, to take in enough air. I coughed, spluttered, gasped, like I too was drowning. Lewis shuffled over to me and rubbed my back with his oversized hand. I could see that it was painful for him to touch me, but he carried on and I let him.

'But you knew for certain…it wasn't suicide.'

'Yes. Absolutely.'

'Didn't anyone else see what happened?'

'There was a security guy, but he was distracted by an incident at the other end of the bridge.'

'No one else?'

'The local cops turned up, of course. But, I'd gone by then.' He straightened up, pain forcing his eyes shut. 'There was CCTV footage, but I was never identified. On film, it must have looked like a straightforward case of suicide. The coroner's verdict was never questioned.'

I had to swallow hard to keep my rising nausea at bay.

'I loved him,' he said, so quietly I didn't see his lips move.

A strain of awkwardness shot through the room, but quickly dispersed. A smothering sadness took its place. We weren't adversaries. No one was the winner here.

I didn't look up. 'So did I.'

Nothing happened. I was aware of a lot of noise going on inside my head, but around me there was a protracted silence. Lewis could have left the room by now for all I knew.

'I didn't push him,' came his voice, faint, but unwavering.

As my brain tried to assimilate what all of this meant, I realised the noise I could hear was my own panting, like an animal who has been chased in a hunt and has finally shaken off its assailant. I knew deep down in my gut that Lewis was telling the truth. Jeff had died, not by suicide as I'd always thought, but by accident.

I rested my forehead in my hand and thought for a while about what difference it made. It didn't take me long to know it was considerable.

'Thank you…for telling me.'

'Elly always said God would see fit to punish me for what I did to her,' he said. 'I lost Jeff and thought that was the price I had to pay. I didn't know there'd be more. The business with Linda. That was all my fault.'

'I don't think you can take the blame for what Linda did. Nor Jeff, for that matter.'

'They were both trying to prove something to me, trying to win my love - in the most insane fashion.' He shook his head. 'How could I let it happen…twice? I should have seen it. Stopped it.'

'You can't get inside other people's heads, Lewis. You weren't to know.'

Thinking back to the fire, I couldn't believe, given the bond they had, that Linda had left Lewis in the lock-up with the whole place about to explode. She'd left him to die. The one and only person in the world she had rooting for her. She'd abandoned him. That realisation could hardly have escaped him. I didn't want to rub salt in his wounds by drawing attention to it, but I did still have unanswered questions.

'You could have got out - of the lock-up,' I said. 'It could have ended with the fire. With me out of the picture, no one else would have gone any further with Elly's campaign. Stefan didn't know the full truth.'

'Linda tried to pull me outside, but it had gone far enough,' he said, simply. 'She knew I couldn't let her get away with it. In that instant, I became the enemy. Besides, dental records would have pulled up both you and Toby.'

I was about to say *thank you* for his part in the rescue, but it seemed a stupid statement to make at that moment. Maybe there would be another time.

'How come Linda had so much hold over her little gang? They seemed entranced by her.'

'Money. Isn't it always? She borrowed Maggie's credit card and bought their loyalty with a string of weekly "rewards".' He rubbed his eyes. Sleep was something he hadn't been acquainted with recently. 'Plus she's smart - a risk-taker - other kids admire that, don't they?'

'What will happen to her?'

'She caused the deaths of two people. Toby's wasn't exactly intentional, but Elly's was. And she attempted to kill the two of us...' He waved his arm vaguely. 'Even now, she can barely see that she's responsible. What kind of a mess must she be in?'

'No one saw it.'

He gritted his teeth. '*I* should have done. She was desperate to gain my approval. I should have seen it.'

'She'll get the treatment she needs.'

'Yeah.' He dropped his shoulders. 'Some appalling secure unit…'

There was a long silence. It was time to go. 'Just one more thing,' I said. 'Why did you take me for a bike ride? Why were you so…nice to me?'

He stretched out his legs. 'I felt bad, after the incident with your bag at Micheldever. I hated scaring you, but I could see no other way.' His head sank. 'I had some making up to do.' He cleared his throat. 'And, I liked you. After you mentioned Jeff, I checked the police records and realised exactly who you were. I can see what Jeff saw in you.'

I didn't know what to say. He sensed my awkwardness and stood up. 'By the way…I've resigned from the force.' It wasn't a surprise. I'd presumed it was only a matter of time. 'I thought I'd get in first before my boss politely suggested it. Business as usual is difficult when everyone knows you've got a murderer in the family.'

And you're a criminal yourself, I wanted to add. But didn't.

He looked up, making eye contact properly for the first time and gave me a weak smile.

• • •

Stefan said, 'What are you reading?'

I was sitting on the veranda outside the café and hadn't heard his footsteps. He was wearing an Aran jumper with a long stripy scarf wrapped around his neck. He looked cute with his scruffy bed-head hair and deep dimples that reminded me of the hollows in warm apple-pie. I held up the book.

He grimaced. '*Child Delinquents: Treatment and Care* - you've gone all scholarly, all of a sudden.'

I tutted and put it face down on the table. 'How's tricks?' I said, stretching my arms back with a yawn.

'You're looking chilled out.' I beamed at him. He was right. I was feeling good. 'I'm glad,' he said. 'Life's pretty good for me, too. I'm going to Istanbul for a scoop next week. Caroline's coming. Did she tell you?'

'She might have mentioned something...'

Stefan stared at the river. 'I still can't quite believe it,' he said. 'It's scary at any age, but in a nine-year-old?'

The waitress came to the table and I ordered another latte and a cappuccino for Stefan. I watched a man with a dog, in a rowing boat, disappear under Richmond Bridge and come out the other side.

'I thought you should know,' said Stefan. 'I heard today from Harry.'

I leant forward, noting the seriousness in his voice.

'Lewis Jackson has confessed to the rape. He just turned up at the police station in Brixton and made a statement. Looks like an officer will be in touch with you soon to request Elly's underwear, so they can run that DNA test.' I didn't know what to say. I stared into space, seeing nothing. He touched my arm. 'He must have had a crisis of conscience. It's good news, isn't it?'

I stroked the spine of the book. The coffees arrived and it gave me the few moments I needed to take in what he'd said.

'Yes. It's good news.' I couldn't work out why it didn't fill me with jubilation. Instead, it made the wall of my stomach shrink like a slug dropped in salt.

'It carries a minimum sentence of five years.' I'd taken a sip of coffee and swallowed it hard. 'Elly will get justice,' he said, sitting back. 'And because of the case against Linda, Elly's suicide verdict will be overturned to unlawful killing.' He looked like a little boy who had just scored his first goal for the school team. 'You did her proud in the end.'

'I wouldn't have lasted the course without your help.'

'We make a good team.'

I watched a waiter hastily scribble a bill at a nearby table and tuck it under a saucer. 'I always knew Elly's suicide note was all wrong,' I said.

'Yes – turned out the note she'd drafted on the computer was meant for her college tutor - that letch Dr Bell - to say she was leaving the course.'

'"*I'm sorry, I've had enough. I've tried - I really have, but I can't do it anymore. I don't suppose you'll understand. I can't carry on,*"' I recited.

'You know it off by heart?'

Until that moment I don't think Stefan had realised how much Elly's case had got under my skin. He stirred his coffee and stared into the creamy swirls.

'You don't feel any kind of vindication? Any sense - just a tiny-weeny one - of achievement?'

I laughed. 'Okay…a bit,' I conceded. I sighed, louder than I'd meant to. 'Mostly I feel overwhelmed with sadness. All the stuff about Jeff. It's been fairly traumatic.' I stared across at the river where two swans were gliding serenely, side by side.

'Yeah. I know. I'm sorry. That must have been pretty shitty.'

'I don't know what to do about the coroner's original verdict. It was wrong, but I don't know whether I should drag it all up.'

'Because of his parents, you mean?'

'Is it worth it, do you think? It would be a terrible ordeal for Jeff's family to get the verdict changed from suicide to death by misadventure. It would mean them finding out about his sexuality, for a start. They've had two years to come to terms with his death and learn to live with it. The dust has settled.'

'Lewis isn't going to go around spreading it about, so there's no reason for anyone to ever know.'

'I've always thought getting the truth out into the open was the most important thing. Now, I'm not so sure...'

He did his usual trick of scooping the froth from the inside of his cup to catch the last dregs. 'It must make a big difference...knowing it wasn't suicide.'

'It does. Jeff wasn't as unhappy as it first appeared,' I said. 'Life with me *wasn't* so unbearable that he committed suicide, after all. He was just hoping for a new start...' I flicked a soggy leaf that had blown on to our table. It barely moved. 'Okay, it was going to be a new start without me, but we would have been friends, I'm sure of it.' The leaf blew away of its own accord. 'Knowing that makes a massive difference.'

He sat back with a sigh. 'So what's next?'

I did a double take. 'What do you mean?'

'Any more mysteries to get our teeth into?'

'Not a chance!' I slapped my hands on the table. 'I'm going back to my quiet, ordinary life writing tame features for magazines - thank you very much.'

He looked perplexed. 'No miscarriages of justice to investigate? No treasure trails to get our adrenaline pumping?'

'I've had more adrenaline rushes in the last few months than I'd ever want in my entire life,' I said. 'Everything's going back to normal. Calm, pedantic and unimaginative - that's my life from now on.' My fingers closed around the gold locket I always wore around my neck: Elly's locket. 'I can stop dashing around like a maniac chasing after cryptic clues. I can stop hearing footsteps behind me in dark alleyways. I can finally get some sleep. What a relief.'

He grinned, jogging my elbow with his arm.

'So, you'll miss it, then.'

I stared at him over the rim of my cup, reluctant to answer.

A large boat passing under the bridge blew its horn.

'I couldn't possibly say.'

THE END

Printed in Great Britain
by Amazon.co.uk, Ltd.,
Marston Gate.